Ezzedine C. Fishere is an acclaimed Egyptian writer, academic, and diplomat. He has written numerous successful and bestselling novels, including *Embrace on Brooklyn Bridge* which was shortlisted for the International Prize for Arabic Fiction (the so-called "Arabic Booker"), and he also writes political articles for Arabic, English, and French news outlets. He currently teaches at Dartmouth College in the US, where he lives.

Translator of the winning novel in the Independent Foreign Fiction Prize and twice winner of the Saif Ghobash Banipal Prize for Arabic Literary Translation, **Jonathan Wright** was formerly the Reuters bureau chief in Cairo. He has translated Alaa Al-Aswany, Sinan Antoon, and Hassan Blassim. He lives in London in the UK.

The Egyptian Assassin

Ezzedine C. Fishere

Translated by
Jonathan Wright

hoopoe
AN IMPRINT OF AUC PRESS

First published in 2019 by
Hoopoe
113 Sharia Kasr el Aini, Cairo, Egypt
200 Park Ave., Suite 1700 New York, NY 10166
www.hoopoefiction.com

Hoopoe is an imprint of the American University in Cairo Press
www.aucpress.com

Dar el Kutub No. 26357/18
ISBN 978 977 416 931 1

Dar el Kutub Cataloging-in-Publication Data

Fishere, Ezzedine C.
　　　The Egyptian Assassin: A Novel / Ezzedine C. Fishere.— Cairo: The
American University in Cairo Press, 2019.
　　　p.　　　cm.
　　　ISBN 978 977 416 931 1
　　　1. English fiction
　　　823

1 2 3 4 5　　23 22 21 20 19

Designed by Adam el-Sehemy
Printed in the United States of America

1

The Eagle

FAKHREDDIN WRAPPED THE TURBAN TIGHT across his face and nose, leaving a narrow slit for his eyes. He leaned over to the camel carrying Omar and pulled it toward him, and the camel complied. He took hold of the turban covering the boy's face. Omar didn't move, apparently indifferent to what his father was doing. Fakhreddin looked into Omar's eyes, and still he couldn't see any glimmer of life in them. They seemed to be frozen. He tightened the turban around the boy's passive face and let the camel resume its normal pace. The sandstorm had just started and they were on an open plain, with no hills to shade them and no caves to provide shelter, so it would not be wise to stop now. As long as their mounts could keep going, they should travel on. Only the sound of the wind and the hiss of the sand broke the silence. The storm would pick up in a while and then the sand would fill the air and cover the earth, like a sea swallowing everything. He had to find shelter before the storm peaked, or else they would perish.

At dawn the day before they had skirted the town of Kutum without going into it, then traveled for nine hours without stopping. Fakhreddin wanted to leave northern Darfur and reach the Egyptian border as soon as possible. He wasn't worried about the tribesmen or the villagers, or even about the foreigners all over the area, but about those he had left behind. He knew there was a place with small caves a ten-hour journey north of Kutum. The storm would be at peak strength in less than an hour and he had to reach it before the sand came. Omar hadn't uttered a word since he had met him two days earlier. The boy didn't appear to see him. He would move in whatever direction his father pushed him, listlessly and without resisting. He hadn't eaten or drunk anything since they had set off. Whenever Fakhreddin passed him the water bag he ignored it, and when he offered him dates and pieces of bread he didn't reach out to take them. Fakhreddin took hold of Omar's hand, opened it, and put some bread into it, but the boy let it fall to the sand. Fakhreddin was angry: the desert was no place to be finicky. But his anger was a waste of energy because Omar took no notice.

General Samir's head was in the crosshairs of the rifle when Fakhreddin's phone began to vibrate. His hand shook and he lost the target in the scope. He hesitated. Only special people knew this phone number. He concentrated on the target again. He moved the sights right and left across the general's head. He held his breath. General Samir turned to his companion to hear something he was whispering and looked through the file he was holding. Fakhreddin could make out his features clearly. There could be no mistaking him. The sight was steady on his forehead. The phone kept vibrating stubbornly. Fakhreddin tensed. General Samir suddenly looked up and Fakhreddin imagined that their eyes met. He pulled the trigger. He fired a single shot that lodged between General Samir's eyes and downed him instantly. The file slipped out of the general's hand and flew through the air. General Samir fell to the asphalt on the path that led from the door of his house to the heavily guarded iron gate. Fakhreddin heard the sound of his head hitting the asphalt and saw the blood spilling from his nose and mouth. He looked through the rifle scope, and on the dead man's face he saw the smile of someone who at the last moment had understood what was happening. Fakhreddin took a deep breath and pulled back from the edge of his hiding place, out of sight. From his pocket he took the small telephone, which was still ringing, and answered it.

At first he didn't believe his ears. The world spun and he imagined he was falling from the eighth-floor balcony where he had hidden and was hearing the words as he tumbled toward the ground.

"What? What did you say?"

"As I told you, he's just been sentenced. The council meeting has just broken up and the group is set on carrying out the sentence at once."

"Sentence? Council? What council? Have they gone mad?"

"Listen carefully because I can't talk long. I did what I could but a majority sentenced the boy to death and Sheikh Hamza took their side. They decided not to tell you but I couldn't hide something like that from you. If there's anything you can do, you should act now because they're determined to carry out the sentence the day after tomorrow at the latest. I have to go back in now. Goodbye."

Then he hung up. Fakhreddin was stunned for some moments. From his hiding place he watched the guards running in all directions and the security officials rushing toward the scene, glancing at the blood-soaked body, then looking away as they went into the building. Men came and started to cover the body. They picked it up and silence reigned. Still sitting on the floor in his hiding place, Fakhreddin tried to piece together the meaning of what he had just heard. He had to leave now, immediately. He dismantled his rifle and put it in his bag, gathered together his few scattered belongings, and left the hiding place, never to return.

He didn't take the car that Hind had left him. That was what they had agreed to do if something unexpected happened. He walked as far as Manshiet Bakri and took the metro to Ramses Square, where he sat to wait for Hind in the cafe they had agreed on. His thoughts were racing. He could get in touch with Sheikh Hamza. Perhaps he could persuade him to postpone the execution for a few days until he reached the group's camp in eastern Sudan and dealt with it himself. But if he spoke to Sheikh Hamza, the group might bring forward the execution. They certainly wouldn't want him to hear the news before the execution because they knew he would try to stop them. Could he reach eastern Sudan by the evening of the next day? There was a plane to Khartoum in the evening but traveling by air wasn't safe; his identity might be detected at the airport, and even if he was only suspected he would be delayed. One night in detention would delay him enough for the boy to be executed. He could take the train to Aswan and then get to the border area. But the border area and Wadi Halfa port were full of security men on both sides and he could be detained there too. The safest way would be to cross the Gilf Kebir desert west of the Nile into northern Darfur and then head to the eastern region, but that would take at least ten days, without taking into account the sandstorms that might delay him further.

The only way was by sea. Fakhreddin looked around, anxiously anticipating the arrival of Hind. The answer was to go to Marsa Alam by land, then take a boat and sail south to somewhere just short of Port Sudan. There was a small harbor there that Fakhreddin had used in the past and that he could easily reach. Sailing was dangerous in that region but the sea was less dangerous than airport security. He saw Hind coming toward the café in her long gray dress, carrying a shoulder bag like a student going home on the train. Just to be safe she settled into a seat behind Fakhreddin's, signs of anxiety on her face. She ordered a mint tea and listened, looking in the other direction. He didn't have time to explain everything. In brief he asked her to take the first plane to Marsa Alam, stay in the best hotel, rent a small cabin cruiser with an engine, and a sail for three days, supposedly for a cruise with a friend of hers, and then to be waiting in the boat one kilometer out of Marsa Alam harbor toward the south at exactly one o'clock the next afternoon. Hind memorized the details quickly while thinking about the measures and preparations she would have to make to do all this without making a mistake or leaving any trail.

She stood up, left the check on the tray, and hurried off. Fakhreddin stayed another five minutes, then stood up and paid the check. He left a standard tip that the waiter wouldn't remember and went to the car that Hind had brought. He got in, turned the key, and within minutes he was on the October bridge heading for the Ain Sukhna road.

Fakhreddin hadn't gotten over the shock yet. He treated the news as a disaster that had to be averted immediately, without thinking much about what it meant or how it had happened. He was good at making plans for assignments and did it as matter of course. Concentrating on averting the disaster helped him neutralize his emotions, because however terrible it might be he could handle it if he broke it down into a series of specific tasks. He focused his mind on defining those tasks, setting out how they were sequenced and how they fitted together in a way that wouldn't go wrong. This spared him thinking about the disaster itself. But he couldn't keep his thoughts at bay as he drove alone at night along the road to Marsa Alam. He tried to push them aside by concentrating on the bends in the road, the unexpected dips and rises, and the oncoming vehicles that blinded him with their headlights, but the thoughts returned and took his mind far away. Could Omar have done that? He couldn't have committed such crimes! That wasn't Omar. There must have been a mix-up. Could Omar have been a traitor? And in such a despicable manner? And when did all this happen? Fakhreddin couldn't understand why no one had told him, so that he could have stepped in and dealt with it. Especially his old bodyguard Abdullah, the man who had contacted him: why hadn't he gotten in touch earlier? Why had no one said anything until things had gone this far? How could they hold a sharia council to try his son? How could Sheikh Hamza take their side? How dare they sentence Fakhreddin's son to death? Half of them owed their lives to him, especially Sheikh Hamza. He thought about it as he drove, but he found no answers. "All this must be a nightmare," he said to himself.

Only the car headlights and the pale blue lights on the dashboard cut through the pitch dark. As he drove Fakhreddin tried to force these thoughts out of his head for a while. It was close to one o'clock in the morning and he still had a long way to go. He gripped the steering wheel with both hands and concentrated on keeping the car right on course as it took the bends. There was no room for error or for risks. He mustn't have an accident or a breakdown; there was no time. He mustn't stop or talk to anyone, except to get through the checkpoints along the road. He concentrated on the sound of the engine and the sound of the wheels as they hummed slightly on the bends. There was no point in thinking about anything else right now. There would be time when he reached eastern Sudan and met them. Then he wouldn't need to guess. He would get his answers straight from the source. He would see Omar and he would know the truth when he looked into his eyes. He would see Sheikh Hamza and the other leaders, and all would become clear. He couldn't believe that things stood as his friend had portrayed them. They must be something else behind it.

At one o'clock the next afternoon a small black dot started to move closer to the boat floating outside the harbor. A black head glinted in the rays of the sun, disappearing under the water, then reappearing and moving toward the boat on a zigzag course. Fakhreddin never took risks; even alone at sea, one kilometer from the harbor, he was taking evasive action. He was swimming underwater more than he swam on the

6

surface, and changing course so that his head shining in the sun wouldn't attract anyone's attention. A few minutes later he appeared alongside the boat and nimbly climbed aboard. Hind was sitting at the helm and looking at him. He glanced at her and, without saying a word, lay on the deck, gasping for breath and recovering his strength. He stayed like that for some minutes, aware that she was watching him as she sat in silence at the back of the boat, almost enjoying the scene.

He stood up and looked at her inquisitively. She nodded to say that all was well. He went down into the cabin for ten minutes, took off his diving suit, had a quick cold shower, put on a pair of jeans and a white shirt, and then came back up. He went to the maps and looked at them as he started the engine and set off. In silence he gradually accelerated until the boat was going at top speed and Hind could no longer hear her voice when she spoke.

"Have you had anything to eat?" she shouted.

He shook his head.

"Would you like something?"

He nodded. She looked at him grumpily, headed for the small galley to prepare something light as she grumbled to herself.

"Here you are," she said as she reappeared on deck. "Some cereal for your highness. Will this do?"

Fakhreddin smiled and shook his head in resignation at her constant sarcasm. He took the bowl from her hand and thanked her with a nod, without speaking. As he ate, he glanced back and forth between the maps and the horizon.

"So what are these maps then?" she asked.

"They're maps of the area."

"Really? I thought they were maps of somewhere else!" she said.

"Nice cereal. Where did you get it?"

"From the supermarket. Where do you think? From the herbalist?"

7

"Same difference."

"What was that?"

He pointed at the maps and didn't answer. She sighed in exasperation.

"Listen," she said. "We've got three days and nights ahead of us on a small boat. That's not much space and I'm claustrophobic, so you have to be nice to me."

"Okay. Instead of ranting, tell me what you did in Marsa Alam."

Fakhreddin stood up, holding the rudder as he listened to her recount in detail what happened in Marsa Alam. She sat in front of him and told him how she had rented the boat in her name and the name of a friend, claiming they had learned to sail together in Italy while they were students. She showed the man in charge the competence certificate he wanted and regaled him with details of the Italian coast and the wind patterns there. Hind loaded the boat with everything she would need to live on it for three days, adding things that sailors might take, such as simple fishing gear and sunscreen. She put her clothes in one of the cabins and put some more women's clothes in the other cabin. She threw a plane ticket in her codename in the cabin and scattered some other things around the boat. After that she changed her clothes and dressed up as her friend, Darqa al-Awsagi. Then she called the man in charge to tell him he should come to the boat immediately because her friend had arrived and they were about to sail. When he arrived the boat really was ready to sail. It had moved forward a little in the water and the engine was running. The man found Darqa al-Awsagi standing on the gunwale in a black bikini with a slightly wet sarong around her waist, her blond hair falling loose over her shoulders and with sunglasses co vering half her face. She leaned down low from the edge of the boat toward the rubber dinghy carrying the man. Flustered by the proximity, he passed her the papers. He stole a glimpse at her breasts while pretending to be looking at the papers. She took the papers, signed them, and waved her passport at him. He gestured that he didn't need to see it. To distract him yet more, she gave him a big smile, a long stare, and a friendly wave. Then she turned and swaggered back into the cockpit, while he stood in his rubber dinghy making incoherent gestures.

"And then I miraculously sailed the boat to here."

"It hardly took a miracle! You just go in a straight line from the harbor to here!"

"Well I've never sailed a boat all that distance," she said.

"What? You're joking?"

"No, I'm serious. I hardly know the basics. I turn on the engine, take hold of the rudder and have my picture taken and so on. You'll have to teach me."

"Why didn't you tell me that yesterday?"

"I didn't tell you anything yesterday. I never claimed I could sail a boat."

"So when you suggested coming with me and taking the boat back alone, what did that mean?"

"It meant you would teach me how."

"You're really crazy. My God, you're crazy."

She insisted on going to Sudan with him and then coming back alone on the boat. He said the idea was crazy but she assured him she could learn during the trip. She would memorize the route, then bring the boat back. She reminded him that leaving the boat on the Sudanese coast would raise questions and would provide a lead for anyone who wanted to follow him and find them. And then, in the end, there was the adventure—Hind sailing a boat across the border alone, without any prior knowledge of sailing. She didn't want to miss the excitement.

The storm had abated and the desert was calm again. The air had cleared, as though the violent storm had sucked up all the coarse grains of sand. The air was still and fresh, and

9

everything had recovered its usual color. To check the weather Fakhreddin came out of the small cave where they had taken shelter. He found the familiar desert in all its colors, stretched out under the sun in the calm after the storm: yellow and red sand, and shiny brown rocks that looked like they had just been washed. Visibility had been zero, the sheets of sand had scoured everything they touched, and the wind had been strong enough to blow away tents and loose rocks, but now there was complete calm. Usually the sight of the desert after a storm made Fakhreddin feel at ease, but that's not the way it was that morning. He brought the animals out, hobbled their legs, put out some food and water for them, then went back to the cave. He called Omar but there was no response. He felt his forehead, and his fever was unchanged. He shook him but he didn't react. He picked him up in his bedding and took him out in the sun. He laid him on the sand and dabbed some water on his forehead. His lips were parched. He took a hand-kerchief out of his pocket and dipped it in the bowl of water, then squeezed it drop by drop on his lips while parting them a little. He did this again until the bowl ran out of water, then he put the handkerchief on the boy's head and stayed sitting beside him. The sun was gradually rising in the dome of the sky, and soon he would have to decide whether they should resume their journey or spend another night in the cave. Prudence required that they leave Sudan as soon as possible. Fakhreddin didn't know what those he had left behind would do. The farther away he took Omar the safer it would be.

But Omar refused to speak or eat and drink, and was so weak that he had fallen unconscious in the middle of the storm. How could a sixteen-year-old boy be so stubborn? What had happened to him? How had he become so difficult? Fakhreddin had tried talking to him in every possible way—gentle, tough, with inducements and intimidation, favors and threats, everything, but he hadn't gotten a word or any reaction out of Omar. The boy didn't even look into his father's eyes, and when he took hold of his head and forced him to face him, the boy didn't resist, but he didn't look at him either. He didn't close his eyes, and didn't avert his gaze, but he didn't look. Fakhreddin didn't understand. Where had his son learned to do that? How had his eyes become so glazed? There was no life in them, no expression, nothing at all.

He tried to control his anger but he couldn't maintain it for long. In the end he snapped.

"It's completely irresponsible. Instead of facing up to the inexcusable mistake you've made, you act stubborn. And instead of looking me in the face and admitting your mistake so that we can work out what to do about it, you refuse to speak! And now you're putting both our lives in danger with this childish behavior of yours. Speak. Or don't speak if you don't want. But eat and drink a little water before you faint and I have to carry you as well."

No response, not a twitch. Fakhreddin stared at him, seething with anger. His face was flushed, his stomach muscles tightened, and he wanted to grab Omar by the collar and cast him loose in the desert, but he suppressed his anger. It would be pointless to shout or get angry. That would only make matters worse.

"So be it. Say as little as you like. Go on hunger strike as you wish. I hope you starve to death. But I'll take you to Cairo anyway, dead or alive."

Then Fakhreddin also stopped talking, and about an hour later Omar collapsed from exhaustion. That was about twelve hours ago and Fakhreddin had been dripping water into his mouth about every hour. "He won't come around now, nor any time today, and we can't wait here long," Fakhreddin said to himself. He prepared a herbal infusion for him and dripped it into his mouth again. He patted the animals one by one and prepared them for the journey. He removed all signs that they had stayed the night there, picked his son up in his arms, and mounted the camel. He sat up straight and settled

11

Omar's body between his arms, and the little caravan set off again toward the north.

Fakhreddin knew the area well. He had traveled the length and breadth of it with colleagues from the group, and sometimes with the sheikh himself. Sometimes he had traveled with young Arab tribesmen who were grazing their livestock and who knew when the storms and rains would come and where the pasture and the wells would be, and sometimes with young Africans from the Fur, Masalit, and Zaghawa tribes who farmed and kept cattle and knew all the tracks and caves. He had climbed Jebel Marra with them many times, and only the local people knew the ins and outs of that mountain. With them he had crossed the deserts of north and west Darfur to Chad, or slipped south into Kordofan and the savannas of the south, moving weapons, money, equipment, and people. Now he took the same route to escape them, changing course every day so that none of them could follow him. It would take longer that way but he could be sure to arrive unharmed by those tracking him. "The real problem is this idiot who refuses to speak, eat, or drink. I wasn't prepared for that. I hadn't taken it into account," he said to himself.

The caravan moved slowly, slower than necessary. Omar was still unconscious. Fakhreddin couldn't hold him between his arms throughout the journey. He tied the boy behind him with a strip of cloth but he had to stop every now and then to deal with the animals, and every time he stopped it was a tricky procedure making sure Omar didn't fall off the camel. Two days passed like this after they left the cave and Omar was the same. Fakhreddin continued to drip the herbal infusion into his mouth. After a while he added some mountain honey and olive oil. He could see from the color of his face that Omar's condition was stable, but the boy would have to regain consciousness if they were to arrive. They couldn't go into the Gilf Kebir with Omar in this state, and the desert track was just a day away.

He was spending the whole day looking after his son, and at night they would resume their journey. Fakhreddin didn't like this state of affairs. Omar's behavior struck him as foolish obstinacy. He asked himself why all this was happening. He watched the camel walk silently through the soft sand under a canopy of stars in the night sky. A silvery light stretched across the land and the cosmic silence was total. It was at moments such as this that his spirit broke free from its bonds and soared. He could be himself and nothing else—not the warrior or the cautious intriguer, not the planner or the adventurer, just Fakhreddin the orphan, the idealist dreamer, and the father who was carrying a disobedient child, sick in spirit and in body, and who did not know what to do.

His plans were always flawless and he carried them out with precision. He was famous for that and no one ever disputed the details of how he made and carried out a plan, because he had an extraordinary ability to put it all together in such a complex and coordinated way that the sheikh called him the group's planning minister. But now his plan was falling apart because of this stubborn boy who might get them both killed. He had been angry with Omar, but now he knew there was no point in getting angry, no point to this resentment. If they went into the Gilf Kebir with Omar in this state they would have to move so slowly they would run the risk of running out of water and food. If they stopped to wait for him to recover, the people on their trail might do them harm. He couldn't go back to Darfur or head toward Chad because the risks would be too great along the way. He couldn't head northeast toward the town of Halfa, where there were troops and a border post. What should he do?

He couldn't force Omar to recover and he couldn't abandon him. He thought what he might do and gradually he realized there was no solution. Little by little he began to understand that his plans were collapsing and all the options available were fraught with danger. If he wanted to keep traveling with his obstinate son, he might have to make do with an imperfect plan. Either that or take him across the desert now in the hope that Omar would recover along the way. But he knew that Omar couldn't make the journey in his present state, and if he went into the Gilf Kebir now his son would die in his arms within a few days. So his only option was to wait till Omar recovered, come what may.

The sea voyage went smoothly for several hours, until he reached the Sudanese border. Fakhreddin took the boat deep into international waters to stay clear of the coastguards. The calm sea helped him sail far and fast, and then he turned south and traveled as fast as possible. The boat's engine groaned from the strain but Fakhreddin seemed confident about what he was doing. He heard Hind muttering something about their speed and the engine but he didn't reply. At the helm now, Hind watched every move he made. He moved around as quick and agile as a panther, doing several things at the same time and not answering any of her questions because he was so focused on his numerous tasks. He knew that Hind didn't need answers. She was watching him as if she were taking pictures of his actions, analyzing them and storing them away in her memory.

He explained the elements of the operation to her in a few minutes: the maps, the gauges, and the things she had to focus on in this area and the later stages of the voyage, the weather conditions, communications between the boat and the authorities, the distress call and how to handle the fuel. He forbade her from using the sails on the way back. At night, on drawing close to the Sudanese coast, they would use the sails so that the sound of the engine didn't draw attention to them. This region had plenty of wind so they could make do with the sails, and there would be more fuel left for her to go back using the engine all the way. If anyone challenged her she could pretend she was a tourist who had lost her way.

It wasn't long before Hind felt that the wind was picking up. Minutes later Fakhreddin turned the engine off and asked her to help him hoist the sails. He pulled out the mainsail and started asking her to do specific tasks: tie this, push the foot of the sail to the other side, push, pull. And all the time he was busy opening, closing, and moving things, untying some ropes and making others fast. The sails were hoisted and secured and the boat set off faster than it had been traveling earlier, with Fakhreddin holding the tiller. The boat was heeling sharply to one side as they raced across the surface of the water. He looked at Hind and could see that she was gradually losing her fear and was starting to move along the sloping deck by holding onto the ropes on the guardrail until she reached the helm. He smiled at her encouragingly.

"I'll hand over the helm to you," he said. "Be careful. Don't let go of it. I'm going to the mast. Stay here until I tell you."

She nodded and he gave her the rudder. He looked at her quizzically and she gestured that everything was under control. He left her and edged his way along the deck toward the mast. Suddenly the boom swung around and pushed him toward the other side of the boat. The side closest to the water rose in the air and the other side fell. The wind forced the sail toward the water until it seemed that the boat was bound to capsize. But it didn't capsize. It kept moving forward at an angle. Fakhreddin fixed the boom in its new position and went back the same way he had come. He slid along the deck, rather than walked. He took the rudder from Hind's tight grip. She sat aside, trying to steady her nerves.

"Don't worry. Everything's going fine," he said.

"Are we going all the way like this?"

Fakhreddin mumbled something affirmative while Hind leaned over the side of the boat and emptied the contents of her stomach into the water. Fakhreddin smiled. She came back in a while.

"Welcome back. You'll feel better soon. Drink something fizzy from down below, but quickly because we're going to do that maneuver again."

Omar woke up for the second time since the morning. He reached out for the plate next to his bed and took a piece of bread. He chewed it slowly, then had a drink. His frail body was curled up on the bed. The air was damp in the rocky cave where he and Fakhreddin had been staying for some days. The light was dazzling outside. Fakhreddin spent an hour looking after the animals, then came back and sat in the cave looking at his son. The boy put him on edge and he wondered what exactly was wrong with him. Omar had been staring into space without moving since waking up. His father looked at him and tried to accept the idea that his son was disobedient. But at least he had eaten something and drunk some water. He went up to him and sat by his side. The boy didn't stir. Fakhreddin asked him how he felt but he didn't respond. He tried to make conversation anyway, describing the journey that awaited them, how long it would be and some of the difficulties they might face. Omar didn't respond. Fakhreddin ventured to say that they could move in two days if he continued to recover his strength at this rate, and he still didn't respond. But he reached out for the plate, took another piece of bread, and started to chew it slowly. Fakhreddin stood up to do some more chores.

Complete silence.

Omar finished chewing the piece of bread and stretched out on his bed again, covering his body and his head. Fakhreddin sat at the mouth of the cave watching the desert outside, impatient to move on. He didn't like this waiting. He didn't like any waiting. He toyed with a stick in the ground and from time to time looked over at his son lying hidden under the covers. What had reduced him to this state? How had all this happened within sight and earshot of the men in the group without anyone noticing anything? He didn't understand. He had found an answer in his stormy conversation with Sheikh Hamza, and that answer was a betrayal of trust. He had left his son in their care, to grow up among them, with them as guardians, and this is what had happened: they had betrayed the trust. But what was worse, what he couldn't understand was Omar's betrayal of himself. When Fakhreddin was his age he used to read about comparative religion and the history of philosophy. He developed a sense of right and wrong and it was beneath him to do wrong or compromise with it. Why had his son stooped so low? And what should he do with him now? He had saved him from the clutches of the group, which had been blinded by anger and the smell of blood, but what should he do now with a silent, thin boy who was stubborn and disloyal, and why had his son become such a person?

The disc of the sun rose gradually from the surface of the sea as Fakhreddin stood at the helm. He was fully dressed and had prepared a small bag containing things that Hind had brought. He looked at the bed and could see that she was still asleep. He leaned over the side of the stationary boat and felt the small rubber dinghy that was tied up alongside it. He called Hind; she got up and walked to the side of the boat. She stepped up to the edge and then slowly climbed down into the dinghy. Fakhreddin followed her and started to row the dinghy gently toward the shore. They arrived within minutes. There was no one on the shore at that time. Fakhreddin jumped ashore and waved to her to go back. He watched her row back to the big boat in silence, except for the sound of the small oars in the water. He had to leave the area as quickly as possible and she would set off in exactly one hour. She would turn on the engine and sail back in a straight line until she reached Marsa Alam, then hand in the boat and go back to Cairo, according to the agreement, and she wouldn't call him until he called her, whatever happened.

He left the coast at speed. He knew the area well and had some Beja friends in a nearby village, but he wasn't going to stop there. He didn't want anyone to recognize him until he reached the village where the group leaders lived and he didn't want to take the risk that word of his arrival might leak out to the group, even with good intentions. Otherwise they would hurry to carry out the sentence. It would also be difficult for Fakhreddin to explain the whole story to anyone he met now. If he told someone there was a disagreement between him and Sheikh Hamza, who could guarantee that they wouldn't be suspicious and take the safest option, which would be to inform Hamza? No, he had best remain under cover until he reached al-Areen. Fakhreddin skirted the village that stretched along the shoreline and walked toward the hills that ran inland. After a while he came across a horse-drawn cart driven by a southern boy. He greeted him and sat on the edge of the cart. He looked like a Zaghawa in his Darfuri gown and the dark sunglasses he was wearing. The cart drove on without them speaking for about half an hour and then Fakhreddin jumped down, thanking the boy for the ride. He walked on foot to a little settlement where he bought a motorbike, filled the tank with fuel, and set off toward al-Areen, the village where the group was based. Along the way he thought about how he would handle his encounter with Hamza and the other leaders.

It was a stormy meeting. Everyone was surprised to see Fakhreddin walking down the narrow lanes of al-Areen. The guards on the security perimeter of the village hadn't noticed him arriving. Fakhreddin had slipped in between them, which wasn't hard as it was he who had trained them and helped prepare the defenses. He reached the door of Sheikh Hamza's house, shook hands with the guards, and asked them to tell the sheikh he was there. Two minutes later the guards came back and took him in.

"Where's Omar?" he asked.

"And greetings to you too, and the mercy and blessings of God."

"Where's Omar, Sheikh Hamza?"

"Still alive."

"Bring him for me to see."

"Sit down, Abu Omar."

Sheikh Hamza came up to him and embraced him. Fakhreddin stiffened. "What happened?" he asked the sheikh directly.

"What brought you so suddenly? When we invited you, you didn't come."

"What happened, Hamza?"

"What have the rats told you?"

"The rats? Is it true that Omar's in detention?"

"Yes."

"And why didn't you tell me?"

"Sit down, Abu Omar, and listen carefully. You know what we mean to each other. You know how much we respect you. But what happened was very serious so, first, sit down and bless the Prophet of God. Open your heart and listen before you rush to judgment. You'll see that I did the right thing and followed God's law."

"Send someone to fetch Omar first. I want to see him."

"Before you've listened?"

"Before I've listened."

"I don't think that would be wise. Let me tell you what happened and then you can have what you want."

"Bring him first."

Sheikh Hamza looked at him and realized that Fakhreddin wasn't sure that no one would harm Omar while they were talking. He gestured to the guard at the door, who disappeared for some minutes and then came back holding up Omar, who was walking slowly and staring into space.

"Omar!" Fakhreddin cried.

He rushed toward him and took him in his arms. He hugged him tight and pushed the guard aside. The guard looked to Sheikh Hamza, who signaled that he shouldn't intervene. Fakhreddin kept Omar in his arms, but Omar was stiff and unresponsive. He turned the boy's face toward him and looked into his eyes anxiously.

"Are you okay? Has anyone done anything to you?" he asked.

He hugged him again but the boy didn't respond. Fakhreddin held the boy's head back a little and looked into his eyes again, but he couldn't see any life in them. Nothing at all. Fakhreddin mumbled some reassuring and encouraging words but Omar was as silent and stiff as ever. Fakhreddin relaxed his grip a little and made an effort to smile, but Omar was far away.

"Has anyone done anything to you? Is there anything you want to tell me?"

When Fakhreddin received no answer, he set Omar on the floor at the end of the room and went back to Sheikh Hamza.

"Omar will stay here," he said. "Now tell me the story."

"In the name of God the Merciful, the Compassionate. You know your status in the jihad and how much we all respect you. We've never come across anything that discredits you in any way whatsoever. You left your son in our care and we looked after him and brought him up well. I took him under my wing and treated him as my son. And believe me, there's nothing harder for me to say than what I'm going to tell you. I was stunned when I heard about it and I didn't take a position until I had seen and heard it myself and the boy had himself confessed. What you are going to hear will be hard for you too, and a test of your faith. Don't let anger and pride blind you, and remember what God says clearly in His book: 'In the name of God the Merciful, the Compassionate. You cannot guide anyone you like, but God guides whomsoever he wishes.' God Almighty has spoken the truth."

"Tell me the story, Hamza, and enough beating around the bush. What happened? Why do you want to kill my son?"

"Your son betrayed us. Your son was responsible for the killing of several members of the group and conspired to have us all killed. If God Almighty hadn't protected us he would have succeeded."

"My son? Omar?"

"What happened was that Egyptian intelligence recruited the son of one of the people working with Sheikh Azzam. They lured the boy, drugged him, abused him, and took pictures of him. Then they asked him to provide them with basic information about Sheikh Azzam and his group. It wasn't important information at first and they threatened to tell the boy's family if he didn't cooperate, so he did. But Sheikh Azzam's group isn't active, as you know, and it turned out later that their real target was not Sheikh Azzam, but us. This is what someone said later. He said they were targeting us in retaliation for operations we had carried out against them. We don't know what operations they were talking about. We haven't carried out any against them since we blew up the consulate in 1995. What reminded them of that fourteen years later? God alone knows."

Fakhreddin's heart sank. What operations were they talking about? Could it be that it was to take revenge on him? For his operations?

"Tell me, have you carried out any jobs and pinned them on us, Abu Omar?"

"No, of course not."

"Maybe one of our members carried out some lone operations and they thought we were behind them. Anyway, they put pressure on the boy to introduce them to one of our children and he did. This boy took your son Omar and went to meet these people in a place they chose, and they did to Omar what they had done to the first boy."

Fakhreddin felt dizzy. Out of the corner of his eye he looked at Omar and saw that he was far away, as if asleep or unconscious and unable to hear what was happening. Fakhreddin watched the sheikh as he spoke, his face as rigid as stone.

"Omar cooperated with them. Sudanese intelligence monitored the meetings, arrested the boys, and told us what had happened. It turned out he had given the Egyptian security agents a list of the names of our members who had fled Afghanistan and the countries where they had taken shelter, the names of those who were in the Damazin farm and in Kutum and in Kordofan. We tipped off as many of them as we could but some of them were arrested, and some were killed. We took Omar from the Sudanese and asked him, and he confessed. We have tapes of his confessions. I sent you an invitation to come but you refused."

"I thought that . . ."

"It doesn't matter now. Some of the members sat down with him and tried to persuade him to repent, out of deference to you, despite the blood that had been shed. He did repent and they sent him to the sharia units to complete his repentance, strengthen his faith, and atone for the offense he had committed. But he ran away and disappeared. After that we found out he had gone back to Khartoum and resumed contact with the agents of his own free will. Then he contacted us and asked to come back and showed remorse and penitence. We weren't convinced that his repentance was sincere but we thought we'd see what it was all about. We brought him back here and two weeks later he made some excuse and went off to Khartoum. We had put him under surveillance and we filmed him in Khartoum with an agent who gave him a bag of explosives. The Sudanese, who were also tracking these agents, arrested him with the bag and interrogated him. He confessed that the agents had asked him to put the bag in my office and detonate it on the day of the weekly leadership meeting. They had trained him to use the explosives. There wasn't any doubt about it. We eventually got the boy back from them, brought him here, and

22

questioned him ourselves. He confessed to me and to the sharia council that was convened.

"The council had a long discussion on the religious law aspect. The boy clearly knew what he was doing. At the trial some members asked him if he knew the penalty for treachery and he said he did. Some of them asked him why he had betrayed us and he said he didn't like us and we weren't his family and that we had no obligations to each other. Just like that! The members had a long discussion with him and it was clear that he hadn't acted under duress, so he was sentenced to death on the basis that what he did was equivalent to conspiracy to murder, and the council endorsed the verdict by a majority vote."

"And why didn't anyone call me? Why didn't you send for me and explain that my son's life was at stake?"

"You chose to go. You decided to leave our group and work alone. And you persuaded the sheikh to let you go despite my opposition at the time, so don't come now and ask us to treat you like a member who lives with us."

"Is that how it is then, Sheikh Hamza?"

"You know that many members opposed your departure and thought it implied arrogance and insubordination. Malicious tongues wagged, wondering how you happened to leave Afghanistan just two months before the Americans started bombing, but I shut them up and, although I wasn't convinced about you leaving, I stood with you out of respect for our history together. You left your son with Umm Yasser while you were on jihad and we looked after him for you. When you came back here you told Umm Yasser you'd leave him with her some time longer because you'd be worried about him in Cairo and you couldn't look after him. So we took him under our wing. We treated him as a son and this is our reward. He was responsible for our members being arrested, tortured, and killed. He cost the group large amounts in expenses, damaged our relationship with the

Sudanese, helped the security people against us, and almost cost us our lives. What do you want me to do? Give him a medal?"

"No. You should have sent for me to come as soon as the problem started and before things reached this stage! And besides, why did he hate you so much? What happened to him? Someone must have done him harm. Do children hate their families like that for no reason?"

"You'll have to put that question to him or to yourself. As far as we're concerned, we did everything by the book to the best of our ability."

"And haven't you ever asked yourself, Sheikh Hamza, how the security people were able to recruit two boys from the group so easily? Doesn't that mean that you're at fault too?"

"The fault is obvious. It lies with the boys, who succumbed to the devil."

"He's a child! He's sixteen years old! How did he come to meet the devil, so that he *could* succumb to him? He's a child in your care. If the devil overpowered him, that's your responsibility."

"No, Abu Omar. He's not a minor. We've examined him and he's not a minor."

"If you're an adult physically it doesn't necessarily mean you're an adult psychologically! Be reasonable, Sheikh Hamza!"

"You be reasonable and don't try to hold me responsible for the boy's deeds."

"So the boy's responsible? How can it be his responsibility? Was it Omar who antagonized the security people and set them against you? He's a young boy you should be looking after and bringing up, rather than throwing him to the lions and then wanting to go and kill him!"

"Omar's not young. The council met and confirmed he's an adult and he himself admitted he was responsible and knew what he was doing, and that was the end of the matter."

"The end of the matter? Something must have happened to your reason. Are you forgetting yourself or what, Hamza?"

"It's not me who's forgetting himself. In fact the situation seems to be worse than I thought and the lack of resolve seems to be congenital."

"Lack of resolve? Congenital? God damn you! You've forgotten the Panjshir, you ingrate. My God, if it wasn't for me, the mountain hyenas would have eaten your corpse years ago."

"Our lives are in the hands of God, so you can't take credit for something that God has decreed for me and for which He has used you as His instrument. Didn't I say arrogance and insubordination?"

"You really haven't changed, Hamza. You're like the pot calling the kettle black. You've always projected your own faults onto others."

"Watch your tongue. Don't go too far."

"You watch your tongue, you thug. If I was a less generous man, I'd have finished you off."

Hamza looked to the guard, who was on the alert and who rushed toward Fakhreddin. Fakhreddin spun around and before the guard could reach him he punched him right in the throat and knocked him unconscious. He went for Hamza, grabbed him by the neck, and lifted him in the air. Trembling with rage, he looked at him and shouted, "You listen to me. If you think those guards will protect you from me, you're mistaken. If I want to punish you, no one's going to stop me having your head cut off."

Hamza made a gurgling noise and his eyes bulged. Fakhreddin maintained his grip. "Abu Omar, I'm choking," the sheikh gasped. "Let me down for God's sake, don't be crazy."

Fakhreddin took a deep breath and put him down, still holding him firm. Hamza slowly got his breath back. He looked at Fakhreddin and continued: "Have you gone mad, Abu

Omar? Do you want to kill me? Listen, I can recommend that the council postpone the execution, as long as you stay here. We'll give you the boy and he'll be in your custody. You can go back to your old position and play your part. We're reuniting the mujahideen who were dispersed by the war in Afghanistan. Some of the ones who went to Iraq and Chechnya have come back, as well as some of those who were in Somalia and Darfur. Hopefully we'll start to operate systematically, and we would reserve an important role for you. You can stay, and together we'll take revenge on those who tempted your son and led him into iniquity. By God, I'll bring you that agent and you can do what you like to him. This is the only way to save Omar. No one will dare demand that the death sentence be carried out against Omar as long as you are among us and the boy repents and you vouch for him, and that would be the end of the matter."

"Why didn't you do that from the start? Why were you going to kill Omar?"

"Enough of that. Now we're here and you have this chance."

"No, enough of *your* nonsense and you listen to me. I've known what you're like for a long time, since the days of the war in the north, when you groveled to the sheikh so he would put you in command, and I didn't care then and I don't care now. But I never imagined you would sink this low. My son? My son, you bastard. If I were to follow your logic I would have to punish you, and now. But your punishment is to be yourself, as you are, and to spend the rest of your life living the same way you've always lived. Listen to me and don't interrupt. This is the end of the line for me and you, for me and all of you. I'm out of here and I'm taking my son with me. No one will stand in my way and no one will come after me. That's the end of the matter. From now on, I don't know you and you don't know me."

Fakhreddin didn't wait for an answer. He just picked Omar up off the floor, threw him over his shoulder, and left.

He walked down the narrow village lanes. Men stopped to look and the guards stood aside in confusion and hesitation. No one stood in his way, but angry eyes were watching him and the son he was carrying in his arms. He went through gateway after gateway and security cordon after security cordon until he reached his motorbike. He sat on the saddle, set Omar in front of him, and put his arms tight around him so that he couldn't fall or run away. Then he set off for the road that led to the Gilf Kebir desert.

2

Bayn al-Sarayat

WHEN FAKHREDDIN WOKE UP AND found himself stretched out on the sofa in his underclothes, he realized that his cousin had carried out his threat. Eissa said he would do it whether Fakhreddin liked it or not, even if he had to drug him. So he hadn't been joking. But it had put his life in danger because these snipers wouldn't stop to check his identity.

He got up and looked out of the window of the little sitting room, immediately spotting the trained sniper on the roof. He felt sorry for him; a sniper is such a failure when he's discovered by his target! He had known from the start that things would come to this. He went into the bedroom and opened the door of the old wooden wardrobe. He reached in for his white galabiya and white pants. He looked for a white pair of socks and grabbed one. He put on a white pair of flip-flops. He threw a farewell glance at his few possessions: the table, the two wooden chairs, the old wall clock, the wide chair with the slightly sunken seat, the edge of the bed showing through the half-open door, a photograph of him when young, herding sheep and goats with Umm Ibrahim. He looked out of the window again, toward the waiting sniper, and left.

It wasn't the snipers stationed on the roofs that upset him, but rather the silence that reigned in the street. How could Bayn al-Sarayat be so silent? How could it close its eyes to him and leave him to fight the wolves alone? What had happened to his ties with the local people? Where was the covenant they had had? Or rather, why had the people unanimously agreed to abandon him when they could never agree on anything else? They had all disappeared under the influence of some mysterious force. Bayn al-Sarayat had left him to face this destiny alone. Now he was alone with these hidden eyes watching him, one pair after another as he passed. Along his usual route he went past the Coca-Cola factory toward Sudan Street. Then he went into his aunt's house to say goodbye to Eissa. A few light knocks on the door and Eissa woke up hurriedly. When he saw him he understood. He made him a quick tea and they sat down in silence. There was nothing to be said. Fakhreddin sipped the tea and felt a calm come over him. He smiled at Eissa, and his vision started to cloud over.

The snipers were puzzled when Fakhreddin disappeared at the corner of Sudan Street. Wireless messages flew on that winter morning toward the command vehicle lurking outside the university. Colonel Samir took a sip of his morning tea and thought for a moment of ordering the snipers to storm Fakhreddin's aunt's house, but decided to wait. His orders were to carry out the operation without causing any disturbance in the neighborhood. He waited. A quarter of an hour later he received a message that Fakhreddin had left his aunt's house. He breathed a sigh of relief. Eissa sensed the secret presence that was waiting and watching for him. He kept walking. At exactly 6:45 a.m. that morning, October 1, when Eissa reached the back of the Coca-Cola factory, the shots rained down from the rooftops and riddled Eissa's body from all directions. He slumped to the pavement instantly, his shredded body bleeding profusely.

Fakhreddin heard the bullets before he got off the sofa. He ran as he'd never run in his life before, but it was too late. When he reached the scene of the incident the snipers had left and Eissa's body had disappeared. He found blood on the ground and empty cartridge casings scattered around, but nothing else. He fell to the ground sobbing. Fakhreddin couldn't believe they had done that to his cousin. When the Meccan pagans discovered that the Prophet Mohamed had given them the slip and escaped with Abu Bakr, leaving his cousin Ali asleep in his bed, they didn't kill Ali, although there were many of them and, if they had killed him, responsibility for the killing would have been shared out between the tribes. But although they were angry they didn't kill Ali, whereas those snipers had killed his cousin, and maybe they didn't even know who they had killed.

He sat on the ground in Eissa's blood. He didn't know where to go or what to do. Two children on their way to school passed by him. They looked at him warily and then went on their way. He recognized them and he knew their father. He had been to their house several times the previous year to help them with some schoolwork. He stood up from the patch of blood, which had seeped into his clothes—his cousin's clothes. He picked up an empty cartridge he found on the ground. It was still hot. How did the cartridge come to be so close to the body? Could it be that the snipers were not satisfied and came and shot him while he was lying on the ground? Fakhreddin headed back to his house, in tears. "I swear I'll avenge you, Eissa. How could you do that to yourself, and to me and your mother?" he asked himself.

But he stopped on the way. He couldn't keep walking. The people of Bayn al-Sarayat started coming out of their houses and he could no longer look them in the eye, and neither could they. The rift had taken place and that was the end of the matter, and Fakhreddin didn't feel he could go back to living among them. He stopped halfway and retraced his steps to Sudan Street. He crossed the railway lines, went to Hussein's house in Kerdasa, and knocked on the door.

Hussein grew more and more anxious until Fakhreddin woke up and left his room. Hussein wasn't used to friends coming in the morning with their clothes dripping with blood and then collapsing in his arms, waking up only to doze off again and sleep for three whole days. He was really anxious, because he had never seen Fakhreddin in such a state. Hussein was from southern Egypt, in his early thirties, strongly built, fairly dark, with curly hair and a bushy mustache. His voice was a little hoarse from constant smoking. He had come to Cairo to study and then settled. He had volunteered with Fakhreddin in the network of lawyers they had set up to provide legal aid to the poor and needy. His apartment was on the ground floor of the house, with no other residents. His reputation as a respectable lawyer and the free legal aid he had provided to the people of Kerdasa over the previous year had enhanced his popularity in the village. Hussein sat in the small sitting room smoking and drinking tea, and looked at Fakhreddin sitting at the dining table without touching anything Hussein put on it.

"You have to eat something. This won't do!" he said.

"I'll eat, but not quite yet."

Then he sank into silence. After hours of persuasion by Hussein, Fakhreddin finally began to tell him the story.

"What did we do to them? There was a network of lawyers defending poor people. What was it that upset them about that?"

"I'm sure the big lawyers objected."

"Besides, if they just want to close down the network, why are they killing us?"

"Well, they stopped you working and that didn't work. People started coming to us in the coffee shop, instead of us going to them. On the contrary, the network expanded."

"So they started killing us?"

"Obviously the idea went much further than we had imagined. It took on other dimensions. People believed us and trusted us and followed us. And that's what most upset the government."

"Upset them so much that they'd kill us? We're lawyers."

"What do you mean, lawyers, Fakhr? We were running a government out of the coffee shop. Anyway, it went further than that. Now the government's not joking. The fun's over and it's time for everyone to take cover."

Fakhreddin looked at the blood on his clothes and didn't reply. A tear glistened in his eye and Hussein came up to him and sat next to him.

"Listen, Fakhr," he said, "I'm very sorry. Eissa was precious to all of us, but what matters now is that you get out of sight. They think they've killed you. Let them think that and you disappear for a while, till things calm down."

"But I don't want to run away, Hussein. I'll stay. Let them kill me. I'll make sure everyone knows they killed me."

"Okay, but what's the point of that? That's what happened today and people just closed their eyes so they wouldn't see. Is it your responsibility to prove to people something they've known for hundreds of years? Or is it your responsibility to save yourself and stay strong enough to help them? Fakhr, listen to me, and please make a decision with your head, not with your heart. We don't have to prove anything now. Eissa's gone, gone so that you can stay. His sacrifice wasn't a waste. You have no right to throw your life away to make a point that's already been made. We want you to stay alive. That's all that's required of you now. For Eissa's sake and my sake and for the young men who abandoned their lives and followed you. It's no good abandoning them now. It's your responsibility to protect yourself from an enemy with an iron fist."

"And then?"

"And then you rebuild your strength and come back. The confrontation will mean something then."

"Strong individuals will never be enough to take on the power of the state. The only solution is that people discover the strength they have in their own hands if they act jointly and in an organized way."

"I'm with you. But what you're doing is defying the state as an individual. You've just seen what the people of Bayn al-Sarayat are like. They don't react at all."

"This time they didn't react, but if things like this happen again and again a day will definitely come when they react."

"Okay, just take time out, no more than that. We'll think about all these things and see what we'll do."

"And Eissa?"

"I and the group will follow that up till we find out who killed him. We'll expose them wherever they are. I swear by my mother's life, we'll shame them in public. But the important thing is that you disappear somewhere safe."

"And my aunt Maryam? She doesn't have anyone but me now."

"One thing at a time. First we'll get you somewhere safe and then we'll solve the problem of your aunt. Go to my family in Upper Egypt. I have a brother in Asyut and you can hide in his house."

"Isn't that your jihadi brother?"

"What do you mean? It's not a question of jihadis or anything else now. What matters is providing you with somewhere you can be safe. And besides, those jihadis have stopped operating. All they do is pray and hold study and discussion sessions. You don't need to bother with them. Don't go and pray with them if you don't want to, and no one will say anything. He's my brother and you're his guest. No more than that. Does anyone but me know you're still alive?"

"Well, several people from Bayn al-Sarayat saw me after the incident but I don't think they'll say anything."

"Good. From now on, you'll be your cousin, Eissa al-Naggar. I'll go and get his papers from the house. I'll tell your aunt that he's gone away and sent me to fetch some things for him."

"You mean we'll lie to Aunt Maria and hide from her the fact that her son's been killed?"

"Delaying the bad news won't do any harm. We'll tell her that Eissa had to go away suddenly to get his grant, that they said he had to travel now so that he wouldn't lose the grant. And later you can tell her in your own way when you come back, I hope."

The two friends talked like this all through the day and for part of the night: Hussein with his common sense, and Fakhreddin committed to an ideal and resistant to any deviation from it, even temporarily. But Fakhreddin had suffered a succession of blows recently: State Security had harassed him at university in recent years and then the union had stopped him working the previous year, Shireen had left him, and he had been arrested in Hafr al-Batin when he incited the troops not to take part in the 1991 Gulf War against Iraq. It was a real miracle that he had survived all this and had remained undaunted. He was wounded and the wounds were deep, although he suppressed the pain. The killing of Eissa had sapped what strength he had left. He could no longer bear this ordeal. If he had decided to leave himself to his enemies and wait for them, when he knew they were coming, that was not only because he wanted them to be held accountable for killing him but also because he was tired and felt he couldn't go on. He wanted a rest. Deep in his heart he wished the snipers had shot him behind the Coca-Cola factory, rather than his innocent cousin. He knew that Hussein was right and that he owed it to himself and to those who loved him and followed him to lick his wounds and move on.

"In the meantime, Ali, Ashraf, and I will submit statements about the killing, but based on the premise that it was you who was killed, until the investigations reveal the truth, and then you can reappear. On my honor I promise you I won't shut up until I've exposed the people behind it. Ali and Ashraf will help me, but only the four of us need know you're still alive. From now on you're Eissa, not Fakhreddin, until the issue's resolved."

"Make it five people. My aunt has to know that I'm alive. Don't tell her about Eissa now. Tell her Eissa's gone away, as you suggested, but she has to know that I'm alive and that I'll look out for her from a distance until I can come back or I send her a message."

"Agreed."

Hussein got up to call his brother in Asyut from a public telephone and tell him that a friend who was dear to him would come to their house the next day and stay a week.

"He won't ask me why, and I'll contact you through him."

Fakhreddin didn't answer. Hussein patted him on the shoulder affectionately, smiled encouragingly, and left.

Ali went up the stairs feeling anxious about the encounter. But Aunt Maria had prepared herself for the worst, because news travels fast in Bayn al-Sarayat. When she saw him on the doorstep, she took him by the hand, pulled him inside, and closed the door quickly. She hadn't found her son at home when she woke up and the local women had told her that the streets had been full of security men since early in the morning and there had been some shooting. Some of them swore they had seen Fakhreddin in a pool of blood behind the Coca-Cola factory. Since then she had stayed at home praying. Ali assured her that Eissa and Fakhreddin were well. It was hard for him to lie, especially to Aunt Maria, but he had no other option. He told her that Fakhreddin was wanted by the police. People thought he had been killed and it was best to go on believing this until things calmed down. He told her that Eissa would also go into hiding and would try to leave the country for France as soon as possible, so that he wouldn't be arrested and lose the grant he had been awarded to study there. He asked her to pretend to be mourning for Fakhreddin. She said she already carried enough sorrow for the whole country and she had no need to pretend. He agreed with what she said, asked her to tell anyone who asked that Eissa had gone to France on his study grant, and again emphasized the importance of keeping the secret in order to protect her sons, and so it was.

Aunt Maria really did carry sorrow enough for a whole country. Ever since she and her husband Youssef had left their village, driven out of the house of his sister, Fakhreddin's mother, they had faced a succession of troubles. Having lost everything they owned in their village, they ended up living in another village as impoverished outsiders. Youssef couldn't find regular work that would provide them with a decent income. Then their elder daughter died from a fever, and Youssef fell ill and had to give up work entirely. One night Maria and Eissa came home to find an ambulance parked outside and two watchmen ominously muttering prayers. At first they stopped them from going inside, but let her through when she started screaming. When she rushed in, the paramedics were putting the bodies of Youssef and her two other daughters into the ambulance. The neighbors said they had died of carbon monoxide poisoning. Aunt Maria thanked God for her lot in life but in her heart of hearts she didn't understand why God had chosen to inflict all these misfortunes on her and her family, who had never in their lives harmed another living creature. But she accepted it; she accepted it and asked God for forgiveness.

She couldn't spend the night at home. She and her son Eissa went to live with some neighbors, then she sent Eissa to Fakhreddin to ask if they could come to live with him in Cairo. Her husband had revered Fakhreddin, saying he was the only real man left in the family. She didn't know exactly where he lived, just that he was a lawyer and that people were bound to help Eissa find him. And indeed, Eissa found him the first day he arrived in Cairo, in a coffee shop in the Bayn al-Sarayat district near the university. Fakhreddin welcomed his cousin and his eyes teared up several times that evening as he listened to Eissa's story. He not only accepted his aunt's request; the next morning he got up early, went with his cousin to where she was staying, and brought her back himself. At first she and Eissa lived in the small room he had been using on the roof of a building, while he moved in with his friend Ali. A week later he found them a small apartment in a street nearby. Fakhreddin provided for his aunt and her son and, more importantly, looked after Eissa like a brother. He helped him apply for a place in the law faculty at Cairo University, helped him with his studies, and encouraged him until he graduated and then earned a master's degree. Eissa did so well at university that he won a scholarship to do his doctorate in France, and Maria was convinced that all the credit for this should go to Fakhreddin.

But her sons, as she called them both, were caught up in politics and she knew deep inside that nothing would deter them from that; it was something almost hereditary in the family. But she wished they would give it up. Why did those she loved always have to take on the burden of defending justice? Wasn't it enough what had happened to her husband? He had been evicted from his home and driven out of his village for standing up against Selim, the family patriarch, when he robbed Fakhreddin of his inheritance. And he had stood up against him again when he tried to force Fakhreddin into an arranged marriage to extend his own wealth. He stood for justice, at a terrible cost. His own sister sided with her husband the patriarch. And it killed him, long before the gas leak finished him off. Before that there was Fakhreddin's father, who had protected them all from the cruelty of Uncle Selim, and Aisha, Fakhreddin's mother, who had stood up to Uncle Selim to defend her and her son's rights until Selim finally had his way. Did the children have to relive this saga of lost struggle? If Selim and the likes of him always triumph, why should we waste our lives resisting them? That's what she asked herself in silence, and sometimes she would let slip a word to Fakhreddin or Eissa, and then hastily retract it, because she knew that what happened was inevitable. Everything was ordained and predetermined.

*

Ali drank his tea, gathered together some of Eissa's papers and other stuff, and emphasized to Aunt Maria for the tenth time that she should pretend not to know anything other than what the local people were saying. Maria was reserved by nature and Ali wasn't worried she would say anything, but these were Hussein's instructions and he was carrying them out.

Fakhreddin sat by the window on the train to Asyut. He looked different today. Ali had given him some different clothes and changed his hairstyle. He wondered how long the trip would last. He didn't feel at ease leaving the house and the neighborhood where he had lived all those years. Despite everything he didn't approve of running away from a confrontation with injustice and malicious lies. He had never run away before, or even backed off an inch, neither in the village with his uncle, nor in State Security detention in his university days, nor even in the field of battle in the midst of war. So why should he retreat now? How could he agree to compromise? As he sat on the crowded train, he wondered whether this moment marked the end of the integrity he had always tried to maintain inside himself, and whether this was the end of him, banished and unsure where the train would take him. But they had tried to kill him before, and he wondered what he would gain if they really killed him. He would lose, and justice would gain nothing. He told himself this and calmed down. Then he went back to thinking that by this logic he would have done better to compromise as a lawyer, keep his name on the register of lawyers, and defend people who had been wronged. Was making compromises the beginning of an endless sequence of concessions? Or was Hussein right when he said that Fakhreddin was now defending his cause and had a duty to stay alive and refuse to die a gratuitous death from which no one would gain anything?

He found no answer. But he vowed he would return, even if it took a long time. He would come back to defend his causes. He wouldn't give up and compromise. He would disappear to protect himself from this crazy violence. But he would build up his strength and return. A strong believer is better than a weak believer, and better than a martyr. From now on he didn't want to be weak or a martyr. No. He would arm himself so that he could come back and triumph in the cause of justice. It would be a long battle and this was only the first round. The Palestinian poet Mahmoud Darwish told the defeated fighter: "Lay down the bag of storms at the first rock, and pick up your emptiness and my defeat." But he no longer wanted to be defeated. No, he would carry the bag of storms with him and go on to triumph in the cause of justice, and the day would come when he would tip the scales with his hand.

Ashraf, Ali, and Hussein prepared a number of anonymous statements and mailed them from various post offices. The statements contained the facts about the day of the shooting. One of them said that Fakhreddin had disappeared from his place of residence and another said he had been killed and included a drawing of the area where the shooting took place. A third included details of Fakhreddin and the addresses of his family and acquaintances. A fourth provided details of some local people who knew him well, and so on. Taken together, the statements included everything that an investigator would need if he wanted to look into the incident seriously. They asked their friends in the prosecutor's office how the investigation was going and a few days later they heard that the prosecution had decided to file the statements away. Then they started looking at ways to put pressure on the prosecutor's office to order an investigation.

Ashraf approached Dr. Nashaat Ghaleb, their professor at college and the director of a human rights organization. Ashraf saw him as a model for professors who combine academic work and a sense of responsibility toward their students and their country. The professor had helped him when one of his relatives had converted from Christianity and run into trouble, and after that his relationship with Nashaat had grown stronger. When they started their free and unofficial legal consultancy network out of the coffee shop in Bayn al-Sarayat, Nashaat took an interest in the experiment. Ashraf invited him to come along one evening and introduced him to Fakhreddin, and he spent the evening with them. But he expressed reservations about the experiment, saying it was unrealistic and doomed to failure. Nashaat said it was wrong to give people false hope if you couldn't help them when they needed you. When Ashraf asked him why he wouldn't be able to help them, Nashaat shook his head and didn't answer.

Ashraf explained the murder of Eissa to Nashaat and how the public prosecutors did not want to start an investigation.

"Of course they won't investigate the statements," Nashaat said.

"Why not?"

"Because if it was an assassination, as you say, then they won't investigate. And if it was all imaginary, they won't be interested."

"Of course it wasn't imaginary."

"Are there any witnesses?"

"There are the local people."

"Where were they at the time of the incident?"

"They were in their homes."

"And of course they didn't do anything."

"No."

"Could any of them testify?"

"I don't think so."

"Well, what then?"

"What how?"

"What do you want? Even if there is an investigation, who would they question?"

"The people who committed the crime!"

"Are you joking, Ashraf? When will you lot come to your senses? I hate the expression 'I told you so' but is there anything surprising in what happened? When we spoke months ago, didn't I tell you that this is how it would end? Are you really living with us in this country or in some other country? No one else would do what you've been doing."

"Okay, so what have we been doing? Do you like what's happening around you? What are we expected to do? Accept it? Just sit and watch?"

"No, we don't accept it and we don't sit and watch. We act prudently, not jump in at the deep end. I told you it was childish and it couldn't go on. The sensible thing is to carry out proper legal work so that no one can stop you. You're lawyers, not cheerleaders at a demonstration. You should work according to the law and in the framework of the law. Use the law to expand the margin available to you."

"Okay, but you've been doing that for fifteen years, and have you gotten anywhere?"

"I think we've been doing good work. The office hasn't been closed down and it's still doing its duty serving at least a few of those who need help, and the proof of that is that you're here today."

"Okay, so what should we do now?"

"Let me see what I can do. I have contacts that can help. I'll do what I can, but think about what I told you anyway, and about giving up these small gestures and starting to work in a sensible, institutional way."

"Okay, but please do see what you can do about an investigation."

Hussein went to meet Nasser al-Khudari, who was an old friend of Fakhreddin's though the relationship had languished in recent years. Hussein didn't like Nasser, or even respect him. He saw him as a young nihilist who lived a bohemian lifestyle free of responsibility and justified his frivolous way of life to himself with confused ideas about the difficulty of the historical circumstance. Hussein was a man of action who hated theories that didn't match the obvious logic of things—what he called intellectuals' talk. Hussein was from Saqultah near the southern town of Sohag. He was educated in government schools and worked while studying to help his family cover its increasing expenses. When he went to university he worked in the carpet trade at the same time to support himself and then to help his retired father in his village. As he struggled to feed himself, pay the rent, and cover the costs of studying, he had no energy left for conversations that are remote from practical reality. Hussein lived with his neighbors in Kerdasa and cooperated or argued with them over the immediate aspects of life—providing drinking water, the broken sewage pipe, the bridge the government planned to build that would divert traffic and affect the shops that were people's livelihoods, the young men who harassed female tourists, the problems associated with street children working in workshops, and so on. His relationship with his neighbors, the people of Kerdasa, and politics as a whole was defined by the struggles, agreements, and alliances involved in dealing with these issues. Because of this he was inclined to look for solutions that sought to protect the immediate public interest and buy time until circumstances were more favorable.

So he went to see Nasser, who worked in a news agency, to see if he could push the prosecutor's office to open an investigation into Eissa's murder. But Nasser wasn't any use. He cried when Hussein told him that Fakhreddin had disappeared and was rumored to have been killed. He faulted himself for failing to keep in touch with him in recent years. Then he started explaining why this had happened and about the incident that had taken place when he was working as an engineer in an electricity project, before he started working as a translator in the news agency. Then he went on about his friendship with Fakhreddin, how complicated it was and how, although he liked him very much, he hadn't been able to stay in touch with him over the years because of the complications. When Hussein interrupted him and asked impatiently if Nasser could help, Nasser asked innocently what he could do if Fakhreddin had been killed, and that was the end of the matter. Hussein asked if he could write something on the subject in a newspaper or magazine, to stir up public opinion and put pressure on the prosecutor's office to act. But Nasser told him he was a translator and not a journalist. Hussein asked him about his journalist friends and acquaintances and whether one of them might do that if he met them and gave them the necessary facts. Nasser thought about it for a while and then asked for some time to look into it. He gave Hussein his telephone number and left.

> Coming down from the old wound to the contours of the country,
> The year when the sea was separated from the cities of ash
> And I was alone
> Then alone
> Oh alone? And Ahmed
> Between one bullet and another the sea was gone,
> Leaving a camp that grows and gives rise to thyme and fighters,
> And an arm that grows strong in forgetfulness
> A memory that comes from the trains that pass by
> And platforms without jasmine or people to welcome the passengers.

Fakhreddin stared at the Darwish poem and thought about the camp and the fighters there. What did the camp look like? Was it a collection of old tents battered by the wind and rain, or was it scattered, dilapidated buildings like the ones he was sitting among? The sun was shining on the courtyard of the house, saturating the dirt floor and reflecting off the cracked walls of the house. The spots of whitewash on the walls shone like little mirrors. Outside it was calm and the little streets were silent at that time of day. The men had gone to work and the women had stayed home. He was sitting immobile in the courtyard, like a statue made of the mud that was all around him. He wasn't thinking, just sitting staring into space and giving free rein to his wandering thoughts. He asked himself if what he was doing was a waste of time, and he didn't have a convincing answer. He asked himself for the thousandth time: "Why am I sitting here now? What next?" Hammam, Hussein's brother, his bearded and silent companions, and their women in the hijab behind the walls knew what they were doing. But he was sitting still, uncertain what he would be doing the next day. The sun was shining in Asyut, and where there had once been fields there were now houses. Dust covered the streets of the city and there were barricades around the local security headquarters. He thought back to the clashes that had taken place in the city after President Sadat was assassinated in 1981 and wondered why Asyut was special in this regard. Then he remembered the clashes that had taken place in Mansoura when he was a boy and that were related to the extremist group Takfir wa-l-Higra, Shukri Mustafa (the group's leader), and the kidnapping of Sheikh al-Dhahabi, the former minister of religious endowments. He was a boy at the time and didn't understand much about it. But he remembered the trucks full of police in the streets, the cordon around a heavily populated area, and the sound of gunfire. And many people told stories about the young fundamentalists and the clashes with security.

He wondered what his uncle Selim would be doing right then, and also Selim's daughter Leila. He thought about the kind of man who had agreed to marry Leila for ten acres of land, when she was pregnant by another man, only to divorce her right after the birth. He thought about Selim's son, Ahmed, and how he had inherited so many of his father's traits: he had contrived to take land and a business from Fakhreddin's disabled father and had cheated his sister, Leila, just as his father had done in the past.

He walked through the dusty streets of Asyut, sat in the sunny courtyard, and wondered whether being just or unjust was hereditary. The mud house was easy on the eye and on the spirit, and the courtyard welcomed the sun and gave the residents a sanctuary where they could move around in comfort. Why didn't they build houses like that in Cairo? Why did everything have to be so frenetic? He sat still or walked around aimlessly, wondering where his old companions and old friends from university were now. He thought about Shireen, who married a man she hardly knew and went abroad with him. He sat and walked and slept and wondered why everyone he loved had disappeared.

He had so much on his mind and needed to unload some of the excess. This stay in Asyut might prove useful as a chance to sit in the sun and clear his mind. He was someone who went from one ordeal to another. Each ordeal left its mark on him and soon paved the way for another ordeal in the future. Hussein said that God tested those He loved with these ordeals. Ali laughed and, in his Aswani accent, asked sarcastically, "So of all His people the good Lord loves only Fakhreddin!" Ashraf stepped in to stop Hussein and Ali from reviving an old debate, saying something about Jesus Christ and his sufferings, but neither of them listened. Fakhreddin, unlike his friends, didn't think the ordeals he had gone through were anything out of the ordinary. He didn't believe they were tests set by God, but rather injustices that human beings inflicted on themselves and on each other. These ordeals only made him more determined, but now he was tired. Tired and on the run from a regime that was armed to the teeth and had plenty of foot soldiers. The regime had escaped from the rule of law and wanted to cut off his head. All he wanted now was to rest, to sit still in the sun waiting for something that he couldn't name, something he would do that would give him the strength to return.

Nashaat Ghaleb called Ashraf and told him that after exerting pressure on some of his contacts he had won a promise that an inquiry would be opened into Eissa's murder. But he warned him that the inquiry wouldn't go anywhere unless there were witnesses willing to speak. Nashaat told him the investigator who would take on the case was diligent and honest. He urged Ashraf to try to persuade two or three of the witnesses to tell the investigator what they had seen and heard, suggesting this might be their only chance to expose the conspiracy to kill Fakhreddin.

Ashraf didn't dismiss the news. He called Ali and Hussein, who met on the afternoon of the same day. Ali wasn't enthusiastic and doubted any of the local people would testify, because if any of them were brave enough to testify they would have acted when the security forces came and took over the roofs of the buildings where they lived, or at least they would have warned Fakhreddin. Ali was angry with the people of the neighborhood, and didn't think any good would come of them, given that they had left Eissa or Fakhreddin to be killed within sight and earshot of their homes. But Hussein said they would lose nothing by trying and thought they should understand the fears and concerns of the local people. Who would protect them from the government's brutality if they disobeyed it? If the government could crush Fakhreddin, who was supposed to defend them and protect their rights, how could any of them be expected to resist? Besides, in the end each of them hoped that someone else would act first, and that was normal. They had another discussion later, and as usual Ashraf came up with a compromise, and the three of them agreed that Hussein should make another attempt with the people in the neighborhood, those who had close links with Fakhreddin, without raising anyone's suspicions. With that in mind, Hussein spent the rest of that day, and the following day, in Bayn al-Sarayat, talking to the local people.

On November 1, Mahmoud Bey, the public prosecutor's office manager, called in Omar Fares, one of his investigators, threw a file at him, and asked him to have a look at it. The case was causing too much trouble. There were endless statements being made and journalists were calling to ask why the matter wasn't being investigated. Then came a call from a senior intelligence officer called Ahmed Kamal, asking about the implications of the case, and Nashaat Ghaleb had also chased him personally to open an investigation. Mahmoud Bey explained to Omar Fares that the public prosecutor had received numerous requests to investigate the incident and was interested in discovering the truth, but he also led him to believe, without saying so explicitly, that the case should be quickly wrapped up and buried, properly and professionally. Omar Fares asked how much time he had for the investigation, and without blinking Mahmoud Bey said, "No more than a week." In effect, it would be swept under the carpet. Mahmoud had deliberately given the assignment to Omar Fares because Omar was known to be competent, intelligent, and professional, and in this way he would fend off suspicions of a whitewash. He was also well aware that a competent person such as Omar could not do anything of value in one week and, since he was about to conclude an important and complicated drugs case that he had been working on for months, he wouldn't waste much of his time on this case.

Exactly a week later, after several inquiries and interrogations that led to nothing, Omar Fares decided that there was no case to investigate. He filed the reports away and submitted his report to Mahmoud Bey, who assured him he was confident of his good judgment. At the time Omar Fares did not understand what Mahmoud Bey meant by this strange comment.

Hussein sat opposite Fakhreddin in the sun-drenched court-yard and smiled.

"Hammam says you sit here without moving from the time you wake up till sunset," he said.

"That's right."

"Good, you deserve a rest."

"Is there anything you need?" Hussein added after a pause.

"No thanks. Just send my regards to Aunt Maria and tell her I hope to come and see her soon. Make sure she has everything she needs. I'm sure Ali's taking care of her, but she likes people to ask after her."

"That goes without saying," said Hussein. "Don't worry, things will look up soon."

"There must be a way forward, but I can't find it. I'm sure there's a way. Sometimes something's right in front of you and you don't notice it. Like when water keeps rising and then suddenly there's a flood."

"My God, that's what I'm really worried about—that flood. Can't you see where things are heading here?"

"I can. Aren't those people your friends?"

"No, my friends are rather less serious than those people. My friends are people who pray and fast, grow their beards, and follow sharia. But those people have gone right to the dark side. They denounce my friends as infidels. Haven't you spoken to any of them?"

"No, I'm not up to it and they're not very sociable anyway. One of them came and spoke to me a little in the beginning and then disappeared. Apparently he was checking me out. Hammam told me that some of them have come back from waging jihad against the Soviets in Afghanistan and they saw horrible things there. They don't speak much and they don't want to be disturbed. He clearly asked them for permission to give me shelter here."

"He did indeed."

"And I haven't seen a single woman since the day I came. They're very strict about men and women mixing too."

"That's right."

"What I don't understand is why they're all concentrated in one area like this and the government leaves them alone. I didn't like to ask Hammam in case he gets anxious."

"There's nothing to it. They have an agreement with the security people: the police leave them alone and they don't engage in any activity."

"Really?"

"Really. They came back exhausted and made a decision not to carry out any operations here. They don't bother the government in any way."

"But they've created a separate society here. It's like we're in another country."

"All the better. It will never occur to anyone that you're here."

Fakhreddin wasn't unhappy to be staying in Asyut. On the contrary, it provided him with rest that he sorely needed. What occupied his thoughts was his next step. If the investigation had been closed down, it meant that the powers lying in wait for him had the upper hand, and so he couldn't reappear for a long time, or if he did reappear, he would just be killed. He could live in hiding until things changed, but that could take years. And then, what would he do during that time? That was what preoccupied him as he sat there in the courtyard of Hammam's house: caught between thinking his future over, remembering the past, and pondering unanswerable questions.

The same questions preoccupied Hussein, Ali, and Ashraf, who also worried about their own fates. While Fakhreddin pondered his next move, the three of them were busy trying to persuade Omar Fares to reopen the investigation.

The information they had on Omar Fares suggested he was a serious and honest man, diligent and the top of his class in college. His father was a retired judge and his mother was active in charity work. They were from a family with a history in the law: his grandfather had been minister of justice in the 1930s and had carried out important reforms in the judiciary. Omar Fares was unmarried and spent all his time in the office or riding horses on Friday at the Equestrian Club. He lived alone in a small apartment on Qasr al-Aini Street that seems to have belonged to his father. He had a friend he met once a week for dinner at a kebab restaurant in the Madbah district and he visited his parents and his sister, who lived with them, for lunch on Friday, and no more.

Ashraf tried to persuade Nashaat Ghaleb to press Omar Fares into reopening the inquiry, but Nashaat told him to forget it. Hussein went to meet Nasser again and found him incoherent and apparently very drunk, although it was the morning. They made other attempts with their contacts and with Fakhreddin's old classmates from university, some of whom were now prominent in the world of journalism, law, and politics. They would smile and play down the importance of Fakhreddin's 'disappearance,' noting that he had disappeared several times in the past, and giving assurances that he would reappear. Other people avoided meeting them altogether.

Ashraf then suggested preparing a large dossier on the real story of Fakhreddin and sending it to Omar Fares. At first Hussein was wary of the consequences, but as time passed they began to lose hope of finding an effective way to reopen the inquiry and resume their normal lives. Hussein remained opposed to the idea until he discussed it with Fakhreddin during his short visit to Asyut. Fakhreddin agreed to the idea and so the three began to prepare the dossier.

They put a variety of things in it: his and his family's documents; papers about the inheritance that his uncle had appropriated; some pages of the diary Fakhreddin had written while still in his village, about the shameful deeds that his closest relatives had developed a taste for; letters his school friends had written at a time when their consciousness was maturing, despite the intellectual and psychological repression imposed by the education system; photographs and short stories; poems he had written while at university; excerpts from letters that he and Shireen had sent each other before she left him and got married; documents about Fakhreddin and his friends' repeated encounters with repression at university, betrayals by colleagues, and police brutality; glimpses into his military service, when he and his colleagues were sent to take part in the attack on Iraq in 1991 and he was court-martialed in Hafr al-Batin after refusing to fight; then, details about his dismissal from the office where he was working and his suspension by the Bar Association; and the empty cartridge that Fakhreddin had picked up next to Eissa's body.

They put everything into a large envelope, and waited till Omar Fares had finished the big drugs case that had kept him busy. He lost the case and all the alleged smugglers left the court smiling at their acquittal. The next day they sent the envelope to his home address, sat down, and waited.

The die was cast.

Nashaat Ghaleb told Ashraf he had met Omar Fares, who said he had tried to reopen the investigation but that his superiors had categorically refused to do so. Nashaat found Omar confused and said he claimed that Fakhreddin had visited him in a dream. Immediately after the dream he had received an envelope with a set of documents signed by Fakhreddin and a box containing an empty cartridge. He thought Omar Fares was going through a difficult period after losing the drugs case because of a procedural error. This may have contributed to his request for a leave of absence, during which time he decided he would look into Fakhreddin's case. Nashaat reiterated that what Omar Fares was doing was in a personal capacity and his investigation had no official status. It would have no tangible effect other than to clear Omar Fares's conscience at the most. The fact that he had gone on leave in the wake of this case was powerful evidence that the investigation route was well and truly stymied and now they had to find another approach.

But no one could see any other approach. Fakhreddin admitted to Hussein that he hadn't hit upon a viable solution, but at the same time he didn't want to spend the next few years lazing in the sun. He hadn't been officially charged with anything, so he couldn't hand himself in to the police and face the charges. He didn't know what he could do now, other than go back and let them kill him in the street as he had wanted them to do from the start. Ali and Ashraf suggested he stay in hiding a while longer, far from Cairo, and pose as his cousin Eissa. Hussein came up with a bold idea: Eissa had a scholarship to study for a doctorate at the Sorbonne in France and Fakhreddin could go in his place. Ashraf and Ali supported it immediately but Fakhreddin didn't because it felt too much like appropriating his cousin's life. But there were not many options available and it didn't make sense for him to waste his life to no purpose. Fakhreddin was a brilliant lawyer and a scholar who loved law, so this would be an opportunity to pass the time at a safe distance from the people who wanted to kill him, and at the same time to improve himself. He had the papers ready, there was a certain resemblance between him and his cousin and no one looks too closely at the old photographs on academic certificates or passports.

"The only obstacle will be the airport, and the calmer and more self-confident you are, the smoother things will go," said Hussein.

Fakhreddin still had reservations about the idea but it really was his only option. He wasn't going to sit idle waiting for Omar Fares's investigation, which was no longer a real investigation according to Nashaat Ghaleb. "Good luck to him," Hussein said, and it was decided Fakhreddin would go. He would go so that one day he could return.

The friends sat in the airport cafeteria waiting for Fakhreddin to go through. He signaled to them from behind the barriers after checking in his bags and getting his boarding card. Then he went to passport control and they held their breath. They wouldn't be able to see him from where they were. They had agreed with him that he would go straight through to the transit lounge and wouldn't try to come back and wave to them, so as not to give anyone a chance to ask any questions. After clearing passport control, he would go into the transit lounge and call Ashraf's house from the telephone office and ask Ashraf's mother whether he was at home. If anything untoward happened he wouldn't call. Every five minutes Ashraf got up and called home. Half an hour later his mother told him that Fakhreddin had called to ask after him.

The three friends sat in the cafeteria until the plane took off.

"What shall we do now?"

"I don't know. I'm thinking of going to Asyut to see my brother."

"And join that group?"

"Isn't that better than sitting around doing nothing? What are you going to do, Ali?"

"Nothing. I mean, what can I do? I'll wait till God provides relief."

"And you, Ashraf?"

"I really don't know. Maybe I'll join a monastery."

3

Saint-Denis

As THE METRO HIT THE bend the carriages shook and the wheels screeched. The train picked up speed as it turned through the tunnel like the ghost train at a funfair. Moments later it slowed down to stop at Place de Clichy station. The people who got off to go to the nightclubs close to the square were white, or they were tourists, while the blacks and Arabs who lived in the banlieues stayed on board. Fakhreddin finally sat down and took out the small book he was reading. He had hated the metro ever since he had arrived in Paris. All his life he had heard about the Paris metro, and he had been eager to see this thing, which must surely be a model of efficiency and elegance. When he reached the airport he had looked for it. After going up and going down and dragging his heavy suitcases amid glares from travelers who resented him blocking the narrow escalators, he found the metro. He squeezed into it, found a seat, and sat down. The metro set off with a speed and a quietness that matched its reputation, and then went into the tunnel and the smell in the air was stifling and unpleasant. At first Fakhreddin thought there was a local problem—maybe there was a sewer nearby or a fault with the water supply and the smell would pass. But it didn't pass: it was there every time Fakhreddin stepped foot in those horrible metal carriages.

On his way from the airport, he felt the other passengers looking at him disapprovingly because he had so many bags. One man muttered something he didn't understand, then an old woman yelled at him, asking if he couldn't see that he was getting in people's way. Before he could reply, she got off, sighing in exasperation. From then on, whenever he ventured onto the metro, in the early morning or in the evening, he prayed to God that he would find a secluded place to sit apart from the other passengers, where he could try to read his book in peace. But the silent war between the various ethnicities among the passengers prevented him from focusing. There was a free seat next to a black passenger, who was listening to loud music that spilled out from the headphones he was wearing. A blond woman stood looking at the empty seat, but refrained from sitting there. At the next station, the man playing the music got off and the woman immediately sat in the empty seat. A woman wearing a hijab, and carrying many plastic bags marked with the name of a cheap supermarket, tried to gather the bags in front of her feet, while the man next to her showed signs of annoyance every time one of the bags touched him. Two teenagers were kissing passionately, pretending they couldn't see anyone, and those around them were busy pretending that nothing unusual was happening in front of them. Then a woman got on dragging a girl of around six behind her, and trying to win passengers' sympathy by saying she was a poor woman from Romania with no father or family and she needed money to have her daughter treated for various diseases. She went from carriage to carriage and Fakhreddin didn't see anyone give her a single franc. Then came the unkempt musician with his loud guitar, stinking of alcohol, playing, singing, shouting, collecting francs, and moving on. An Arab passenger looked Fakhreddin in the eye, trying to ascertain his identity, as if asking him whether he was with him or against him. An American tourist surveyed the scene, trying to work out whether the man sitting opposite was a good foreigner or a scary one. Then a woman with a lonely-looking face, and another who was depressed, and more and more of them till Fakhreddin felt dizzy. He went back to his book, but a man sat next to him and knocked his thigh into him, as he manspread his legs. Fakhreddin cowered where he sat and tried not to look up from his book.

The metro reached the end of the line and Fakhreddin hurried out to find the Basilica of Saint-Denis at the top of the metro station stairway. He wrapped his coat tight at the neck and smiled as he remembered his aunt Maria claiming that all members of their family suffered from cold necks and insisting that he do up the top button on his shirt, even in summer. The smell of *merguez* sausages filled the square in front of the cathedral. Fakhreddin stopped at the Amine restaurant and bought a large sandwich filled with the North African sausages, which reminded him of Saber's sausages in Bayn al-Sarayat. The street was crammed with shops selling halal meat. Plump women with colored scarves covering their hair were coming and going, dragging behind them large plastic shopping carts with wheels that didn't run smoothly on the cobbled street. The groceries smelled of Arab foodstuffs—Damietta cheese, mulukhiya, couscous, and Tunisian chili pepper. A group of youngsters was standing in a circle on the paved area in front of the cathedral door, watching two young men on skateboards jumping between the benches on the pavement. He decided against sitting there to eat. He packed up his sandwich in its box, put it in his bag, and went on toward the bus station.

The apartment where Fakhreddin lived was about an hour and a half from the university. When he arrived in Paris he found that the institute that had awarded him the scholarship had arranged for him to live in university dorms in an isolated tower block. But several nights in the block persuaded him that he had to move into private accommodation. He hadn't imagined he could find any university accommodation grimmer than the dorms in Abu Qatada in Cairo. Every time he went into his room, he felt as if he was in a cell on a submarine that had gone missing. The room was cold and depressing, with bare walls. He couldn't read or sit or do anything in it. It rejected him whenever he went in, like a womb that was contracting and wanting to get rid of him. He would go back to the room late so as to sleep immediately. He saw the room as just a large bed suspended in the air in a gloomy building, and for the rest of the day he took refuge wherever he could, to recover and feel more comfortable. He would hang out in the nearby park or around the university buildings, trying to read or study, but he needed a house to relax in, if only for a short while.

Then came the sounds of people making love. The sounds seemed very close, as if they were with him in the room. It wasn't just the screams that came at the end, he also heard the whisperings and the moans and groans that came earlier, and even the sound of kissing. He hadn't known that kissing could make a noise. The first time he heard these noises, he jumped out of bed and stared at the wall in disbelief. He thought of making a noise to let them know that someone could hear them, but he was too embarrassed to interrupt what sounded like a heated encounter. In the morning, and every morning for two weeks, he tried to find the person in the room next door to tell them how the sound traveled, as well as to see this formidable lover who never tired or lost interest. But he never succeeded. Every day he saw new faces in the corridors and in the shared bathrooms in the middle of the floor, and in the end he gave up.

Then came the cold, which was so resistant to all forms of heating that he would wear all the clothes he had at night, and, along with it, was the sound of the wind and the doors slamming in the wind. And there was the deadly feeling of isolation and silence: when he walked across the small garden that separated the street from the university campus he felt as if he were crossing the border between the real world and a submarine that was part of a nightmare from which there was no deliverance.

At the university he asked how he could look for private accommodation, and the woman in the office advised him skeptically to ask in the accommodation center. She didn't forget to point out that his monthly allowance was only four thousand francs, which didn't give him much leeway to afford the high Parisian rents. He went to the center, where they gave him a long list of addresses, telephone numbers, and details of rooms and apartments of every kind. He spent a week viewing rooms for rent for less than two thousand francs a month, which was all he could afford. These were either maids' rooms on the top floors of houses, where half the room had a sloping ceiling and you could stand up straight only in the other half, rooms on the dark side of a courtyard, or rooms squeezed in next to or under the staircase. None of them had bathrooms. He saw these rooms and thought of the Egyptian writer Tawfik al-Hakim, the "Sparrow from the East" as he called himself in his book about his stay in France as a student. At first he went to Montmartre to look for a room, but the smiles of disdain in the realty offices soon taught him to look elsewhere.

When he grew increasingly desperate about finding suitable accommodation, his friend Mohamed Buheiri, who knew Paris intimately, advised him to look in the Saint-Denis neighborhood, where he found a very small apartment in one of the government housing projects known as "moderately priced accommodation." The government had let the apartment to an Algerian family but the family would be away for two years and wanted to sublet the apartment to someone at a slightly higher rent, without telling the authorities so that the family didn't lose it. Mohamed Buheiri said this was standard practice, especially among poor immigrant families who wanted to keep these apartments for when their relatives came back. Out of necessity Fakhreddin moved into the apartment.

The bus arrived, half empty at that time of day. The driver, waxy-faced, did not return the passengers' greetings and watched them warily. When a young man in baggy clothes playing loud music got on, he took the man's metro travel card and asked to see his identity card. The man objected with wild arm gestures, incomplete sentences, and an accent characteristic of banlieue residents. The driver waited indifferently for him to finish his objections and then repeated his request in a monotone, as if he hadn't heard a single word of what the man said. Fakhreddin, sitting in the middle of the bus, took out the *merguez* and started to eat. He looked out of the window at the buildings in the industrial zone through which the bus was passing. The streets were deserted and the buildings all looked like warehouses. Small shops that sold cigarettes appeared from time to time. A police station, a train track, and bridges leading to the Paris ring road. Concrete bridges, then concrete walls, streets of asphalt and concrete sidewalks. The only colorful thing was the graffiti young people had sprayed onto the walls with metallic paint. The bus drove under the ring road. A little bell rang. The bus stopped for less than a minute, then moved off again. It went past a shopping center and a small cinema. Neon lights that hummed constantly spelled out the name of the shopping center. One of the letters was dark, and a neighborhood beggar loitered around the shopping center, pushing a shopping cart. Empty fruit and vegetable crates were piled up, waiting for the garbage truck. Teenagers were gathered in the square, skateboarding without enthusiasm. He pulled the cord by the window and listened as usual to the sound of the little bell. A few moments later the bus stopped. He went down the stairs, the door opened, and he got off.

When Fakhreddin first rode on a Paris bus, he stood on the back stairs waiting for the door to open, but it didn't. He called the driver, who didn't answer. The bus moved off with him still on board. He made his way through to the driver and told him he had wanted to get off at the stop, but he hadn't opened the door for him. The driver didn't turn to him or reply. Fakhreddin repeated his remark but the driver remained silent. The bus stopped at the next stop and Fakhreddin rushed out of the front door despite the protests of an old woman who wanted to get on. After that one of his Arab colleagues at university told him that the bus door only opened if you put your hand on the door window. Fakhreddin didn't understand why the driver hadn't told him this.

He pushed open the door of the building and went into an empty lobby. He pressed the lift button and waited. The red paint on the metalwork in the lobby and the lift relieved the gloom a little. The lobby door opened and the mailman came in, heading for the mailboxes. Fakhreddin followed him to see if he had any letters. He heard the elevator door open and close and someone inside cursing the unknown people who had pressed the elevator button for no reason. He wished the mailman a good day and the mailman returned his greeting without looking up from the boxes where he was putting the letters. Fakhreddin said nothing and waited. The mailman muttered the apartment numbers as he looked at the boxes. Fakhreddin heard his apartment number and said, "Yes, that's me."

The mailman ignored Fakhreddin's outstretched hand and put the envelope in the box. He finished putting the rest of the letters in the other boxes, and then left. Fakhreddin took out his key, shaking his head in disbelief, took out his letter, closed the box, and moved off. He looked at the letter as he waited for the elevator. It was from Nasser; at last a letter from his old friend. He would go up to his little apartment, put the heating on, make some tea, and sit down to read the letter. Nasser's letters were like a warm breeze in the emotional wasteland around him. Everything about the letter had an effect on him: Nasser's handwriting on the envelope, the stamp with its pastel colors and its primitive design, the envelope with the edges colored blue and red and unnecessarily marked "Air Mail." Even the smell and feel of the envelope moved him. He tried to read the letter slowly to spin out the time he spent with it, but he always ended up racing through it. As he was going up, the elevator door opened and a tall blond woman came in, wearing a short black dress, thick socks of the same color, and a woolen hat. She smiled at him and he was taken aback. It was the first time a woman had smiled at him in Paris. He asked her which floor she wanted and pressed the right button for her. He thought for a moment, then asked her if she lived in the building. No, she said, she was from the social services department. He smiled and laughed inside. He wished her success in her work and got out of the elevator.

He sat on a chair near the small balcony, where he had put a small plant. The glass door of the balcony was firmly closed to keep out the cold. He turned the electric heater on, and sat in front of it with a cup of tea from which steam was rising invitingly. He picked up the letter again, smiled at it as if he were greeting a lifelong friend, and opened the envelope.

Cairo, March 30

Dear Eissa,

I heard you were in Paris and that was a pleasant surprise. Thank you for telling me and I promise you I won't spread the news, as you say in your letter. Don't worry, the agency hasn't been publishing that kind of news for some time, and even when it does no one notices what we say. I had intended to write you a long letter and I wanted it to be warm, emotional, and powerful. I wanted to tell you how much I've missed you since your first departure, and your last departure, and your permanent departure. I wanted to tell you (that I still haven't recovered from your previous absence or from your purported murder, which pained me (and I now want to go and punch your friend Hussein in the face). More importantly, I haven't forgiven you for either and maybe I never will. I have prepared the words in my mind on my daily journey from death in the stupid agency to death alone in my desolate apartment, to death in my love of Sahar, who comes and goes, and who I forget when she goes. I wanted to tell you many things but as soon as I get home I no longer feel like writing anything.

I sat down at that white draftsman's board that you make fun of, picked up a pen, kept staring at the board, and asked myself why I have kept it all these years. And why I've kept you, and myself, and all the trivial things in my life. I stood up and poured myself a glass of whisky without ice. The taste was horrible because it was that local brand that might be made under the stairs in the building next door (have I told you about the building next door and what goes on there? Maybe not). I'd like you to come back and visit, to pour me a proper whisky, and some wine (though I don't really like it), and some French coffee so that I can make myself a cup with that machine you sent me with your friend who brought me the letter and explained it to stupid me—I no longer remember his name. But the coffee machine is in fact useless because there aren't any coffee beans apart from the ones that Amm Mohamed, the cleaner at the agency, buys for me.

I don't really want to talk and I have nothing to say, but I do want to write to you. I've thought about traveling, as you suggested in your letter. But I'm not sure that I want to leave. Where would I go? To Paris, too? What would I do there? I don't want to study, as it's boring, and I don't speak French, and my only chance would be to go there with the agency, but I'm not a real journalist. That's what your friend Hussein doesn't understand. I told him I'm not a journalist, but a translator. His contempt for me was obvious, although he tried to pretend otherwise. I've wanted to punch him ever since (and now I want to do so even more—did I already say that?). That guy thinks that anything can be done. I hate this excruciating naiveté and these enthusiasts who appoint themselves as representatives of the world's conscience. Sometimes I wonder if I hate you too for these same reasons. But I don't hate you, just as you don't hate me for accepting the squalor in which I live.

I'm part of this squalor, and I love you because you understand that and you love me nonetheless.

And now I feel a slight numbness creeping into my writing hand. I've only drunk a few glasses, but even so. And as usual I don't know how to end this stupid letter or whether I'm going to send it. If it reaches you, you'll know that I sent it and that I love you.

Yours,
Nasser

Going back to studying was a life-saver for Fakhreddin, after all the disasters he had recently faced. Studying law was one of his passions, and he was at France's oldest university, a beacon of legal studies. He felt he had been given a rare chance to make a fresh start, so he tried to put what had happened behind him and view it as a painful past that should not prevent him from going forward. He went to the university with an open heart and a deep desire to learn, thirsty to study in the literal sense of the word. When he sat down in the lecture hall he felt that the words and ideas were seeping into his mind, filling gaps in it, lighting up corners of it, and enriching him intellectually. He discovered how superficial his knowledge of law and the legal sciences had been. His days at Cairo University had passed quickly and the overcrowding, the pressures, the shortage of books and other resources, and the lack of original texts by the founders of legal theory meant that he had only scratched the surface of the subject. Now windows had opened that he had not previously known existed, and his main preoccupation was to improve his French so that he could acquire all the learning available.

But he also felt like someone swimming in the ocean without a compass. He hadn't thought about a subject for his dissertation before he arrived. How could he have done so, unless of course he had chosen to write about the denial of justice and extrajudicial killings? They assigned him a supervisor based on the preliminary proposal that Eissa had sent with his application papers. It was a subject that neither he nor Eissa knew anything about, but a professor at college had recommended it so that Eissa could get his papers ready in good time. Fakhreddin met the supervisor and tried to explain his thoughts, but the supervisor didn't have much time and told him brusquely that it was up to the student, not the supervisor, to decide the approach he should take.

"Mr. Naggar, when someone doesn't know where he wants to go it's hard to help him get there. My task is to help you, but not to think for you."

"I understand that, sir, and I know it's my task. But I was looking forward to your advice so that I could make a good choice of research topic, so that I won't have to change it at a later stage."

"There won't be any changes in the future. This is my first piece of advice. Because any change will cost you many months of hard work and sleepless nights. This is not a university where it's easy to get a degree. There are other universities that do that, but not the Sorbonne and not the law faculty."

"Yes of course. I didn't mean . . ."

"Tell me precisely how you want me to help you."

"As I said, I feel from my preliminary readings that I'm adrift at sea and I'd like you to show me what I should focus on."

"Listen, Mr. Naggar. First, swimming in the sea is something you'll have to get used to. Scholarship is like swimming in the sea. Second, I'm the supervisor for your doctoral dissertation and not your private tutor. If you haven't studied properly in your home country, then maybe you should reconsider what you are doing. My task, as I said, is to make sure that what you write in your dissertation is not rubbish, that you're not reinventing the wheel, that your research doesn't overlook important scholarship, and that you don't go astray in your analysis. That's my task, not to manage your private affairs. Is that clear to you?"

"Yes."

"Good. Now, you'll have to keep swimming in the sea you chose, on the understanding that you come back here in two months and tell me what direction you plan to swim in, and then we'll see what we can do."

Fakhreddin told Damian, a new friend of his, about his meeting with the professor. Damian had a good laugh and told him this was the usual way professors addressed their students in Paris.

"Don't expect to get any help. It's all up to you and your own efforts. He doesn't have the time or the energy, or any interest in adopting you."

"I don't want him to adopt me, God forbid, but a little guidance wouldn't kill him!"

"He was generous with you, I'd say. Ask the other students about their meetings with their professors. You're lucky he didn't tell you how ignorant and stupid and what a waste of time he thinks you are."

"And also that he didn't slap me."

"I'm not joking. Handholding is out of the question here. The prevalent view is that the students have to climb the mountain of scholarship, while the professors throw rubbish at them."

"Can't you find a slightly better analogy?"

"Well, think of it as doing the hurdles. You're running and clearing the hurdles, and the professors are pelting you with more obstacles, and if you manage to get through all that, it means you're worth the effort, and if you don't, then you don't deserve it anyway."

"What effort? And why does he always call me *vous* when he speaks to me? I feel like he's talking to some other people."

"Well, if you need anything, I'm ready to help."

Damian was about to finish his doctoral dissertation. He would smile whenever anyone asked him when he would finish and say he preferred to stick with "about to finish," because no one knew exactly what that meant. He was short and thin, acutely intelligent and extremely polite, always smiling and greeting people left and right, although many of his greetings were not returned. Damian had excelled as a student and had received the best education France could offer to a young man from an elite family, thanks to his father's money and influence. He was from a Lebanese family of Armenian origin, though he had spent most of his life in France, where his father had settled after the first Lebanese civil war in 1958. Damian said his father realized early on that once these things start, they never end; that once the Lebanese started killing each other, they would never stop. And so he had left. Damian was born and brought up in Paris with his brother and sister, but he had preserved what he called his "Lebaneseness" at home, where they spoke Armenian, Arabic, and French together, and ate the same food that his mother use to make in their house in Ashrafiyeh in Beirut. Damian had no problem with life in Paris. It was his mother who complained that she missed life in Beirut and that nothing in Paris could compare to Beirut: not the food, the air, or the sea, of course, nor the civility of the people, the beauty of the women, the cleanliness, or even the taste of the fruit and vegetables, especially the mint and the citrus fruit. Damian had no illusions about his identity: he was Lebanese, Armenian, and French as well, as he often said.

But Damian, pleasant, cheerful, intelligent, successful, from a rich family, and culturally diverse, didn't have any friends among the other Arab students. None of them liked him or spoke to him. Even Fakhreddin didn't like to be too close to him.

"It's because I'm 'effeminate.' Isn't that the term you use among yourselves when you talk about me? Don't get upset. I've been told dozens of times, and worse things too. I've grown used to other people rejecting me. When I told my father the truth about my sexuality in my twenties, he was silent for a while and then he said, 'You have a life of loneliness ahead of you.' At the time I didn't know what he meant, but I've come to understand over time, and I'm trying to adjust."

Fakhreddin didn't know how to reply.

"It's actually a flagrant injustice. I've never done anyone any harm or mistreated anyone. I've never harassed anyone, not even one percent of the harassment other men inflict on our female colleagues. I don't know if they reject me because I'm different from them, or because they have homosexual tendencies that they're trying to suppress."

"Maybe they hate what you represent."

"But I don't represent anything!"

"You do. You represent a different basis for society. Accepting homosexuality means undermining the foundations of the family and social relationships. It's not just a matter of individual freedom. There are consequences for society as a whole, and there's also the religious prohibition."

"I'm a Christian from a very religious family. And the last thing I want is a sermon on prohibitions from someone who's ignorant. Besides, how can the fact that I don't like women undermine the foundations of the family? It's all about ignorance and hatred of anything that's different. They see me as an extraterrestrial, something they never imagined dealing with or touching. Of course they think I'm mentally ill, or that the concierge raped me when I was young and corrupted my morals, or that my mother betrayed my father in front of me and I developed some complex, or that a gecko stepped on me while I was asleep, or any of the nonsense about homosexuality that Arab folklore is full of. Whatever happens, as far as they are concerned, I'm a creature with a tail, or some creature that looks like them but isn't a 'normal' human being, and of course the fact that I'm Armenian doesn't help my case."

"In fact, it does help."

"How?"

"Because it gives you an excuse!"

Fakhreddin laughed to relieve his embarrassment and end the discussion, which he hadn't wanted to open. The truth was that his feelings differed from those of his friends only in degree. He didn't hate Damian, but he couldn't bear the idea of homosexuality. At most, he could accept it as an exception within certain bounds. If it was amenable to treatment it could be treated, and if it wasn't, one could hope that the person prospered and was treated with compassion, provided he kept his distance, remained an exception, and wasn't normalized in way that gave him legitimacy. But in any case, it was the least of his concerns and he didn't feel the need to discuss it.

Damian smiled.

"I'm sorry to impose all this on you for no reason. Why don't we go for a drive? Let me show you Paris by car."

Fakhreddin hesitated for a moment and Damian burst out laughing. "I swear that was an innocent invitation. What's wrong with you?"

It was a letter from Ali that gave Fakhreddin the news that Hassan Mahmoud had died. He was distracted for the rest of the day. The news brought to mind things that Fakhreddin had buried: the way his heart sank at the mention of Shireen's name, the smell of her hair when she pushed it aside or tied it up with a colored ribbon, the way she walked through the lobby of the High Court building, the distinctive sound of the heels of her shoes, the barrister's gown thrown carelessly over her shoulder as she rushed along to make up for her perpetual tardiness. He remembered the palm of her hand when she took his hand, her eyes when she looked at him deeply and drew him in, and his love for her that had shattered on the rock of social class. Should he call Shireen to offer his condolences on the death of her father? Was she here or still in Cairo? She must have gone to Cairo to attend the burial and the condolence ceremonies. Had her husband gone with her or was he too busy with his important work? Could he bear to meet her in the presence of the man who had taken her from him so unfairly? Could he see her again after she had abandoned him so unlovingly? He looked at Ali's letter and his mind wandered further. So Hassan Mahmoud was dead. The icon of tradition and proprieties was dead. Shireen had given up love for fear of angering her father, and now he was dead. He had died as all men die. He had died and come to an end, just as everything comes to an end, so what had been the point of us parting? Many other questions followed in quick succession, leaving him no time to think or answer. He decided to call her to express his condolences, in the hope that she was still in Cairo, so that he could leave her a message and that would be the end of it. Of course he could have sent a telegram, but the fact was that he wanted to hear her voice and he was afraid to admit this to himself. He didn't want to have to think openly about this desire, which had been working away inside him ever since he had stepped foot in France. He picked up the receiver, called the embassy, and asked for her husband. The secretary said that he wasn't in, so Fakhreddin said he was an old friend and he asked for his home number so that he could give his condolences to him and his wife. She gave him the number. He hesitated again, then picked up the receiver quickly before he could change his mind again. He dialed and heard her voice come down the line.

"Hello," she said.

It was a strange conversation between the two former lovers, who had never recovered from their love for each other. There was as much silence as conversation. He expressed his condolences on the death of her father and she said, "Thank you," or something similar, and then paused. Then she cried. He cried inside and said nothing. Neither of them knew for sure if they were crying at the death of her father or at the love they had suppressed. He said something about hearing the news late and apologized. She said she should apologize and then they were silent. He said how sad he was when he heard, and she mumbled something and stopped. She asked him what he was doing in Paris and he told her it was a long story. She said she had heard a strange rumor about him disappearing, from their mutual friend Manar. He said his decision to come to Paris was connected with that and that he was in Paris under the name Eissa al-Naggar. He asked her not to say anything about his real identity to anyone, either in writing or by phone. He asked her if she needed anything and she thanked him, but didn't say anything that suggested she was ending the conversation. On the contrary, she asked him if he needed anything and he thanked her. She asked him how long he had been in Paris and he said it had been about three months. She reproached him for not calling, at least as an old friend. He said nothing and she stopped too.

As one might expect, this was not the last phone conversation between them. She called him next, to thank him for his condolences; the conversation lasted longer, there were fewer silences and there was more talk. In the conversation after that, she peppered him with questions and he spoke at length. Then she asked him if he would like to meet and give her his condolences in person. He hesitated; he wanted to ask how her husband would feel about him being there, but instead he said something meaningless about not wanting to cause any inconvenience. Then they met. He went to offer his condolences at her home, and she met him in the small garden attached to her elegant house. She didn't invite him in but an Ethiopian maid brought tea and coffee to where they were sitting in the sun in the garden. She was wearing a simple black dress and a black shawl of light wool decorated with little red

71

flowers. Her face looked fresh, without any make-up, just as he liked it. Her eyes were slightly red, with a trace of dark rings underneath. Her hair was tied at the back with a black ribbon. She was just the same, unchanged.

She greeted him and left her hand in his for a couple of seconds. They didn't know what to do with their hands. How could they touch like strangers? How could he take her hand in his and not embrace her? His hand was stiff while hers was warm and tender. Then his relaxed, but the two seconds allowed to friends were over and she withdrew her hand, just as his began to thaw. Their dilemma was how to look at each other in an ordinary way, in a way that didn't violate the protocol for such a visit, and that at the same time was not the way strangers looked at each other. He tried to shift his gaze into the distance or look at her with indifference, but his efforts proved in vain and he ended up looking at her in the only way he knew how.

Then Maryam, her daughter, arrived and saved him. She came running across the garden, almost falling at every step. Fakhreddin was suddenly face to face with a little version of Shireen, as he had long imagined Maryam, with her hair in a ponytail, completely innocent, and with a charming smile. It wrenched his heart to see this wonderful creature emerge from his dreams and stand in front of him as a real being, not of his own creation. She mumbled something, kept close to her mother, and looked at him with a mixture of curiosity and playfulness. Fakhreddin sat still, then took his leave and left, so as not to distract the mother from her daughter.

As one might expect, this wasn't their last meeting. The next time was when Shireen was walking around the Latin Quarter, looking for a carpet for the house. She had been told there was one in an antique shop there, and she had called him the day before and invited him to have coffee at the university between his lectures. After three other meetings they finally talked about the past and their relationship. There were no recriminations, no accusations, or anything like that. They just reminisced about the past and Shireen told him they could now be friends. She explained that her husband knew about their meetings and said that this was a friendship they could acknowledge in public; there was nothing about it that needed to be hidden. A few weeks later they argued, each accusing the other of responsibility for the breakdown in their relationship. Shireen cried bitterly that day and she was still crying when she left. Then she called him, apologized, and asked to see him again. The next time they didn't argue, but spoke about their lives since they had broken up. Fakhreddin explained what had happened to him that made him come to Paris using his cousin's name. They started to meet more often and he spoke to her husband, Sherif, when he answered the phone once, but the two men didn't meet face to face.

Then she admitted that she wasn't happy with her life. She explained how she had tried to acclimatize to her new life, but had failed. She confessed that, in a moment of despair, she had tried to kill herself and said that the doctor who treated her after she recovered had advised her to talk to a psychiatrist. She did that and it calmed her down considerably, along with some tranquilizers, of course. She said she ended up accepting the idea of not being happy and made up for it by being contented and psychologically stable. She had given birth to Maryam, the apple of her eye, and built a stable structure for herself and her little family.

"But there's something missing. It's like living in a black-and-white film. There are no colors, nothing to stir me or move my heart. There's nothing I want to tell Sherif. We have nothing to say to each other. I always do my own thing and he does his."

It wasn't long before things reached their natural conclusion. She admitted that she had never loved anyone but him and that she still loved him. She said she had tried life without him and found that it had no flavor. He confessed that he loved her and had never loved anyone else, and that life without her had always been bitter.

Mohamed Buheiri had taken on the task of solving Fakhreddin's practical problems soon after his arrival in Paris. Buheiri was an old colleague from the army who had been assigned as a reserve officer in the missile unit in which Fakhreddin had served. He had gone to the Gulf with him and had been there when Fakhreddin refused orders and was court-martialed. At the time he had tried to dissuade Fakhreddin from refusing to deploy to Hafr al-Batin—not because he was committed to the war but, on the contrary, because of his calculation of the gains and losses. He told Fakhreddin he should bend to the storm until it passed, but Fakhreddin was as inflexible as a steel rod. Buheiri was angry at his obstinacy but he admired his valor and held him in high esteem ever after. Buheiri left Egypt because he couldn't find a good job when his military service ended. Some of their friends arranged for him to go on a tourist visa to Paris, where he was met by an Algerian "brother," who employed him in the house-painting business. With time he prospered, became a partner in the business, and married the man's sister, who had French nationality. This enabled him to sort out his legal status. His business gradually expanded, especially after his brother-in-law left the country. He started buying and selling cheap real estate in the suburbs, alongside his decorating business. Buheiri bought himself and his small family a small house with a small garden on the edges of Saint-Denis. He had three children and became known as Abu Yasser, after his eldest son Yasser. He settled down as an authority figure for Egyptian workers and refugees in Paris. He helped find shelter for those who needed it until they found their feet, and did his best to employ those seeking work. Sometimes he helped them marry French Muslim women of Algerian origin whom his wife knew, and provided other forms of assistance and charity.

Fakhreddin didn't know all this before he arrived, but Hussein sent him a telephone number that led him to Buheiri, who undertook to introduce Fakhreddin to as many members of the Arab communities as possible, especially his Algerian relatives. He would drop in on Fakhreddin at times, take him to the Saint-Denis market, and walk around arm-in-arm with him, as if Fakhreddin were his younger brother. He greeted the shopkeepers as he went from street to street, introducing them to Fakhreddin as "the doctor," and urging them to look after him. They would have tea and smoke shisha at a coffee shop run by Sheikh Naimi, a Palestinian who had settled in Paris. On Fridays they would finish off their tour by performing prayers in the Saint-Denis mosque—Fakhreddin saw the name as an amusing oxymoron but no one else seemed to notice. In the mosque, Fakhreddin met even more members of the Arab community and realized that Buheiri's influence went beyond housing and finding work for young people. In their army days he hadn't noticed Buheiri's religious interests, but from the discussions that he and Buheiri attended in the mosque it was clear that Buheiri was well versed in religious law and hadith. He spent hours after Friday prayers arguing with young people on points of law: on whether it was permissible to work in banks, French government institutions, or restaurants that served alcohol, and on other matters of interest to the Arab community in France. After these discussions Buheiri would complain to Fakhreddin that the young people were too strict and had been influenced by imams from Pakistan, Saudi Arabia, Afghanistan, and Algeria who had strong ties to militant organizations. He said they pushed the young people toward extremism in their daily lives, which made it hard for them to live in France and drove some of them to leave the country after they had ruined their own prospects of making a living there. Fakhreddin asked him where he had acquired his interest in religious law. Buheiri laughed and said, "Have you forgotten I'm an engineering graduate? You learn two things in the engineering faculty: the first is religious law, and the second is to take your chances."

He had in mind the vast influence that the Islamic groups had in engineering faculties and Fakhreddin asked him how no signs of this were evident during his military service.

"Are you trying to get me into trouble?" he said with a smile. "Doesn't the army teach you that government service is government service, and then there's everything else? Well, this is everything else."

He added that he had benefited greatly from serving in the army, but it was a phase in the past and now he was focusing fully on his new life in Paris and on serving the Muslim community there.

Paris
May 3, 1993

Dear Nasser,

Let me tell you how I have found myself. Here in Paris, the City of Light, I finally discovered who I am. I, sir, am an "unusual Arab." If I say anything intelligent, the people around me are surprised. If I behave politely and treat others with respect, they're amazed. If I order wine, they're impressed. If I turn up on time, they're astonished. If I get high grades in an exam, they're stunned. If I speak concisely and ask someone what point exactly they are trying to make, they're puzzled. If someone is present on three of these occasions, they say I'm not your "usual Arab."

But I'm not writing to you because of all this, but to ask you what's happening. Your recent letters have been disturbing. Why are you drowning yourself in despair so much? I know how frustrating things are in Egypt, but does that mean that drunkenness and wallowing in indolence are the way to salvation? Or is it a slow death that you have chosen? I don't know the Sahar that you talk about, but from what you say she doesn't seem to be like the other short-term women, and if I'm right, make sure she doesn't end up short-term too.

You can't continue in this state. You're slowly killing yourself. Remember that there are people who love you and depend on your friendship for their emotional stability, you fool.

Eissa

Fakhreddin had accepted Damian's invitation to go for a drive. Through the window of the fancy car he saw another Paris, without the queueing and fighting on the metro. He discovered that places were closer to each other than he had thought and that the routes between them were not always straight lines. They drove down the Rue de Rivoli, which Fakhreddin hated because the metro stops were so far apart, and he discovered that it was a pleasant street. They drove around the old opera house and Place de la Bastille, and made a quick tour of the modern opera house that had recently opened. Damian took him to the new La Défense district and they went up the new triumphal arch, which contained offices. With a laugh Damian said that this really was France's new triumph. They took a long route back to the old Arc de Triomphe and drove around it. He didn't know that was possible. All he knew was that he walked down long tunnels from L'Etoile metro station to reach it. They went to Rue Saint-Denis in the city center and Damian told him that it was the traditional red-light district. He saw some of the prostitutes standing around waiting for clients. Damian pointed out some of the hotels nearby that worked in the same business. Fakhreddin commented that most of the women were from Africa, the Pacific Islands, and the Maghreb, and Damian said there was a new wave from Poland and Russia but they operated in other areas. They went up to the Sacré-Cœur basilica and had lunch in a small café in the Place du Tertre, which was packed with tourists.

"And where have the square's artists gone?" Fakhreddin asked.

"They've gone home, my dear. Artists today aren't like the ones in the time of Van Gogh—the ones who didn't have enough to eat and died of tuberculosis. Most of them work with companies, producers, and agencies, and also in advertising."

They went to the Île Saint-Louis in the Seine behind Notre Dame Cathedral. Fakhreddin didn't know there were people living in houses here, with balconies looking out on the lovely view. They went to the Institut du Monde Arabe, the Pompidou Centre, the fourth arrondissement and Le Marais, the old center of Jewish life in Paris. As darkness fell Damian drove to the Bois de Boulogne, where Fakhreddin saw the new arrivals from Poland and Russia that Damian had mentioned, and also people cruising for sex. He saw young men selling themselves to men. Not wanting to stay, he asked his friend if they could leave. They went back to the Latin Quarter and sat in the famous Café Deux Magots.

"What's all this?" Fakhreddin asked.

"This, my friend, is what you could call total chaos."

"I'm trying to imagine what Sartre and Camus would have been saying when they were sitting in this café fifty years ago."

"They would be saying whatever it was they said at the time."

"Was it always like this here?"

"Of course. France has always been total chaos, and out of this chaos emerge thinkers, writers, philosophers, deviants, and war criminals."

"And law?"

"Law too. Don't forget that lawyers are the ants of the socioeconomic system. They and the ENA graduates."

"ENA?"

"Yes, the Ecole nationale d'administration, the largest of the 'grandes écoles' where the big politicians, senior civil servants, and company executives graduate. They are all one elite and they share out the jobs among themselves, like musical chairs."

"And law?"

"Again? Law, sir, is what holds all this together. That's why the students fight to enroll in the faculties of law. That's why the professors fight over the reputation, prestige, and status of the law faculty. That's why lawyers are paid such massive fees. That's why they occupy the top rungs on the social ladder. It's a fight to preserve their livelihoods, my dear. The lawyers are the high priests of the system, just like the Egyptian scribes in the pharaoh's court."

"Hor? Have you met him too?"

"Sorry?"

"Never mind."

"Are you shocked by what I'm saying? Did you expect anything different from studying law here?"

"Yes, in fact. I had hoped to be studying the role of law and how it relates to social change. I mean, as Rousseau and Montesquieu wrote."

"Rousseau and Montesquieu? You must be joking! Those are ideals, my friend, models in our dreams. But the reality is a law office at 750 francs an hour. That's the reality."

"Good morning, law, and welcome to rule by the elite."

"Of course, welcome to rule by the elite! The elite has always ruled. Didn't you learn that back home?"

"It's one of the ironies of fate that I should learn that in the land of the French revolution."

"That's because you're a dreamer, my dear. The French revolution was led by an elite and its ideals were defined by an elite. The masses were their fuel, but it was the elite that led and that lead today. Shall we resume our tour?"

"No, I think that will do for today. Could you take me to the nearest metro station on the blue line?"

"Where are you going?"

"The Saint-Denis Cathedral."

"Ah, Algerian France, the land of *merguez*! Have a nice trip."

In September Shireen left her husband and came to see Fakhreddin. The doorbell rang at his house and he jumped in surprise: no one in Paris came without making an appointment first. He opened the door and found Shireen standing in front of him. He stood there, stunned. She threw herself into his arms and started to cry. After all these years, he was finally in her embrace.

He shut the door and sat her on the sofa. She rested her head on his chest and gradually calmed down, as he patted her head and pushed her hair off her face. Then he went back to her eyes, wiping away the tears with the edge of his hand, drying his hand on his shirt, and then wiping away more of her tears. She laughed through her tears and raised her head a little so that she could dry her eyes and clear her nose.

"I'm sorry," she said.

"Not at all. Don't say that."

"I don't know what to do or where to go."

"What happened?"

Shireen started to tell him what had happened between her and her husband Sherif over the past weeks and how things had grown worse since Fakhreddin had reappeared in her life.

"Don't worry. You're not the reason," she said. "He's the reason. I'm the reason. Me and him. We're not living with each other. All your appearance did was remind me that I'm still a human being with feelings and that there's more to life than silence and just getting along, more than talking about Maryam and her clothes and the nanny and her holidays. Something more than air tickets and receptions and boring people that I have to put up with, and the pills that I can't sleep without. My dad's death was the start of it, and then you turned up, and then I couldn't take it. I can't bear living this way any longer. Just his voice or any comment he makes and I can't bear myself. I can't bear him. And he's not stupid. Of course he understood right from the start. That's all. I took Maryam and the nanny and I left."

"You left?"

"Yes. I told him I wanted a divorce. It's nothing to do with you. It's all about me. I won't go on with this living death. That's what I told him and he agreed."

"And where are Maryam and the nanny?"

"Downstairs."

"Downstairs?"

"Yes."

Fakhreddin reminded her that an hour had passed since her arrival. They went downstairs but didn't find anyone in the car. Shireen started screaming and ran down the street looking for them, and he ran after her, hoping to calm her down.

"They must have gone to the shopping center nearby. Come on," he said.

They were in fact sitting in a small shop that sold candy and sodas. Shireen ran in, hugged Maryam tight, and told off the Ethiopian nanny, who started to apologize. Fakhreddin sat down, made Shireen sit down, and asked her what she wanted to do. He suggested letting them stay in his little apartment and going to sleep at a friend's place nearby. Shireen smiled and thanked him and said she had booked two hotel rooms in the city center until she could make other arrangements. She reminded him she had inherited a fortune from her father and, if she wanted, she could live in hotels for the rest of her life. He tried to drive her there but she just thanked him for the offer. She put Maryam in the child seat in the back of the car and the Ethiopian girl next to her, waved goodbye, and drove off toward the city.

*

"And the solution?"

"There is no solution," Damian replied with a smile.

"But if liberalism is so cruel and peaceful methods to bring about change are thwarted in this way, then there's only violence left."

"And is violence a solution? Violence destroys the perpetrators first and foremost."

"But it's the last resort of those who no longer have any other way," said Fakhreddin.

"Violence is not a solution."

"So what do you want people to do? Submit?"

"Submission is better than violence."

"Submission is cowardly."

"It's better to be a coward than to be a savage."

"Now I know why the Arab students call you a wimp, not because you're gay, but because of your ridiculous opinions."

October 14

Eissa,

I wrote to you this morning to wish you a happy birthday but I was very drunk and I don't remember exactly what I told you and I don't want to open the envelope.

I can see your look of disapproval from here, and I'm telling you to stop it. Stop telling me what I ought to be doing. I received your letter, in which you describe me as a fool. It was me who gave you the right to play the role of honest advisor, and now I am saying, thank you, I don't want any more of your advice that I can't act on. It's like your gifts that I can't use. Have I told you about the damned coffee machine that took up half the worktop in the kitchen and sticks out its tongue at me? After a massive effort I managed to find the kind of coffee that can be used in it, but then it turned out that the bitch needed

82

paper filters as well! Of course there's no trace of such things here—we who can scarcely find water. So I made a filter out of tissues and put it in the machine. But when I turned it on, it made strange noises and smoke came out of it and it blocked up completely, and it's refused to produce anything ever since.

We have parted ways. You are now on an ill-defined path but it is a path, while I have jumped like a parachutist into the swamps in which I float, sometimes live, and often dive and wait.

I think I wrote this identical sentence, completely identical, in a previous letter.

Now I'm going to pour myself a glass. Happy birthday.

Nasser

Fakhreddin's next meeting with his dissertation supervisor was no better than the previous one. Fakhreddin still hadn't figured out what he wanted to work on. The supervisor asked him how long he planned to spend writing his dissertation and he said he had two years. The supervisor had a fit, reminding him that he was seeking a serious academic qualification and that the average time for completing a doctorate was five to seven years. At his current rate of progress, Fakhreddin would need ten. He gave him another appointment in six months' time and dismissed him with a wave of his hand.

Shireen settled down in her separate life. After a few weeks in the hotel she found herself a grand apartment in the seventh arrondissement. Fakhreddin didn't comment on the astronomic rent she was paying, but he clearly noticed how fancy the place was. Shireen smiled, half apologetic, and said she could live only on the Left Bank, where there was cultural life, schools, universities, and libraries. It was also close to her husband's office, so the nanny could take Maryam to him when he had time off. She mentioned in passing that she was going to stay in Paris and maybe resume studying for the qualification that would enable her to work as a lawyer in Paris. He asked her if she really wanted to be a lawyer here and she said she wanted to live in France and resume the life that had come to an end when she got married. She was a lawyer and she couldn't have her life back without working. She said she would specialize in commercial arbitration. Fakhreddin smiled mischievously and reminded her that she had inherited a vast fortune and didn't need to work in one of the most lucrative branches of law. She laughed and said he hadn't changed, and explained that she wanted to work in a branch that she could take with her wherever she went. That way she could benefit from what she had learned and do it anywhere.

Maryam started going to the nursery every day, while Shireen roamed around Paris. She wouldn't start studying before January, so she decided to make use of this period by discovering Paris without the constraints of her previous life. Fakhreddin went with her on these walks. She was exuberant when she got on the bus or pulled the cord that told the driver that passengers wanted to get off, but she was frightened of the metro, clung to him the whole time, and then asked to avoid it because it made her depressed. At night, they drove around in her car and sometimes Maryam came with them. The little girl was now friends with Fakhreddin: she'd hold his hand whenever she saw him and wouldn't let go till he left. Fakhreddin really loved her—loved her because she was a miniature version of the woman he loved. But Shireen was always thanking him for being so good with Maryam. He thought it strange to be thanked and said she was mad if she thought it was a matter of "being good" to Maryam. He explained that he saw Maryam as an innocent version of her. Shireen laughed and then seemed touched. She thanked him again and he laughed. On weekends the three of them would go out in Shireen's car for most of the day, to places Fakhreddin had never seen, such as the vineyards in the Champagne region, Mont Saint-Michel, Fontainebleau, where Napoleon said farewell to soldiers of his defeated army, and often to the Palace of Versailles, where Maryam loved being free to run in the groves. And when they came home, the nanny would have prepared dinner.

"What's her name?"

"Who?"

"The Ethiopian girl."

"Maryam."

"Her too?"

"Yes. That's why no one calls her by her name. Only Maryam is Maryam."

"So what do you call the nanny?"

"The Ethiopian girl. We say, 'Take this, girl. Go there, girl.' And if you ask her who she is on the phone, she'll say she's the Ethiopian girl."

Shireen still hadn't obtained a divorce. Sherif asked her to wait, then he objected to her retaining custody of Maryam if she remarried in Paris. So Shireen spent her days being pushed and pulled by the divorce issue. She would call Fakhreddin and tell him that Sherif had agreed to a divorce and to her keeping Maryam and had apologized for the inconvenience he had caused her, justifying this by saying that he wanted to stay with them. But a few days later Shireen would show up at Fakhreddin's door weeping bitterly, and saying she felt as if she would meet the same fate as Anna Karenina and that Sherif was determined to take Maryam from her and not give her a divorce, and so on.

During this tug-of-war Shireen was growing closer to Fakhreddin. Nothing had happened between them except when she had come to his house in Saint-Denis, that first time, and he had hugged her. After that he was careful to keep his distance from her because he knew how much he desired her and knew he wouldn't be able to stop if she came one step closer than was necessary in the normal course of events. He was burning with desire for her. Ever since their time at university, she had excited his imagination and monopolized his desire so completely that he felt nothing for any other woman. He hadn't gone near another woman since she had left. He loved her tall curvaceous figure, her neck, the curve of her hips, her knees, her hair when she lifted it up and it fell loosely on her face, the smile that lit up her face, and her piercing eyes. She enchanted him every time he saw her, and he didn't need to see her to want her. He was truly her slave and he knew that if he touched her he wouldn't stop and so he forced himself to keep his distance, when touching her was the one thing he wanted.

They were growing closer and spending more time together, but they often disagreed and argued too. The points of contention were mundane, but the vehemence of Shireen's reaction would take him by surprise. Once they were discussing Fakhreddin's studies and the intractable question of his dissertation. She advised him to choose an ordinary subject that wouldn't take much time, so that he could finish his doctorate as soon as possible. He told her he didn't want an ordinary subject; he wanted to write something that would make a difference in the study of law. He said that was the only justification he could see for spending five years of his life doing the research. He said he wanted to lay the foundations for international law from a Third-World point of view, and specifically from an Arab–Islamic point of view, as Grotius had done but from a non-European perspective. Shireen said nothing, her face clouded over, and she claimed she suddenly had a headache and was going to bed. That night Fakhreddin left her house bewildered. She disappeared for three days straight, then called him and said she wanted to end the relationship and she couldn't be tied to someone like him, and that only now did she understand why they had disagreed in the Bayn al-Sarayat days. When he asked her why, she said he was a megalomaniac and she couldn't spend her life with such a madman. She hung up and disappeared for another week.

Then she turned up at his door in Saint-Denis, as on the first occasion. She cried, apologized, and said how much she loved him and how she couldn't live without him, and they made up. But the very same story recurred, this time when Fakhreddin talked about wanting to go back to Cairo to try to find a way to put right the things that everyone thought were wrong and that they were doing nothing to fix. She told him this was a sign of immaturity and that she had left a stable life and her husband for someone who was immature. Fakhreddin was upset this time and protested she had told him before that she wanted to leave her husband anyway, and it wasn't for his sake. He said he couldn't agree to be a substitute for her husband, and she left. Then she came back a week later and assured him she hadn't meant what she said, and they made up again. But two weeks later she again said something similar that made him angry and he stopped speaking to her. They made up a week later, and so on. Sherif announced that he wouldn't give her a divorce, either with Maryam or without. Shireen broke down completely. She called Fakhreddin and asked him to come over. When he reached her house, he found her asleep and the nanny told him she had taken some tranquilizers. Maryam was spending the weekend with her father. Fakhreddin stayed over in the sitting room and at about three o'clock in the morning he heard Shireen calling the nanny. Without moving he mumbled that the nanny was asleep and asked if she wanted anything. She started crying, and then the crying turned into sobbing. Fakhreddin hurried to her room and found her curled up in half the bedding in the fetal position, crying bitterly. He held her, hugging her as the sound of her sobbing grew louder. He rocked her in his arms until her crying died down and her breathing was more regular. She held him tight and went back to sleep. Fully dressed and with his shoes on, he lay by her side with his arms around her. She clung to him and fell into a deeper sleep. He stayed like that for an hour or a little longer, looking at her. She opened her eyes and saw his face next to hers on the pillow. She smiled and kept looking at him. Then she moved closer and kissed him on the cheek. He didn't know how to react, but he smiled and didn't move. She moved her whole body closer, gave him a long kiss, wrapped her arms around his neck, and shut her eyes. He kissed her, put his hands around her shoulders, and pulled her toward him. She pressed against him, with her breasts resting on his chest, her face close to his, her eyes open, and her luxuriant black hair covering them both. She raised her arms and slipped out of her blouse, revealing the white body beneath. He shivered when she rested her chest on his stomach but the heat of her body overwhelmed him and he gave free rein to his suppressed passion. She pulled his body toward her and her whole body was his. They made love till morning came and they were exhausted.

Ali called him one night at his apartment and explained to him that his aunt's psychological state had seriously deteriorated despite attempts by Ali, Hussein, and Ashraf to reassure her. She now believed that her sons were dead and that her friends were hiding this from her. Ali said she was scarcely eating, that her diabetes and high blood pressure were growing worse, and she needed constant care. Fakhreddin also understood indirectly from what Ali said that his friends were running into brick walls more than ever. He told him that Ashraf really had started the procedures for becoming a monk. He had passed the first tests and was now in seclusion in a monastery on the North Coast to test his commitment. Hussein was working in a law firm that specialized in defending members of the Islamic Group—a firm run by the famous lawyer Dalia al-Shenawi. And Ali spent all his time hanging out in coffee shops.

Fakhreddin was disturbed by what Ali said and wished he could make a short trip to Cairo. But the dangers made that impossible. He had had one lucky break and it wouldn't be wise to tempt fate by traveling back and forth. On arrival the security services might want to speak to him, and then everything would be revealed. No, he couldn't go back to Cairo yet. He told Ali he would arrange to make a phone call to his aunt to explain the situation himself. He asked him only to tell her it was important to be discreet during the conversation, in case someone was listening. He also asked Ali to arrange another call with Hussein on any evening that week.

"How are you spending your time?" Fakhreddin asked.

"I don't do anything. I see your aunt if she wants me to do anything for her, and that aunt of yours is very tough, my God. She knows exactly what she wants. And then I read the newspapers, go out and see a friend, or sit alone in a coffee shop. I might sit there for hours and then find the day's over, so I get up and go home."

"And what do you do for money?"

"The good Lord provides. I go to the village and get money from my family. Anyone who passes by to see me and has any money will give me some. That's how things are. You don't know whose money it is in the first place. Someone's sold some land. Someone's bought some land. Someone's sold his crops. It could be anything. People keep giving me money. They seem to have given up hope in me. They say, 'That guy looks in a bad way, he looks hopeless, we'd better give him some money or else he'll go and cause us trouble.' Sometimes I do chores for people, like registering a piece of land, selling livestock, any old task, and if they give me something I don't say no. And then I go and eat at your aunt's because she forgets to eat when she's alone, and so I eat at her place almost every day."

"Well, that's great, Ali. You're clearly living the life."

"Look, don't make fun of me. To be honest, I don't feel like doing anything. I mean, what difference does it make whether I do anything or not? None at all. And what's Ashraf going to be doing in the monastery? Do monks have anything to do? They plant olive trees. Okay. Well, I look after your aunt and keep her company. And, for God's sake, that's more useful than Mr. Ashraf's olive trees. So treat me like Ashraf—he's a monk in the monastery and I'm a monk in the coffee shop."

"Excellent."

Ali laughed. "Nothing better than that," he said. "They don't want us to work, right? Very well, then, we won't. I'll just sit around for them. Don't they say that the simple-minded make a living off the mad?"

"And Hussein?"

"Hussein is doing well, thank God. He's working with that famous lawyer woman who's on television every day. What's her name? Leila or Dalia al-Shenawi, something like that. They're laying into people, them and the guys from the Islamic groups. Anyone in our hometown who can't find anything to do now goes and works with them. They've got companies and offices and they give you money to start up businesses and it's great. Now he's working on legal protection for people who've been arrested. And then they file *hisba* cases. Like, if you said something I don't like—if you wrote an article or a book that contains something I don't like—I go to Hussein and file a lawsuit asking the court to annul your marriage because what you said means you're not a Muslim and so you can't remain married to your wife."

"And what if she said the same thing?"

"Then you'd both be infidels and someone would come along and shoot you. End of story and isn't that great."

"Whatever God wills."

"Don't say 'Whatever God wills' and leave it at that. You have to say, 'Whatever God wills happens, and whatever He doesn't will doesn't happen.' You're going to get your soul in trouble, my friend."

*

"If you want to stay in France, you have to get out of Saint-Denis," said Damian, playing with his car keys.

"Why? What's wrong with Saint-Denis?"

"Saint-Denis is the land of *merguez* and decorators. Do you want this to be your destiny here? If you want to be a lawyer or a professor, you have to escape from here."

"I have to escape and abandon all my friends?"

"Exactly. Either you stay with your friends in Saint-Denis and become one of them, or else you escape and integrate into French society."

"Can't I combine the two?"

"No. Polygamy is illegal here. Look at me. Why have I been accepted as French? Because, thanks to the excellent education paid for by my father, I managed to prove to others that I was a worthy member of the elite. If you're of Arab origin you have to choose between joining the elite, on more demanding terms, and selling halal meat or decorating apartments in the banlieues."

"But I don't want to run away from my friends. That wouldn't make sense. If I wanted a personal solution, a solution just for me, I wouldn't have put up with all the hardships I've been through. I could have been that kind of person long ago, without having to go abroad and live in exile."

"But now you're here, aren't you? And you have to choose. You can either stay with the others and be a 'bad Arab' like them, or you can save your skin and be a 'good Arab' like me."

"I'm an 'unusual Arab.' That's what they tell me."

"Really? That's good news. Congratulations. That means the door's open for you to join the elite."

"To join on my own?"

"No one's forcing you. A metro ticket costs six francs and it'll take you to Saint-Denis in less than an hour."

Fakhreddin didn't believe it when he heard his aunt's voice on the other end of the phone line. "My dear, my son," she said, then stopped. But he could hear her holding back her tears. She asked him how he was, and he asked her how she was. They talked about everything but she didn't mention Eissa, her son. Fakhreddin steered clear of the subject and felt that she knew. He talked about his life in Paris, his studies, and people he'd met, then he expressed regret that Eissa hadn't been destined to see all these things. His aunt said nothing and he could hear her sobbing. After another pause she spoke in a shaky voice:

"Fate can be cruel and kind. My heart felt it right from that day but, thank God, sometimes one fate is easier to bear than another. I thought the two of you were gone, but thank God you're well, my boy. It's fate and destiny, and what can we do? Can anyone change his destiny? You were like brothers. My God, I used to confuse the two of you. God has given me you to make up for the loss of Eissa."

"Don't despair, Auntie. One day I'll come back and make the person responsible pay the price for what he's done."

"What good would that do, my boy? Don't let the past ruin the future."

"You mean we shouldn't speak out, Auntie? We should accept it and keep our heads down?"

"Look, my boy. I'm going to tell you something and you listen to me carefully. You and your brother, I swear no one could beat you at talking, but I'm your mother and my gray hair has its value too, so listen to me and think hard about what I tell you. Half the kids in this family are dead because they couldn't keep quiet when they saw injustice. That's fate. Do you think I didn't know what was going on when you were sitting around talking for hours and coming and going at strange times with strange people? It was nonstop—telephone calls and appointments and people asking for you. A mother, my dear, feels these things. I just prayed to the Lord for things to turn out well. Fate is kind and we thank the Lord and praise Him. So your brother's gone, and I won't tell you to give up what you're doing. Stay the course, my boy, and may the Lord be with you. But I want you to promise that you'll come back safely to me. Do what you have to do, but come back safe. That's all, my boy. Think of your mother and look after yourself because you're all I have now. Everyone goes, but the salt of the earth remains. The peasants remain, living and tilling the soil and planting and harvesting. Please keep this in mind, for your mother's sake."

"Okay, I won't forget, God willing."

"And I have another request."

"Anything."

"I want you to arrange for Leila your cousin to come and stay with me."

"Leila?"

"Yes. She's wilting like a flower, I'm sorry to say. That criminal brother of hers has done to her what his father did to his sister. Like father, like son."

"Very well, I'll tell Ali to sort that out."

Fakhreddin and Shireen were now almost living together. The nanny took Maryam to Sherif on Friday mornings and Fakhreddin came from the university at noon and stayed with Shireen till Monday morning, when he went to university and she went to pick up Maryam. During the rest of the week, they went out together, sometimes with Maryam. Fakhreddin was uneasy about the lack of any clear agreement on a date for divorce or how it would happen. They often discussed how to overcome Sherif's various objections and whether it would be wise to put pressure on him through relatives or by starting a lawsuit. One day Fakhreddin said he was willing to go to Sherif and tell him openly about their relationship. Shireen said straight out that she had already done that; he knew but he still insisted there would be no divorce. Fakhreddin didn't like this triangular relationship and what sometimes looked like acquiescence to it on Shireen's part. She was angry when he told her and they fell out for a week, then made peace and went back to the way they had been. But Fakhreddin's unease didn't go away. It grew as Shireen resorted to tranquilizers to get to sleep. She said that she was used to them, that everyone in France took pills to sleep, and that she hoped to stop taking them completely when she was done with her previous life, which didn't want to leave her. He suggested she file for divorce in France, where the law treated women more fairly. But she thought it unlikely the courts would give her custody of Maryam, since Sherif could prove she had been unfaithful. There was also the scandal that would come with it. She asked him to wait a few more months so that she could work gently on Sherif. Fakhreddin agreed, but he wasn't happy.

They often quarreled, and every time it looked like they were going to break off their relationship. Shireen sometimes hinted that she would go back to Sherif, and Fakhreddin would get angry. Then she would backtrack and say she couldn't go back to her old life because it wasn't a life. Shireen didn't know what to do. Even if she knew she couldn't go back, she wasn't sure she could build a new life with Fakhreddin.

"What's changed?" she asked him.

"Sorry?"

"I mean why do you now think we could build a life together?"

"Maybe because we've learned that life without each other is no life."

"I know that, but how about you? What's changed in you?"

"I don't know. Maybe I'm less naive now."

"You think so?"

"What do you think?"

"I don't know. Sometimes I believe it and then you go and say something that makes me think the opposite."

"Like saying I'll go back to Cairo and go on doing what I was doing before?"

"That kind of thing, and like when you insist on living in Saint-Denis."

"What's wrong with Saint-Denis?"

"Yes, that's exactly what I mean: 'What's wrong with Saint-Denis?' Remember 'What's wrong with Bayn al-Sarayat?' The same attitude."

"And you'll leave me this time too?"

"No, I won't be able to leave you this time. But I'm still not sure I'll be able to stay with you."

"Hello. Is that Eissa?"

"Hi, Hussein. Congratulations on the new job. Dalia al-Shenawi? So now we're officially working for the Islamic Group?"

"It's a law firm. It's not as if someone else offered me work and I turned it down, as you can see. Do you want me to be like Ali and sit in a coffee shop sulking, waiting for the government to make up with me? Or Nasser, who's never sober? Or join a monastery like Ashraf?"

"Okay. But what about the group's puritanism and the violent methods they use? And the assassinations? Do you help with that?"

"I don't help with anything. You're going to get me in trouble. Our role is to defend the legal rights of young men accused of violence. Doesn't a murderer have the right to a fair trial? Doesn't the prosecution have to prove that he killed someone, not just go and grab anyone with a beard and pin a charge on them?"

"And the violence?"

"No one forces anyone to take part in that. And besides, do you think the government—and they are, I'm afraid, listening to us—are sending them flowers? The solution to violence is to contain it. Look, not all of them think the same way, as you imagine. There are disagreements and lots of internal discussions. The group is changing and there's a new generation coming up. Take Dalia, for example. When did the group ever have women? There is narrow-mindedness, but the more open-minded people there are in the group, the more they'll take on the narrow-mindedness, and that's for the best. The real battle is inside the group, not outside. The framework in which the Islamic groups operate is the cultural framework that will win and prevail, because it's the community's real identity. And would you abandon the field to narrow-minded points of view, rather than introduce and support more enlightened attitudes?"

"Can't you see you're giving yourself a justification for cooperation with these people? Can't you see that the extremists always swallow up and use the open-minded people?"

"Not at all. And anyway, as I told you, if you have a better option, I'd like to hear it."

"If I had one, I wouldn't be where I am now."

"Okay, look after yourself and best regards to everyone. Bye, my friend."

"Bye, bro."

Dear Nasser,

I've read your last letter ten times. In it you make clear, leaving no room for doubt, that you now believe that the only solution is to surrender to what you yourself call docility and nihilism. I understood that you let Sahar leave after disagreeing with her on this point. I want to ask: "What makes you think the problem isn't with you?" In the sense that you're afraid of trying. You're afraid of there being a solution, because when there is you'll have to act and face the possibility of success or failure. You're afraid of failing.

Now I'm worried about the effect that saying this will have on you. I'm ready to slap you if necessary to bring you to your senses, but I don't want you to dismiss what I say, withdraw into your shell, or drown my words in another bottle of whisky. Be a man and face the problem.

You're not weak. If you were weak you would no longer be alive, you wouldn't have escaped your old life in Mansoura, left your job at the Talkha electricity project that was killing you, or put up with what you've gone through in order to change your life. If you were weak you'd have died in the corridors of that wretched news agency. If you were weak, all those women wouldn't have loved you and you wouldn't have abandoned them. Your supposed weakness, in my opinion, my friend, is just an excuse you use for not taking responsibility for your deeds.

I think you owe it to yourself to at least be honest about who you are. I think it's time for you to stop this nonsense and take responsibility for yourself. The world is bad and living in it is often painful. God knows I understand that. But both of us must try not to just lie down and die.

I was very reluctant to write this letter to you. But I'm sure that our relationship permits me to be frank with you at this critical time. If I have gone too far, my excuse is that I love you and that you are a brother to whom I am tied by unconditional affection, and you know this.

Best wishes,
Eissa

Shireen was in the bathroom when Fakhreddin heard her cry out. He rushed in to see her sitting on the floor, her hair disheveled and with a white tube in her hand. "Blue, blue! Take it and look at it. It's blue, isn't it?"

He glanced around and saw three other tubes lying on the floor. He looked at her for an explanation. Her eyes red and her hair covering her face, she shouted, "Don't you understand? You never understand anything. It's blue. Do you know what blue means? Look. They're all blue. Blue. Blue. Can you hear me? Blue!"

He understood. Now he understood. He moved closer to hug her but she pushed him away. She kept shouting frantically, looking for the instructions written on the box. Then she stood up, ran to fetch her phone, called a number that didn't answer, then threw the phone in the bath, which was full of water. She cried, held her head in her hands, and whenever he tried to approach her she shied away. The nanny came and gave her some pills. She took her by the hand, led her to bed, and pulled the covers over her. After half an hour of quiet sobbing, she fell asleep.

Shireen was pregnant.

When she woke up her face was firm. She looked determined and clear-sighted.

"Just to be clear, this pregnancy cannot continue," she said.

"What do you mean?"

"Look. I don't want this craziness. I've had enough. My being a married woman aside, I can't go through with this pregnancy. I'd been taking Prozac since Maryam was born, I stopped a few months ago but my whole body's full of chemicals. It wouldn't be right to expose a fetus to something like that."

"Prozac? What's Prozac?"

"Prozac, the antidepressant. Haven't you heard of it?"

"No. But that's something for doctors to decide, not you."

She took a deep breath and spoke with exaggerated precision: "I was addicted to Prozac. I didn't just take it. I was addicted. I went to a clinic to stop taking it. I spent three months there. The doctor told me explicitly that I shouldn't get pregnant."

Fakhreddin stopped to think for a moment, then said, "But you're pregnant now and we don't know what's happened in your body in the meantime."

"I'm married to another man," she said, raising her voice now. "I'm not divorced, so I can't have a child with you. There's nothing for us to discuss. A baby is out of the question."

"My dear, you're pregnant now. We're not discussing something that might happen. You're pregnant. The divorce is bound to go ahead. Maybe this will prove decisive."

"What do you mean, the divorce is bound to go ahead? What's that exactly? The punchline from some old movie? There's no way any pregnancy's going to continue. There's no way there'll be any children. I don't want a child that would share Maryam's inheritance."

Fakhreddin was at a loss what to say.

"Inheritance from who?" he asked.

"The fortune my father left me. Isn't that Maryam's inheritance?"

"Her inheritance from you?"

"Yes."

"Are we making inheritance plans already? Really? Okay, but you might have had another child as a brother or sister for Maryam, anyway, before we met. So what difference does it make now?"

"Well I haven't had another child. And I don't want her to share her inheritance with anyone."

"What inheritance, Shireen? Have you gone mad? And besides, let's hope you stay around for her. You mean you think she might be short of money?"

"The inheritance isn't spending money. Do you think I could spend the millions my father left me? Even if I frittered it away every day it wouldn't run out. The inheritance is social capital that defines your status in society."

Fakhreddin didn't respond. In fact he had never thought about money in this way before. Money for him was a means to buy things. He patted her on the shoulder and told her to calm down. She pushed his hand away and said she wasn't mad, and the fact that she had been addicted to Prozac for a time and had once tried to kill herself didn't mean she was mad. She didn't say anything else for the rest of the day. The nanny brought some food but she waved it away. She sat motionless until night fell. Fakhreddin took his leave and went off home.

At two o'clock in the morning the telephone rang in Fakhreddin's house. The nanny begged him to come at once because her mistress was in a bad way. When he arrived he found Shireen asleep. The nanny said Shireen had spoken with her doctor, taken some tranquilizers, and gone to sleep. He sat next to her bed all night and in the morning she woke up calm. They had breakfast and she apologized to him for troubling him in the middle of the night. But she had felt she was losing control and had told the nanny to call him. She patted his hand and thanked him for coming and for being patient with her. She got out of bed and they went for a short walk around the house.

"I'm prepared to consider keeping the baby, on only one condition: if you give me a sign that you can be a responsible person," she said.

"You need a sign?"

"Of course."

"Like what, then?"

"For example, if you tell me clearly what you intend to write about in your doctorate, when you plan to finish it, and what you'll do for a living. Will you be a law lecturer, for example, and settle in France or will you go back to Cairo? And if you go back, will you go back to lead the revolution, or will you go back and be a responsible person?"

"But I don't want to lie to you or promise you something I'm not sure of. I don't know if I could stay in France or not."

"Why not?"

"Because I'm not French and I can't switch to the French way of life."

"That's nonsense. You know you're a hundred times closer to the French way of life. Egyptians treat you as a foreigner."

"Even if what you say is true, it's still no use. You know what that means? That means walking around with a sign on my chest saying, 'Not like other Arabs,' doesn't it?"

"Yes, and that's what anyone sensible would do. You're not like other Arabs. You're not like the annoying people who don't respect other people's privacy, who turn up late for appointments, leave a mess everywhere around them, go around with a hundred screaming kids, and flunk out of college. You're not like the freeloaders and all the other types you know. You're not like that and I'm not like that and I've no reason to stick with them."

"The only solution is to stick with them, because trying to prove that you're not one of them means you despise them. And it's no use, anyway. They'll stay stuck to you, whatever you do."

"You know what your problem is? Your problem is you're blind. You have chances to escape but you're determined not to see them and you refuse to take them. You stay trapped until you suffocate and then you complain that the world's standing in your way. But in fact it's you who's standing in your own way."

"Why do I feel we've had this discussion before?"

"That's exactly what I'm worried about. Come on, please, take me home."

When he called her the next morning she wasn't there. He called every hour until he found her, at nine o'clock in the evening. She was crying. She had told Sherif she was pregnant and he swore he wouldn't agree to a divorce unless she gave up custody of Maryam and gave him assurances about what she would do in the future. Shireen tried everything with him, from begging to threatening him with scandal, but he wouldn't budge from his position. She didn't eat anything all day and she refused to have dinner with Fakhreddin, who rushed to her house. She went to bed, leaving Fakhreddin to sit around anxiously. At about three o'clock in the morning

Shireen got up, went to the bathroom, and disappeared inside. Then Fakhreddin heard a commotion and a few minutes later he saw Shireen come out, leaning on the nanny's arm. She went to the sofa and stretched out there. He asked what was wrong and, between tears, she told him she had been bleeding and she might have miscarried. He got dressed quickly and took her to the hospital, despite her protestations that they should wait till the morning.

The doctors confirmed that the fetus was fine and that the bleeding had stopped but might resume. Their diagnosis was that Shireen had not been eating well and was severely anemic. Her blood pressure was irregular and this was dangerous for mother and baby. They gave her something to help her sleep and decided to hold her for observation for a few days. The next day her private doctor came to examine her. He looked at the results of the tests they had carried out and at the report from the doctors who'd seen her overnight. After deliberations between the doctors, they recommended she be kept under constant observation until she was due to deliver. The doctor explained that the pregnancy was in the beginning of its fourth month, and that the baby was doing well and there was no reason to believe it had been damaged by the tranquilizers and "other things" that the mother had been taking. It was medically possible for the pregnancy to continue and for the baby to be born in good health. The real danger, the doctor said, was that something unexpected might happen to the mother and it might not be possible to give her the medical attention she needed in time, or that the mother might do something harmful to the fetus, and that's why she should be kept under observation.

Shireen put up no resistance. The doctor clearly had influence over her. He had been her doctor since she arrived in Paris and had been with her through her depression, her addiction to antidepressants, and her suicide attempt. She behaved like a child in the presence of its father. She agreed to stay in the hospital without much discussion, and they took her to a more comfortable and more spacious room, away from the bustle, so that she could bring her own things and stay for the remaining months of her pregnancy. She was so docile that she seemed almost to have surrendered. Fakhreddin was worried about this, and his anxiety was well founded.

Cairo

August 15, 1993

Dear Eissa,

I received your letter. First I'd like to thank you very much for your honesty and for many things. Thank you for your many attempts to save me from falling into the abyss of nihilism. Thank you for a long and deep friendship, for putting up with me and with my many stupidities for all this time. Your candid letter was as thought-provoking as it was hurtful—very much so, that is.

The time has come, my friend, for me to be honest in return.

I'm not a child and you're not my father. I admit that I've treated you as a father for many years. This was a mistake on my part, and that's my personal problem, rather than your mistake. But the time has come to move away from that style of relationship.

I may not be as weak as you say. I might use weakness as an excuse for avoiding the responsibilities you say I should shoulder, but I don't know what responsibilities you are talking about or who is placing them on my shoulders. I can do what I like, even if I fail to meet your expectations of me, which are your business, not mine.

Yes, I have abandoned you in the past. Yes, I did let you go off alone and I broke the pledge we had made. But that happened many years ago, and I have paid the price for that myself, and I will not spend the rest of my life expressing regret.

So that I don't abandon you again, I say now: thank you, I don't want to come and live in France. I prefer to get drunk here, rather than chasing after news that has no value in a capital that I won't necessarily like.

I have found a job or, more precisely, a job has found me, as a translator with the United Nations in New York. I know it's a pointless job, but I don't care. I've accepted it. I have the tickets and I'm leaving for New York tomorrow. I'll be there when this letter reaches you. You will tell me not to accept it, not to waste my time on another dead-end job that might kill off whatever soul I have left in me. But from now on I don't want to follow your advice, and I will live in a place where I won't feel your presence every day.

With love,

Nasser

In the weeks that followed, Shireen was slowly losing strength. First, she accepted Sherif's decision to keep Maryam with him throughout her stay in hospital. Maryam came to visit only twice a week, stayed an hour, and then left with the driver. Shireen grew thinner and still wasn't eating enough. She said nothing for long periods and communicated with signs more than with words. At the beginning of the seventh month she bled again, and her life and that of the baby were in danger. Although she recovered from that crisis, her gaze wandered and she couldn't concentrate as she could before. Her doctor said he was worried she might revert to the deep depression she was in when he first met her. Fakhreddin asked what she'd been taking in recent months and was surprised to find that she'd continued to take tranquilizers. He had thought she was cured of her addiction. With every week that passed, Shireen became more withdrawn, so much so that sometimes she didn't seem to notice her daughter when she came to visit. The doctor said there wasn't much he could do at this stage, except focus on feeding her and strengthening her body to help her safely through the last weeks. Fakhreddin stayed at the hospital most of the time. He left for home late at night and came back in the morning. He stopped attending lectures at university and canceled appointments with his supervisor when they came up.

But Shireen had completely succumbed. When she started bleeding for the third and last time at the start of her eighth month, and went into what appeared to be a coma, the doctors decided to intervene surgically before it was too late. They held consultations and called in her husband to brief him and for him to sign the papers. Sherif arrived and Fakhreddin kept out of the way. Sherif had discussions with the doctors and they decided to operate, while Fakhreddin stood in the waiting room, taking no part in the discussions or the decision-making. Sherif, in his capacity as next of kin, agreed and the doctors went ahead. The operation took a relatively short time and then the nurse came out pushing a small incubator with the baby in it. Fakhreddin ran and looked at its wrinkled red face, which had just come out of his beloved's womb. He tried to touch the baby but the nurse prevented him and took him to the intensive care unit. Sherif left after signing the necessary papers, while Fakhreddin sat in the corridor leading to the operating room. An hour later the doctors came down the corridor shaking their heads sadly. The private doctor took Fakhreddin aside and told him with real anguish that they had done what they could, but Shireen had passed away.

A chill fell over Fakhreddin. The light seemed to have suddenly gone from his life. Colors disappeared from around him, as Shireen used to say to him: "The world's turned black and white, or rather gray and white." He was like a ghost.

He would sit among people but wouldn't hear what they were saying, and sometimes he wouldn't see them. Sometimes he would stand up and suddenly leave, as if he had seen something they couldn't see. He was like someone who has lost his hearing. He didn't hear the sounds around him, only a distant humming. He might hear a noise in the distance but he couldn't make out what people were saying most of the time. Things lost their sharp edges and turned into vague shapes that seemed to obstruct his path as he walked. Sometimes he passed through them and sometimes he felt they would collide with him, so he suddenly started and changed course. His mind was so disturbed that things appeared to him as flashes of light that produced a humming in a sea of silence.

Fakhreddin found himself alone in the Parisian winter holding a newborn baby boy, with no idea what to do with him. He still didn't understand what had happened or how it had happened. How had Shireen died? He had understood when she had left him. He had understood when their differences proved too much for them and drove them apart. He had even understood when she married another man and abandoned him. That had hurt him deeply but he understood why she'd done these things. But now he didn't know what her death meant. Like a child that has lost its mother, he told himself that she had gone away and was bound to come back one day. But he wasn't a child and he knew she wouldn't come back.

Sherif came and took away Shireen's body—a bitter reminder that she was still legally his. He didn't object to Fakhreddin registering the boy in his name, in the name of Eissa al-Naggar, that is. Sherif even asked, with a sneer, if Fakhreddin thought he was going to bring up the boy for him. Fakhreddin looked at him and couldn't understand how he had the gall to behave like this. In return Sherif asked Fakhreddin to waive any inheritance rights the baby might have claimed. Fakhreddin signed: there was nothing he wanted more than to distance himself and his son from the misfortune that had consumed the life of his beloved. He called the baby Omar, and registered Eissa al-Naggar as the father and Shireen Hassan as the mother. He mused that fate had conspired to prevent their names ever appearing together, even on their child's birth certificate.

Shireen was gone and Fakhreddin felt that his heart had gone with her. He didn't stop to ask himself why he had loved this woman, and why she had become so important in his life. He didn't ask himself where this complicated and unjust relationship had led him—a relationship in which he always paid the price for her weakness and sometimes her selfishness. He didn't ask himself these questions, because people in love never question their love.

Shireen was gone but she was still with him. He often saw her in his dreams at night and sometimes when awake by day. He woke up and felt her presence by his side. Not some phantom, but her real self. Sometimes he spoke to her and people looked at him suspiciously, but he didn't care. He scolded her for abandoning him again and she apologized. She told him that life was too much to bear and she had had to let go of the reins because she could no longer take the pressures. She said she couldn't go on so she had left the details of life to those who put pressure on her and had become his alone, because he was the only person who could really see her. She promised she would stay with him and would never leave him again. She hugged him and he could feel her stretched out beside him, comforting him till he dozed off. When he woke up in the morning he couldn't find her but he saw her during the night. He spoke to her even when he couldn't see her, and he could hear her reply. He told her about Omar and how he was looking after him and asked her for advice on things, and she would answer. He asked her about Maryam and her eyes would wander and she'd look down and say that Sherif wouldn't let her see her. He felt her hand on his hand and heard her asking him to go to see Maryam. He went to her school and saw her from a distance but he was worried he might cause her problems with her father if he spoke to her, so he left and never went back to see her.

Despite the humming noises in his head and Shireen's ghostly appearances, Fakhreddin looked after Omar, holding the baby's life in his hands—a soft lump of flesh that made demands with such regularity that Fakhreddin had no space for sadness. He had to look after the child. He learned what to feed him and how and when. He would get the night bottles ready and put them next to him in bed in warm water so that he could feed Omar when he woke up screaming in the depths of the night. He learned how to bathe him, change his clothes, and so on. Buheiri and his wife helped him look after Omar, and their house was always open to him when Fakhreddin needed to run an errand. But staying in Paris became patently absurd. Fakhreddin had given up studying many months ago. He had never really started in the first place, and he had grave doubts about its value. He spoke at length with Damian, who was strongly opposed to him leaving. But Fakhreddin wanted to leave the place where death had left its mark on him. He could no longer see any reason to stay. In Paris there were doors that had always been firmly closed and he felt there was no place for him. Shireen's death was the last straw, but he had known for a while that his departure was only a matter of time. But where to? He couldn't go back to Cairo and he didn't know where else he could go. He spoke with Buheiri, who told him he had friends in various Arab countries and he might be able to find him work as a lawyer or certified accountant, and Fakhreddin nodded in agreement.

A week later Buheiri came back with the good news that he had found him work with a Gulf investment company that wanted a lawyer to look after the legal aspects of its investments in Sudan. Fakhreddin would need to learn more about accounting procedures too but he would have accountants to help him with that until he was up to speed. They would pay him an attractive salary and arrange his housing and the other practical aspects, including a nanny for the baby. Fakhreddin quickly agreed and two weeks later he and Omar began their first journey together.

4

The Amarat District

FAKHREDDIN ARRIVED IN KHARTOUM AT night after a long flight. Omar was three months old and it hadn't been easy to feed a baby, change his diapers, and amuse him on such a long journey. The change of pressure in the plane also hurt the baby's ears, which put him in a generally bad mood, so he spent the flight either grizzling or screaming, while Fakhreddin tried in vain to calm him down. The plane finally landed. When Fakhreddin stepped outside, the hot air was like a slap in the face. It was humid and heavier than ordinary air. There was no bus waiting, but a security man wearing blue waved him along the pathway to the terminal building. He walked with the other passengers, carrying Omar. He was surprised at the size of the building: it was a small one-story structure with a small control tower and an aluminum door. The entire terminal was the size of Mansoura railway station and there were many mosquitoes. He opened the door and went in. The neon lights were humming, there were soldiers deployed inside, and an aluminum barrier with a small kiosk in the middle, also made of aluminum. A long line of passengers was queueing at the kiosk. The barrier had other openings, with similar kiosks that were closed. These ones had signs saying "Sudanese," "Arabs," and "Foreigners." All the passengers were standing in the one line and it took Fakhreddin half an hour to reach the kiosk. The soldier looked at him through the window, took his passport, then gave it back and asked him to fill in an arrival form. Fakhreddin left the line and looked around for the forms until an experienced passenger showed him where they were. He wrote in the information and went back to the line. After another half-hour his passport was stamped and he went through the barrier.

Omar was scowling and still in a foul mood. Fakhreddin looked for his bags and tried to keep the mosquitoes off Omar's soft skin. The conveyor belt wasn't working. The passengers gathered near the belt and after a while two workers came in pushing a metal cart piled high with suitcases and started to unload them onto the stationary belt. They then left and came back a quarter of an hour later with another load and so on. Fakhreddin eventually found his bags and headed for the exit. A policeman stopped him and directed him to another gate. At the other gate he found more police, male and female, with badges on their chests saying they were customs officers. One of them asked him what was in his bags, then pointed dubiously at one of the suitcases and asked him to open it. Fakhreddin opened it, but by then the man had gone. When he came back he waved him on without looking at the open bag. Fakhreddin went out and found himself in a large open space with vehicles, people, and dust everywhere. A man came up to him and asked him if he was Dr. Eissa al-Naggar. "Yes," he said. The man said he was glad he had arrived safely and that he was from the company. He helped Fakhreddin with his luggage, and it took them a few minutes to walk to the pickup truck that took them out of the airport area.

The streets were quiet, half-lit, and almost deserted at this late hour. They were dusty and reddish in color. At a checkpoint a soldier exchanged greetings with the driver and asked him who he had with him and where he was going. He stopped a moment to think about something, then told his colleague to lift the barrier and let them pass. The truck drove on through the quiet night, and was stopped at another checkpoint. There was no one in the streets except for these soldiers. After about ten more minutes the car reached the road that ran along the bank of the Nile.

It was close to three o'clock in the morning. The Nile flowed majestically and the dark red water hinted at the silt it was carrying northward. Fakhreddin had been looking forward to this moment. He looked at the dark, fast-flowing water and mused: "This is the secret of life—the tiny grains of soil carried by the waters of this powerful and munificent river. They will settle on the banks and become Egypt, creating it and recreating it every day. These are the waters that have irrigated a whole civilization over thousands of years. What river, other than you, holds this honor? What other river holds within it the life that you have held?" His train of thought was interrupted when the vehicle turned and suddenly stopped. The driver pointed to a yellow three-story building and started to unload the bags. Fakhreddin left Omar in the truck and went to check in but he didn't find anyone in the lobby. At the reception desk he found a large sign in Arabic and English that said, "The hotel does not accept major credit cards." He smiled and took this as a good omen. He looked for some staff, but couldn't find anyone. He started calling out and after a while a young black man appeared, thin, extremely tall, and looking like he'd just woken up. Fakhreddin greeted him but he didn't respond. He just put out his hand without speaking to Fakhreddin, who handed him his passport. He took it and put it aside without looking at it. He took out a key and asked Fakhreddin about his bags. Without another word he went off to pick up the bags. Fakhreddin asked him what the room number was but the man just pointed in the direction they would take. Fakhreddin fetched Omar from the truck and joined the silent young man in a long corridor. They went through a courtyard with some plants and Fakhreddin was struck again by the redness of the soil and the smell of the rain that had seeped into the ground. He liked that. They reached a room on the ground floor and the man opened it, put the bags down, and left. Fakhreddin put Omar on the bed and went out to thank the driver but he had also gone. He hurried back to Omar and noticed with irritation that there were mosquitoes in the room. He called reception but no one answered.

He saw a small electrical anti-mosquito device next to the bed. "Ah, so the mosquitoes are a permanent feature of the room!" he said to himself. He plugged the device into the socket and turned the air conditioning on, but it made a very loud noise. He started unpacking his clothes. He opened the wardrobe and found that the shelves were covered in dust. He looked at the bed and the chairs and found they had obvious stains. He moved the heavy curtain: the wooden rod clattered but didn't move. From behind the window a yellow light was shining and there was a soldier standing on the other side of the street, so Fakhreddin put the curtain back as it had been. The temperature in the room hadn't changed despite the noisy air conditioning. He went into the bathroom. The neon light was buzzing and there was no hot water. He sat down on the bed and wondered what Shireen would have done if she had been with him. She would have had loads of suitcases, spread around the room. She would no doubt refuse to put her clothes in the wardrobe, so they would stay in the suitcases. Would she insist on leaving for somewhere else on the same night—maybe on leaving Sudan completely? What would she do with Omar? He hadn't often seen her taking care of Maryam: it was the nanny who did that. He wondered how Maryam was now, and what her emotionally detached father had told her. Had he gone home and told her that her mother was dead, or had he pretended that "Mother has gone away"? Maryam was bright and would no doubt understand. He wondered if Maryam had visions of her mother, as he did: Did Shireen come to her in her imagination too? He could see Shireen now, sitting there at the end of the room on that rickety chair, grumbling and pouting. It was late, Omar had finally fallen asleep, and Fakhreddin was exhausted. He leaned back on the headboard, overcome by exhaustion, and fell asleep in his clothes on the thick bed cover that hid the dirtiness of the bed.

When the driver came by in the morning to take him to work he was surprised by Fakhreddin's complaints. "But sir, this is the best hotel in Khartoum," he said.

"Maybe it was just the room that wasn't good."

"For sure, sir. They say it's the best hotel in Khartoum."

"No problem, inshallah."

"No, no problem. Everything will work out, God willing."

But of course nothing did work out. Fakhreddin spent two weeks in the room, trying every day to persuade the hotel management to repair the air-conditioning unit and the hot water, get rid of the mosquitoes, and provide clean blankets. Every time a different member of staff would promise him all this and then he would come back at night and find nothing had been done, until he gave up asking. When his apartment in the Amarat district was ready he moved into it with no regrets. The apartment was small and cold and almost unfurnished, and the electricity was off most of the day. The owner of the building said they were going to install a generator soon, but it never happened. Amarat was the grandest neighborhood in Khartoum, but the dusty streets were flooded with rainwater at that time of year. There was a grocer at the end of the street who had everything that was available in Khartoum and there was a small restaurant that made various dishes with dubious ingredients. Next door there was a coffee shop that consisted of a small room with a boy who was reluctant to serve the customers and a couple of chairs set out in the dusty street. Cars drove by and sprayed dirt up into the faces of the few customers there were, and no one seemed to care. Beyond the coffee shop, there was a fruit and vegetable shop, then nothing. The rest of the neighborhood was made up of buildings like the one he was living in, and dirt roads flooded with rainwater. There were boys hanging out and a few vehicles, most of them pickups.

Fakhreddin didn't venture far from the neighborhood. His colleagues told him there was nothing worth seeing in other parts of the city, and the only place he could seek out for diversion was the bank of the Nile. Fakhreddin loved the river. He walked along the narrow pavement that followed the riverbank, passing in front of the Egyptian consulate, which had originally been the headquarters of the Egyptian inspector of irrigation. He would keep walking as far as the entrance to the presidential palace, which was originally the residence of the British governor. There the guards blocked his path and he would walk back the same way. Every time he walked past the yellow hotel where he had stayed he felt a lump rise in his throat.

Fakhreddin left his baby with Umm Fatma in the morning, then dropped in at her place in the evening to pick the baby up. After a while Umm Fatma agreed to work for him full time, and then she started coming to the apartment in the morning. She looked after Omar while Fakhreddin was at work, and then stayed and left at the end of the evening. Umm Fatma was a kindhearted woman from the Fur tribe in western Sudan. She didn't speak much and Fakhreddin didn't understand her well when she spoke, but they managed to communicate one way or another, and Omar loved her.

Then Sultan appeared. One day, while Fakhreddin was sitting reading on the balcony, he saw a cat staring at him. It was a Persian cat, with masses of hair, young and thin though the hair made it look bigger. It came and stopped close to him and began to stare at him. Fakhreddin started stroking it: he had always liked cats. But the cat didn't respond. Fakhreddin ignored it for some moments and it came closer and started scratching at his clothes. He pushed it off but the cat continued. He ignored it in the hope that it would give up but the cat grew fiercer. He shouted at it and it shut up, but a few seconds later it went back to scratching him. Fakhreddin stood up, shooed it away, and it withdrew. Then it came back, approaching slowly, extending its claws and scratching him. A few moments later it jumped onto the table next to Fakhreddin and stretched its head toward a plate of cheese on the table. Fakhreddin tried to shoo it away and threw a piece of cheese on the floor, but the cat didn't move and started to meow. Fakhreddin ignored it but the cat went on meowing monotonously and incessantly. A quarter of an hour later Fakhreddin stood up and left the balcony. "That's all I need: a stupid, stubborn cat. Where did this woman find it?" he thought. He called Umm Fatma and asked her, and she said it had been visiting the house for some days and she didn't know if anyone owned it. She had been giving it food and water, and it came and went as it pleased. Then she had made a little shelter for it in a corner of the large balcony, and the cat had settled in.

"And it's going to live with us, is it?"

"He's a sultan and he behaves like he owns the place."

Sultan was really annoying, because he was always in the wrong place. Fakhreddin might open the fridge and Sultan would stick his head inside without Fakhreddin noticing, and when the door was closed on him, the cat would squeal in pain. Then he would do it all over again, as if nothing had happened. Whenever Umm Fatma opened a door, the cat would slip in and hide, either in a bedroom, a cupboard, or the bathroom. When she went out again she would close the door on the cat without anyone knowing it was trapped. It could meow for hours until someone figured out where it was and let it out, and so on. What annoyed Fakhreddin most was the cat's constant meowing at night, for which there was no obvious cause. At first he thought it was lonely so he took it into his room, but Sultan would run around the room all night, sometimes pulling the cover off Fakhreddin, sometimes pulling at the bedsheet or attacking the mosquito net above him. Fakhreddin couldn't sleep so he would turn the cat out and have to shut the bedroom door on him. But then Sultan would come and stand by the bedroom door and meow.

Fakhreddin put up with the cat anyway until it started attacking Omar. Fakhreddin had never seen a cat attack a baby but Sultan apparently thought that Omar was a big cat that he could play with. Fakhreddin came into the room and found Sultan had taken all the covers off Omar and was standing on top of him about to pounce. Fakhreddin almost threw Sultan out of the window, but he restrained himself and put him out gently, and warned Umm Fatma never to leave Omar alone with the cat.

Fakhreddin started work as soon as he arrived. The group of companies urgently needed a certified accountant because the previous one had left unexpectedly. Fakhreddin asked why his predecessor had left so hurriedly but he didn't receive a clear answer and he didn't push to find out. His job was to audit the accounts of the companies in the Wadi investment group, which was owned by several wealthy Gulf Arabs. These companies were engaged in a variety of activities. There was a real estate company that owned houses and other properties in Khartoum, Port Sudan, El Fasher, and other places in Sudan. There was a company that specialized in farming, with a big farm in Khartoum North and others in Damazin near the border with Ethiopia, in Port Sudan, and in Nyala in the south of Darfur. Then there was an import–export company, a tourism and travel company, a construction company that built roads, bridges, ports, and airport buildings, a company that distributed foodstuffs, and a transport company that dealt with air freight, sea cargo, and moving livestock and building materials across the vast country on trucks, river barges, and sometimes even camel trains. Each company had an independent management structure and staff, who didn't necessarily know those in the other companies. But the accounts from all the companies came to the investment holding company, Wadi, and had to be audited in order to monitor their activities, and also because the investments involved the Sudanese government, taxes, and the like, as well as the non-resident Gulf investors who owned the group of companies.

The chairman of the group's board of directors had moved to Sudan about a year, or a little more, before Fakhreddin arrived. He was a dignified sheikh of few words. He met Fakhreddin when he began work and advised him to comply with legal principles and not to tolerate the slightest error, because people's money was at stake and he would not accept any financial impropriety. He urged him to be god-fearing and emphasized his interest in the ethical commitment of those who worked with him. He said that if it hadn't been for Buheiri's recommendation, he wouldn't have hired anyone he didn't know personally for such a sensitive position. The sheikh warned him that he would be on probation for three months, and if he proved competent and performed well he would give him a contract for a fixed term, but he should understand that he would be under permanent observation and scrutiny. Fakhreddin promised to do his best and assured him that he had done similar work before, that he wasn't frightened of the assignment, and that his only concern was his work and his son, and so there was no need to be anxious. The sheikh left an impression on Fakhreddin: he was one of these people that you feel can look deep into your soul. They speak slowly and with such sincerity, clarity, and confidence that you don't want to disagree but only to listen more. The sheikh said goodbye and Fakhreddin left wondering who this thin man might be and why he might have left his own country to settle in Sudan. He was no older than his mid-forties and yet he managed a vast commercial empire.

Fakhreddin excelled in his work so quickly that everyone was amazed. He finished off the audits shortly after arriving, saving the group from the crisis that had arisen when his predecessor had suddenly left. He made no mistakes and left no room for any ambiguity. His way of working made life easier and smoother for everyone. He maintained a good relationship with the accountants and auditors in all the companies in the group. Even those who initially treated him with skepticism, as an outsider to the group, soon conceded that he was honest, intelligent, and trustworthy. After several weeks studying the operations of the companies and the legal framework that governed the group, he suggested to the sheikh some adjustments that would save the company millions. The sheikh was dubious and advised Fakhreddin not to propose new ideas until he had properly understood all the activities of the companies. But he sent the suggested changes to the group headquarters in the Gulf for them to look at. The headquarters approved them and praised the Sudan branch. Gradually, the sheikh and the staff in the group had more confidence in Fakhreddin, in both his knowledge and his morals. Without giving it much thought, he started to spend all his time at work, leaving Omar in the care of Umm Fatma, who devoted herself full time to the baby. He had a closer look at the company budgets and how the companies operated. He liked the idea of investing in Sudan. The country was dear to him, not least by virtue of the sentiment that ties together all the people in the Nile valley. It was a poor country that had been torn apart by wars, despite its resources and vast potential. He didn't understand the details of the conflicts that had ravaged Sudan and its people, but he reckoned that a little economic development was bound to reduce the severity of those conflicts. His enthusiasm for the work of the group was enhanced by his sense that the sheikh was honest and that the investors were trustworthy. It was clear that their aim was not profit, because they often reinvested their profits in the country rather than transferring them abroad, or else they spent as much on charitable projects as they had earned in profits—projects such as building new roads and providing food for displaced people and so on.

There was nothing distinctive about the company staff. Like the Gulf company, they were of diverse nationalities—many Egyptians and Palestinians, some Levantines,

Moroccans, and Yemenis, many Sudanese and Eritreans, and a number of Indians and Pakistanis. The security guards were something else: really tough, physically and in their tolerance of harsh conditions. They never spoke to anyone but their superiors and they were all strictly religious. They lived together in the Khartoum North farm with their families and left the farm only to work. When Fakhreddin asked about this, he was told that Salman Ahmed, the group's security official, was a former officer in the special operations unit of the Pakistani army and applied the same rules that had applied in his army unit. This was necessary, he was told, to protect the group's investments from any risks, especially as the Sudanese security forces were not wholly reliable because of corruption and internal conflicts. So the group had asked the government right from the start to let it have its own independent security operation, and the government had agreed, though there was close coordination between Salman Ahmed and the local security agencies. Fakhreddin was surprised when he examined the budgets and found wide discrepancies between the prices for various consignments of livestock. Fakhreddin knew he was no expert in the livestock trade, but the discrepancies seemed odd. Sometimes a consignment of cattle would cost a certain amount and on another occasion it would cost twenty times as much. He asked the financial officer about the fluctuations.

"It's based on the market price. The market's volatile," the man said.

"But these fluctuations are very dramatic—twenty times the price and sometimes more."

"Ah, those variations are because of the different types of livestock."

"What types? They're all cows."

"Yes, but cows come in different kinds."

"So much so that one's worth a hundred dollars and another two thousand dollars?"

"Of course, and more. Don't you know that cows come in brands, just like clothes? There are Australian cows, English cows, and so on, and each kind has its price."

"Well, to reach prices like these, these cows must be Versace."

The financial officer roared with laughter, till there were tears in his eyes. Fakhreddin noticed his childlike delight at the joke and the innocence of his laugh, although the man looked tough. The expression spread among the group to describe livestock consignments of this kind.

The sheikh was balanced in everything he did or said. He spent his time monitoring business and inspecting the companies and the investment locations on the ground. In his free time he rode horses at the Khartoum North farm. He had three wives and several sons, though Fakhreddin didn't know exactly how many. His family was reclusive and didn't mix with the other families. He didn't like excess, either in the display of emotion or in conferring praise or blame. He always counseled careful deliberation and thorough study before acting, and avoiding haste, which he saw as a sign of arrogance and overconfidence. Although the sheikh was very pious, he advised those around him to make decisions and judgments based on reason and he never tired of telling people that trusting in God did not mean fatalism or failing to plan ahead, since God has told us to use our reason and act prudently. He said that strong believers were better from God's point of view than weak believers and more resilient. Although he admired Fakhreddin and had growing confidence in him, he never said so openly or showed excessive appreciation of him. In fact, he was always testing him, placing obstacles in his path from time to time to see how he would cope, and rewarding him every so often to see how he would react. He gave the financial officer instructions to raise Fakhreddin's salary and move him from his simple apartment to a more comfortable one in the same neighborhood. He gave him direct supervisory responsibility for the accountants in all the group's subsidiaries, and then observed him. Nothing changed in Fakhreddin's behavior. He wasn't condescending toward anyone and his tone didn't change when he spoke to colleagues who were now his subordinates. He didn't claim more expenses, he didn't work shorter hours, and his commitment to doing his job properly did not wane. The financial officer told him that from now on he wouldn't check Fakhreddin's work, but would send it straight to the head office. But he did check it in secret and didn't notice any decline in the quality of the work. On the contrary, Fakhreddin was now more meticulous and checked his reports himself several times before sending them to headquarters. The sheikh accompanied him several times on his visits to subsidiaries in various parts of the country, and traveling with him was a chance to test him further and observe him at close quarters. One night, as they were having tea at a rest house on their way out to the Damazin farm, the sheikh said, "Have you found yourself a wife yet?"

Fakhreddin was surprised by the question and answered slowly: "But I am married."

"Who's your wife?"

"Omar's mother."

"And where is she?"

"She passed away."

"May God grace her with His mercy, but now you have a duty to your body and to your mind, and the only things that can harm or help Omar's mother now are the things she did in her own life."

He stopped and Fakhreddin didn't respond. On another trip, when they were on their way to Nyala in south Darfur, as Fakhreddin was sitting on a rock to have a rest, the sheikh rode up to him on his horse and asked, "Do you know how to ride?"

"No," Fakhreddin replied.

"I really don't understand you Egyptians. How can a man be a man when he doesn't ride horses?"

Then he called the guard, told them to fetch a docile horse, and invited him to ride it. Fakhreddin mounted the horse and it walked a little. Then the horse began to gallop and Fakhreddin didn't know how to stop it. He bounced up and down and struggled to stay on the horse's back. He was soon panting for breath. The guard rode up alongside him, grabbed the horse, and stopped it. The guard took the two horses back, leading Fakhreddin's horse by the halter as Fakhreddin sat on its back, trying to get his breath back. The sheikh smiled and shook his head. "You need to get fit, my boy. You need to do some exercise, go running until you're in better shape. Don't try riding till then."

Then he dug his heels into his horse's flanks, let out the reins, and raced off, leaving a cloud of dust behind him.

These trips taught Fakhreddin more about the sheikh, but he never initiated conversation with his boss. On the contrary: he said nothing, watched what was happening, and tried to understand without asking. The sheikh noticed that and liked it. Once, he told him that what ruins men is too much talking. One night in the Eastern Desert, Fakhreddin got up to light a fire near the tent they were sleeping in. The sheikh watched him, called him over, and asked him where he had learned to do that. Fakhreddin explained that he had been brought up in the countryside, in Sharqiya province near the desert, and he often went out to graze sheep and goats with his foster mother Umm Ibrahim. The sheikh beamed and told him that the Prophet Mohamed had also been a shepherd. Fakhreddin blushed in embarrassment and replied, "*May God bless him and grant him peace.*" The sheikh nodded and didn't say anything.

The next day the sheikh told him off sharply for something trivial that wasn't even his fault. Fakhreddin promised to fix it and then called the person responsible and asked him to sort it out, and that was done on the following day. But the sheikh kept his distance and didn't make conversation with Fakhreddin for the rest of the trip. The sheikh would joke with him at times and be tough with him at other times, saying or doing things in front of him that required a reaction, and observing him. And every time, he grew more confident that this newcomer was a man of honor, trustworthy and upright.

These trips were the best part of Fakhreddin's work in Sudan. Shireen often came to his mind on these trips. She once said that she hadn't realized she would like the open air and the desert so much, after living all her life in big cities, without ever imagining that the desert offered so much beauty and peace. Fakhreddin smiled and said there are many things we don't know because we have never experienced them and that most beautiful things don't cost much, apart from the effort of trying them, and that this is what he had tried so often to explain to her. She was angry at what he said, and told him his impatience was unbearable. Instead of letting her discover this for herself, as usual he was trying to force her to adopt his attitude in a way that was quite intolerable. She lost her temper and said he hadn't understood anything she had been saying all those years, even after she died and left him.

Fakhreddin traveled all over Darfur with the sheikh, discovering the mountains, the valleys, and the people of the various ethnic groups and tribes with their different customs. They went to Kutum and Kulbus to the north, El Geneina to the west, and as far as the border with Chad, to El Fasher, Tawila, Nyala, and other places—dozens of villages and small towns spread across the land. Sometimes the terrain would be bare desert, sometimes savannah, and sometimes mountains where only the local people ventured. He noticed how the tribes revered the sheikh and received him warmly. That took him by surprise, because investors don't usually receive such a welcome. The sheikh had deep ties with the tribal people and he always left them gifts in the form of livestock or some of the goods they carried around with them. He would even leave containers full of "Versace" consignments for some of them, especially the Arab tribes. In the east, the Beja tribes, who claim to have their origins in the Arabian Peninsula, feted him as if he were one of them, and the sheikh behaved as if he really were one of them, and he knew those areas like the back of his hand. But the place closest to Fakhreddin's heart was Damazin, near the border with Ethiopia, where he felt he was close to the great sources of the Nile. The waters of the river seemed to generate an energy that he found irresistible.

During these trips Umm Fatma would bring her only daughter to the house and stay with Omar until Fakhreddin came back. When he went to Darfur, she would give him presents and money for her relatives in El Fasher. Umm Fatma was gentle and took good care of Omar, the house, and Sultan, the annoying cat. On several occasions, Umm Fatma asked Fakhreddin for permission to get rid of Sultan, who had "missed the boat on being clever," as she put it. His behavior made it hard for her to move around the house and complicated her work. She couldn't leave the cat in the same room as Omar out of concern for the baby's safety and she couldn't leave him alone with food because he would devour it. If she locked the cat up, it meowed constantly, which "got on the nerves of the angels," to use her words. Fakhreddin smiled and showed understanding, but urged her to take good care of Sultan. He liked cats in general and despite the problems that Sultan's presence created, Fakhreddin hated to throw out a weak creature that had sought refuge in his house. Shireen also liked the look of the cat and urged him not to mistreat it, saying that tolerating Sultan's stupidity and antics would be good training for Fakhreddin to put up with the shortcomings of others and not to push them too hard.

Following the advice of the sheikh, Fakhreddin started exercising. He started jogging in the street in the early evening. Salman Ahmed, the security officer, then told him that some of the residents had complained about him running, on the grounds that their womenfolk sat outside their houses in the evening. He advised him to go jogging at the Khartoum North farm instead. When Fakhreddin said the farm was too far away and he didn't know anything about the place, Salman said he had sought permission from the sheikh and had assigned a guard to act as his guide, who could also train him. He had chosen a young Zaghawa man from Darfur called Abdullah, who was tall, well-built, and extremely dark-skinned. Abdullah undertook to train him gradually: he took him to the farm for two hours a day during siesta time, when the people of Khartoum closed their doors, and brought him back after the afternoon prayers. After some weeks of running and exercising, Fakhreddin had recovered some of his fitness and started swimming. A few weeks later he started riding horses.

The exercise served him well. He had ignored his body for years, but he began to notice it again. He was aware of his legs, his waistline, and his arms. He felt lighter when walking as his leg muscles awoke from the long slumber imposed on them by a life of using public transport and sitting on chairs for too long. His breathing improved and he felt new strength seeping into him. This improved his general state of mind and helped him feel less dejected. Little by little the invisible barrier between him and the world around him began to lift, and the clouds that separated him from life began to disperse a little.

Abdullah stayed close to him even when he wasn't training, and Salman told him that the sheikh had requested protection for him, as an important element of the group's operations. Fakhreddin was rather surprised but he didn't mind. Abdullah didn't like Umm Fatma and she couldn't stand him either, so they interacted with each other as little as possible. Umm Fatma offered him tea and food when he was in the house with Fakhreddin and answered his questions in the morning as curtly as possible, but he avoided her as much as he could. Fakhreddin was surprised by this, since they both came from the same area and he had expected they would be close. Abdullah smiled when Fakhreddin asked him about this.

"Umm Fatma's a Fur and I'm a Zaghawa," he said.

"So?"

"There are problems."

"Between you?"

"Between the tribes."

"Really? But I thought the problems were between the tribes of Arab origin and the tribes of African origin: the Arabs and the blacks."

"No. There are problems between all of them."

"How so?"

"The Khartoum people don't want the Darfur people, whether they're Arabs or blacks. And all the Darfur people have problems with each other."

"But you get along with the Khartoum people, don't you?"

"Everyone gets along with everyone, but no one likes anyone else in this country."

"My God."

"It's always been that way with us, God help us."

On July 1, while Fakhreddin was sitting in his office checking the final accounts of one of the companies, he heard someone say, "Aren't you ever going to have a break from those calculations of yours? They all turn out wrong anyway."

He looked up from his computer screen to find Abu Yasser Buheiri standing there, smiling with his arms open. They embraced. Fakhreddin was delighted to hug his old friend from his Paris days again. Thoughts of Shireen flooded back and Fakhreddin's voice choked with emotion as he welcomed him. Buheiri was in a good mood, laughing and making jokes. Fakhreddin asked him how he was, about Paris and his family, and his work there.

"All's well. Umm Yasser's well and Yasser's in good health and all the children are well. They're with me here."

Fakhreddin looked at him in surprise.

"We're here to stay," said Buheiri. "I wrapped up my affairs in France, brought the children, and came."

"Here? You wrapped up your affairs in France and you're going to settle in Sudan?"

"It's just that France isn't fun any longer."

Fakhreddin looked at him quizzically.

"To be honest, they've cracked down on us more than necessary," Buheiri continued. "I don't know what happened but suddenly the police were on our case. At first, they kept closing down our business. They set themselves up in the metro and in Saint-Denis and in the streets and started rounding up young men who don't have residence permits, and deporting them before anyone had a chance to do anything. Then they started cracking down on us at work and rounding up people working informally and fining us. They cut off our livelihood. Who's going to give you a job if the police are going to come in after you? And besides, how can I work without the lads who work informally? If I took on people with work permits and paid taxes and insurance, what difference would there be between me and French companies? I couldn't give customers the prices I was giving them and I couldn't make a penny in profit. But let's get out of here and go for a walk. Do you have anything planned?"

Fakhreddin picked up his papers, closed down his computer, and went out with him. They walked a short distance to a nearby coffee shop and sat down. A young southern waiter came and asked them what they would like, and they ordered hibiscus tea. Buheiri continued: "After that they set to work on the guys in the mosque. They said the imam's an extremist and they issued a deportation order. Of course we knew he was an extremist and we'd been saying that for years, and why were they silent then? They waited till he'd recruited half the young men and then they noticed? Anyway, they deported the man and someone even worse appeared. Then they deported that one too and arrested a few young men and deported them. The ones deported were Algerians. We later found out they'd been tortured and one of them had been executed.

The others started to get cold feet and they rarely came to the mosque. They started meeting in other places. Then some incidents took place and they started rounding up everyone and handing them over to the security people in their home countries. Everyone ran for cover, and whoever had a place to go went there, and so here I am. I'm here and you're here, and tomorrow you'll see, these things they've done won't pass unnoticed, and tomorrow they'll pay the price. The people who've been deported back to their home countries are done for, but their blood won't be forgotten. The ones they could get hold of were the poor guys like me—the ones who help people travel and find jobs and the ones who attend classes in the mosque and so on. The heavyweight people are still there, the ones I hope will hurt them."

"Are you going to work with the group here or will you start up something of your own?"

"No, with the group, of course. Where do you think I got the money I worked with there? From my mother?"

"What kind of work are you going to do? Decorating here, too?"

"What do you mean, decorating? Have you forgotten I'm an engineer? I'm going to work at the Khartoum North farm."

Fakhreddin hadn't forgotten that Buheiri was an engineer. Even when Buheiri was at work painting and renovating apartments in the suburbs of Paris, Fakhreddin would look at him and feel sad for the state of the world and its loss when an aerospace engineer turned to decorating. Apart from being acutely intelligent, Buheiri was pleasant company, hated disagreements and conflict, and was always able to reconcile people and bring an end to rivalries, and Fakhreddin liked him for that. He asked after Umm Yasser, his wife, and Buheiri told him that she had asked after him as soon as she heard they were going to Sudan, and that she would be with the children in the Amarat for a while and then he would decide whether they should move to the farm with him. Buheiri took

Fakhreddin to meet her after they had dropped in at Fakhreddin's house to pick up Omar. Omar wasn't even one year old yet and so he hadn't changed much since they were in Paris. Umm Yasser was delighted to see him, as if she were meeting a child of her own that had been taken from her, and she made Fakhreddin swear by everything he held dear that he would leave Omar in her care.

"You're all by yourself," she said. "You don't have a wife to look after him and you don't have enough time for him, and do you think the woman at your place will look after him better than me? I'm practically his mother. I mean, has he had anyone closer to a mother than me, since the day he was born? That little guy came out into the world and found me, right before him. See . . . ? See how he calms down and keeps quiet when he's with me? So, leave him here, and come see him whenever you like, and treat the place as your home."

Fakhreddin loved to hear her trying to speak the Egyptian dialect. He thanked her for her generous offer, but turned it down. Although what she said was logical, he couldn't be parted from Omar. Omar was his link with the world and he felt that if he left him in anyone else's care he would find it hard to go on living.

He would just sit down and do nothing but think about Shireen's absence and about the life he had lost when she died, and then fade away quietly. But with Omar, he felt he had to keep going because there were things he had to do for him. That was the last remaining thread linking him to the world and he didn't want to let go of it. He thanked her and promised her he would drop in once a week and leave Omar with her for a whole day, or for a day and a night. And so it was.

Fakhreddin spent the next months learning, training, and traveling around. He grew stronger and tougher, physically and mentally. He acquired a ruggedness that city life had suppressed. His many travels in the desert and the bush took him back to basics. He rediscovered how few needs a human being has: a drink of water, a piece of bread, clothing against the cold, somewhere to lie down when he feels sleepy, somewhere to defecate, and not much more than that. Physical exercise made him better able to endure hardship. The person that Umm Ibrahim had nursed and taught to be a shepherd in his boyhood had suddenly reappeared. In the calm of the night in the desert, when his soul felt at peace, lying on the sand in a tent, or as he looked up at a sky filled with stars, or on a walk that lasted days across the sands, through the bush, or over mountain passes, Shireen came to him often, embraced him, wiped some of his sorrows away and set others aside. She told him he had never been a whiner or a crybaby, and reminded him that he always used to say that God created us to strive, that He has made everything in our lives a matter of endeavor and exertion. Life brings both obstacles and opportunities, challenges and disasters, such as hunger and thirst. All of them force us to stand up and take our fate in our hands. How can we leave others in control and then bemoan our luck? Shireen told him she would like to follow him when he was out riding, an activity he had finally learned and even mastered. Sometimes, on Friday at the Khartoum North farm, the sheikh would race with him, always beat him decisively, then smile at Fakhreddin and tell him he had to "make more effort."

Fakhreddin became more active. He spoke even less than he had done before and moved more, with agility and resolve, and accomplished his work faster. His accountancy work was now peripheral and he finished it off in an hour or less a day, all the while looking forward to his next trip to Darfur, Damazin, Suakin, or Port Sudan. He fell in love with Kordofan and they would pass through it on their way to the south, where they went into the bush and the swamps. He didn't catch malaria although he refused to take the anti-malaria pills they had given him in Paris, because the damage in the long term could outweigh the benefits. Umm Fatma gave him some herbs that supposedly protected him from malaria mosquitoes. He started eating the same food as the local people and drinking what they drank, and his body built up a natural resistance that came from local products.

When he first went to Juba he stood at the end of the main street watching the Nile gliding along and turning at the end of the houses, beyond which there was nothing but lush greenery as far as the horizon. His eyes filled with tears for the first time in months as he remembered the Nile in Mansoura when he was young. The Nile bent in the same way as here, and the banks of the river were equally verdant. The soil grows more and more red the further south one goes, there are fewer roads and more water, the green is lusher, and the trees are taller. Fakhreddin made friends with camels, discovered them, and learned their natures and how to handle them properly and control them. He understood their fears, their courage, and their points of weakness. He learned how to sail on the river and steer a barge through the marshes. He also learned to navigate by the stars at night in the wilderness. He learned to tell the difference between a wind that will bring rain and a wind that heralds a sandstorm that will block out the sky. He learned about human character and how people vary. He finally understood that God had created them with differing natures and ethnicities, and that it was futile to expect anything else from them. He began to wonder why he hadn't understood this earlier and how he had walked through the world so long without seeing it.

The trips, the training at the Khartoum North farm, and the growing confidence that everyone had in him, gradually revealed to him another aspect of the group's activities. When Buhciri arrived and settled down at the Khartoum North farm, he finally saw what he had long suspected, but had been afraid to ask about. He realized that the consignments of "Versace" livestock were a cover for containers full of weapons and ammunition, and that the big farms included training camps for fighters. He met them, mixed with them, and came to know them, and they came to know him. Buheiri laughed as he explained to him the work he did, making simple short-range shoulder-held missiles and training the fighters to use them. He saw the reason for the strict security measures, the prestige the sheikh enjoyed among the Arab tribes in various parts of the country, the group's close relations with the government, and the mysterious transactions that the financial officer removed from the official budget under the category of "facilities." He discovered the nature of the field work that the group financed. The operations manager briefed him on secret details related to financing the training of young men and sending them off to Afghanistan, Pakistan, Libya, Algeria, Yemen, Eritrea, Somali, Bosnia, Chechnya, Indonesia, and the Philippines. Fakhreddin had never imagined he would end up in the middle of such a major network. But the doors that had been closed in his face one after another had brought him here. The group had provided a comfortable framework for his life and no one had asked him to take part in any of its secret activities. His role was only to do the accounts and accompany important shipments as the sheikh's representative. In its investment activities, the group was the model of an honest and responsible company, and he saw nothing shameful in doing this kind of work with them—quite the opposite, in fact. Buheiri's arrival helped to reinforce these bonds of affection. Although Fakhreddin did not take part in the group's other activities, he persevered with his daily physical training and horse-riding. This very much helped clear the sorrows from his mind and soul.

This framework was suddenly shattered. Salman Ahmed told Fakhreddin that Hussein was in Khartoum and wanted to meet him. Fakhreddin was delighted to hear the news, but he realized that this visit must mean bad news. What had brought

Hussein from Cairo to Khartoum? Salman Ahmed didn't answer, but he mentioned in passing that Hussein was going to stay some time in Khartoum. All the way home, Fakhreddin had a sense of foreboding.

When Fakhreddin saw Hussein, he didn't recognize him. He was sitting on an old chair at the end of the courtyard, staring absentmindedly. He looked up at Fakhreddin and nodded. Hussein had once had curly black hair, but now he was completely bald and no longer had a mustache, and his brown face was frozen in a scowl. He tried to smile, without success. Fakhreddin went up to this person sitting there, and tried to recognize Hussein in his features. Hussein stood up, and only then did Fakhreddin believe that this tall, thin man really was his friend from Kerdasa. They embraced and Hussein's body trembled in his old friend's arms for some moments, then he recovered his composure. They sat down and Fakhreddin asked Umm Fatma to make them some tea and take away Sultan, who was meowing monotonously in a corner of the courtyard.

Hussein was sullen and curt, despite his attempts to seem relaxed. Fakhreddin had a thousand questions: about Cairo, his friends, his aunt Maria, everything. Hussein told him he would tell him everything, but a great many things had happened since they had last corresponded when Fakhreddin was in Paris. He gave Fakhreddin condolences on the death of Shireen and congratulated him on the birth of Omar, saying he had seen the boy at Umm Yasser's that morning and that he looked very much like him. He asked Fakhreddin about his life and Fakhreddin told him he was living from day to day, until he felt at ease again and could think about the future. Fakhreddin explained that he didn't really notice what was happening around him and that he lived his life robotically, as if it were someone else's life and he was watching from above. He felt there was a glass barrier between him and life, the people he met and the things he saw. He expected to wake up one day and find that this barrier had shattered and disappeared, and until that happened, he wouldn't make any decisions or do anything other than doing the accounts for the companies in the Wadi group. Hussein nodded and said that what he said was logical and made sense. Umm Fatma brought the tea and put it on the table behind them. They stopped talking till she went back into the house. Then Fakhreddin asked him what he'd been up to and what was happening in Egypt. Hussein took a deep breath, warned him that the news was very bad, and asked him if he was prepared to hear it.

"Is my aunt Maria all right?" Fakhreddin quickly replied.

"She's fine and sends you her regards."

"So what's happened?"

"Nasser al-Khudari, may you rest in peace," he began.

"What?"

"Nasser, he had an accident in New York, on the subway."

"Nasser?"

"In fact he. . . . The New York police report said he committed suicide. He'd also sent a letter to that famous journalist friend of his in Mansoura. What was his name?"

"Ashraf Fahmi?"

"Yes. Nasser had written to him from New York and told him he planned to commit suicide or something like that. Ashraf went to New York to see him, but when he arrived he found Nasser was dead, so he brought the body back home."

"*There is no power or strength save in God*," Fakhreddin intoned formulaically. He put his face between his hands and said nothing more. There were so many ideas at work in his head that he couldn't speak.

"Unfortunately, that's not the last of the sad news," Hussein continued.

Fakhreddin looked at him questioningly, and Hussein went on:

"At the end of last year, around October, Younis came back to Egypt. Remember Younis? He was with you and Ali

136

in the army. Younis turned religious after his military service, joined a group from Luxor, and went to Afghanistan with the mujahideen. When the jihad ended and the mujahideen factions started to fight each other, he left Afghanistan and came back to Egypt with everyone else. Anyway, he stayed with Ali. You know they had known each other well before they were in the army. He stayed with Ali for about a month and a bit. He shaved off his beard and changed his appearance, of course, but you know Bayn al-Sarayat. Word spread and he decided to find somewhere else to stay. He came and stayed at my place in Kerdasa. I found work for him there and he began to sort himself out. After a while, maybe two months, a detective came and asked Ali about him. Ali told him any old story. Two days later, the security people summoned Ali. I told him not to go, but he went. They asked him about Younis and he told them he was a friend of his from the same hometown and they were together in the army, and that Younis had visited him and left and he didn't know where he was. Of course, they didn't buy his story. They let him go and monitored him until he met Younis at my place and they picked up his trail. They followed him quietly. Little by little, they monitored everyone. At the end of January, they started rounding everyone up. They arrested lots of people in Kerdasa and Giza and came to arrest us too. We had nothing to do with it, but since they'd been monitoring us too, they decided to take us, just in case, so to speak. Ali and I went into hiding when they started picking people up, each of us in a different place. We stayed in hiding and they kept going to our houses, asking after us and leaving messages saying we needn't worry and we should hand ourselves in, as it was just for questioning and so on. But what happened was that they were picking people up and not a single one of those people ever came home, and there was no news of any of them after that. They rounded up about a thousand people, mostly people who'd come back from Afghanistan. There was no way

137

we were going to turn ourselves in. How could we prove we had nothing to do with them? And what we heard about the interrogation techniques made death seem preferable to handing oneself in. I mean, by the time you proved you were innocent, what would have happened to you? We stayed in hiding and moved from place to place. And after that, things started to get worse."

"How?"

"They arrested your aunt and Leila, your cousin."

Fakhreddin was speechless. Hussein continued, speaking more slowly now:

"They arrested them and left a message telling Ali to go and collect them. Our information, from previous cases that is, was that they put pressure on the relatives so that the people they wanted would hand themselves in. People get beaten up in detention, until the wanted men turn up. Sometimes the beatings are severe and the longer the fugitives stay in hiding, the greater the pressure they exert. Your aunt and cousin are okay, thank God. They say it wasn't too bad. Leila says so. Your aunt doesn't say anything. She just says it's all in God's hands. Leila said it was just a matter of a few slaps, a few insults, a few pushes, and general mistreatment, but nothing major. God alone knows, of course. When I was working in the Shenawi office I saw some horrible things, but it differs from place to place, depending on circumstances. We didn't know what the situation was, but Ali went crazy when they arrested Aunt Maria and Leila and he decided to turn himself in. I tried to persuade him not to do it. You know how dear Aunt Maria is to us all, but what happened had already happened. Ali wouldn't listen and he handed himself in, and they let Aunt Maria and Leila go the same day."

"And Ali?"

"I heard from some colleagues who were with him that the interrogation was brutal and Ali refused to speak. I don't know the details exactly. I mean, I heard contradictory things.

It's clear that something went wrong and Ali couldn't take it, the poor guy, may he rest in peace."

Fakhreddin choked. He felt that someone was squeezing him so hard he almost snapped. His head felt heavy and he could hardly breathe. Hussein's face was a blur and his voice faded out.

"The security people said he'd had a heart attack, that he'd had a diabetic seizure—the usual things they say in these cases. They wrote the medical report the same day and took the body to Aswan in a police vehicle with an escort and buried him in the presence of his father and his brothers only. They posted a guard in the cemetery for about a month and put pressure on the father not to breathe a word to any living creature. The police chief supervised the condolences ceremony and everything took place in silence. May God have mercy on his soul."

Fakhreddin couldn't move. His face froze and not a muscle twitched.

"Then my turn came. They rounded up every living soul in Kerdasa and called it 'the Kerdasa cell.' It wasn't a cell or anything of the kind. Everyone we knew was arrested, whether they were connected with an organization or not. Some of the jihadis they arrested were active and planning operations, but others weren't active at all. They had come back exhausted after what they had seen and just wanted to live their lives without causing trouble. In other words, they picked up every mother's son with a view to sorting them out later in their own way. I hid with a group I know in the desert outside Luxor, where no one would know how to find me. Many of the people they caught know me. You know I'm like an Arab sheikh and my house is open to anyone. Everyone they caught told them they'd been to Hussein's place before. They said things like Hussein arranged for me to travel to Sudan, or Hussein put me in touch with someone in Yemen, or Hussein introduced me to someone in London. They thought Hussein was the organization's chief of operations. They concentrated on me. They detained my brother in Sohag and the whole household in Asyut: my brother, his wife, my father and mother. I don't want to tell you what they did to them. My father's a sick man, if you remember him. Suffice it to say that if you saw any of them today you wouldn't recognize them. I didn't recognize him when I saw him. I won't tell you about the women and what was done to them. And this is Upper Egypt. You know what it means if you arrest a woman in Upper Egypt? Or if your mother is arrested and roughed up in detention? They held them for a month, but still that wasn't enough for them. They sent a bulldozer and demolished the house. Remember the house where you stayed? They sent the bulldozer and waited a week, and when I didn't show up they sent a police squad and knocked down the house. Within an hour, they had razed it to the ground. After that, they set the women free and then my father and my brother in Sohag. But my other brother is still in detention, just like that, without any charge or anything. They're keeping him till I appear. They've held a trial, charged me, and sentenced me to death in absentia."

"To death?"

"Yes, to death. I got my stuff together and came here straight from the mountains."

Fakhreddin sat immobile and in silence. It was as if he had aged since they sat down. Hussein stopped speaking. They sat there in the courtyard in Khartoum, shielded from the glaring sun over their heads by an awning of thick cloth. Another dark shadow fell on Fakhreddin's heart.

"I forgot to tell you. Condolences for one more."

"Who else?"

"Omar Fares."

"The prosecution guy?"

"Yes, the one who was investigating your case. Dr Nashaat's friend, remember?"

"He's dead?"

"A car accident. A car hit him in a side street near his house in Qasr al-Aini. Hit and run, though it's a narrow street and there are no fast-moving cars in it. But, surprise, surprise, this one was going fast. It hit him and didn't stop and miraculously disappeared onto Qasr al-Aini Street."

"May God have mercy on his soul."

"May God have mercy on us all."

They fell silent again. A long time passed before Umm Fatma came and called them to lunch. They mumbled that they wouldn't eat. Hussein stood up and left and Fakhreddin went off to his room. He sat in silence on the edge of his bed. Shireen came and sat next to him. She was silent too and her eyes looked sad. She looked at him but said nothing, and he said nothing either. He wanted to cry. He wanted to throw himself in her arms and burst into tears. But he couldn't, he couldn't muster the strength to cry. There was nothing left but a coarse sadness that was as hard as an ugly piece of rock. He looked at Shireen but couldn't see her face properly. His eyes were red but he wasn't crying. He tried to force the tears out of his eyes. He wanted to cry for his friend Ali, and for Nasser, and for all those who had been killed, and for Leila and his aunt and all those who had come to harm. But he sat there speechless, neither crying nor stirring, and the features of his face did not change. Sultan was meowing at the door of his room, but Fakhreddin didn't move. All he could hear was a distant buzzing and the meowing. Otherwise complete silence. Evening fell slowly on Fakhreddin as he sat there, his head about to explode. Sultan was still meowing. Umm Fatma came, took the cat away, and asked Fakhreddin if he wanted anything before she went home. She asked if she could take Omar to spend the night with her and when he didn't reply, she picked up Omar and left.

Complete silence descended on the house. Fakhreddin collapsed from exhaustion and fell asleep. He slept for an hour and dreamed of Ali, Nasser, Omar Fares, his mother, his aunt,

Leila, and Hussein's family. They were all in a big house with the doors and windows locked and bulldozers were knocking the walls down. The people were screaming and trying to get out but they couldn't open the doors. Fakhreddin woke up in a sweat. He could hear the sound of scratching coming from the door. He pricked up his ears. Sultan was scratching at the door with his claws, digging them into the wood and then pulling them downward, over and over. Fakhreddin jumped out of bed, leaped to the door, and opened it, completely out of control. He picked up the cat by the scruff of its neck and started to hit the door with it. Suppressed anger surging inside him, he bashed the stupid cat's head against the door until it was completely shattered. He looked at the smashed head and saw the same stupid look in the cat's eyes. He flew into a rage again, grabbed what was left of the head, and tried to separate it from the cat's body. But the head refused to come off and clung to the body by the skin. Fakhreddin held the cat's head with one hand and tore at the skin with the other. Then he started to pull the cat's body apart with his bare hands. His hands were drenched in the cat's blood, which was still hot and oozing from the flesh. He ripped the frail body to pieces and threw the pieces out of the room. Fakhreddin sat down on the bed, surrounded by spots of blood and bits of flesh and fur and crushed bone. He felt the beginnings of a sense of relief, as if a demon had escaped his grasp. "All these people were killed by the same hand and here I am doing the accounts, making trivial decisions, and saying yes or no. The bulldozers drive over me and I'm still wondering what should be done," he thought.

Umm Fatma brought Omar in the morning. Fakhreddin took him from her at the door and told her to leave. He gave her some money and asked her not to come back. He didn't answer her questions, just shut the door in silence. At noon, he left Omar with Umm Yasser and asked her to take good care of him. Then he went to the Khartoum North farm.

*

It was Hussein who suggested blowing up the Egyptian consulate in Khartoum, but Fakhreddin objected to killing innocent staff there and was skeptical about the benefits of such an operation.

"Innocent? You think they're innocent? Brigadier Ahmed Kamal, the guy in charge of combating religious activity, is innocent? Are these intelligence agents and spies innocent? So my mother they beat up would be what: a criminal? Was it my mother who killed Eissa and Ali and tried to kill you and sentenced me to death and roughed up our families? Was it my father who ignored the law, blocked the inquiry, ruined our lives, and killed Omar Fares when he didn't do what he was told? Was it my mother and father and your aunt who arrested a thousand people and tortured them and threw them in jail? What do you mean, innocent? Wasn't it Ahmed Kamal who tried to recruit Dalia al-Shenawi and have her get us all in trouble? Wasn't he the one who followed us here, even after we left the country?"

Fakhreddin tried to dissuade him from taking this approach. He reminded him that they shouldn't reduce the problem to a particular person, and that, even if Ahmed Kamal was responsible for some of these crimes, blowing up the consulate wouldn't do anyone any good. It would kill many people who had nothing to do with the government's abuses. It would open the gates of hell and lead to an endless cycle of killing and revenge without solving anything. Fakhreddin suggested two options: either to plan a major operation in Egypt that could change the situation that was responsible for all this injustice and killing or, if they wanted revenge, to target directly those who had done them harm—those who had actually killed and tortured people and those who had given the orders, but not to kill people at random.

But Hussein was past the point where he would listen to advice. He told Fakhreddin he had made preparations to carry out his plan and had persuaded Buheiri to take part. He had consulted his other colleagues and obtained everyone's approval. There was a fatwa that it was legitimate to kill government employees, even if they had not taken part directly in the government's crimes, because they had acquiesced and facilitated those crimes. Fakhreddin objected to the use of such fatwas and warned Hussein and Buheiri that it was dangerous to take this path. He tried to convince them and the others throughout January and February of that year. But when March came Hussein asked him to stop arguing because planning for the operation had already started. He told him that a Pakistani group had agreed to carry out the attack on their behalf, while they provided backup in the form of diversionary operations in Sudan. Fakhreddin asked if the sheikh was aware of all this and Hussein told him that they hadn't spoken to him about it explicitly. They had decided to act independently of the sheikh's group, but Salman Ahmed was their contact with the Pakistani group and they were leaving it to him to judge how much the sheikh needed to know. Fakhreddin said nothing. He knew it was impossible for one person to control everything. It was a big group, its decisions were made by consultation, and no one had the right to monopolize the process.

Buheiri had been in charge at the Khartoum North farm since he arrived, and over time he had converted the farm into a headquarters for young men coming from Egypt. Hussein divided his time between lessons in religion and physical training. He received plenty of military training and excelled at everything. Within a few months he was the one of the most proficient fighters on the farm and all his trainers praised him. He trained as if he were actually fighting, with determination and a steely will. Nothing could stop him or stand in his way. He trampled on all obstacles, overcoming them without emotion, and emerged from them unscathed.

Fakhreddin was also training with an enthusiasm that took even him by surprise. He soon mastered shooting and learned about various kinds of weapons, from small pistols to machine guns that could be mounted on vehicles. Within a short time, he could regularly hit the targets, however small or distant they were, even if they were moving and regardless of whether the weapon had a telescopic sight or not. He was able to do this without any great effort. When the target appeared he raised the gun, hit it immediately, without a single muscle in his face twitching, and then went back to sitting still. He lost what remained of his cheerful smile and his face assumed a rigid expression that never changed.

On June 1, Buheiri told him that the basic elements of the operation were ready, with some details and the timing yet to be decided. They settled on August as the time to carry it out, because a UN conference on human rights would be taking place in Khartoum at the time and the city would be full of foreigners of every kind, which would make it easier for the bombers to enter and leave the country, and to move around. They had been monitoring the consulate and its staff for months and had worked out the staff's routine—when they came and went and who they were. There were some diplomats there but they were not part of the intended target. There were some security agency personnel, headed by Ahmed Kamal, who used the consulate building as their headquarters. They calculated how large an explosive charge would destroy the consulate but not the neighboring buildings. They prepared places to lodge the team that would prepare the bomb in its final form—as a briefcase full of TNT. The detonator would be the key to the briefcase. One of the team, trained and eager for martyrdom, would carry the briefcase into the building and detonate it.

Two details remained: how to reduce the number of civilians visiting the consulate on the day and how to mislead the security people if any news of the operation leaked out before it took place. Buheiri explained the importance of this aspect; something always leaked out to the security agencies, however devoted the participants were to their mission. Some security agent always learned about a part of the plan, or someone would come to know a member of the team; word would leak out or someone in the team would make a mistake because of the psychological pressure on them. So there had to be a diversionary plan that would send the security agencies in the wrong direction and waste their time and effort.

"So in other words we need a decoy."

They thought for some moments, then Fakhreddin said slowly, "I'll be the decoy."

They looked at him puzzled and he started to explain his idea to them.

Dr. Nashaat Ghaleb was the go-between. Fakhreddin contacted him and pretended to be a petroleum engineer working in the United States and an old friend of Ashraf's. He said he had things he wanted to pass on to an Egyptian intelligence official, quickly and without any fuss. Nashaat suggested he meet the consul and made him an appointment with Ahmed Kamal at the Hilton after afternoon prayers, as Fakhreddin had requested. The Hilton café was empty at that time and the road along the Nile outside was also almost deserted. A few cars passed toward the Omdurman bridge and there were a few people milling around.

Fakhreddin went into the hotel through a side door and went down a floor where there were some shops. He took the lift to the fourth floor and then another lift down to the lobby. He came out of the lift and immediately caught sight of the Egyptian officer sitting in the café looking around him. Fakhreddin smiled to himself and said, "I probably have guilt written all over my face." Fakhreddin had grown a short beard, trimmed it, and dyed it chestnut. He was wearing green contact lenses and looked like an American university professor. He went up to Ahmed Kamal and reached out to shake his hand.

He sat down confidently and ordered an espresso, while Ahmed ordered a Turkish coffee without sugar. Fakhreddin spoke slowly and hesitantly, lacing his sentences with English expressions. He told him he was working for an American oil company and had come to Khartoum on company business. He asked Ahmed who he was with and the man said in surprise that he was the consul.

"I know. I meant are you intelligence or Foreign Ministry?"

Ahmed gave him a long look and then said, "Intelligence. Isn't that why you asked to meet me?"

Fakhreddin smiled. There he was, sitting a few feet from one of the people responsible for killing his friends, yet Fakhreddin was the one scheming, playing games with him. "Very good. You'll find you have a file on me."

"I don't work for State Security."

"I'm not making any insinuations. You don't seem to understand. We're not in Egypt, and if I wanted to hit you now there aren't any policemen around you could call, to lock me up and teach me a lesson."

"I know."

"Anyway, I'll tell you the story as time's getting on and I'll have to go. I'm settled down in America, married to a Muslim woman who's American, and I've been living a quiet life far away from Egypt. Anyway, to keep it brief, I arrived in Khartoum a month ago and my family was supposed to join me to spend the school vacation with me. They arrived three days ago and just by chance my wife found something strange in our son's suitcase—blocks of some strange substance, like wax and carefully wrapped, and some pieces of paper that seem to be instructions for making bombs. She told me about it and of course I went crazy. I pressed the kid until he confessed. He said it was a package he was supposed to deliver to some friends in Khartoum. They would contact him, and he didn't know what the package was or why he needed to carry it. So, tell me, what should I do? Should I throw the stuff in the Nile and forget about it? And what should we tell the people when they call him about the package? The kid says he can't throw the stuff away because he's sworn an oath to hand it over to them, and the penalty for breaking an oath is death. Should I tell the American consulate? Common sense, logic, and duty say I should tell them. The lives of innocent people are at stake. But does it make sense to inform on my family and fellow Muslims to the American police? So, should I tell the Sudanese police? But they don't respect human rights and, God forbid, they might kill all of us because of it. So, what should I do? I decided that the only solution was to hand over the package myself and tell them that from now on the kid has nothing to do with it. The fact that I handed over the package would be a sign of my good intentions and so they would react calmly. At the same time I decided to inform you. When I contacted Dr. Nashaat, I asked him if he knew anyone and he mentioned you."

"Very well then, and where would the package be now?"

"I gave it to the group an hour ago."

"You're saying you gave it away?"

"That was the only solution I had to save my family's lives. You can't imagine how hysterical they are. They don't take things lightly, like us. They're Pakistanis and Afghans who've been fighting the Russians and they're ruthless, and woe betide anyone who shows a trace of weakness."

"Yes, yes, and who was it you gave this damned thing to?"

"That's your business. What else have you got to do? Or maybe the only thing you're good for is bullying the poor in Egypt. As Adel Imam puts it, aren't you the government, don't you know everything?"

"Adel Imam? Are you joking? You've carried explosives for terrorists and you're making jokes?"

"Listen, Officer. I could have told you this by telephone without showing you my face in the first place. And I could have gone back where I came from without telling you anything at all, so please calm down and let's talk sensibly."

"And what would be sensible, then?"

"I'll tell you who I gave the stuff to, without mentioning anyone by name, and in return you write me an undertaking that if anything happens I'll be a witness in the case."

"Sure, I can do that."

"Between you and me, I don't trust the word of our intelligence people. Don't take me to mean you personally. I'm speaking in general. But the piece of paper might be useful in the American courts if it ever comes to that."

"I told you I'd give you a note, so there's no need to be rude or say anything more."

Fakhreddin took out a sheet of paper with writing on and gave it to him. The officer read it perfunctorily, then signed it, and handed it back. Fakhreddin stuffed it in his pocket, smiling to himself, and stood up. "The package was delivered to the imam of the grand mosque in Omdurman. Goodbye," he said, and then left.

The three of them sat at the window watching the entrance to the consulate. It was hot and the time was approaching ten a.m. Hussein was the tensest and could hardly stay still, whether sitting or standing. When Salman found out that Fakhreddin had met Brigadier Ahmed Kamal, he had flown into a furious rage. He told them they were amateurs and didn't know what they were doing. When they looked at him in bewilderment, he was even angrier. Salman asked them impatiently how someone could carry explosives in a plane across the ocean without the scanning devices at the American airport detecting them and without them exploding during the flight because of the air pressure. The three of them stood there speechless and Salman was amazed that Brigadier Ahmed Kamal didn't pick up on this point. Hussein played down the danger, saying the intelligence people were incompetent and relied on luck rather than attention to detail. Salman Ahmed didn't like what he heard, and answered disdainfully that they were the ones relying on luck. If Ahmed Kamal had his wits about him, he would realize that Fakhreddin was a liar, and this would be a first lead that would end in the operation being thwarted.

Fakhreddin stood watching the entrance to the consulate in silence. Deep inside he hoped that something would happen to prevent the operation. Buheiri was apprehensive and cautious. Hussein was anxious and tense but was trying to control himself. At exactly 9:45 a.m., the bomber appeared. Buheiri was the first to see him: he stopped talking or moving and fixed his gaze on the bomber. The others noticed and looked in the same direction. "At last," Hussein said with a sigh.

"Is that him?" Fakhreddin asked him anxiously.

Buheiri nodded in silence. The bomber was Pakistani and was wearing distinctively Pakistani clothes. He had a long beard and a small backpack on his back. Fakhreddin was surprised that the bomber was dressed so obviously.

"Do you think they won't search him?" he asked anxiously. "He looks really obvious."

"It's too late for questions like that," Hussein replied spontaneously. The others were stock still, their eyes pinned on the man's footsteps. The bomber walked toward the consulate gate. He walked past a truckful of Sudanese troops lurking at the beginning of the street and no one stopped him. He reached the gate and nodded at the guard. The guard stopped him and exchanged some words with him. The three of them held their breath. The guard went into a small gatehouse and had a short conversation on the phone, then came back and waved the bomber toward the waiting room. The man nodded to him and proceeded toward the old building. Hussein sighed with relief and patted his colleagues on the shoulder. The bomber went into the building at exactly 9:53 a.m.

"Hussein, can't we stop him?"

Hussein patted Fakhreddin's shoulder reassuringly. "Hopefully it'll all go fine. Don't worry," he said. "The rules are about to change. They're going to find out that their crimes won't go unpunished."

He paused and the others were silent too. The hands of the clock hit ten a.m., and the bomb went off. The light came first—a large yellow flash with a ball of blue light inside it. Then there was a slight tremor in the ground and in the air as if the world were a picture that was shaking, and a sound like a deafening rumble. Then the dust came: a vast ball of dust rose in the air and hung there. The three men tried to make out what had happened to the consulate building but the cloud of dust prevented them from seeing what was going on. There was a deep silence across the whole area. Everyone was still shaken by the surprise. The truck full of soldiers didn't move, but two minutes later, two soldiers got out and walked cautiously toward the building. The street was deserted except for the two soldiers walking toward the cloud of dust. The three men watched through the window from their hiding place. Fakhreddin was speechless; Hussein was ecstatic and had to stop himself from leaping into the street to tell everyone that it was all his work. Buheiri looked anxiously at the consulate buildings and the street, and said, "We must go now."

His eyes pinned on the cloud of dust, Hussein replied, "Wait a minute. Nothing will happen. The police won't get to the building for an hour."

Ambulances could be heard in the distance, then a police car arrived, and then another one a few minutes later. The cloud of dust was still hanging there, but the outlines of the building had started to appear. The upper floor had completely collapsed onto the ground floor and in some places the ceiling had fallen in. Some walls had collapsed and others were cracked. The building had turned into rubble, just rubble. A quarter of an hour later the first fire truck arrived but no one dared go into the remains. There was no fire, just rubble and dust and total silence. The three men were thinking about the victims now. Where were the people who had been in the building? What had happened to them? How many of them were there? What would happen next? "We must go now," Buheiri repeated, firmly this time.

Hussein obeyed. Buheiri pulled Fakhreddin by the arm and he followed like a sleepwalker. They left the apartment. It had been rented in the name of someone they knew and nothing in it pointed to them. They went down to the street. At the junction leading to the road along the Nile, Hussein said, "I'm going to the consulate."

"Are you mad?" Buheiri asked.

"I'm coming with you, Hussein," said Fakhreddin.

Buheiri looked at them in surprise. "What's wrong with you? Are you kidding?" he said.

"Don't worry, Buheiri," said Hussein, his eyes pinned on the site of the explosion. "You'd expect Egyptians to go to the consulate to find out what's happened. It's the most natural thing in the world."

"You're wrong. It's not a good idea."

"You go and we'll catch up with you."

"That's not how this works, Hussein. We're a group and what one person does affect everyone. Look, if you have to go, just don't stay too long. I don't want you to appear on television."

Buheiri went back to the farm while Hussein and Fakhreddin went to the scene of the bombing. Policemen had started to pour in, but they were still in their vehicles awaiting orders. Fakhreddin stopped at the consulate wall, while Hussein went past the barrier and inside. Fakhreddin tried to stop him, but Hussein pushed him aside and went on. He couldn't be stopped. Fakhreddin stood there, the smell of the dust hanging in the air around him and filling his nose. But there was another strong smell—the smell of roasting meat. He was surprised. He didn't remember a kebab shop in the street. Besides, it was too early in the day to be roasting meat.

Then he realized what was happening. The smell of roasted meat was coming from inside, from the rubble.

The Sudanese authorities were furious and asked the group to leave the country immediately. The number of deaths was not high: three security guards and a junior diplomat who happened to be in the consulate at the time of the explosion, as well as the Pakistani bomber. Ahmed Kamal the consul was injured and medevaced to Cairo the same day, along with three Egyptians who were visiting the consulate. All four were put in intensive care. But what really angered the Sudanese authorities was that a small, recently formed group had carried out such a major operation on Sudanese territory without their intelligence agencies detecting any preparations. They told the group they had crossed red lines, set up a state within the state, and embarrassed them in front of the Egyptian government and the international community. The group tried to persuade the sheikh to mediate, but he refused to do so, since he hadn't been consulted on the operation. They told him they had consulted Salman Ahmed and he told them to appeal to him. In the end, they had no option but to leave the country.

Fakhreddin was sad and upset, as was Buheiri, while Hussein seemed proud of his capacity for meticulous planning and implementation, and elated at having taken revenge. This was a source of anxiety to Fakhreddin. He watched Hussein giving free rein to his anger and worried what this might lead to. As far as Fakhreddin was concerned, the operation had failed to achieve its basic objective, which was to punish Ahmed Kamal, who had survived though he was seriously injured. The operation had also injured innocent people who had been in the consulate, such as Dr. Nashaat Ghaleb, who had often offered them a helping hand, Ashraf Fahmi, a journalist who had nothing to do with them, and Dalia al-Shenawi, the owner of the law office where Hussein himself had worked before fleeing Egypt. But Hussein said she wasn't seriously injured and was recovering, and if she were asked, she would have preferred martyrdom. As for Nashaat, he was an opportunist and his alleged assistance had never been useful. Ashraf Fahmi was a fraud. Buheiri stood in the middle: he shared Fakhreddin's annoyance with what had happened to Dalia especially and described that as a mistake, saying he never expected her to go the consulate and that they had done what they could to make the Egyptians tighten up their security procedures and reduce the number of visitors. Maybe she should have been warned specifically, but no amount of vigilance can avert fate. Buheiri said that what mattered now was to deal with the crisis, organize the departure of the group, learn from the mistakes, make arrangements for the families, and decide who would stay and who would leave.

The Sudanese authorities insisted that all the men in the group should leave, along with any boys over fourteen years old, and within a week at the most. The only concession the authorities were willing to make was that women and children for whom the sheikh was willing to take responsibility could stay. The sheikh agreed to take responsibility for many of the families, including Umm Yasser and her children and Omar. The men soon began to leave. Groups of them went to Yemen and others to Somalia, while a limited number dispersed in the Balkans. Fakhreddin, Buheiri, and Hussein made up their minds to go to Afghanistan, where Salman Ahmed promised to make arrangements for them. But that would take time and the Sudanese authorities were insisting that they in particular should leave the country immediately. Fakhreddin left Omar in Umm Yasser's care and went to Darfur with his colleagues, where Abdullah, his guard, arranged for them to travel with some of his fellow tribesmen from Darfur to the south, across Kordofan. From there, they crossed into territory controlled by the southern rebels and then to Kenya, where they hid with acquaintances until Salman Ahmed could arrange for them to move to Afghanistan.

Fakhreddin was subdued throughout the trip. They spent weeks in their hiding place in Kenya waiting for instructions from Salman, and they started to get bored, since they were used to activity. Finally the signal came, but they had to go to Tanzania and meet someone who would give them the papers they would need for the trip and explain the travel arrangements to them. They had a discussion and decided to go to Tanzania across Lake Victoria to avoid going through the airports. They found a ferry that carried passengers, vehicles, and goods from Kenya to Tanzania across the lake every other day, so they bought tickets and boarded.

The journey cheered Fakhreddin up a little: he liked anything that brought him close to the waters of the Nile. They spent a day on the ferry watching the variety of passengers, who numbered more than a thousand. They made jokes about whether the rickety ferry could really carry so many people, as well as the livestock and the vehicles. Then they went to sleep in their little cabin.

At seven o'clock in the morning, as the ferry was approaching the Tanzanian shore, it suddenly rolled to one side. Hussein and Fakhreddin fell out of their bunks onto Buheiri, who was sleeping on the other side. The ship continued to roll, while the three men, who had been asleep, recovered from the shock. In no time at all, the cabin door was where the ceiling had been. Buheiri acted first: he jumped up and opened the door, but water poured into the cabin.

He climbed up through the doorway, leaned down, and offered his hand to Hussein, who took hold of it. Buheiri pulled him up toward him but water was pouring into the cabin, which was filling up. Fakhreddin tried to open or break the window but he couldn't. The water level in the cabin was rising and Fakhreddin was trying to stay afloat with his head above the surface. Hussein squeezed through the doorway that was hanging in the air and got out of the cabin. Buheiri pushed him down the corridor and pointed toward the exit.

Hussein swam until he reached the ferry door, and then threw himself into the lake. Meanwhile, Buheiri was trying to save Fakhreddin. The water had started rising in the corridor too, now that the cabin was full. Buheiri grabbed Fakhreddin's hair and tried to pull him out of the cabin. He got him into the corridor and they started swimming together along the corridor, which was rapidly filling with water. They reached the opening that led to the exit, but it was narrow and only one person could go through at a time. Buheiri jumped into the opening and sat on the ledge, reaching out toward Fakhreddin, but Fakhreddin was short of breath. He hit the corridor floor and the water swept him back. Buheiri called him but he didn't answer. He called again, but the water kept pushing Fakhreddin in the opposite direction. He was unconscious and motionless. Buheiri looked at the lake outside and at Fakhreddin, who was drifting back down the corridor. The ship was sinking fast. He took a deep breath, dived into the corridor again, and swam until he grabbed hold of Fakhreddin, who was about to drown, and pulled him back to the opening again. The ship was going down faster and faster. Buheiri lifted Fakhreddin onto his shoulders and raised him toward the opening until his head was outside the ship. He pushed him upward, until half his body was through the hole and above water level. Fakhreddin came around and his lungs filled with air again. He found himself slipping down the deck toward the surface of the lake. He grabbed the door and stopped sliding. Clinging to the door, he waited for Buheiri, but Buheiri did not appear. Fakhreddin took a deep breath and stuck his head into the opening to look for Buheiri, but a massive surge of water suddenly gushed down the corridor and through the opening, throwing him through the air into the lake. At the same moment the ferry sank below the surface, with Buheiri and the rest of the passengers inside it.

5

The Panjshir Valley

FAKHREDDIN WAS DESOLATE AND HEARTBROKEN. The desolation drove a wedge between him and other people and the rest of the world. His face was rigid; instead of being a window into his soul it looked like a still life, devoid of movement. He no longer had anything to say. What could he say? Should he console his friend? What was the point? No, nothing was better than silence. Throughout the month that the journey took, hardly a word passed his lips. He traveled in train carriages packed with people, on decrepit buses, in dodgy taxis, on African roads that were sometimes paved and sometimes made of red dirt, through ports controlled by militias and checkpoints manned by wretched soldiers and corrupt civil servants, on green mountain roads in Pakistan, on trucks and buses painted in garish colors, along deserted and rugged mountain tracks. He traveled them all without saying a word.

Everything happened amazingly fast. It was as if he had fallen from a mountain peak and, as he rolled toward the foot of the mountain, he unconsciously made adjustments to restore his balance and save himself from hitting the rocks at the bottom. Then he reached the bottom and stopped rolling for a moment. He tried to think over recent events but couldn't believe what had happened. All these people killed? He had hardly anyone left. Even he had almost drowned. He knew that if it hadn't been for Buheiri he would now be a corpse floating in Lake Victoria, or trapped in a small cabin being eaten by any fish that could get inside. Was that how men died? Buheiri had been right there, and then, within minutes, he was gone. There had been three of them, and now there were two. All of them had almost died in vain. He thought about his loved ones who had died over a matter of a few months, and Buheiri who was gone in minutes. He saw the people around him as floating corpses.

He pressed his face against the dirty window of the vehicle he was traveling in and could still taste the lake water in his mouth. He saw Buheiri's face as Buheiri pushed him through that damned opening. He saw lines of dead people standing outside, looking at him through the glass. He saw them as if they were sitting beside him, and he could see their faces reflected in the window pane. He looked around at the other seats like an automaton, as if he could see dead people in them, and then he went back to looking at the road. But he could still see their faces in the window, and he wondered if he had lost his mind. He wondered if all this had really happened.

He repeatedly asked himself how it could have happened. Those around him had suddenly started to fall. They had killed everyone he knew, either directly or indirectly. They had killed his close friend and college roommate Yahya Ibrahim in the State Security prison when Fakhreddin was at university. They had killed many of his comrades indiscriminately in the 1991 Gulf War. They had been sent to a battlefield they hadn't chosen—those who died died and those who came back came back. Then they had tried to kill him several times and they had killed Eissa. Then they had killed Ali. And Omar Fares. Hussein had escaped at a high cost to himself. Those were the victims they had actually murdered, but they had also killed Shireen, and Nasser, and Buheiri, and many others. They had trapped them in cages and they had wasted away. Like plants, their stems had dried up and then collapsed spontaneously.

Fakhreddin was finally convinced that his colleagues, from university times onward, were right when they said that oppressors only understood strength. That was the only language that their antennae could detect. Everything else was irrelevant. No law, no common sense, no mercy even. Eight letters: S T R E N G T H. Nothing else. He had an overwhelming sense that he had wasted many years to no purpose, with Colonel Samir, the university administration, the military court, the Bar Association, and even Shireen's father. None of them had understood anything he said: he might as well have been speaking to them in Chinese. The more ways he tried to explain to them, the more they misunderstood. With unwonted bitterness, he asked himself what he had done to deserve having them come after him with such a vengeance, trying to kill him. What crimes had he and his colleagues committed? Who were these people who wreaked death and oppression on mankind? They had no right to do any of it, but they had a sense of power, sheer power; they had their tanks, armored cars, weapons, prison cells, and henchmen.

He sat on buses and trains and wondered what could be done to counter this brute force. Would he be a man and stand up to resist this tyranny or would he submit while they continued with their serial killings? Damian had said that violence rebounded on the perpetrators and turned them into monsters, and at the time Fakhreddin had retorted that surrender was unmanly. As he traveled, he remembered these discussions and dozens of others. And now, after all the arguments and all the brouhaha, if he had to make a choice, would he be a monster or a wimp?

This time the answer was glaringly obvious, to both his heart and his mind. He had resisted the logic of force for a long time, but every other way had failed. He said he would make sure they were held responsible for his death and leave this world with a resounding cry that would rouse even those who hadn't cared. But the list of victims was growing longer and there was no redemption. Hussein had been correct from the start: people wouldn't follow you unless you could protect yourself and protect them. Those who remained silent were not unaware of their rights, but they realized they couldn't resist or pay the price for resisting. They didn't need anyone to remind them of their rights; they needed someone to give them the strength to win their rights back.

Strength was now at hand, within his reach. Strength meant that the world would submit to your will. Now he felt it, and the will of the other young men in these organizations was many times stronger than that of the men in a regime that was weighed down by its own might. The sources of strength were available to all but whose will would triumph? He knew that blowing up the consulate was not a noble act, but it sent a message of strength, a message that they were able to hit back and penetrate the lair of the oppressors. He knew that the victims were innocent and his heart trembled at that thought. But he could no longer see any other option. When a bulldozer is on its way to demolish your house and bury everyone in it, do you step aside to think how noble your allies are or do you grab the nearest weapon and accept help from your neighbor, even if you don't agree with what he does?

Fakhreddin could not take any more discussions. He no longer saw any other way forward. He had long resisted taking this path, but they might as well have been pushing him toward it. The idealistic dreamer was dead. Fakhreddin was finally dead and now, in these moments, from the fangs of death that pursued him and among the floating bodies, a new person was born: strong, not a coward; a doer, not a whiner; a man who would make a triumphant return, albeit after a while.

That's what he told himself on the desolate road to Peshawar. That's what he told himself as he sat with Hussein in a grill on a rooftop in Peshawar, listening to the Pakistani fixer boasting that the territory from Peshawar to as far as the eye could see was under the control of the mujahideen. That's what he told himself when they were in an inconspicuous vehicle slipping through the streets of Peshawar and snaking along tracks deep in the mountains; when they mounted donkeys and followed narrow, rugged paths to climb a perilous mountain; when they stayed at a base and spent the night in tents with fighters of unknown identity or intent; when they took off their usual clothes, put on Afghan-style shalwar kameez, and resumed their journey to the border; as they went through the Khyber Pass into Afghanistan with a guide whose identity they didn't know and who brazenly bribed the soldiers. That's what he told himself during the three days they spent in rocky mountains and then in green mountains with amazing plants and trees. And that's what he told himself when they reached Abu Hafs's base, but once there, he no longer needed to tell himself anything at all.

They arrived close to nightfall and the guide handed them over to someone who smiled broadly but said nothing, not by choice but because he had a speech impediment. He led them across an open space surrounded by hills on all sides, to a small dormitory with mats and eight mattresses spread on the floor. They would spend the night there. A few minutes from the dormitory there was another building with lavatories, a place to have a shower, and a small kitchen next door. The ground was rocky, brown in color, and covered in gravel. The man with the smile made signs for eating and showed them where to find bread, honey, and cheese. At the end of the open space there was a small mosque, and then some other dormitories. He signaled to them not to go to those buildings, emphasizing his point by frowning. The hills around looked desolate and deserted, but Fakhreddin knew that behind them lay the rest of the base and training centers. The man with the smile signed that he would come back in the morning, or that's what they concluded from his hand gestures, and the two friends went straight to sleep.

They woke up at dawn to the sound of activity on the base, and when they were about to go out the man with the smile stopped them with a hand gesture. They stayed in the dormitory, from where they could hear the sound of the dawn prayers. The imam's voice was faint and reverent. Fakhreddin's heart melted when he heard the dawn recitation of the Quran amid these wild mountains. Much as he felt homesick, he also felt grateful for these men who had abandoned their lives and their homes to follow the right path, as dictated by their consciences. He also faulted his own country, which thought so little of its young people that it banished them to the far ends of the earth. After prayers the man with the smile came up to them, greeted them, and then led them along a twisting path that climbed between two hills until they reached a largish tent. They didn't ask the man with the smile any questions, just waited to see what would happen. The tent was empty but for some mats on the ground. He gestured to them and they sat down. After about half an hour, three men came in. The one who seemed to be their leader came first, greeted them, and sat facing them.

"I'm glad you arrived safely. How was your trip?" he began.

"We thank God for everything," replied Hussein. "We lost our colleague in the lake."

"Yes, the brethren told me. May God have mercy on him. Buheiri was a leader and a scholar. He is a big loss, but if God wills, He will compensate us with good things through you. Salman Ahmed has told me wonderful things about you and what you did in Sudan. If it hadn't been for his praise for you, and the fact that the sheikh vouched for you, I wouldn't have agreed to receive you here. You're Fakhreddin, aren't you?"

"Yes."

"And you're Hussein?"

"Yes, I'm Hussein."

"If you want to stay with us, you'll have to take what comes. If you don't want to stay, we can help you go somewhere else or go back if you like."

"We hope to be staying," Hussein replied quickly.

"God willing. All of us here are from Egypt. There are some Arabs who come for training but they move on to other bases after that. The brethren here are usually put in groups according to their country of origin, but sometimes we do take non-Egyptians too. There are two Libyans, three Palestinians, an Algerian, a Tunisian, and two Saudis who chose to stay with us after training, but the rule is that everyone should go with their fellow countrymen, because there are things related to jihad in their countries that they have to discuss together without interference. If you stay with us, you'll go through various levels of training. How long you spend in training depends on you and on how fast you learn, but it won't be less than several months. After the training, you can move elsewhere if you like: we do our work to serve God and jihad. If you choose to stay with us, you can either take part in our operations or you can become instructors. If you choose to take part in operations, you'll swear an oath of loyalty to the jihad commander, and then you'll be obliged to obey him, though he will have a duty to consult you.

"If you choose to stay and train, the only oath is to the camp commander. We'll start tomorrow, if you decide to stay."

"We'll stay, inshallah," said Hussein.

"Don't be hasty, brother. If you stay you'll swear an oath of loyalty to the camp commander—that's me—and then we start training. The training will be long and hard. If you can't go on, we'll give you one or two chances to try again, but the third will be the last, and then you either leave or stay to work in maintenance or camp administration, without training or fighting. You could concentrate on matters of Islamic law at that stage, if your academic record permits, but that's not my area of competence. Starting today, you'll have different names, your jihad names, God willing. Never reveal your original names or the details of your lives to anyone. It's best to be cautious. We're all brothers here and the only qualities that matter are piety, valor in jihad, and loyalty. We're all equals and, as I told you, you'll have to obey your commander and he will have to consult you. But if you decide to leave at any time, you'll have to make an agreement with us on that. Such things require time and security precautions. We can't open the camp to people who come and then leave and talk about us and what we're doing. It's not a question of treating people as traitors, but just a precaution. And so, you now have to decide if you're prepared to make that commitment. If you stay, you're with us in this endeavor and you can leave only after you've consulted us, obtained our approval, and made the necessary arrangements. I'll give you until dawn prayers tomorrow. Think about it together and I'll meet you tomorrow. But don't wander around the base. Stay in your dormitory, the bathrooms, the kitchen, the mosque, and the space between them, and don't go anywhere else."

There was no need for the time he had given them to think it through. Fakhreddin had never been a fundamentalist: in fact, he had more questions than he had faith. He remembered a story he had read when young, about a priest who lost his belief in God but who went on performing his duties—taking confessions, giving blessings, and baptizing babies—because he asked himself: who was he to disappoint a flock who relied on him to regulate their lives? And what would he have to give them, if he refrained from performing his ecclesiastical duties? This fundamentalist faith that he rejected was the only remaining resource that protected these young men from apathy and submission, so who was he to dissuade them or plant doubt in their hearts? And what did he have to give them in its place? Nothing but questions. He couldn't deprive them of a source of solace and protection in exchange for questions. The more he thought about it the more convinced he was that Hussein had been right from the beginning: only absolute faith could rally these thousands of young men around a message of change. The skeptics, the sophists, and the outright intellectuals should thank God for the gift of faith that He had granted to these fighters. They should work with them and thank them for giving them shelter and taking them in. There was no need to wait before answering.

The man with the smile came back in the afternoon and took them to the kitchen, where they ate alone and then went back to the dormitory. The same thing happened in the evening and then they went to bed, but they didn't sleep well in anticipation of the following day. After dawn prayers, the man with the smile appeared at the door and led them to the tent again. They went in and waited till the camp commander arrived, followed by the two silent men. He greeted them, sat down facing them, and asked what they had decided. Speaking as one, they said they would stay. The man's face lit up and he smiled for the first time. He reached out his arms to welcome them, pulled them toward him, and embraced them. He told them to go with the man with the smile to perform their ablutions, and then come back. The man took them somewhere they could wash and gave them new clothes. They hadn't shaved since they were in Tanzania, and their faces had caught the sun. They looked like the local men. They put their new clothes on, including the distinctive turbans that Arab fighters wore. When they came out the man with the smile had disappeared with their old clothes. One of the two men who walked behind the camp commander came up to them and told them to follow him. They took a new route and went into another tent, where they found the commander and ten young men. They greeted them and the young men stood up and greeted them in return. The commander recited some verses from the Quran and then asked Fakhreddin if he had made up his mind to join the ranks of the mujahideen in the camp, and he said he had. The commander put a copy of the Quran in his hand and recited the oath of allegiance: "I swear by Almighty God that I, Abu Omar the Eagle, will hear and obey the camp commander, Abu Hafs al-Misri. He has my allegiance and he will hear my counsel, within the limits set by the law of God Almighty."

Fakhreddin repeated the oath after him.

"I swear by Almighty God that I, Hamza the Lion, will hear and obey the camp commander, Abu Hafs al-Misri. He has my allegiance and he will hear my counsel, within the limits set by the law of God Almighty."

Hussein repeated the oath.

The young men shook their hands. Some of them embraced them and congratulated them, then they left Fakhreddin and Hussein with Abu Hafs. The commander said it was the sheikh himself who had chosen their new names and these were the names that he and Salman Ahmed had used in their contacts while arranging their journey. Abu Omar was his patronymic and the sheikh had chosen the epithet 'The Eagle' because of the accuracy Fakhreddin had shown during sniper training on the Khartoum North farm, and because of his tendency to be silent and withdrawn. He had named Hussein 'Hamza the Lion' because he had detected in him courage, strength, and the ability to challenge his opponent face to face, and defeat him. He went over the base rules and procedures and asked them to spend the day praying, reading the Quran, and having some food. He assigned the man with the smile to show them the other parts of the base, while they waited to start training.

The man with the smile woke them up before dawn prayers. They joined other groups and everyone had a light breakfast of bread, honey, dates, and cheese. They prayed in the mosque, led by Abu Hafs, and after prayers the man with the smile took them to a place far from the dormitory area and signaled to them to wait. Then the training began.

First was hiking. Their trainer, Abu Azzam the Libyan, told all of them to take off their shoes and walk barefoot. The small stones cut into their feet and the small cuts soon grew deeper and bigger. The young men's feet bled all along the way, as they hurried after Abu Azzam. They took a winding path up the hill, and then the path twisted sharply up the side of a mountain. They left the track and clambered up rock after rock, apparently without end, but no one said a single word. Fakhreddin and Hussein—Abu Omar and Hamza—were extremely fit. Their training at the Khartoum North farm had proved its worth, but their feet were bleeding. They did hours of nonstop climbing, with just short breaks to drink water. With time, they lost sensation in their feet. In the evening, the man with the smile brought some disinfectant and cleaned their cuts skillfully. He gave them an infusion of local herbs, some dry bread, honey, and two onions. The next day the process was repeated. After a few weeks their feet had grown accustomed to the stones and rocks in the mountains, and the hiking was plain sailing.

Then came the running. Suddenly, Abu Azzam started running. He told them not to lose sight of him because they wouldn't be able to get back to base on their own. And so it was. They ran until they felt they were about to drop dead. Hussein stopped first, Fakhreddin right after. They lost sight of Abu Azzam and after resting a few minutes to get their breath back they resumed running in an attempt to catch up with him, but he had disappeared. They tried to go back the way they had come but the rocky hills all looked the same and they spent the day in the mountains without finding the right path. As evening fell, they were hungry and exhausted and could hear wolves howling, but they held out. They found a cave where they took shelter. At sunrise, the man with a smile turned up with food and water. Within minutes, Abu Azzam arrived at a run. He didn't look at them and didn't say anything, as if it were still the previous day. They resumed running behind him and they didn't lose him this time. Over the coming days they ran the whole way to the top of the mountain. Within a few weeks, they could climb to the top of the mountain barefoot and half-naked, hardly aware of their tough, strong bodies. They were like beasts of burden: their bodies no longer rebelled against them.

Fakhreddin and Hussein hadn't spoken much since they survived the disaster in the treacherous waters of Lake Victoria. Something between them had drowned with Buheiri. Fakhreddin felt that Hussein secretly blamed him for their friend's death, because Buheiri had been so close to him at the time of the sinking. Hussein didn't say anything about it. When Fakhreddin asked him, he denied it, but his heart told him that this was how his friend felt. It crossed his mind that Hussein wouldn't have risked his life to save him, as Buheiri had done. He had been one of the first to jump into the lake. But they were silent for other reasons. Fakhreddin was taciturn by nature and was lost in his own musings most of the time, but Hussein was preoccupied with his anger and his plans for revenge. One day, Fakhreddin asked him, "Did you know I can see them?"

"See who?"

"Buheiri, Ali, Nasser, Eissa, even Omar Fares."

"May God have mercy on them all. They're always on my mind. Them and my family."

"I see them as if they're right in front of me."

Hussein patted him on the shoulder and didn't reply. Fakhreddin felt that Hussein hadn't fully understood him, so he held back. Although they didn't speak much, Abu Hafs once overheard them and was angry; he reminded them that conversations at the base should be conducted only in formal Arabic, even if all those present were Egyptian. He also forbade them from using their original names.

"This is not a game. It's a security measure." he said.

From then on, they used their new names and spoke in formal Arabic. That helped to break the barrier of silence between them, as if they were now new people, as if they had met for the first time in the mountains of Afghanistan:

new names, new clothes, new relationships, new habits, and a new life.

Next was the weapons training. Abu Omar was issued with a small pistol and a sniper's rifle, while Hamza received a similar pistol and an automatic rifle that hung over his chest all the time. On top of the training in hiking, running, jumping, and climbing, which continued, they started shooting practice, initially from fixed positions and later while running and climbing. At this stage the two men were separated. A special trainer took Abu Omar and concentrated on improving his skills as a sniper. He taught him to use the wind direction and the echoes off the mountains so that his opponent didn't know where the shots were coming from. Another instructor was responsible for teaching Hamza how to use more advanced weapons, especially shoulder-held anti-tank and anti-aircraft missiles.

The Arab fighters had plenty of good weaponry. They bought weapons from neighboring countries with money from the sheikh and other donors, but most of their weapons had been obtained from the defeated Soviet army. Most of the fighters who had taken part in the war carried at least one weapon they had plundered as a trophy after battles with the Russians. Their base was in an area close to Jalalabad that was known only by those who visited it. Neither Abu Omar nor Hamza would be able to leave it, or return to it, because the route was so complicated and the hills and tracks around it were so similar. The area had previously been under the control of Burhanuddin Rabbani's Jamiat-e Islami party, but then a branch of the party defected during the conflicts that broke out between the mujahideen factions after the defeat of the Soviets. This branch was close to the sheikh and it allowed his group to operate in the area. The sheikh decided to focus his efforts on training and kept the group out of the fighting that took place between the Afghan factions.

Abu Omar and Hamza joined the group training program, but they each had an additional individual program.

In the evening they had lessons in sharia, the Quran, juris-prudence, and the saying and doings of the Prophet and his companions. Fakhreddin looked forward to these lessons and found food for thought in them. He had often studied religion in the past and dreamed of studying sharia and Islamic juris-prudence in greater depth, but al-Azhar had refused to take him as a student. When he asked why, he was told that the university only accepted graduates from the Azhar institutes. He would never have imagined that he would end up studying these things here.

Hussein resented these classes, but he persevered until he had memorized the whole Quran and they started calling him Sheikh Hamza. Fakhreddin concentrated on religious law and continued to attend some of the sessions even after the obligatory lessons were over. In the little spare time that they had, Sheikh Hamza practiced dismantling and cleaning his weapons, while Abu Omar went out for night walks in the mountains. At first they weren't allowed to wander around alone, and then Abu Hafs gradually gave them more free-dom. It was a big base: apart from the dormitories, the dining rooms, the mosque, and the open space, there were tents for families, rooms for studying, a place for the camp's consulta-tive council to meet, underground storage space for weapons, and other buildings, with functions unknown to Fakhreddin or Hamza, that extended into the mountains further than they could see. The base had a security system and Abu Hafs spent most of his time dealing with that. The residents were distrib-uted according to how long they had spent at the base and whether they were married or not. Abu Omar never saw a woman in the camp, since the women kept to their section and did things assigned to them, such as teaching the children. Abu Hafs ran all this efficiently without anyone feeling that he was exercising too much authority over them. He was strict in an understated way that reminded Fakhreddin of the sheikh, and he later learned that Abu Hafs had been the sheikh's disciple.

They improved at long-range shooting and the time came for hand-to-hand fighting. This was where the cats came in. Abu Omar, Hamza, and their instructors went into a small room and could hear loud meowing. Fakhreddin immediately remembered Sultan. In the room, they found five other young men and seven sacks hanging on the wall. The meowing was coming from the sacks and something was moving inside them. The men greeted each other and put their weapons by the door, as Abu Azzam had instructed them to do. Then they were given old rifles with bayonets fixed to the end of the barrels. They stood in a line to the right, and Abu Azzam explained the procedures. He told them to step forward and they all rushed toward the sacks full of cats. Each of them stabbed his bayonet into the sack in front of him. Abu Omar stuck his bayonet in and could feel the blade sink into something soft. When he pulled the bayonet out it was wet with blood. He stuck it in again but this time the sack was thrashing around violently and the bayonet didn't hit anything. He tried again and had the morbid sensation of the blade sinking into soft flesh. The screeching grew louder and louder as the stabbing continued. Hamza was the first to finish his assignment by silencing all the cats in his sack, and at this stage Abu Azzam ordered everyone to stop. He pointed at Hussein, went to the sack, took it off the wall, and put it down on the floor. He took out the slain cats and counted them: one, two, three . . . seven. Abu Azzam applauded him and the others congratulated him. Abu Azzam asked everyone to put their weapons by the door and gave everyone a pocket knife. Then he told them to take all the sacks off the wall and empty them out. The cats that had survived came out terrified and ran madly around the room. On orders from Abu Azzam they chased the cats, grabbed them one after another, and cut their throats with the knives.

"Don't torture the cat by stabbing it too much or killing it slowly. You have to hold it by the back of the head with a steady hand and slit its throat quick and deep so that the artery is completely severed. Keep hold of the cat's head so that it doesn't hurt you when it shudders in its death throes, until you've drained out all the blood, then put the head in your pocket and look for another cat quickly."

After the last cat had been slaughtered, each man had to count the heads he had in his pocket, and the one who had the fewest heads had to clean up the blood and the bits of flesh in the dormitory, supervised by the man with the smile.

The cat training continued for several weeks until the trainees' performance had improved and they could kill the cats in the sacks in just a few minutes, and then the man with the smile would bring extra cats to train them in cutting their throats. On day, Abu Omar asked Abu Azzam where all these cats came from, and Abu Azzam said the mountains were full of cats and some families bred them for this purpose, as it was a good way to keep the children busy after school.

After about two months the trainees could finish the cat training in less than an hour, and so Abu Azzam moved on to the next stage. They took it easy during the day, doing only a bit of physical exercise and plenty of studying. At night, they started a new form of training. Abu Azzam, or one of his assistants, took them to the mountains in groups of two, and they would spend the night walking barefoot in light clothing. Every trainee had a pocket knife. They stopped in an area in the mountains and lit a small fire. Then Abu Azzam would slaughter a cat or two and leave them at the mouth of a cave to attract wolves. Things then proceeded according to the number of wolves that appeared. If there were up to three wolves, Abu Azzam would stand at a distance and leave the trainees to face the wolves alone with their knives. The aim was not to frighten the wolves away but to lure them, then catch them one after another, and cut their throats with the knife. If the trainee became really skilled, he could lure a wolf to its fate and slit its throat without stabbing it anywhere on the rest of its body, but the only people who reached this level were Abu Azzam himself and Hamza the Lion.

During this training, the trainees were often injured, sustaining either superficial cuts or more serious injuries when a wounded wolf dug its teeth into someone's shoulder. Abu Azzam once had to shoot a wolf in the head because it was about to kill a trainee. When the man got back to camp at dawn, they had to amputate the trainee's arm. But the other trainees came through training safely.

During this period, Fakhreddin stopped having visions of Shireen. Although he often shared his thoughts with her, she refused to appear for him, even in his dreams. He missed her terribly and complained about her to the ghosts of his old friends—Ali, Eissa, and Buheiri. He asked them what kind of wife would abandon her husband for so long. But they just looked at him without replying.

During this period, the Taliban started to appear on the scene. At first, they were just a group of Islamic law students who carried out an operation to save two girls who had been kidnapped and raped, but they showed such resolve and integrity that people supported them, especially as the two main mujahideen groups, led respectively by Rabbani and Hekmatyar, were busy fighting each other. Toward the end of the year, while Abu Omar and Hamza were completing their combat training, the Taliban were advancing on the capital, Kabul, which they entered in September. Hamza went to Abu Hafs and told him he was bored with killing cats and wolves and wanted to volunteer to fight on the Taliban side. Abu Hafs forbade him from doing that, saying he hadn't finished his training and that the nature of the relationship between the Arab mujahideen and the Taliban had not yet been decided. The group's consultative council was committed to staying neutral in the wars between the Afghan factions and no one was allowed to violate this commitment. Hamza gave way after Abu Hafs promised to inform him as soon as an opportunity arose for him to take on a combat role.

The training with wolves was the final stage in their training as a group. In the presence of Abu Hafs, Abu Azzam congratulated them and said he had finished his work with them. After that, each man would be trained in the field in which he had excelled. It was clear that Abu Omar would specialize in sniper operations and Hamza in hand-to-hand combat.

One morning at dawn, Abu Azzam took Abu Omar and handed him over to the sniping instructor. Abu Omar spent two weeks with him and then the instructor sent him back to Abu Hafs because he thought he was ready for work. Abu Hafs asked Abu Omar what he wanted to do, and Abu Omar replied that there were still things he needed to learn: self-control and how to be more disciplined. Abu Hafs nodded and promised to help.

A few days later, Abu Hafs took him to the master, an old Uighur man who hardly spoke Arabic. He handed him over and left. Abu Omar spent several days practicing physical disciplines of the kind he had done in Khartoum, such as yoga and tai chi. The master asked him to come and stay with him in a more secluded place. Abu Omar spent the next months learning jujitsu, kung fu, aikido, taekwondo, and other martial arts whose names he didn't know. He spent days meditating with the master, preparing food or training to carry out these exercises, all in complete calm. He learned how to stand still for hours at a time, how to control his respiratory rate, how to go without water for long periods, and how to reduce his metabolic rate. He also learned the energy points in the human body and the points where pressure can make your opponent lose consciousness within moments. He learned how to kill with a single blow and without making any noise. He learned how to wait patiently and live alone. It reminded him of the days he had spent under Umm Ibrahim's supervision, herding sheep and goats, and he liked that.

Fakhreddin spent plenty of time meditating in seclusion and was alone for most of the time. He would go to the furthest limits of the base, to a rocky, barren area, and spend the day in the desolate hills, then go back at sunset along the road that led to Jalalabad. On his way back, one day, he met Hind for the first time.

He saw her lying on the ground close to the road to Jalalabad. She was holding her ankle and her face showed she was in pain. Fakhreddin was surprised to meet a woman in this deserted place, especially as she wasn't wearing a hijab. She had a pretty face, fair with dark eyes. Strands of black hair showed from under her loose headscarf. He thought she must be a figment of his imagination, so he stopped and had a careful look. She looked at him, raised her hand to wave, and shouted, "Yes, yes, please, don't go. Yes, please, come here."

He approached her cautiously. "Are you Egyptian?" he asked.

"No. Palestinian," she replied.

"So why are you speaking in an Egyptian accent?"

"Oh, I thought you were Egyptian! Could you help me first and leave the interrogation till later?"

"Help you? Who are you? And how did you come to be here? And how do you know me?"

"I'm Hind al-Qudsi from the Czech News Agency."

"Czech!"

"Yes, but look, my leg seems to be broken and I can't move. I've been here an hour and I have an important meeting and it looks like I'll miss it, if I haven't missed it already, that is. . . . Argh, my leg, please, I can't move it."

"Okay, and what do you want me to do?"

"I don't know. But surely you can do something to help me. Are there any taxis here?"

"Taxis! Do you know where you are?"

175

"Yes, I do. I'm not stupid. Look, I had an appointment with an important person, but the driver who brought me said he couldn't take me any further than this and told me to walk the rest of the way. It's my mistake. I should have waited for the news agency driver but he wasn't around today because his sister's getting married and I didn't want to miss the interview."

"Driver? Sister? Czech News Agency? What is all this about, lady?"

"I just want you to help me find a car that will take me there. Aren't you with the group that's here? Can you take me to the person I'm going to meet?"

Fakhreddin sat on the ground some way from her and watched her in silence. She kept talking but he wasn't listening. She was saying roughly the same thing as before. He slowly raised his pistol and pointed it toward her. She was stunned into silence. He started thinking quickly: what was this idiot doing here? If anyone else had seen her here it would all have been over. If anyone saw them now, he would be under suspicion. She was a disaster in human form; a woman, an Arab, her hair uncovered, and a journalist working for a dubious or nonexistent news agency. With the pistol pointed at her head, he asked, "Have you worked in this area before?"

"No, I work more in Hekmatyar's areas."

"Really? Well, that's just great. Have you come to get yourself killed?"

"What do you mean? It's only a minor injury."

"I'm not talking about your injury, for God's sake. Hasn't anyone told you there are rules for journalists coming here?"

"But what have I done?"

"Okay, you stay here until the base official comes and sees what you're up to."

"Please, no. I've come without a permit."

"Without a permit!"

He pulled out the aerial on his satellite phone and told the communications center at the base to send someone to investigate. Hind couldn't move, so he left her, assuring her that the car she had asked for was on its way.

He knew that the meditation exercises were the last stage in his training, and he began to wonder what he should do next. One morning the master told him that he no longer needed his help and from then on the master left him free to organize his days as he liked. He could go into retreat in the wilderness or stay at the base. They met only rarely, to go over some of the more arduous exercises together. This was another sign that he would soon move on to a new stage. But one night when Fakhreddin was alone in seclusion, he was attacked by an unknown person.

He was lying in a small cave in the mountains, trying to sleep, when he heard a sound like gravel moving. It wasn't a wolf. He knew the sound wolves made. This was the sound of footsteps. He braced himself inside the cave and pricked up his ears but the sound disappeared. He thought for a moment it was just one of his hallucinations, like his friends' faces. While he was turning to go back to where he was lying, someone attacked him from behind. Abu Omar resisted, but didn't try to hurt him in case it was part of the training process. He pushed his assailant off, but the assailant pulled out a dagger and tried to pounce on him again. Abu Omar dodged him but the attacker turned with the agility of a professional fighter and stabbed Abu Omar in the shoulder. Abu Omar put his hand to his shoulder and couldn't believe how much blood was pouring from it, while the attacker pounced on him again, aiming the dagger at his chest. Abu Omar pushed back the arm that was holding the dagger and turned it toward the attacker's heart. He planted the dagger deep inside his chest and twisted it between his ribs, now aiming to do as much damage as possible. He pulled out the dagger and pushed the attacker's body, which fell onto the floor. He stood in the center of the cave and listened carefully in case there were others. There wasn't a sound. He looked at the blood-soaked body and leaned over it to examine it. The dead man's face wasn't familiar and it offered no clues to his identity. At that moment his Uighur master and Abu Hafs appeared together at the mouth of the cave. The teacher came up to him, took hold of him, cleaned the wound, put a bandage on it, and tied it up, jabbering some incomprehensible but clearly disapproving words. Abu Hafs came forward, patted Abu Omar on the shoulder, and congratulated him on graduating and surviving the encounter.

"What?"

"Yes, this was the last test. The training program's over now."

"And the dead guy?"

"He had been sentenced to death."

"Who sentenced him to death? And why did he attack me?"

"The sharia council sentenced him to death. He'd been cooperating with Pakistani intelligence and he confessed. It's a capital offense, and we gave him a choice between death by the sword or fighting one of the new trainees. He chose to fight."

"And what about me? Did I choose to fight, too? You made me take someone's life. This dead man was a human being. I've just killed someone."

"He'd been sentenced to death."

"And did I tell you I wanted to be his execution squad?"

"But you didn't execute him. You were defending yourself."

"What kind of twisted logic is that? It was you who sent him."

"I didn't send anyone. He wanted to kill you in order to survive."

"Great. That's great. And what if he had killed me?"

"I wouldn't have put you through this test if I'd had the slightest doubt."

"Abu Hafs, you sent an armed man intent on killing me to my retreat. How can you be sure of anything?"

"I was standing here all the time with my gun, to save you if necessary."

Fakhreddin was stunned by this logic. But there wasn't time to dwell on it because Abu Hafs had something far more urgent to tell him, something that had to be dealt with immediately. He asked him to say goodbye to the Uighur master and go back to the base with him at once. On the way, he told him of the developments that had taken place during his months away.

"The Taliban went into Kabul but the disagreements between the Afghan factions have persisted and the fighting's continued. Those who were enemies—Hekmatyar, Rabbani, and Dostum the Uzbek—are now allies and have refused to obey the new government the Taliban set up in Kabul. The fighting's still intense. Although the Taliban have had success on the battlefield, it's not clear how the war will end, especially as the alliance receives significant foreign backing."

"What's this got to do with us? Aren't we neutral?"

"Not any more. The Taliban have been hospitable toward us. They've allowed us to work in our camps and our bases in their areas without interfering in our affairs, but now they're under pressure and they're asking for help. Besides, the situation in Sudan has deteriorated since you left and it looks like the authorities there are running out of patience, which has prompted the sheikh to approach the Taliban about the possibility of him coming back here."

"The sheikh? He's going to come back here?"

"The sheikh *is* here, in a house close to Kandahar. In return, he's agreed to help the Taliban."

"But what happened to the fatwa that said we shouldn't fight with Afghans against other Afghans?"

"A new fatwa was issued after Rabbani and Hekmatyar joined forces and starting cooperating with foreign powers. By doing that they made themselves and their fighters into soldiers in the service of non-Muslim powers."

"And us?"

"The brethren discussed the situation in the consultative council and the majority favored accepting the Taliban request, but the jihad commander opposed it. He said the Taliban were extremists. Anyway, after long discussions and pressure from the council, the jihad commander stepped aside and the brethren elected me as the new jihad commander."

"You? And the base?"

"Abu Azzam is in charge of it now, with God's help."

"Have you actually started working with the Taliban?"

"Not yet. We hope to start soon. We're still getting ourselves ready and working out who wants to take part. As I told you and Hamza when you arrived, we don't force anyone to wage jihad. Hamza has volunteered to fight and he's eager to start."

"Yes, he was bound to take part."

"And you?"

"I don't know. I hadn't reckoned on this."

"Think hard. You've completed your training and done very well. The truth is you finished your basic training many months ago but the master saw you and chose you for the Chinese training, which is additional and we don't require that mujahideen complete it. He says you have the necessary instinct and talent and that you could become a master in your turn if you kept training with him. So, now, you have to decide. You can volunteer to join the jihad or you can keep on training with the master until you become a master in your turn. But think about two things: the first is that there are skills you can never acquire by training and that you have to join the fighting to master. The second is that, under these circumstances, we need everyone who can fight. The pressure is intense. If the Taliban are defeated and the alliance wins, they will throw us out and hand us straight over to the authorities in our countries of origin. That is part of the price that Hekmatyar, Rabbani, and Dostum will pay to their masters, who have given them money and weapons. These governments have realized that they made a mistake when they helped the jihad in the 1980s, and now they want to correct their mistake, but using the same people. So it's not just about the Taliban, but about us and the future of jihad in our countries. Think about that. You have until dawn the day after tomorrow to tell me what you decide."

Abu Omar and Hamza met on the base after months without seeing each other. They embraced and were happy to see each other. They sat down, but found they didn't have much to say. They asked each other about their training and both said it was "Excellent, praise be to God." They asked after each other's health and Abu Omar explained how he came to be injured in the shoulder and why there was a bandage with fresh blood on it. Hamza told him he should rest and walked with him to the place where he slept. Abu Omar asked him if he was going to spend the night in the same place, and he said he had to spend the night with his comrades with whom he was going off to jihad. Hamza asked him what he thought about the new situation, and whether he had decided what to do, and Abu Omar said that he hadn't. Hamza nodded and didn't reply. Then he said he had heard that Abu Omar had done well in the training and Abu Omar said he had heard the same of Hamza. They smiled and nodded, and Hamza went off to go to bed.

Abu Omar spent the whole night and the next day thinking. He went out in the morning, climbed to the mountain peak barefoot, and spent the day meditating there. He looked at the caves in the mountains, the valleys, and the shadows that the scorching sun cast on the ground. He looked at the faces of Eissa, Ali, and Buheiri, which visited him almost daily, and then he looked again inside himself. He did breathing and concentration exercises and looked for the calm inside himself as much as possible.

He made his decision. He knew this was a crucial moment and he would follow the path to the end. Either you are something or you're not. There can be no fighters without fighting, and you can't be strong without bringing your strength to bear. This strong body, this sharp eye, this steadfast mind, this determination, this steady fist, this steely will—all were fruits that it was time to pluck. It was time to use them to serve a meaningful cause. After dawn prayers, he met Abu Hafs and told him he would join them. He met the brethren and took the oath of jihad. A few days later he left the base to join the ranks of the Arabs fighting for the Taliban.

Abu Omar spent the next five years as a sniper. Some people say that professional killers take drugs so that they can do their job without feelings. Fakhreddin didn't need to take drugs: the thick glass screen that separated him from the rest of the world was enough. The sounds he heard seemed to come from afar, drowned out by the constant ringing in his ears. He saw people as characters in a 3D film. The nature of his missions helped him do that. He worked alone, chose his position, looked for the target in the distance, tracked it through the scope of his rifle until it was right in the crosshairs. Then he squeezed the trigger gently and the man disappeared from the telescopic sight, never to be seen again.

A person who lives with war grows inured to death. He may be standing with someone, or walking beside them, or hugging them, or waiting for them to shake his hand, and suddenly they fall. He could be drinking tea or waiting for a colleague, who's gone to relieve himself in the ruins, and suddenly the wall of the decrepit building collapses onto him and he hears the sound of the shell less than a second later. There's no time to run. The only solid piece of rock in the wall lands on one of their heads and crushes it. Pink brain spurts out through the fragments of a skull. One of the two of them was there and is no longer, or it could have been both of

182

them. There's nothing more to say about it. Death accompanies him wherever he goes. All around the devastated streets of Kabul, there were women hidden behind thick pieces of cloth that guard against all manner of evils; young boys scattered about the place; and men slumped on either side of the street waiting for who knows what. Suddenly he finds out. A hail of bullets descends from somewhere unexpected, and he fires back at people he doesn't know. When the guns fall silent, he'll look around and find one, two, or more dead bodies, depending on the crowd. The dead person might have been sitting next to him a minute ago, annoying him with his smell or by poking him with his elbow, or it might have been him, or both of them. It's just a matter of fate, which may place him in the path of the bullet or the shell. A hair's breadth separates life from death, and the two always travel with him. Death advances one pace, or life, and he only feels the result when it comes down on him. The more time passes and the more people die around him, the less he cares about the difference.

Afghanistan spun out of control: it become a massive killing field. In these fields, the Taliban rose and thrived. They tried to impose their control in the way they knew best. Pickup trucks patrolled the villages and towns. They stopped anyone they deemed suspicious. Two men would get out of the vehicle to speak to the suspect. They might come back quietly, or one of them might put a bullet or two in the man's head, and then they'd drive off. Sometimes, after the vehicle had passed, someone might take out a weapon, fire at the vehicle, and blow it up, killing everyone inside. That's where Abu Omar's role came in. He would sit at the back of the truck. He wouldn't get out or speak to anyone, in the vehicle or outside. His orders were not to intervene, unless he saw someone about to attack the vehicle. In that case he would raise his sniper rifle and within moments Abu Omar would have slain the attacker. That was his assignment—protecting the Taliban patrols. They told him from the start to save the lives of the fighters at any cost. "If you kill someone by mistake, ask God for forgiveness. But if you allow an attacker to open fire on you, then may God have mercy on all of you. And asking for forgiveness is a hundred times better than asking for mercy." One hair's breadth made the difference between one man dying and another man surviving, maybe to find the man who tried to kill him.

He went into many towns and villages and they all left one of two impressions: either a cloud of dust constantly hanging in the air, a scorching sun, and barren mountains, or a cold that froze one's fingers and toes, dreary clouds, and mountains covered in snow. In both there were rows of damaged houses, with the light shining through the holes left in the walls by shells and high-velocity bullets, the streets broken up by rain, tanks, and other tracked vehicles, boys pretending to play, and many one-legged men. It seemed impossible to tell if the women were coming toward you or moving away, and their male companions had stern faces and identical beards. And always present were the many weapons and gunshots, the explosions and dead bodies that were soon covered with dust and abandoned.

Pickup trucks scattered life and death, and Abu Omar the Egyptian Eagle crouched in one of them, loading his gun in silence, surveying the scene in search of a soul that might intend to attack them. He would extinguish it before it could snipe at them. He only looked down to clean his weapon or signal to one of his comrades.

Amid these scenes, his visions of his old friends ceased to haunt him. He wondered whether they had abandoned him or whether they had found peace and departed. From time to time he remembered them and missed them. He didn't have any friends in Afghanistan. He sometimes felt sad about that and then he remembered that he didn't have friends anywhere else either.

He saw Hind again. She was in good shape this time and walking on both legs. He had left Jalalabad after delivering a message from the sheikh to some 'brethren' in the town. After passing through a checkpoint on the edge of the town, he found Hind walking by the side of the road and waving at the vehicle. He recognized her immediately and stopped. She smiled when she saw him and jumped into the vehicle without asking permission. That wasn't allowed, but she begged him to give her a lift to the next town. She told him complicated stories about drivers and appointments and he didn't object this time. In fact, deep down inside, he was delighted to see her again. As long as she had survived whatever interrogation the committee would have put her through when he had called them about her that first time, she must be harmless from a security point of view, and just a foolish woman.

She told him many stories along the way. She told him she was a Palestinian from Jerusalem and her family became refugees in Gaza in 1948. She was born and grew up there. Her parents were members of the Popular Front for the Liberation of Palestine—the PFLP—and arranged for her to go to the Arab University in Beirut with a grant from the PFLP. There, she had trained in technical work in support of the resistance, such as forging documents, how to disguise herself, and sheltering fugitives. After that they sent her back to Gaza to help the front with operations inside the Gaza Strip, but the cell was discovered, all the members were arrested, and she spent about a year in jail. Then the Israelis expelled her and her family from the Gaza Strip. She settled in Egypt and completed her university studies there. In the meantime, the PFLP arranged for her and her family to obtain political asylum in Prague, where she worked for the Czechoslovak News Agency. They sent her to their Islamabad office a few months before Czechoslovakia split into the Czech Republic and Slovakia. She told him the news agency continued to operate as the Czech News Agency and she was covering the situation in Afghanistan.

She asked him many questions, none of which he answered, so she kept on talking about herself. Before he reached the next checkpoint, she asked him to let her get out, and she put her hand on his arm as she thanked him and said goodbye. It was the first time in years that a woman had touched him, and although his arm showed no response, the touch had an emotional effect. It was like a gust of cool air on a hot day, and it reminded him of something he had forgotten. His face remained expressionless, but the gesture stirred his imagination and disconcerted him for a moment, and then he drove on.

Abu Omar's star rose and the Taliban started calling him "The Eagle" too. They sent him with a detachment of Arab fighters to join the Taliban campaign against the Northern Alliance in the Panjshir valley, where battles were under way that might decide the country's fate. Abu Hafs himself was leading the Arab fighters and Hamza was with him. The day after Abu Omar arrived, Abu Hafs sent him to reconnoiter the area that lay between their camp and the Northern Alliance forces. Close to dawn Abu Omar noticed that the Alliance forces were deploying large quantities of troops and equipment in the flat area between two mountains, maybe to surround the Taliban from that direction. He deftly infiltrated enemy lines and took up a position between the two mountains. He howled like a wolf to check the direction of the echo, then started to open fire at the attacking force. He shot dead six men before any of the attackers could reach for their weapons, and continued to pick them off one by one. The sound of his gunshots echoed off the mountains and the men in the attacking force couldn't figure out where the shots were coming from, so they started shooting in all directions. The attacking force soon clashed with forces from the Northern Alliance camp because each group thought the other was their enemy. Amid this chaos Abu Omar sniped at the soldiers one after another, slowly and carefully until he ran out of ammunition. That night he killed thirty-three men himself, not counting the ones who were killed in friendly fire. Then he slipped back while the raiding force continued to clash with their allies. The Taliban forces attacked the fragmented Northern Alliance forces an hour later and drove the ones that remained out of the area.

A week later, Abu Omar woke up to a commotion. The Northern Alliance had sent a special force to take revenge and had infiltrated their camp. They fought hand-to-hand inside and between the tents. That day Abu Omar saved Abu Hafs from an assailant who was about to plunge a knife into his back. Abu Omar pushed his commander aside before the attacker fell on him. The assailant fell to the ground. Abu Omar jumped on top of him and slit his throat with one cut. Abu Hafs was amazed at what had happened. It was a real massacre that night, with many killed. A week later Abu Omar and a Taliban raiding party went and besieged Mazar-e Sharif, then attacked it and killed many of the fighters there.

Toward the end of the year, Fakhreddin left the north, where the battle lines had stabilized, and went back to Jalalabad, where the sheikh was living, and joined his bodyguard detail. The sheikh started sending him on operations like the ones he had carried out in Sudan. He traveled in a variety of convoys—from four-wheel-drives to horses, camels, and donkeys, as well as motorbikes. These trips took him to all parts of Afghanistan—narrow, rugged tracks to the top of towering mountains to deserts with sandy dunes that stretched away in endless undulations, riverbeds that were so dry one month that you could drive across them but were raging torrents in another month, green valleys and glorious meadows that he hadn't known existed in the country. He traveled across Pakistan to the Chinese border, went into China, and came back with another convoy.

Then the sheikh went away and entrusted Abu Omar to one of his allies in the Taliban leadership. Some Taliban leaders had been assassinated as a result of internal rivalries and Abu Omar was assigned to protect the sheikh's ally. He didn't know the man's identity but everyone revered him. He went with him to attend a reconciliation session with a rival about whom Abu Omar knew nothing either. When the fighters got out of the vehicles, he remained alone in the vehicle with his rifle. The well-wishers came forward, shaking hands and embracing each other. From his hiding place, Abu Omar noticed a man pull out a gun and point it at the sheikh's ally. Once again, he found himself aiming his rifle at an unknown assailant and shooting him dead before his opponent had a chance to fire a single bullet. The Taliban chief was grateful and happy to have his life saved, despite the chaos that broke out after that. But Abu Omar's only concern was that he had managed to kill this wretched assailant before he fired a shot. That was his job and he had done it well.

He started seeing Hind often. He would usually find her lost somewhere, looking for a car or late for an important appointment. She never asked him for any information: on the contrary, she told him what was happening in Pakistan and the current news about international plans for dealing with Afghanistan and about the Northern Alliance. She also filled him in on what the news agency was saying about the Taliban's excesses and the brutal acts they were perpetrating in the areas under their control. He listened to all this with indifference. There was nothing new in what she said. He had heard the same stories before and had witnessed some of these events himself, even if he hadn't taken part in them. But when Hind told him these stories he felt as if she were drawing these events out of his memory and presenting them to him in a new light, as if she were showing him images that he had previously glimpsed only from the corner of his eye. Little by little he began to trust her, or trust the accuracy of her information. She never told him about anything that hadn't happened, and when he asked her about things she didn't know, she didn't pretend to know.

She would often get carried away when she told him these stories and in her enthusiasm her scarf would slip off her black hair. He would draw her attention to this and she would put it back in place while engrossed in finishing the story. But every time he waited a little longer before drawing her attention to it. He liked black hair and hadn't seen a woman's hair since coming to Afghanistan. She had so much hair that it often broke out from under her loose headscarf. Her forehead was white and soft, and when her hair hung down over it looked even more attractive. He couldn't remember seeing such a soft brow. She noticed that he was looking and smiled complicitly, warning him of the consequences if any of the Taliban found out what he was thinking. He pretended he didn't understand, ended the conversation, and drove on.

He went back to the Arab fighters embedded with the Taliban in the north to fend off the Alliance's attempts to regain control of the center of the country. They ran daily patrols along the lines between the two sides and one day a stray bullet hit Abu Hafs, killing him instantly.

The jihad commander was dead. Everyone prayed to God to have mercy on him, then went back to their work. That's how it was—one moment he was the jihad commander, and then a stray bullet hit him. No one had even aimed at him. It was a just a stray bullet flying through the air in search of a skull to settle in. It chose him, or he got in the way and it lodged inside him, like a mosquito bite that would leave you prey to malaria for the rest of your days. The comrades ask God to have mercy on him, read the first chapter of the Quran over his dead body, and trust that God would count him as a martyr. Farewell, commander.

The consultative council met and decided unanimously to pledge allegiance to Sheikh Hamza as the new jihad commander. He was seen to be the fighter best able to lead the group under these circumstances and was someone that the sheikh trusted. Some of them had reservations about his knowledge of Islamic law, but the majority, who supported him, countered that he had memorized the Quran and that the most important quality in a jihad commander was his fighting abilities. The sharia council could discuss matters of religious law and it was not for the commander to make unilateral decisions on such things. Hamza received oaths of allegiance from Abu Omar and the others. Hamza took Abu Omar aside after the ceremony and asked him, "Do you have any reservations about this, Abu Omar?"

"Why would I have any reservations about pledging allegiance to you?"

"Abu Omar, you used to be my superior. Can you pledge allegiance to me as commander without resentment?"

"Your superior? Me? When was that?"

Hamza smiled for the first time in ages and whispered, "In Bayn al-Sarayat."

"Come on! That was another life."

Abu Omar was honest in what he said. As far as he was concerned, Hussein had been Sheikh Hamza for so long that he only thought of him by that name. The past, the names from the past, and everything about the past had disappeared with the dead bodies. All he could see was the fighting, which seemed to be endless.

Abu Omar was driving one of the sheikh's cars, carrying a consignment of cash for one of the brethren, when he met Hind again. This time he gave her a lift without hesitation. She asked him what he was really doing in Afghanistan, and he said he was a driver. She didn't respond. After a while, he spotted a motorbike coming from behind at high speed. He kept driving, looking at the motorcyclist in the mirror out of the corner of his eye. He was still approaching at speed. Hind looked behind anxiously and asked, "What's up with that guy?"

"I don't know."

"Is he Taliban?"

"No, he's . . ."

Before Abu Omar could finish his sentence, the man fired a shot that shattered the back window of the car and skimmed past Hind's head. Abu Omar slammed on the brakes as hard as he could and the car spun a half circle to face the motorcyclist coming right toward them. The attacker fired at them again, but didn't hit them. Hind ducked under the car seat while the motorcyclist turned back toward the car. Abu Omar waited till the attacker reached the car window and then, with lightning speed, put a bullet in the man's head, killing him instantly. For a few seconds the only audible sound was the motorcycle's engine that was still running. Abu Omar drove the car a short distance away from the motorcycle; as he moved off, he stuck his head out of the window and fired another bullet at the motorcycle, blowing it up. When he stopped, he turned off the engine and sat still. Hind raised her head little by little. She looked at him, threw herself into his arms, held him tight, and started to tremble and weep.

When he found her in his arms, he was taken aback and his body froze. But she clung to him tighter and started to sob. He held her around her waist and her shoulders with his arms. She trembled even more and buried her head between his neck and his shoulder to smother the sound of her sobbing, and wrapped her arm around his neck. He began to stroke her hair, which had slipped out of her scarf. The sensation of touching her hair came as a shock—he had forgotten that feeling. He buried his hand in her hair as it fell loose and then moved his hand up toward her scalp, patted her head gently as it rocked from side to side, submitting to his hands. She leaned her head on his chest and shoulder, and he could see her reddened cheek and her closed eyes. She was crying quietly now. He reached out and wiped the remaining tears from her cheek, then wiped her eyes. She moved her head a little and he wiped her forehead and nose.

His hand began to caress her under her chin and around her neck. She let out a slight sigh, her lips parted, and her cheeks flushed. He held the back of her head, raised her head a little, and before he had time to think he had planted his lips on hers. He felt as if she were melting. She seemed so limp that he thought she was going to fall off the car seat. He pulled her up to stop her falling and, again, found himself pressed close against her soft, warm body. He felt a surge of desire and pressed her lips so hard that she tried to pull away, but he held her tight. Then his desire subsided as suddenly as it had started. He calmed down and, embarrassed, loosened his grip on her. He leaned back in the car seat and she looked at him with wide eyes.

"What did you tell me your job was?" she asked.

"Sorry?"

"You? What do you do?"

"I'm . . . I'm very sorry. I don't know how that happened."

"Did something happen that I didn't notice?" she said with a laugh.

He got out of the car and didn't know what to do. He wasn't sure if he was embarrassed about what he had started or that he hadn't continued with it to the end. He walked toward the wreckage of the motorbike and examined the dead body. The man was an Uzbek, but he didn't have any papers on him. He went back to the car and asked Hind if she had any contacts with the Uzbek groups. She said she had met Dostum, the Uzbek leader, and done an interview in which he attacked his allies as agents of the United States. She said the interview caused a stir and created problems between Dostum and Rabbani and Hekmatyar, and later, she came under pressure from Dostum's people to publish a retraction of some paragraphs and to say she had mistranslated them. But she refused and said she had his words on tape. Since then, she hadn't been to the Northern Alliance area for fear for her life, and this was why she had come to the Taliban areas.

"And you don't plan to tell me what exactly you do for a living?" she asked.

"I drive."

"And you're a marksman as part of your driving?"

"That's self-defense."

"Oh, spare me. Don't waste my time. Tell me, why do you kill the people you kill?"

"Sorry?"

"Listen. I'm not stupid. I'm well aware who you are and what you do. Besides, I've told you who I am and what I do, so why don't you stop acting dumb and tell me straight?"

He opened the car door and asked her to get out.

"You must be joking!" she said.

"That's enough now, Hind. I don't want any trouble."

"Where will I go, if I get out here? Look around you, for God's sake."

"You can manage. Since you managed to get here, I'm sure you'll know how to get back."

"How rude! Didn't anyone ever tell you you're supposed to give your girlfriend a ride home after you've finished? I swear I'm not getting out."

She closed the car door and sat tight. He drove on in silence till he reached a checkpoint on the way into Jalalabad. He made a sign to her and she hid under the seat. He knew them and they knew him. He waved to them and they waved to him, and he didn't need to stop. When they were past the checkpoint she came out from under the seat. He stopped the car, opened the door for her, and she got out.

The Northern Alliance made many attacks on the front lines, and the task of defending the area became more onerous. An attack would take place somewhere, almost every night. Abu Omar would snatch some sleep when he was stationed at his position, waking up at the slightest sound. Sometimes he used his rifle and sometimes the fighting was face-to-face. Every day, Abu Omar saved one of his comrades from the clutches of death, aiming his fist, his dagger, or his rifle at the attacker and slaying him before his comrade figured out what was happening around him. One night, the comrade in question was Sheikh Hamza. They were in the Panjshir valley and Sheikh Hamza was fighting off an attacker, while Abu Omar was busy shooting at a source of heavy gunfire. Suddenly, another assailant appeared, out of sight of Sheikh Hamza, and raised his dagger to stab the sheikh in the back. Abu Omar saw him out of the corner of his eye and punched him hard at the base of his neck. The man fell on Hamza's back, and Hamza still hadn't seen him. It took him a couple of seconds to understand what had happened, but he managed to slit the throat of the man he was fighting, then pushed the body of the other man off his back. Hamza had thought he was done for and it took him some time to pull himself together. Although he had been fighting for years, was brave, and had a reputation for combat skills that had spread far and wide and won him the command, he had never been so close to dying before. The incident affected him, and twice more in the same month in the same valley, where there were fierce battles between the two sides, Abu Omar saved him from certain death. Hamza said later that the Northern Alliance had been targeting him as commander. One of the fighters suggested he stop taking part in the patrols they sent out, and the others supported him. After that, Hamza didn't go back to the front lines.

Those months saw the fiercest fighting Abu Omar had witnessed in Afghanistan and he no longer knew how many people he had killed each day. Some days he would go to sleep thinking he had killed three or four and then remember when he woke up that he had killed two other men who had attacked their positions earlier. Then he stopped counting or remembering the dead, and killing became easier.

But the military pressure didn't stop. The sheikh came up from the south and Taliban leaders came and met Sheikh

Hamza and the group's consultative council, which included Abu Omar. Everyone said that the pressure on the ground was the result of an increase in the support that foreign governments were giving the Northern Alliance to help it wipe out the Islamic emirate. So they decided to declare jihad against all these foreign powers, or what they called "the distant enemy." Some people objected because they preferred to focus on the "proximate enemy," meaning the Northern Alliance forces. They said that jihad against foreign states was meaningless and that jihad should be restricted to an immediate objective. But the dissidents were a minority, and jihad was declared against the West.

Abu Omar had spent more than two years in Afghanistan when the group made that decision, and he then spent roughly another three years there. But the seeds of his decision to leave were sown on that evening. "This is not my cause," he told the sheikh. "You think it's important, and maybe it is, but it's not my cause."

"Do you want to leave, then? There are brethren who have left," the sheikh replied.

He was still learning. He was learning how to be strong and it wasn't yet time for him to leave. But he wanted to warn the sheikh that he wouldn't be staying forever.

"Not yet, but soon," he said.

"Since you're staying, we'll have time to talk about this later."

He missed Hind. He denied it but he knew it. Whenever he remembered what had happened in the truck on the side of the Jalalabad road, he tried to think of something else, but deep down inside he knew he missed her, very much so. Whenever he found himself alone on the road between two towns, he remembered her. He would see the outline of a woman wrapped in an Afghan burka and hope inside himself that it was Hind.

Then he saw her. She was standing on the road, as usual, outside Mazar-e Sharif, just as he was on his way back from an assignment for the Taliban commander he was working with. He stopped alongside her.

"What are you doing here?" he asked. "The sun's about to set."

"I can't find a taxi."

"Why are you always so perverse?"

She got in the car and he drove off at speed before she'd shut the door properly.

"Do you have to do everything so fast?" she asked.

He shook his head in disapproval of her boldness, and didn't speak. She put her hand out, held his right hand, which was on the gearshift, and laced her fingers with his.

He put his hand over hers on the gearshift and squeezed it for a moment. She left her hand in his and played with his hand and fingers with both her hands. They didn't exchange a word. The sun went down and in silence they drove on into the twilight.

"This is dangerous. If a patrol stopped us we'd be in trouble," he finally remarked.

"Why are you worried? Aren't you an important person?"

"Don't count on it. Some twenty-year-old kids might stop us and shoot us."

"What nice friends you have! So what's to be done?"

"We'll find somewhere to stay till the morning."

"Okay. Let's find somewhere."

He drove on for some minutes, then turned down a side track. He turned off the car lights and drove by the soft light of the moon for half an hour, then stopped. They got out of the car and walked along a rocky track until they reached a small cave. He took her into the cave, gave her a blanket to spread out, and went to inspect the place. He came back and said it was safe to spend the night there. She gestured to him and he sat next to her on the blanket.

"You haven't missed me?" she asked.

He didn't answer. He looked at her pale face, and her eyes looked at him inquisitively. He turned her head to look him right in the face, moved his lips toward her mouth, and kissed her. He took her lower lip between his lips and pressed it until it relaxed. She pushed his turban off his head and pulled his head to her chest. He pulled off her dress and took hold of her almost naked body. He kneaded her bare arms and caressed the soft roundness of her shoulders. Touching her warm skin inflamed his desire for her. His inhibitions, all the rules, no longer counted for anything. She pulled at his shirt and bared his chest. She touched him with her hands and he felt his temperature rising. He took off her underclothes, held her at the waist as his eyes feasted on the wonderful sight of her firm young body. He cradled her bare breasts in the palms of his hands, fondled them, squeezed them, and kissed them. He licked her neck as her body writhed in his hands. He held her at the hips and planted kisses on her stomach. Her sighs and moans grew louder as his lips gradually moved down her stomach to between her legs. She breathed faster and faster, then finally let out one long scream that echoed off the walls of the dark and silent cave. Silence fell again and her body slumped onto the blanket spread on the rocky ground. She gave a small smile and was about to speak, but he put his hand over her mouth. Within moments he fell asleep.

He woke up in the middle of the night and it took him some moments to remember where he was. He looked at the woman sleeping beside him, and pricked up his ears. There was no sound from outside the cave. She was still naked and uncovered. He touched her body in the darkness and she stirred. She got up, leaned toward him, and looked at him.

"Are you happy here, in Afghanistan, with what you're doing?" she asked.

His face clouded over and he said nothing. She kept looking at him.

"I mean, it's a phase and it'll pass," he finally said.

"And do you like your Taliban friends?"

He waited, then mumbled slowly: "It's a phase and it'll pass."

His face turned darker and gave no clues to his feelings. He seemed to be detached from everything around him, to be living in another world. She reached out to him and pulled his head to her breast. "Never mind," she murmured. She kissed him and put her arms around him again, and they stayed like that for a while, until he started to relax again. She kissed him on his lips and he held her face to stop her, then he gathered her hair in his hands, suddenly lifted her up, and had her straddle him. Suddenly he lifted her up and had her straddle him. Her eyes widened and she gasped as he entered her, holding her body on top of him, his hand pulling at her hair from behind. The surge of pleasure swept him away, like welcome rain flooding land parched after years of drought. Her sighs and moans transported him to a world where their bodies merged into one. She rose and fell on top of him until finally she let out a quick succession of short screams. He relaxed. He didn't move and she didn't move. She stayed like that a while, then moved off him and lay on her side on the blanket. He lay beside her and they dozed off again.

When he woke up, she was no longer beside him. He found a small piece of paper saying she had left at sunrise so that she could reach Kandahar for an appointment. He wondered in amazement how she would reach Kandahar.

"She's crazy," he said to himself.

There was a weak spot in Abu Omar's training and he knew it. It was diving and swimming, about which he had had a complex since Buheiri had drowned in Lake Victoria. He asked Hamza for permission to go somewhere where he could learn. Hamza looked at him at length and asked if this would be the prelude to his departure, but Abu Omar denied that this was the case. He nodded without conviction and sent him to the sheikh, who sent him to a secret center in the middle of the desert where people were trained to swim and dive. He spent several weeks there, until he was proficient, and he also took lessons in the theory of marine navigation and boat mechanics. After that, he crossed the Pakistani border and traveled on to a tourist resort that the sheikh owned in southern India. There he was trained for some months to sail and handle motorboats.

He went back to Afghanistan. The training course in India hadn't helped to alleviate the sense of listlessness he had felt since the beginning of the year. He was well established as a first-rate fighter. He continued to train and maintained his proficiency in all aspects of fighting, especially as a sniper, which he liked more than anything else. After achieving full control over his mind and his body, he moved on to planning operations and was so good at it that the sheikh often sought his help. But boredom was taking its toll. He could stay and keep fighting, but for how long? And for what purpose? Several times in the middle of an operation he caught himself wondering what he was doing. He might be in a building, behind a hill, or in a vehicle, waiting for some target to appear so that he could gun it down. It wasn't the killing that upset him but the loss of meaning. He wanted to fight a real enemy, an enemy that meant something to him directly, not "the far enemy" or its proxies in the Northern Alliance and in the intelligence agencies.

In the heat of an operation, in Taliban vehicles or in the sheikh's car, he would say to himself, "What's the point in being the best sniper in a country that I don't really care about? And against an enemy that isn't my enemy?" As far as he was concerned, all this fighting was just training for an ulterior purpose. He had come to learn how to be strong, and now he wanted to end the training and move to the real battlefield. He wanted to go back to his first vocation, to his first love and his first enemy. He wanted to go back to Cairo.

Hamza objected strongly when he brought up the matter with him. He told him all the Arab fighters planned to go back to their own countries and change the situation there, but everything had its time and the time for that hadn't come yet. He explained to him that the group wasn't yet ready to operate in Egypt and that the far enemy took priority. Fighting the Americans and their allies was the key because it was they who supported corrupt and despotic regimes. Abu Omar made it clear that he disagreed, and asked what the point of fighting the Americans was when they were just secondary factors and not the primary cause of misery in the Muslim world. He said that logic and common sense mean we have to change things inside ourselves first and then look at what others are doing to us, and not the other way around. Hamza wanted to continue the discussion, but Abu Omar said he had decided to leave and that was the end of the matter. Hamza asked him to commit himself to whatever the group had decided and to avoid causing dissent in the ranks. Abu Omar replied that he had done that for many years and now it was time to go. Hamza objected and reminded him of the oath he had taken. Abu Omar gave him a sneering look and asked him to prepare himself for his departure. Then he walked off.

After a few days of animosity between the two men, Hamza dropped in on Abu Omar and told him he wouldn't force him to stay if he wanted to leave. But he asked him to be patient for a few months because they were organizing a big operation and needed him. A week after this discussion, the sheikh dropped a hint that he was aware that he wanted to leave, and backed Hamza's position on the need to wait. He promised him good news by the end of the year. Abu Omar agreed to wait and toward the end of August Hamza assigned him to travel north with a group that would arrange an opportunity for him to kill the military commander of the Northern Alliance, Ahmed Shah Massoud. Abu Omar asked about the purpose of the operation but Hamza refused to go into detail, saying only that it was part of a bigger operation that he was not authorized to discuss. Abu Omar refused to take part, and the two men had a heated exchange.

"Why not? I want to hear a convincing reason why you've refused," Hamza said.

"Because we have a truce with the alliance, and if you want to kill him now that means there's some major fighting coming."

"Maybe, but what's wrong with that?"

"I wouldn't be able to leave then. I couldn't leave when fighting like that starts."

"We'll cross that bridge when we come to it."

"No. I want to go, and we've agreed."

"Stop this, Abu Omar. Remember that you took an oath to listen and obey."

"As long as we aren't violating the sharia, commander. Killing Ahmed Shah Massoud would violate the sharia because we have a truce with the man and killing him would break a pledge."

They went on wrangling to no purpose. Hamza sent Abu Omar to the sheikh, who met him on September 1 and urged him to carry out the operation, but Abu Omar did not relent. It was the first time he had turned down a direct request from the sheikh. After hours of arguing, the sheikh realized that it was all over as far as Abu Omar was concerned and he gave him permission to leave, as long as he promised to keep the Ahmed Shah Massoud operation secret from everyone, even from those in the group. Abu Omar swore not to reveal anything he knew, and the sheikh arranged for him to leave Afghanistan for Pakistan. He assigned someone to meet him in Peshawar, facilitate his journey, and arrange the necessary travel documents for him. Abu Omar asked to go back to Sudan first to see his son. The sheikh agreed and promised to arrange it with the Sudanese authorities, as long as he didn't stay in Pakistan for more than three days, and the same period in Sudan, so he would be on his way to Cairo within a week of leaving Afghanistan. He left the sheikh's office and started to make preparations for the journey. He didn't have time to go and say goodbye to Hamza in Jalalabad, so he just called him by telephone. The call was even briefer than what was required by security precautions. The next day, September 2, he set off to Peshawar, remembering the way he had come into the country for the first time six years earlier.

He met his contact at the Khan Klub Hotel, an old building in the Afghan style that had been renovated and had become a popular choice for visitors to Peshawar. His contact gave him a Yemeni passport, a ticket to Khartoum via Abu Dhabi, and some money.

Hind caught him unawares as he was sitting in his room in the hotel. He heard a light tapping on the door and when he opened it he found her right in front of him, with her wide eyes looking straight at him. "You didn't think you could leave without saying goodbye to me?" she said. "Aren't you ashamed of yourself?"

She pushed the door, came in and closed it behind her. Then she threw her arms around his neck and hugged him.

"I'd like to know where you sprang from."

"From your black magic! Aren't you embarrassed after everything that you tried to leave the country without saying goodbye to me?"

He didn't have an answer. This was war. You're here today and gone tomorrow. You've either gone somewhere else or you're dead. Don't look back and don't say goodbye to anyone. If luck's on your side, you shake hands or embrace whoever's at hand and wish them well, then each person goes his own way. You might meet again, but death might get to you first. It was four o'clock in the afternoon and the hotel was quiet. The weather was still hot. He put the ceiling fan on and it made a monotonous drone, but the rush of air that it produced cooled the room. The bed was on a raised part of the room, right under a domed ceiling and close to the fan.

"That's weird!" she said.

She put down her bag and told him she wanted to hear everything from him—why he had now decided to leave, whether he would come back, where he intended to go, and his plans for the future. She said she was going to take a quick shower and expected him to have his answers ready when she came out, though maybe she also knew that he didn't have the answers in the first place.

He sat down to think, listening to the sound of the water from the shower. The bathroom was made of rough old marble and half of it was taken up by the shower. If you wanted, you could sit in it with four other people. He felt an urge to go in after her but his shyness got the better of him.

She came out and saved him from his thoughts. She was wrapped in a large blue bath towel. Her legs, shoulders, and arms looked bright white and radiant. There were drops of water on her skin that sparkled in the heat of the room. He reached out spontaneously and touched the droplets. She stopped, smiled, threw her head back, and whispered, "I missed the touch of your hand."

He held her by the shoulders and turned her toward him. She pulled back a little. "No," she said, "you go and have a shower first, like me. The water opens up the pores of the skin."

He went in and came back out wrapped in a similar towel, but couldn't find her. He looked around anxiously and saw her blue towel lying on one of the chairs. He was puzzled. He looked out of the window and heard her teasing laugh coming from the bed on the upper level.

"Did you think I'd run off? Are you always so suspicious? I'm here, waiting for you."

He went up the narrow stone stairs to the bed. The upper half of the room had a low ceiling and to reach the bed you had to go on all fours. She stretched her foot out to the towel wrapped around him and pulled it off as he made his way to the bed.

"It's better like that. It's hot," she said.

He reached her, pulled her toward him, and embraced her. Their bodies touched in the stillness as if they were charging each other. As they lay there, he gradually moved close and closer. He entered her and felt her tightness gripping him, both of them hardly moving. The pleasure drove them to desire more pleasure, in a loop that fed on itself until they climaxed together. They held each other tight, her eyes looking steadily into his.

"Won't you tell me what you plan to do?"

"I'm going back to Cairo."

"What are you going to do there? Work as a driver too?"

"I don't know yet, but I have to go back. There's no longer any need for me to be here."

She put out her hand to touch his chest. He pulled her close. "And what will you do?" he said after some hesitation.

She sat up sharply. "I'll stay here until my contract with the agency comes to an end. There are five months left," she said.

"And then where will you go?"

"Where do you think? The Republic of Palestine?"

"Why not?"

"How would I get in? I was expelled."

"So Lebanon or Jordan?"

"And do what there? Work with other militias who think they're fighting an occupation when in fact they're chasing their own shadows? It's all an illusion."

"You're very harsh today."

"It's not me that's harsh. It's the world. But that's your good luck. When I finish my contract, I'll come to see you in Egypt."

"Really?"

"Really. But tell me first what you plan to do."

"I'll tell you, but first, you have to lower your voice. You'll get us into trouble. Here, I'm a well-known Yemeni businessman."

"In that case, I'll let the whole of Peshawar know how good Yemeni men are!"

She tied her hair back, turned to him, and kissed his neck, his chest, his stomach, his legs, his feet. Then she turned him on his back and massaged his body with her own body. He took hold of her and placed her on top of himself. She recoiled a little and turned without escaping him. She relaxed on top of him again, with her back to him, and let down the jet black hair that she had tied up. It fell down her back in full view of his greedy eyes. She rose and fell, her hair cascading with her, brushing his face and the edges of his chest. It drove him mad with desire. He held her by the waist as they both moaned in pleasure. She moved faster and slower in turn and he held onto her hair, pulling it to control her movement on top of him. She played him to perfection, almost breaking free at one moment and then plunging down the next to take him to the hilt. He held her at the hips, pulling her down onto him as if he were drilling into her and then releasing her upward. She gasped as if coming up from under water, and then he would press her down again. The noises she made must have been audible throughout the hotel and they grew louder the harder he pressed. The rhythm picked up pace until she finally reached orgasm with a scream. She collapsed on top of him in exhaustion and they fell into a deep sleep.

The sheikh's representative put him in a car, which then took him to Islamabad early in the morning. He reached Islamabad around midday and headed for the airport after a short rest that included lunch at the Marriott hotel, which was frequented by foreigners and spies. As at the Khan Klub in Peshawar, the idea was that the people who monitor people's comings and goings would notice him and he would be listed from then on as an important Yemeni businessman. After lunch, he went to the airport and boarded the plane to Khartoum. It landed during the night after a long layover at Abu Dhabi airport. He found his old guard Abdullah waiting for him at the airport. All those years and nothing had changed here—neither the red color of the soil, the strong brown Nile, the checkpoints, nor the smell of the humid air. It was as if he were moving back in his life. Memories came back to him, along with old faces and emotions, but they did not linger. On the contrary, they came and then receded, like a wave that tries to grip the sand on the beach but then drains back into the sea.

In the morning, he visited Umm Yasser for the first time in six years and their meeting was warm. Omar and Yasser were at summer camp, so Abu Omar left them some things he had bought for them at Abu Dhabi airport. He made an agreement with Umm Yasser that Omar would stay with her a while longer, so that he could finish off some business he had in Cairo. She agreed willingly. She didn't ask him how long or what kind of business it was that prevented him taking his son with him, and she wished him success. She didn't ask about Buheiri and their last days together, and Abu Omar didn't bring up the subject either. But he suddenly said, "May God have mercy on him. He died as he had lived—generous and giving. A man in every sense of the word." He said the words rapidly and then paused. He was in a hurry. Then he left her in order to arrange his return to Egypt. He met Abdullah, who was waiting for him outside the house. They knew that their every movement was monitored and so they wanted to be brief. They took a domestic flight to El Fasher in Darfur, where Abu Omar said goodbye to Abdullah and took a vehicle to northern Darfur. There he met an old acquaintance from when he was living in Sudan before. The man arranged a small caravan of two camels and a horse, along with some equipment and supplies. On September 8, the deadline the sheikh had set for him to leave Sudan, Abu Omar started his journey across the Gilf Kebir desert between Sudan and Egypt.

6

The Red Line

ABU OMAR SPENT FORTY DAYS in the desert before reaching
Asyut. Forty days along the same route he had often traveled. He remembered his travels in Darfur with the sheikh,
and his adventures in the desert when he was protecting the
Versace consignments coming from Libya, but the memories
came without any nostalgia, as just reminiscences of places
and events. He had left Egypt a defeated outcast, but he was
coming back as a man whose fate was in his own hands, determined to settle old scores. He was not coming just to exact
revenge, but to set right the scales on a balance that was faulty.
He was coming back to establish justice in a cause that the law
couldn't see because it had been suppressed. It didn't require
an inquiry because he was well aware who had killed Ali and
Nasser and driven the others into exile. He would come back
to settle scores and set the scales right, nothing more and
nothing less. Throughout forty days of travel in the desert,
with two camels and a mare, under the stars that shone so
bright at night and the scorching sun by day, he thought about
the practicalities of his plan. What identity should he adopt?
Was he still Eissa al-Naggar or should he resume his old identity? Should he declare his arrival to family and friends, or stay
in hiding? How would the security agencies treat him in each
case? What work would he do? The sheikh had provided him
with enough money, but he would have to find work. What
could he do? And where would he live? Where should he start?

In Asyut he sold the animals, got rid of his desert clothes, and shaved his beard. Now he looked like a secondary-school teacher on his way to spend a vacation in his hometown. He sat at a café drinking tea and reading the newspapers. It was then that he realized what had happened. He looked at the front page of the newspaper and the news stunned him. He devoured the news reports to understand properly what had happened in the past forty days. Now he understood why they had insisted on killing Ahmed Shah Massoud and why the sheikh had insisted that he cross into Egypt before the end of the first week of September. He had known that the security on the roads and at places of entry would be tighter after that. The newspapers said that the United States had started bombing Afghanistan and Taliban rule was collapsing. They were abandoning the towns one by one and the Arab fighters had dispersed. He looked at the papers and could hardly believe that all this could have happened in just forty days. It was like driving through a tunnel and when you come out at the other end you find that the city's roads and landmarks have changed. He had known that things were moving toward a confrontation of this kind, but the confrontation was much bigger than he had expected. He thought about the fate of his comrades. The Americans would thrash the fighters: many would be killed and the networks and organizations would collapse. The leaders would leave, but from the dust of the bombing new leaders and new organizations would be born. Other networks would emerge that would be more complex and more robust. That was the law of survival and that's how the combat skills of organizations developed. Abu Omar looked at the newspaper and realized that this conflict would never end.

He took the train to Cairo and went over the parts of his plan. The train passed through fields that had retained their appearance: nothing about them had changed. Nothing had changed on the banks of the Nile except that there were more houses close to the river and on land that had once been fields, so much so that sometimes you couldn't see any fields at all. Nothing had changed on the way into Cairo except that the neighborhoods were more brutal and the poverty was more obvious. He got off the train at Cairo's central station and took another train going to Alexandria. He'd loved this station since he was young. On this platform, he'd smoked his first cigarette—a Super in a soft pack that didn't stop the cigarettes from getting broken. You'd take a long cigarette out of the pack and pray it would be intact. You'd run your fingers along it to straighten it out and check it didn't have any holes, then light it and draw a puff that had to be long because smoking was a guilty pleasure. It was here that he felt for the first time that sudden buzz in his blood-stream. He had started here and now he was back. Here his heart had wept and here he had enjoyed happy moments. Here, by night, in these carriages with broken windows. But all that was in the past now and all that remained from those days was images of the past. It was like a story that had happened to someone else. As if Fakhreddin really had been killed that day in Bayn al-Sarayat.

As soon as the train arrived he looked for the minibus station and found it in its usual place. He smiled to himself. He took a minibus toward Marsa Matrouh and after about an hour, at the police checkpoint at the town of Hammam, a man in plainclothes asked the driver for the identity cards of the passengers. Abu Omar gave him his old card. The man went away for some minutes and then came back. He put his head through the window, called someone, and asked him to get out. Then he looked at Abu Omar, handed him his identity card, and told him to get a new card as his would expire soon. Abu Omar nodded as he took the card, and the bus drove on, abandoning the passenger that the police had detained. Nobody asked why. A few minutes later the bus drove past the Abu Makar monastery. Five minutes later, Abu Omar asked the driver to stop. He got out, walked back toward the monastery, and was soon at the gate.

He was met with great kindness and affection by his old friend Ashraf, whose name was now Bishoy. He hugged him when he saw him. He looked older in his dark, loose monk's habit and with his long beard, but his face was as cheerful as ever. Bishoy held him in his arms a long time and Abu Omar felt that his old friend was about to cry, so he wriggled until Bishoy let him free. The two men looked at each other as if measuring how much of their lives had passed. They held each other's arms for a while, then Bishoy remembered his obligations as host and noticed the monks passing by and giving them quizzical looks.

"Come, I'll show you where you'll be sleeping. Put down your bags and everything. You must be tired from the journey," said Bishoy.

Abu Omar nodded and followed Bishoy along the monastery passageways and through the gardens. The monastery was carefully organized. There was an olive farm that extended behind some small buildings, with gardens and small plants in the middle. The paths at the monastery were paved with white stone, and beyond the walls you could see the blueness of the sea and white sands that reflected the rays of the sun. All you could hear here was the distant sound of the waves, the monks' footsteps on the stone paths, and the creak of the gate as it opened. Bishoy left him to wash and relax, then brought him some food. Right after that, Abu Omar fell asleep and didn't wake up till the morning.

Life in the monastery was simple and as regulated as a beehive. For the first few days, Abu Omar did nothing but walk, exercise, and spend a lot of time sitting and meditating in the olive grove. He felt at home in this place, which resembled Abu Hafs's base in its simplicity and neatness. He and Bishoy swapped stories without going into too much detail.

He said nothing about his time in Afghanistan and Bishoy didn't ask him. They didn't go over past times or refer to the events that followed. They just exchanged pleasantries and made sure that the other was well now, like survivors of a storm who didn't want to talk about their ordeal. Bishoy took great interest in Abu Omar's comfort but left him alone most of the time, and that was best for Abu Omar. The past was gone and vanished, and neither of them wanted to dig it up. Now they were Abu Omar and Bishoy and they felt comfortable with each other because they had a shared history. After a few days, Bishoy asked him what his plans were and whether he planned to stay in the monastery for some time, so that he could arrange things for him. Abu Omar said he would like to stay a while, maybe a month or more, and he expressed a desire to join the monks in their work so that he wouldn't be a burden to the monastery. They agreed that he would work in the olive grove under Bishoy's personal supervision, and so it was.

Abu Omar spent the next three months in spiritual catharsis and preparing the work ahead. The many years of fighting had made him accustomed to austerity, and he found peace in the life of the monastery. There was no electricity, nothing beyond what was necessary. He'd started to hate material things and tried to have as few possessions around as possible. He divided his time between working on the olive farm, meditating, and physical exercise. He went out at sunrise after a breakfast of bread, areesh cheese, and olives, and ran five miles along the beach, which was deserted at that time of the year. He would swim in the cold waters of the sea, go back to the monastery, wash, clean his room, and start work on the olive trees or in the press. In the afternoon he spent several hours doing meditation exercises and clearing his mind, and he drank plenty of water. He would have a nap for a while and then a light supper shortly after sunset, usually soup, vegetables, and sometimes a little fish. He spent some time working in the olive press, then went out for another walk after supper, then came back and went to bed.

He met Bishoy on the olive farm every day without them saying much—just a few words about this or that olive tree, land that needed turning over or leveling, weeds that needed to be removed, fertilizer that was about to arrive and that would need to be spread on the ground, windscreens to be set up, or lubrication for the olive press. Bishoy was the right arm of the prior, who devoted himself to worship and left Bishoy to look after the monastery's practical affairs. Bishoy was active and energetic: he flitted around the monastery so fast he seemed to be in more than one place at the same time. He looked after the farming, helped the monks in their cleaning work, took part in the religious rites, looked after the visitors who came to the monastery for one reason or another, and negotiated the sale of the harvests. He ran the library and sent for new books he'd hear about from mysterious sources. He would sit down to listen to a lesson from the prior, take part in complex theological discussions, or stand in the kitchen helping to prepare the simple food that the monks had for supper. He did a hundred things at a time, as if he were trying to distract himself by keeping busy. Abu Omar watched him from a distance without speaking. He saw him and thought to himself: "An aerospace engineer wastes the prime years of his life painting houses for French people and then drowns in an African lake. A promising lawyer tries to escape from himself by running around in circles on an olive farm. But where's the man who sent them all to their ruin? What's he doing now, I wonder? Does he see these young men and hold himself responsible, or is he happy with the emptiness he's creating around him?" He had learned in physics class that nature abhors a vacuum and that matter will fill an empty space as soon as it appears. This killer must be made of some substance that defies nature, a substance that generates emptiness. The man was sitting there in his hideaway and this substance poured out of him, devouring everything and leaving behind it only death and emptiness. Like a black hole that is gradually devouring the universe. His mind wandered and he thought how he had escaped this killer, had transformed himself into someone who resembled his killer superficially, and had now come back to take him on.

Abu Omar followed the monastery's strict regimen for three months, and then decided that it was time he started work. He told Bishoy that he planned to leave. Bishoy nodded sympathetically as if he had expected the decision. The same day, while Abu Omar was working among the olive trees, he saw Hind talking with Bishoy. He looked at her in amazement, at once happy and worried to see her. Happy that she was back because deep down he missed her as much as a body misses a hand that has been amputated, though he tried to drive her out of his thoughts all the time. And worried because, if she had found him, that meant others could. She recognized him instantly despite his changed appearance. She looked away and went on talking to Bishoy. He continued to work robotically among the olive trees, thinking what he should do. While he was deep in thought, he suddenly found her standing before him. He looked around and couldn't see anyone else.

"What are you doing here?" she asked.

"What are *you* doing here? This is a monastery, for monks."

"As if you're a monk! Last time I saw you, weren't you with the other guys? Did September 11 make you tattoo a cross on your wrist and turn Christian? Another farm with religious people! Is there any chance you'll ever be normal, like other people?"

"Come on, now. What's up with you? Why are you always so sarcastic?"

"Ok, so it's my fault for coming to ask after you."

"Yes, but tell me, what do you say when you ask after me? 'Has anyone seen the Eagle of the Taliban?' I mean, how did you find me?"

"Calm down, my pious friend, and bless the Prophet. I'm here to write a news story."

"Still with the Czech News Agency?"

"That's right. Look, it's a long story. I came here by pure chance and suddenly I found you right in front of me. I swear, I haven't been following you and I didn't know if you were dead or alive. Listen, I'm living in Cairo, so when you come to Cairo, call me. Here's my phone number. I have to go before anyone sees me with you."

He left the monastery the same evening. He took a minibus going to Alexandria and from there he jumped on the 10:15 p.m. train to Cairo. The winter was bitterly cold. The Coptic month of Touba was handing the city over to the stormy month of Amsheer. He sat in the second-class carriage in thick clothes and a woolen hat. If he had been asked to describe himself, he would have said: "He wore thick winter clothes, thoughtful, a little sullen and undecided." That's what he was like at university, in the army, in the death pickups in Afghanistan, and in the mountains.

When he reached Bayn al-Sarayat, the neighborhood was asleep. The man who sold fava beans was gone, the kofta shop was closed, and even the café had shut its doors. But otherwise, it was just as he had left it nine years ago. The sight of the street after all those years did not bring him any sense of pain, nostalgia, joy, or anything else. He walked down this street that he knew like the back of his hand. The last time he had walked along it was the day the snipers shot his cousin in the belief that it was him. He went back to his house, without enthusiasm or sorrow. It was just a walk down a narrow street with potholes full of rainwater. His mind was working fast on what he was going to do next, how he would carry out the tasks he faced. First, he would go to his aunt's house and knock on the door until he woke her up. It would be a long night, and he would tell her and his cousin Leila, if she was still there, stories about the places he had been. In the morning, he would go out and meet some of the local people. After that, he would make a start on things.

And so it was.

He reached his aunt's building and went in through the old wooden door. The entrance was even further below street level than before. He went up the narrow stairway as panicked cats fled from his path. Abu Omar looked at them and thought these must be different cats from the ones that were there nine years ago. He reached the apartment and knocked gently on the door, until he heard a voice. A young man that Abu Omar didn't know opened the door, but the man recognized him, smiled, and shouted, "Oh my God! Uncle Fakhreddin's back, Mama!"

This was Leila's son Tamer, who had grown up and greatly changed during Fakhreddin's long absence. Leila came running. She was older and plumper, but the shape of her face hadn't changed much. She stood and looked at the new arrival for some seconds, then gasped, beat her chest with her fist, and shouted for her aunt to come. Then she took him in her arms, muttering unintelligibly. His aunt woke up in alarm—she was used to disasters coming through that door—and came into the sitting room. She recognized him as soon as she set eyes on him. "My son! My love!" she shouted. She hugged him tight for a long time, weeping silently. Fakhreddin was kind to his family, but calm and composed. Leila made him some tea and something to eat, while he sat and told his aunt, his cousin, her daughter, and her son, who was now a man in his mid-twenties, where he had been all those years. He told them he had gone from France to Libya, where the chances of life took him to work on a livestock farm, in building, farming, and fishing, which made it possible for him to send them the money he had been sending. He told them he'd been married and had a child, but his wife had died and he had left his son with the boy's grandmother while

215

he sorted out his affairs in Cairo. Then he would send for him. He told them other details of a story he had prepared in advance. Aunt Maria could see that the story was a fabrication, but she didn't want to know anything that he didn't want to divulge, convinced that he must have sound reasons. After hours of storytelling, she asked him what he planned to do, and he said he would stay with them, taking Eissa's old room on the roof if it was still available. She said it had been empty since Ali died, and they all asked God to have mercy on him and on Eissa. His aunt repeated the question and Fakhreddin understood what she meant, and he assured her he planned to look for a suitable job and keep out of trouble so that he could settle down and then send for Omar. Then he would live the rest of his days quietly among his family. She approved what he said but without great conviction, and just before dawn everyone went off to bed.

In the morning, Fakhreddin went out to buy beans for breakfast. He didn't find Amm Abdu, but instead there was a boy of about fifteen serving the lines of local women in black abayas and children holding plastic bowls in their outstretched hands. He bought some beans and went to buy a newspaper. Instead of Ibrahim al-Sayegh, he found a fat woman he'd never seen before. He went past Amm Sayed's barber's shop and found it had been converted into a women's hair salon. Inside he spotted two young men with fancy hairstyles, new chairs, and various decorative features. He went home with the beans and the newspaper and, as he went into the building, he noticed that Amm Suleiman's window on the ground floor was boarded up with a wooden plank. He asked his aunt about them and she said that Amm Abdu, Amm Ibrahim al-Sayegh, and Amm Suleiman had died of various diseases over the last few years. Amm Abdu's son was the one at the bean cart and it was Ibrahim al-Sayegh's last wife who had taken over the wooden stall, after a fight with the sons of his first wife. Amm Suleiman's apartment had been sealed shut by order of the court that was looking into the dispute between his heirs and the landlord of the apartment.

After breakfast, Fakhreddin went off to the government department that issued ID cards. He filled in the papers needed to obtain a national number, well aware of where this might lead. Then he went back to Bayn al-Sarayat and sat in a café. The old café owner recognized him and reminded him of days gone by. Fakhreddin replied curtly that that was the past and was gone. He asked the man if he knew of anyone who had a taxi for sale. The man asked in surprise why he was asking. When Fakhreddin told him he was looking for work, he was puzzled and asked about his work as a lawyer. Fakhreddin smiled wryly and reminded the café owner that he had been struck off the register of lawyers more than ten years ago and that he had spent recent years doing manual work in Libya and he was no longer fit or willing to be a lawyer. He told him a short version of the story he had told his aunt the day before. The man promised to ask his acquaintances, but added, "It's a shame, Mr. Fakhr. You were a brilliant lawyer." Fakhreddin nodded and said that fate was everything and the taxi might bring in more money than practicing law. Then he left the café and went for a walk. After so many years not many of the people who knew him were left—a few old people recognized him, after they had examined his face for some time. He went to buy a SIM card for a cell phone and did the rounds of the car shops, leaving his telephone number for anyone to contact him if they found a taxi for sale. Then he went home.

Tamer showed great interest in the mysterious uncle he had heard about for years. Aunt Maria would pray for him, Leila would ask Tamer to remind her of something she wanted to ask Fakhreddin for, through the intermediary who transferred money to them every few months, people had spoken of Fakhreddin's generosity and decency, Leila had urged Tamer to do his homework so that he would grow up and be like his uncle, and so on. All those years he had wondered who this uncle really was. Deep inside, he hoped Fakhreddin would come back and live with them, compensating for the absence of the father he had never known. But Fakhreddin hadn't come back. Tamer had lost hope, and then he'd found his uncle standing at the door. But he didn't know how to get through to his uncle, whom he didn't know. He wanted to sit with him and tell him about the hope, despair, anger, and love that seethed inside him. He wanted to cry and laugh and tell him everything. If he had overcome his inhibitions, he would have thrown himself into Fakhreddin's arms and asked him to adopt him, but he didn't do any of this. He couldn't. He had to respect the fact he hardly knew this newcomer, who must have a thousand other things to worry about. He had to make do with hovering around him, keeping close to him, and waiting till the channels of communication gradually opened up between them.

They spoke several times, as they sat in the café together. Tamer explained what he did: designing websites. Fakhreddin thought that rather odd. How could a young man be satisfied with such work? What was so attractive about it? Tamer spent most of his time in his room in front of a computer screen. He came out to eat, drink, or do whatever else he needed to do, but the rest of the time was spent in front of the screen. Even his telephone calls with the girl he seemed to be attached to took place on the computer. Fakhreddin didn't want to drag him into anything against his will, and certainly not into things that might do him harm and infect the next generation of the family with the disease of politics. He told himself that if Tamer wasn't disposed toward that, there was no justification for dragging him into it. Leila was watching the situation and was reassured by her cousin's approach in dealing with her son.

There was another aspect to this interaction that Fakhreddin didn't admit to himself. It wasn't just that he was anxious not to involve Tamer out of fear for his future, but also because, in his eyes, Tamer still symbolized a mistake, his mother's mistake when she falsely claimed he was her husband's son. It was her father, Selim, who forced her to marry that man, for the sake of a few acres, while she was pregnant with Tamer. Fakhreddin tried to help her marry the man she loved, incurring Selim's wrath. But Leila was too weak and chose the safety of her father's approval—and the land—over her love and honesty. He reminded Fakhreddin of the false symbol of honor that his uncle Selim had driven out because it mattered more to him than the true honor that Fakhreddin was trying to defend. Tamer didn't know anything about this. But Leila knew and Aunt Maria knew, and Fakhreddin hadn't forgotten. If he had agreed to let Leila and her son come and live with them years ago, it was out of pity for her, after her brother had grabbed the land and the flour mill and had made her life hell, and also because it was what Aunt Maria wanted. But he hadn't forgiven or forgotten the mistake.

It didn't take the police long to show up. A detective dropped in at the house and asked after Fakhreddin. Leila told him he was in the café. He found him there and told him he was wanted at the State Security office. Fakhreddin, pretending to be surprised and anxious, asked the reason. The detective said casually that all he knew was that he was wanted at eight o'clock that evening. Fakhreddin had dinner early, drank two cups of tea in readiness for a long night, and headed for Dokki, where the office was. He remembered the place well. He'd been taken there for questioning when he first took part in campus demonstrations. It was here that Colonel Samir had roughed him up for whole days and nights. Yahya Ibrahim, his friend and university classmate, had died there, and maybe it was where Ali had been killed too.

Unexpectedly, the meeting didn't last long. He arrived at exactly eight o'clock and, after waiting for only fifteen minutes, the policeman took him in to see the officer. The officer was a young man in his late twenties, slim and dressed in smart civilian clothes. He waved Fakhreddin to a seat and continued with his phone call, which seemed to be with his wife or mother. He asked about a child and its health, and what the doctor had said, and things of that kind. He ended the call in some embarrassment and turned to Fakhreddin.

"Glad to see you're safely home, sir. How did you get back?" he said.

"How do you mean 'how,' sir?"

"Are you going to play dumb?"

"Not at all, sir. I just don't understand the question."

"Come on, listen. I'm not in the mood for this. I have quite enough on my plate. So, are you going to talk straight?"

"I'll talk, sir."

"How did you get back into Egypt, and where were you coming from? There's no record of your entry from anywhere."

"Across the desert, sir."

"Is there a desert between us and France that I don't know about?"

"Sorry, sir. I meant across the desert from Libya. I left France about fifteen years ago, went to Libya, and settled down there. My passport expired and I stayed in Libya minding my own business, and then I came back from there across the desert."

"And your passport?"

"I have it."

"You realize that this is impersonation?"

"I'm clean. If you don't mind me saying, there's nothing to say I've been abroad in the first place. I have an identity card and I don't have a criminal record. I'm no troublemaker and I told you, sir, what happened in full."

"Okay, show me the passport."

"Okay, sir, but give me an assurance."

"Give me the passport and I won't do anything to you."

"Look, sir, I brought the passport with me to prove my good intentions. But if you don't mind, if this is going to be official then this is the passport of my cousin, who disappeared in 1992 and we don't know if he's alive or dead. There's nothing to prove this passport has anything to do with me. So if you press charges I will stick to my deposition: I was in Egypt all this time."

He took out the old passport and it had an exit stamp from France when he left and an entry stamp for Libya that was genuine and matched his story. The group knew that the security agencies cooperated closely with each other and if they were suspicious about him they would ask the Libyans to check their entry and exit records—where they would find a record of his entry on that date under the name of Eissa al-Naggar. The officer examined the passport carefully, then put it in his desk drawer. He asked him what he'd been doing in Libya and Fakhreddin replied with the story he'd prepared. The officer wasn't listening carefully, but looking at some papers in front of him while Fakhreddin spoke. Suddenly he interrupted him: "Okay, you've got plenty of stories. I don't understand why they were so interested in you."

"Nor do I, to be honest, sir."

"And what do you plan to do now? What's brought you back? Are you planning to play dirty again or will you come to your senses and be well-behaved?

"I gave up that stuff long ago. I tell you, sir, I was working on livestock farms and in construction and I left only when they fired me. Those old things of the past, their time is gone. I want to make a living."

"And how are you going to make a living?"

"A taxi, sir. But I need a taxi license."

"Don't tell me: you want State Security to buy you a taxi as well?"

"No, sir, sorry. I only want the license."

"I really don't understand why the officer who started this dossier on you in the old days was so interested in you. Listen,

I'll let you go, but I'll keep an eye on you while I check your story is true."

"It's true, on your honor, sir."

"My honor's none of your business. Do as I say and no bullshit. I'm going to check out what you said. But until that happens don't go anywhere. You won't get a taxi or an identity card or do a single thing. You'll just stay in your aunt's house, close to her and her daughter, until you hear from me."

"Okay, sir, and might all this go on for a long time?"

"Long time, short time, whatever. If you don't like it, find yourself another country to live in. You're clearly a smartass, crossing the border illegally. And you know what the penalty is for forging official documents?"

"I haven't forged anything, sir. You know I was a lawyer and I understand these things. If you don't mind me saying so, if we went to court, I'd be acquitted. I don't want any trouble. All I want to do is make a living and look after my family."

"Okay. So stay put, as I told you. And every week drop in to report all present and correct. Tell them at the door you're coming to see Captain Ayman. They'll let you right through. And keep doing that till I tell you you can stop. And be careful, don't go wandering off. I've got my eyes on you, understood?"

"Understood, sir."

The officer pressed a button nearby and a policeman appeared in a blue uniform like those of railway workers. Captain Ayman nodded to him and the policeman escorted him out of the building. The whole process didn't take more than forty minutes. He spent the rest of the evening arranging his new room on the roof and then came down to spend some time with his aunt and Leila. They discussed their financial circumstances, the state of the world, what had happened in Egypt in recent years, and news about distant family. Then he went up to the roof and fell asleep.

*

The next day he went around some local car dealers looking for a taxi for sale, went to the movies, and sat in a café for a while. He went for a walk through Dokki and as far as Tahrir Square, walked back to Bayn al-Sarayat, and spent some of the day with his aunt. At over seventy-five, Aunt Maria was in relatively good health, but she was beginning to show her age. Some days she couldn't move and some days she was well. He asked her what medication she was on and discovered that she was taking things that various doctors had prescribed for her in the past, but she couldn't remember what they were called, what they were for, or what the right dosage was. He spoke about it to Leila, who complained that Aunt Maria had an aversion to doctors and never followed their instructions. He asked what exactly his aunt's medical complaints were and she said it was mixture of high blood pressure, diabetes, and nerves. That didn't seem very precise. He asked his aunt about her health in passing and she said, "We thank the Lord." He asked her if she'd like to consult a doctor, but she wished him a long life and changed the subject to talk about Leila. She told him that Leila was more than forty years old and she hadn't had a husband since she was abandoned by the man her father had married her off to. Fakhreddin nodded without commenting. She asked him about Omar and urged him to go and fetch him as soon as possible, saying that Leila would look after him well. She said it was important that the boy grow up close to his father. He nodded in agreement and said that everything was in God's hands.

The next day he met Hind. He called her from a public telephone and they met at the zoo in Giza. They sat apart on a wooden bench as if they weren't together. He asked her how she had left Afghanistan and when and she said she had left at the start of the American bombing, and that the bombing had been intense and widespread, as if they wanted to raze the mountains of Afghanistan to the ground, and nowhere was safe any longer, not even the areas controlled by the Northern Alliance. She told him details of the assassination of Ahmed Shah Massoud and how the subsequent power struggles inside the Northern Alliance made matters more complicated. It was like being in a hospital full of madmen carrying deadly weapons and determined to wipe each other out. She told him how she got out with some aid organizations under the protection of US forces, and that even then their convoy was bombed by American planes. She stayed in Pakistan for a month and then decided to leave. First, she went to Dubai and worked as a stringer, then came to Egypt and settled in Heliopolis, where she had lived with her family in the past. He asked her what had become of the sheikh and Hamza, and she said no one knew anything for certain. She asked him about the timing of his departure and whether he had any prior knowledge of what was going to happen. He dismissed the question. He told her he had come back right after meeting her in Peshawar, that he was on his way between Sudan and Egypt when 9/11 took place, and that he heard about it only after arriving in Egypt. He said he intended to stay and avoid political activity, and she nodded without conviction. He spoke to her a little about his aunt Maria and Leila, and how they needed looking after. He told her for the first time that he had a son by his late wife whom he wanted to send for, because he had left him with acquaintances in Sudan for some time, and that he was looking for a taxi or a taxi permit so that he could work as a driver. Hind didn't believe a single word of all this.

"So you're not planning to tell me why you did what you did?"

"What did I do?"

"Why you killed all those people."

"Who did I kill?"

"I'm asking seriously."

"Why do you always insist that you're being serious?"

"Because you never take me seriously."

224

"And do you think there's a reason for that?"

"Oh come on, Fakhreddin, enough rudeness. Please, stop being rude to me. In Afghanistan, I put up with your rudeness and told myself we were in a conflict zone. But this isn't a conflict zone. We're at the zoo. There are animals and they smell bad too and it gets on my nerves, so please let's meet without them from now on. Look, I know you've done things. I saw you myself when you killed that guy on the motorbike. You hardly even had to aim at him, like they do in the movies. And I think you should be nice and share things with me and stop being rude. There are plenty of things I can help you with."

"You want to help me? To kill people as well?"

"Oh, Lord, I'm fed up with the people you send me. Why, God? What have I done to make you keep putting these annoying people in my path?"

"Who are you talking to?"

"To God."

"Really? Would you like me to leave you two alone so that you can talk at ease?"

"You really make me laugh, and that's why I put up with your rudeness. No. It's because I know you're a good person and this killing means something. But I want you to explain to me why you killed them. Or, look, you don't need to explain. Could you just bring me in on it?"

"Okay, I'll bring you in on it next time, but these days I'm on vacation."

"Whatever. In the end you'll bring me in with you. There's something ethereal about me and what I want comes true."

"Well I say we meet up in Abbasiya next time."

"Okay, okay, I'm off, but think it over."

"Okay, as soon as I have a killing opportunity, I'll call you."

He wasn't joking: he knew she could help him. If she had survived the Taliban, the Lebanese, and the Israelis, she must be highly talented. He needed help he could trust, and he trusted her. The question was whether he could bring her in on his plans without running any risks. He decided to test her on simple assignments first and see how things went. He asked her to investigate certain people: a retired teacher in Mansoura, a former prosecutor, a former head of the Bar Association, and some individuals he was looking for, though he knew only their names and where they grew up. He had the impression she was pleased with his request and saw it as her letter of appointment to the guild of killers.

While Fakhreddin was drifting around the streets and alleys of Cairo, waiting for Captain Ayman to make sure his story checked out, and meeting Hind from time to time in a café or park, talking surreptitiously and exchanging information, he was quietly reconnoitering the lie of the land and making plans. Based on information provided by Hind, he initiated some careful research of his own to locate his targets and find out about their movements. He asked her to prepare identity documents for herself under various names, and he started moving around himself. He went in secret to his village in the Nile delta, to Mansoura, Fayed, Ismailiya, Hurghada, and Kom Ombo, and he went through Cairo street by street with taxi drivers, discovering ins and outs and shortcuts known only to people who spend their lives driving around the streets, until they become a part of them. All the while, he never forgot to drop in on Captain Ayman, who would sometimes sit with him and sometimes send him on his way without much to say. After six weeks, the captain had good news for him:

"I'm going to leave you alone temporarily, but behave yourself and play nice. Go to the ID department in Abbasiya tomorrow and get your national number. Find the officer on duty there and tell him I sent you, and he'll sort things out for you."

"Thank you, sir."

"Always willing to help. But forget about going abroad. Don't even apply for a passport, and any funny business and I'll cut your throat. Stay here and make a living—you said that's what you want. If you think about sneaking over the border, I'll get you and no one would be able to save you. I'm making life easy for you, but you don't want to push your luck."

"That's okay, I don't want to go abroad, anyway. I'm tired of traveling, sir. Sorry to bring it up, but what about the taxi permit?"

"What about it?"

"Will you issue me one?"

"Come on, you must be joking. Issue you one? Do I work for you? Go and buy one."

"They cost ten thousand pounds, sir!"

"What's that got to do with me? Did someone tell you I'm the head of the traffic department?

"Sir, you're everything, and that way the government, if you don't mind me saying so, would be compensating me for the ordeal I've been through. You could see it as a charitable loan and I'd be willing to pay it back by giving your staff free rides in the taxi. You could call me a driver in State Security, sir. Any time you ask, I'd come and pick up anyone you want, the detectives I hope, and that way I'd be under your control and within your sight."

After some back and forth, the captain agreed to help and sent him to someone in the Giza traffic department, which issued him with a taxi license. The clerk who handed him the license said he must have pulled some very powerful strings because they'd stopped issuing new licenses years ago. He also got a new identity card with a national number. Then he bought a Fiat Regata with some of the savings from his work in "Libya." He installed a meter and started his new life in Bayn al-Sarayat as a taxi driver.

Aunt Maria watched him and waited. Hind watched and waited. The only person who saw nothing strange in this was Leila, who was constantly praising his aunt for Fakhreddin's morals and support for them, and comparing him with her brother Ahmed. Aunt Maria nodded and prayed she would make a good marriage and have more children. Leila laughed and asked how that could happen when she was more than forty years old and had a twenty-five-year-old son, who also wanted to get married. Aunt Maria said that God was capable of anything, and Leila said "Amen" and went off to do some housework.

Leila was certainly attracted to Fakhreddin, and Aunt Maria could see that and understood it. In Aunt Maria's view, love could grow out of another emotion, such as the affection created by kinship, and it could come about when we admire someone and what they do, so we see them in a new light and fall in love with them. Maria said to herself that circumstances had changed and nothing could be more sensible or more beautiful than Leila and Fakhreddin getting married. They would complement each other: she would bring up his motherless son and he would help her troubled son. She could lavish on him all the emotions that hadn't found an outlet, and he could look after her and be the man in her life. But the idea didn't seem to occur to Fakhreddin and she didn't want to talk to him about it. She wanted him to observe Leila by himself and see that he wanted her. She tried to make him look at her, and to plant the idea in his head, but he didn't pick up the hints. She knew that Leila was thinking this over, and Leila knew that Aunt Maria was thinking it over, but they never spoke about it. When the conversation moved in that direction they looked at each other and sighed, both thinking: "How little insight men have!"

After a few months, the people of Bayn al-Sarayat had grown accustomed to his quiet presence among them and to his new role as a taxi driver. At first some of the people who remembered his previous career sought him out and asked for his help in legal matters, but he told them firmly that he no longer remembered anything of the law or legal practice and he was worried he might tell them something that would harm their interests, and they would go away when they heard about this possibility. Some people came to him seeking lessons for their children and he turned them away in the same manner, reminding them that he wasn't a teacher and couldn't teach without a permit as it might cause him problems. To anyone willing to listen, he repeatedly said that he didn't want any trouble. But he did agree to help their landlady's two grandchildren with their homework as a favor to her, as a big brother and not as a teacher. They were a boy and a girl a year younger; both were in middle school and their mother had died in childbirth. Their father had married again and left the children with their grandmother. The children came up to Aunt Maria's house at eight o'clock in the evening, did their homework with Fakhreddin until half past nine, and then went back home. Fakhreddin liked this time more than any other part of the day: he detached himself from the world he knew and went back to being a child. With them he reviewed geography, history, science, Arabic, and other subjects. Although he was inwardly contemptuous of the narrow-mindedness of the school curriculum they followed, it made him nostalgic for a past that had completely disappeared.

He gave Hind his cell phone number so that she could call him when she needed a ride, and he asked her to give the number to her journalist colleagues who might want a driver who knew his way around and could spare them the trouble of looking for a taxi. Captain Ayman would also send him off with detectives if they needed to go somewhere and there weren't enough station cars to take them. Sometimes Ayman would send him to pick up and drop off members of his family. Then the detectives started calling him directly and he would voluntarily give them and their families rides for free. Captain Ayman's family always paid something, but much less than the usual fare. Fakhreddin was the ideal driver. He was always on time, he was polite and silent, and he knew the routes. He drove sensibly and was never reckless. He was trusted to look after people young and old, and he never objected to the fares he was offered. He gradually became the favorite driver for Captain Ayman's family and their friends, the families of his friends, the detectives, and others from the station, as well as journalists and foreign correspondents. And it's amazing how much information people share in taxis.

He started meeting Hind often but they didn't resume the intimate relationship they had had in Afghanistan. He couldn't explain that, but neither of them showed any desire to revive that aspect of their relationship. It seemed to belong to two other people or another life. But he liked her company because she knew him well and because she had seen the worst things he had done, without it affecting her liking for him. They understood each other and got on well, despite her strange philosophy on life and her occasional aggressiveness. He trusted her, although she was obviously crazy and despite the mysterious way she came and went.

He often drove her around, so much so that he was almost her personal driver. In the taxi, she'd tell him the news that had come her way, which would be plenty. Fakhreddin only had to give her three rides a week to know all the rumors circulating in Cairo that week, and he didn't need to read the newspapers. He did read them though, voraciously. He had started doing that in the weeks he spent waiting for the taxi license from Captain Ayman. He read whatever newspapers came his way, and he also went to the archives of some newspapers and to public libraries and read old newspapers. He wanted to know what had happened in Egypt in the years when he was abroad—not just the news, but the things people were talking about and the things that preoccupied them. He read the death notices and the society news and tried to find out who had been appointed to which jobs, who was related to whom, and who had married whom. In his mind, he built up a picture of society since he had left it, and little by little, from all the sources from which he gleaned his information, he formed a pretty good idea of what had happened in Egypt, and what was happening now. He began to move on toward the next stage in his work.

He thought hard about how to start work. Should he start with the people who most deserved to be the targets of his revenge, or with less important people so that he could practice operating in this new environment? Although he longed to start with those who most deserved to face justice, he decided to be cautious and start with people who were less important and less complicated as targets. He made up his mind, then set to work.

He went to his home village in the Nile delta and in the dead of night sneaked into the building where his now-disabled uncle lived. He climbed the staircase toward the upper floor in silence. He stood on the stairs and pricked up his ears. He could hear noises from the lower floor, where his cousin Ahmed, his wife, and his sons lived. He wondered which of the sons would follow in Ahmed's footsteps and eliminate the other brothers. He lurked between the two floors waiting for the house to settle down. Next to him, there was a window that led to a storeroom and a dovecote and he could sneak in there if anyone came. He stayed like that for about an hour until the building was completely still. He went up to the front door of the apartment and put some drops of oil on the old iron hinge, then opened it quietly. He went in and closed the door behind him. He slid the small bolt across and stood inside his uncle's room. His uncle was asleep in bed, breathing audibly. He stood at the end of the room until his eyes had adjusted to the dark, then he went up to his uncle's bed and stood over him, watching him. He was shocked at how frail his body was, and how thin his face was. The man lying there resembled his uncle in the same way as his ghost or a picture of him after his death would have resembled him. What a difference there was between this bag of bones and his tyrannical uncle, whose household trembled at the sound of his key in the front door. His uncle opened his eyes and then shut them again without seeing him. Fakhreddin shook him a little until he woke up and looked at him.

"It's Fakhreddin," he said.

"Fakhreddin who?"

"Fakhreddin Eissa, Uncle Selim."

"Fakhr? You're back?"

Fakhreddin murmured in confirmation.

"Where have you been, my boy?"

"I was abroad."

"Welcome back."

"So, where's your mother?" asked Selim after a pause.

"My mother? She passed away ages ago."

"Really? May God have mercy on her. And where's your father?"

Fakhreddin took a deep breath and looked at his uncle. "Enough of this nonsense," he said.

"Nonsense? Who's saying it's nonsense? Is there anyone with you?"

"My father? My mother? Have you forgotten where they are? Have you forgotten what you did?"

"Me? What did I do? Did I do something?"

Fakhreddin took another deep breath. He hadn't expected this.

"Okay, let me remind you. Don't you remember why I left the village? Don't you remember where your daughter Leila is? And Ahmed, your son?"

"Ahmed's downstairs, if he's back from the mill, that is. Why are you asking all these questions?"

"And why did I leave the village, uncle?"

"Didn't … didn't you want to go and study in Cairo? Come on, my boy, do I need to remind you? Didn't you say you wanted to go and study at university, away from the filthy peasants?"

"I said that? So who tried to force me to marry Leila, while she is pregnant with someone else's child, just to keep the land in the family? Who robbed me of my own inheritance? And who threatened me when I objected? Who shot me in the leg, when I was 17, and said, 'This time in your leg and next time in your head if you don't leave this village immediately?'"

"Someone shot you? In the village here? Why didn't you tell me?"

"Because it was you who shot me, uncle."

"Me? I shot you? What are you talking about? Have you gone crazy, boy? Me? Shoot you? No way. Something's up with your memory."

They went on talking in this vein for about an hour. At first, Fakhreddin suspected that his uncle was being evasive and pretending to have forgotten, but the deeper into the conversation they went and the more alert his uncle became, the more he was certain that the man had forgotten most things and was confused about those he still remembered. He spoke about his wife as if she were still alive and he asked Fakhreddin to call her so that he could ask her something; he denied he had a daughter called Leila. In the end, Fakhreddin sighed in despair. He told his uncle to ask God for forgiveness when he met Him. When his uncle looked at him in puzzlement, Fakhreddin put one hand over his mouth, grabbed his thin arms with his other hand, and held on to the man, who gradually lost strength until his breathing ceased. He left him a stiff corpse with a look of surprise on his face. He checked his pulse, then left the room, the house, and the village as he had entered.

Fakhreddin had to wait a long time on the highway before a pickup truck stopped for him. He greeted the driver, jumped onto the cargo bed, and wrapped himself in an old blanket he found there. Two hours later, he jumped off at the entrance to Mansoura. He had breakfast in a small restaurant in the station square and had a cup of tea in the café on al-Sikka al-Gadida Street. He was surprised how small everything looked with time. He bought the newspapers on the corner of the street and had a glass of sugarcane juice, though it wasn't in season, then went to Thanawiya Street. He stopped a while outside his old secondary school and remembered how he had suffered there, then he moved on. He went toward the home of Mahmoud Hafiz, the former principal of the school. From his inquiries over the previous months, he had learned that the principal's son had married and was living in his father's house, and the father had had to move to a small apartment near the new automated abattoir, where he had been living alone since the death of his wife. He sat in a small café close to the house and began watching the place. He had lunch and by three o'clock the street was completely quiet. He went into the building quietly and rang the doorbell on the ground floor. No one came to open it. He rang the doorbell again and a third time until a shadow appeared behind the door. The window in the door opened, behind iron bars, and the face of Mahmoud Hafiz, or what was left of him, appeared.

"Yes, who is it?" he said.

"Yes, Mr. Hafiz. I'm one of your old students."

"My students? Who?"

"My name's Fakhreddin Eissa."

There was silence as the man thought.

"Fakhreddin? Aren't you the guy in the scandal over the minister?"

"Yes, that's me."

"Is there anything I can do for you, my son?"

"I've come to settle my score with you."

"Settle your score? For what, for heaven's sake?"

"For your crimes, Mr. Hafiz. Open the door and don't be a coward."

"Really, come on now! How very impolite of you, as ever. It's true that a leopard never changes its spots."

"We'll change them, I hope."

Fakhreddin slipped his hand quickly inside to the door lock and opened it with a thin sharp instrument. He pushed the door, went in, shut the door behind him, and took hold of Mr. Hafiz.

"You have no idea how happy I am that you remember me. I've just finished off someone who couldn't remember anything," he said.

"What! You're crazy. Get out of here before I call the neighbors for help."

"There's no need for that, Mr. Hafiz. You're an educator and you know that violence serves no purpose. Calm down and behave yourself. I only want you to explain something to me. The misery you inflicted on us as kids, why did you take it so far? What had we done to you to make you steal our innocence in such a cruel way?"

"What do you mean? Innocence? Steal? You're mad. Come on, get out."

The man was about to scream, so Fakhreddin gagged him with a piece of cloth and forced him over to a chair close to a small table. He sat him down and tied his hands behind the back of the chair. Fakhreddin kept asking him questions but the thin nervous man just foamed with rage into the gag. Whenever Fakhreddin started loosening the gag to give him a chance to speak, the man started screaming, so Fakhreddin had to tighten it up again. After about an hour, Fakhreddin told the man he'd missed his chance to defend himself. He took a small vial and a syringe out of his pocket. He broke the neck of the vial, drew the poisonous liquid into the syringe, and then injected it into the man, who was trying to wriggle out of his bonds, free himself from the chair, and get the gag off. He plunged the syringe into the man's arm, injected all the contents quickly, and stood up holding the man's arm. He watched his eyes bulge and his body start to convulse until it went limp. Fakhreddin tested the man's pulse, then untied his bonds and his gag. He left him slumped dead in his seat, made sure he had both the remains of the broken vial and the syringe, and left the apartment.

It was a little after four o'clock in the afternoon. If he hurried, he could catch the fast train at half past four. That's what he did. He reached Cairo at seven o'clock, picked up his taxi where he had left it in Tawfiqiya Street, and was back in Bayn al-Sarayat by eight, when it was time for him to help the kids with their homework. He found them sitting at the table at his aunt's. He stroked the little girl's head as he asked her how school was going. He washed his hands and face quickly, listening to her incomplete sentences and encouraging her to complete them. Then he asked Leila for a cup of tea. He sat down, gave each child a piece of the chocolate he had bought at the train station, and started going over their homework.

Fakhreddin spent the next day driving his taxi. He started the day by taking a Swiss tourist to the airport. He had no idea how the man had found his telephone number. He asked him who had given him the number and the man said, "Anne, your American friend." Fakhreddin didn't have an American friend or know anyone by the name of Anne. But he nodded politely. The tourist paid him generously, then asked him if he would like his cell phone SIM card, since he was leaving Egypt for good and wouldn't need it. Fakhreddin thanked him, and took the SIM card and the number. He went straight to one of the phone company's branches and asked if he could make some changes to the account. But he was told that the account was in the name of a foreigner and they couldn't make any changes in the absence of the account holder. He said he was the man's driver, that the man was Swiss, and that they could check the information. The assistant checked the information and said it was correct, but the man still had to come in person. Fakhreddin went out smiling to himself because he now had a cell phone number registered in the name of a Swiss man. After that he started collecting the SIM cards of travelers and switching between them so that he couldn't be traced.

Fakhreddin was no longer in touch with his old group, which had started trickling back to Sudan. But he had told Abdullah, his old guard, where he was and left him the Swiss man's cell number for emergencies. He learned from Abdullah that Hamza was still alive: he had escaped from Afghanistan and gone to Yemen, and he might go back to Sudan soon. He couldn't find out what exactly had happened to the sheikh, who had left him a large sum of money across various accounts that the investment group used and had asked him to use some of these accounts only when necessary. Fakhreddin wanted to tell the sheikh that he didn't need these additional amounts, but the codes he and Abdullah used when speaking meant he didn't understand clearly where the sheikh had gone or whether Abdullah was even in contact with him. So he decided to leave the money in the accounts until the storm died down and the sheikh or a deputy turned up.

"So I'm not going to work?" asked Hind.

He went on driving, apparently indifferent.

"I let you go to Mansoura by yourself," she continued. "You told me my presence would arouse suspicions and I accepted. But I'm fed up with waiting."

The next day Hind and Fakhreddin went to Aswan. He told one of his detective friends he was taking some tourists in his taxi, so that Captain Ayman wouldn't "worry" about him. They took two rooms in a big hotel, one in his name and the other in the name of Aurora Sanchez. When the receptionist looked at him suspiciously, Fakhreddin smiled and said

he was the Spanish tourist's driver. He asked the receptionist where they could hire a car. He pointed to the car hire
office, then leaned over toward him and warned him not to
create a scandal. Fakhreddin told him not to worry because
he would only be driving her. Aurora hired a car, handed the
keys to Fakhreddin, and began her sightseeing tour. They
spent the first two days visiting the sights in the town, and on
the third day they headed to Kom Ombo, where he left her
to look at the reliefs in the pharaonic temple while he went to
have lunch. He bought a bag of gum arabic seeds, which the
local people believe can cure diseases. He then drove to visit
Ahmed, his company commander when he was in the army.
He found him sitting outside his house in the sun. Ahmed
recognized him, welcomed him, and asked him how he was.
Fakhreddin asked him for a glass of water, so Ahmed got up
and went inside. Fakhreddin went in after him, swung his left
arm around his neck, and with his right hand started to stuff
the officer's mouth with the bag of seeds until it was full. He
held the man firmly, blocking his mouth and nose, and listened to him croaking his last breaths until his body stopped
moving. He left him lying on the ground. He took the bag out
of Ahmed's mouth and emptied the contents down the toilet.
He checked that Ahmed no longer had a pulse and then left.

Qutta, the sexual predator, lived a few miles away.
Fakhreddin had met him during his brief—and painful—military detention. What set Qutta a part was that his abuse was
not deliberate or purposeful; it was almost like a habit. A habit
used and encouraged by those who were in charge of the detention room. Qutta was asleep when Fakhreddin came into his
room and he slammed the door behind him to wake him up.
He yanked the cover off him and kneeled on top of him. Qutta
opened his eyes to find that Fakhreddin's steel fist had landed
on his temples. It also forced the man's mouth open. His tongue
lolled out of his mouth and his eyes bulged in horror. In a single sweep, Fakhreddin's knife cut off the man's lolling tongue.

He turned and grabbed the man's penis at the base and before Qutta had time to understand what was happening Fakhreddin cut if off with the knife and stuffed it into the man's mouth. Fakhreddin jumped off Qutta, shut the door of the room from the outside with the bolt, and left the building. He could hear Qutta's hysterical screams echoing behind him but within minutes he was out of the whole village area.

Aurora asked the hotel receptionist the best way to get to Hurghada and asked him to book her and the driver two rooms in a certain hotel there that she had heard about from a friend. She spent the rest of the day relaxing around the pool. On the morning of the next day, Fakhreddin drove toward Hurghada, which they reached in about six hours. They stayed in the hotel where they had rooms booked. Aurora spent the rest of the day relaxing around the pool and in the evening her driver took her on a tour of the town. In the morning he took her on a final tour, then she packed her bags, sent them to the car with the bellboy, and went down to the lobby to wait for Fakhreddin. Fakhreddin carried his own suitcase out of his room. In the corridor he spotted the soldier who had been in charge of the detention center in their unit, who was now working in the team that cleaned the hotel rooms. He rushed up to him and greeted him. The man returned the greeting but then took a close look at Fakhreddin's face.

"Don't you remember me?" Fakhreddin asked.

"I'm trying to place you."

"I'm Fakhreddin Eissa, from the operations branch."

"The operations branch?"

"Yes. The operations branch. The command. The prison. Have you forgotten?"

The former commandant stammered and his face changed color.

"Oh, that was a long time ago."

The commandant paused in embarrassment.

"What? Are you embarrassed?"

"Not at all. That was the army. As you know, when you're in the army, it's not the same as civilian life."

"Of course, but I have something for you from our army days."

Bewildered, the man shook his head and Fakhreddin pre-empted him with a punch to the throat right under the chin. He left him lying on the floor and went down to the lobby. He apologized to the parking valet for leaving his car in the no-parking zone and explained by gesturing toward the Spanish tourist he was with. Then they drove off.

As he handled the bends in the Red Sea coastal road, Fakhreddin shook his head in disapproval when another car cut him off or a slow-moving truck blocked the traffic. He looked at his watch anxiously. He put his foot down on the accelerator, raising protests from Hind.

"You're going to kill us!" she said.

"Don't worry. Our lives are in the hands of God."

He didn't want to be late that evening. He had promised to review the children's work with them before their exams the following day. Their grades in the previous exam hadn't been good, so he wanted to go over their work and make sure they had learned it all properly this time.

As one operation followed another, the working relationship between Fakhreddin and Hind became stronger and she gradually took on a larger role. She began to make bookings, arrange transport, forge documents, and do other such things that she liked doing. As she became more engrossed in the work, she took to it with enthusiasm and complained much less. The cooperation between the two became more system-atical and more harmonious. After the Hurghada operation, he told her he was going to move on to a more complicated phase, and she welcomed that.

He spent two weeks working in the downtown Cairo area monitoring the main office of the newspaper edited by Sayyed

Aboul-Kheir, a university friend who had betrayed the whole group to the security agencies. Since then his political, and actual, weight had grown and he was now the official mouthpiece of the security agencies in the media world or, as his rivals called him, the "pit bull." Hind volunteered to gather information about him and, after two weeks of careful monitoring, they had a good enough idea about his movements. People don't notice how predictable their routines are. They go to the same places by the same routes. They order the same food and mix with the same people, almost at the same time each day. Sayyed Aboul-Kheir moved around in a black car that never changed, with a small police car for protection since he had received death threats in the past, or so he claimed. Hind rented a small apartment in a building with a view of the newspaper offices, using the name Huda Barakat, a Tunisian worker at a foreign bank in the city center whose husband visited her from time to time and then went back to his business in Tunis. Fakhreddin holed up in the apartment to monitor the movements of Sayyed Aboul-Kheir and his bodyguards. Two weeks later, he set up his rifle and waited. Huda paid the rent to the agent in the morning and told him she was going abroad for a week.

At noon, Fakhreddin was sitting at the window of his hiding place with his rifle aimed at the door of the building opposite. At two o'clock, the driver of the black car hurried out carrying his employer's briefcase, and the police car prepared to move. The door opened and out came Sayyed Aboul-Kheir with his bloated body and his dark sunglasses. The glasses were right in the middle of Fakhreddin's sniper scope when he pulled the trigger. Sayyed Aboul-Kheir collapsed to the ground and for some moments those around him didn't understand what had happened. Fakhreddin collected his equipment, picked up the small bag that contained the rest of his belongings, and left his hideout. Within minutes, he was driving his Regata through the streets of Cairo, far from the bustle of the city center.

All hell broke loose. Hind told him how angry the security agencies were that their man had been assassinated. She said they suspected there was a large organization behind the operation because it was so well executed and the perpetrators had left no traces. A few days later the newspapers were promoting the theory that some foreign party had carried out the operation. A few more days later Captain Ayman called in Fakhreddin and asked him about Sayyed Aboul-Kheir.

"Weren't you together at university?" he asked.

"Yes, we were, sir."

"So what do you know about him? Have you seen him recently?"

"I've seen him on television, sir."

"Hey, don't dodge my questions, or else, I swear, I'll have to give you the third degree."

"He's a famous and important person in this country. We were together in college but, if you don't mind me saying so, there were twelve thousand of us in just that one intake. So, multiply that by four, and there were forty-eight thousand people who were his classmates at college."

"And forty-eight thousand of them were organizing demonstrations with him, smartass? Forty-eight thousand of them were in dorms with him?"

"I swear, since the day I graduated, I've seen him only on television."

"Listen, now. If you hear anything and you don't tell me, your day won't end well. This business is no joke."

"Sir, I'm with your detectives all day long. But if I hear anything, I'll tell you."

Fakhreddin's phone rang while he was driving the taxi. He looked at the screen—Leila. He didn't answer the call. He didn't like to talk on the phone while driving. He had a passenger who was going to the airport. There was still about half an hour to go and he would call her back then. He dropped off the passenger at the airport, but someone else jumped in and asked Fakhreddin to take him to a hotel in Mohandiseen, and Fakhreddin agreed. He spent another hour on the road and then called Leila. She didn't answer. He went on working for another hour, then called Leila again and this time she answered. She was crying and he couldn't make out what she was saying, but he gathered that something had happened to Aunt Maria and they were now in the University Specialist Hospital. He put a yellow duster over the meter to show he wasn't taking passengers and set off for the hospital. It was midday and the traffic was heavy. He arrived another hour later. The guard refused to let the taxi into the hospital parking lot so he spent another ten minutes looking for a place to park. He went in and asked for emergency admissions and they showed him the way. It was a big hospital and it took him a while to find Leila. She was sitting on a blue plastic chair crying, with her hands over her face and a scarf over her head. Fakhreddin put a hand on her shoulder and asked her anxiously what had happened. Leila leaned on his chest sobbing and he patted her on the back until she started to speak, through her tears. He gathered from what she said that Aunt Maria had gone out to do some shopping and had lost consciousness on the way. Some young men picked her up in a car and drove around the neighborhood asking people until they found the house. When they arrived, there was no one at home so they knocked on the neighbor's door and the neighbor looked after Aunt Maria till Leila came home. Aunt Maria came around before Leila came home and she drank some water and a cup of tea. She seemed to have recovered. Leila and Aunt Maria then went upstairs. About an hour later, Aunt Maria started to have such violent convulsions that Leila thought she was going to die. She called her neighbor, who tried to calm Aunt Maria down, but the convulsions were recurring every few minutes and they seemed to be losing her.

The neighbor hurried to call a doctor who lived nearby. The doctor examined her, then called a friend of his at the specialist hospital, booked her a place in the intensive care unit, and called an ambulance, which came and took her.

Leila was telling the story and weeping at the same time and whenever she came to describe the convulsions she broke down in tears. They were sitting at reception in the emergency ward and there was constant movement around them—doctors hurrying from room to room, patients being moved on gurneys, relatives of the patients shouting or arguing with a nurse or a doctor.

"How is she now?"

"The doctor says she should stay in intensive care."

"Where's the doctor?"

"Her name's Shayma. She comes and goes in that office with the lights on."

Fakhreddin went to where Leila had pointed, but couldn't find anyone. The room had a plain metal desk with a tablecloth on it, a box of tissues, and some papers scattered around. In front of the desk there were two chairs and at the end of the room there was an examination couch and a small screen that hardly hid half of the couch. He sat on the chair and waited. After a while a male nurse came in and Fakhreddin asked him about the doctor. The nurse said she didn't work in emergency, but in neurology. Fakhreddin asked how he could find the doctor and the nurse said she would come in a while. Fakhreddin went out looking for her. He walked down the corridors of the department asking anyone in a white coat for Dr. Shayma. Everyone was busy, running from place to place, pushing one patient or reducing another to tears. A man and a woman in hijab were hugging and crying together and a girl of around sixteen was consoling them. There was a man carrying his young son and wandering from room to room looking for something. There were patients' relatives struggling to deal with paperwork, counters, and clerks. Suddenly, he saw a tall dark woman in a white coat, with her hair hanging loosely around her face, slightly pensive and leafing through a file as she walked. She bumped into someone and apologized and went back to the file. Fakhreddin asked a passing nurse for Dr. Shayma and the nurse pointed at the woman. He walked toward her. She looked up at him and stared for a moment. She realized that this wasn't appropriate, and looked awkwardly through her papers again, taking care not to look up. She could feel him approaching, but she didn't look up, as if she were hiding from him. He stopped in front of her and asked quietly, " Dr. Shayma?"

She looked up at him quizzically, as if she were surprised to find him there.

"Yes."

"I want to ask about my aunt Maria, the lady who came in two hours ago with a diabetic seizure. They told me you were in charge of the case."

"She's doing much better now. She'll stay in intensive care for a while and then we'll move her to our ward when her condition stabilizes."

"Which is your ward?"

She looked at him in puzzlement, then said slowly, "Our ward. The neurology department."

"Wasn't it a diabetic seizure?"

"Well, it started out as diabetes but it seems to have changed into a form of epilepsy."

"But she's never been epileptic."

"It could be metabolic epilepsy. That's what we'll try to check. That's why they called me. Hopefully she'll be fine. I know the condition looks shocking but, as I told your wife, it's not as bad as it looks."

"My wife? Oh, Leila, she's my cousin. So what's the next step?"

Shayma smiled. "Are you a doctor?" she asked.

"No."

"Then the next step for you is to go home. She'll stay in intensive care until she stabilizes and then we move her to the neurology department until we sort it out. You can come back in the morning."

"Could I spend the night here?"

"I don't know. I don't think there's any point in you wasting your time here, because no one's allowed in the intensive care unit."

"I don't have anything else to do. I'll wait in the waiting room. But could you tell them to let me know of any developments if something happens?"

"Okay, sir. I'll tell the doctor on duty in intensive care to let you know if there's anything."

Fakhreddin thanked her and left. She followed him with her eyes until he disappeared at the end of the corridor. Then she went back to her papers again. Fakhreddin explained the situation to Leila and asked her to go home. She refused at first, then she gave way under pressure. He went to the waiting room, took a seat, and waited. About an hour later a nurse came and asked him if he was Mr. Fakhreddin, and he said yes. He said that Dr. Shayma wanted to tell him that his mother was well and he could see her as long as he didn't make any noise, and he promised he wouldn't. He followed the nurse to the door of the intensive care unit, where the nurse gave him a surgical cap, latex gloves, slippers, and a coat, and then took him into the room. It was a large room with five or six beds with patients who were unconscious and hooked up with wires and tubes in all directions. It was silent except for the monotonous droning of the medical equipment, the air conditioning, and the air purifier. Two young male nurses were working in silence on some of the patients. They were setting things up, taking samples, or changing dressings. Fakhreddin followed the nurse to Aunt Maria's bed. He didn't recognize her at first because she looked so thin and was hidden behind straps and blankets. She was asleep, or seemed to be. The nurse signed to him to sit down on the seat next to his aunt and to keep quiet. Then he whispered to him that he should press the button next to the bed if he wanted to leave.

He sat next to his aunt, looking at her sad face as she slept. He thought how strange it was when one's parents, or people who might as well be parents, fell ill. People tended to take the presence of their parents and their good health for granted, and however old they got and however much their health deteriorated they saw them as they were when they were young. The symptoms of old age seemed to be a temporary inconvenience, like a cold that came and would go. And if it didn't go it was just an irritant, just a decline in their faculties. When a parent became less mobile and less able to concentrate and grew frailer, they didn't see that as the prelude to their demise. Sometimes they thought about that possibility as an intellectual exercise but didn't feel that it might actually happen. Until they had an attack like this one and suddenly they were shocked to realize that they were going, if not this time then the next time. They'd weep bitterly and something mysterious would break inside, and then they suddenly grew older. It's as if the parent was giving up the space that had been set aside for them and then they saying, "Come, take our place, now you're the old ones, and we're going." Maybe it was this that alarmed people most: this wheel that never stopped. It took them higher, and then higher still, and then it took them away and pulled the younger generation into their place, and then they would follow them.

Dr. Shayma walked past the room, looked in at the man sitting by his, and then went off. Half an hour later, she came into the room and examined the patient's details and the paper ribbon coming out of the devices she was attached to. She nodded at Fakhreddin reassuringly and left. As he sat watching his aunt, his mind wandered back to memories of the old house in the village and his aunt when she was young—laughing, teasing, telling him off, preparing food, sullen, everything. How could this life that had nurtured us come to an end? How could we sit here helplessly and watch her fade away like this?

About another hour later the nurse came and beckoned Fakhreddin to follow him. Fakhreddin stood up and went out after him. The nurse told him that Dr. Shayma had given instructions that Aunt Maria be moved from the intensive care unit to the neurology ward and they were going to move her now. He asked if there was anything he should do, and the nurse told him to go and buy some medical supplies they didn't have in the hospital that night. He gave him a list of what was needed.

"And come back here?" Fakhreddin asked.

"No. Come to the neurology department."

"Where's that?"

"Follow the red line."

What was the red line? He went to his Regata and started looking for the medical supplies in the Cairo night. He found a drugstore in Merghani Street in Heliopolis but it didn't have what he wanted and they advised him to go somewhere else, then a third, and then he came to a small drugstore at the beginning of Qasr al-Aini Street that looked more like a grocery. But he found everything he needed there and went back to the hospital at about three o'clock in the morning. He asked for the neurology department and the guard told him lazily to follow the red line. Fakhreddin repeated his question about the red line, and the guard told him to take the first left and walk as far as the stairs, and on the stairs on the ground he would see lines of various colors and he should follow the red one till he reached the neurology department. He went to the stairs and did indeed find tiles of various colors stretching out toward the various parts of the hospital. He followed the red line until he came to the neurology department. Dawn was about to break. A nurse met him, asked him for the medical supplies, and took them from him. He visited Aunt Maria in her new room and checked up on her. The nurse asked him for some additional information and assured him that everything was under control. That did indeed seem to be the case. Fakhreddin went home to reassure Leila, with plans to go back to the hospital in the morning.

For a month and a half Fakhreddin headed to the hospital in the afternoon and stayed there till about midnight. Her condition was still unstable but the team at the hospital was monitoring her carefully and constantly. The hospital wasn't luxurious, but Fakhreddin was surprised at how efficient it was. Dr. Shayma ran the neurology department very competently. Tests were done on time, doctors came from other departments to do examinations, and everyone coordinated in prescribing medications and making sure patients received the right nutrition. Within days Aunt Maria was staying awake for longer periods but her blood sugar level was not responding to the treatment. She went through phases of complaining and giving up hope. She had to take so much medicine, the treatment seemed so futile, and she was embarrassed about the urine bags and the need to call the nurse to help her go to the bathroom. She complained that the food was boring and tasteless, that she was losing her strength, and that life was slipping through her fingers. But she and the nursing team soon made friends. She welcomed Fakhreddin every day with stories about them and their lives. Fakhreddin learned that they all had other jobs apart from their work in the hospital and some of them were studying on the side. He found out who was engaged to whom, who was sending money to his family in which town, and so on. Aunt Maria was especially full of praise for Dr. Shayma, her skill, her kindness, her beauty, and her concern for her. Aunt Maria was amazed by them all and their devotion to their work despite their meager salaries, and by their determination to look on the bright side of life despite the challenges they faced. Fakhreddin listened to her endless stories about these young people, but his mind was somewhere else: on his aunt recovering and going home, so that he could feel confident that her condition was stable and then he could get back to work.

Hind told him that the former prosecutor-general, who had covered up the attempt to assassinate him and the killing of his cousin Eissa, was ill and confined to his bed, so Fakhreddin decided to act before death saved the man from justice at his hands. One day he told Leila he would be late going to see Aunt Maria and asked her if she could stay till the evening. The man had left government service some time ago and was living in his apartment on Taha Hussein Street in Zamalek. Fakhreddin picked up a folder full of papers and went to the man's house at five o'clock in the afternoon, after the maid usually left and while the doorman was having his siesta. He went up to the third floor, opened the door quietly, and went in. The apartment was dark. It had grand old furniture, much of it covered in white sheets. He went into the bedroom and looked at the man's face: he was sound asleep. He half-opened the window, secured the two halves of the window together with the latch, and lowered the lace curtain. He shook the man gently until he woke up. When he saw a stranger right in front of him, he was agitated. In a mumble, as he rubbed the sleep out of his eyes, he asked Fakhreddin who he was.

"I'm Fakhreddin Eissa," he replied.

"Who? What are you doing here?"

"Don't you remember me? I'm the guy in the Bayn al-Sarayat case."

"I don't remember. But what are you doing here and how did you get in?"

"I've come to settle the score. I've come to balance the scales. Wasn't it you who colluded with the security people and closed down the investigation into the case? Didn't you, the prosecutor-general responsible for justice, conspire against me, deny me my rights, and betray the trust that you were expected to uphold."

"What?"

"I've brought you a copy of the case file if you'd like to look it over."

Sitting up in bed, the man mumbled incomprehensibly and put on his glasses. Fakhreddin thrust the file toward him but he didn't open it.

"But I stopped working years ago."

"So what? Is there a statute of limitations for your crimes?"

"But I don't understand what you want now."

"I want you to explain why you did what you did."

"Explain what? You wake me up to ask me about something that happened fifteen years ago?"

"I'm sorry to trouble you, but this is rather important as far as I'm concerned. I mean, since you've ruined my life. If it's not too much trouble, you'd better shake yourself awake before I put a bullet in your brain."

"God almighty. Just what do you want?"

"Tell me why you went along with these crimes."

"For God's sake, what's past is past. Do you expect me to remember? We dealt with thousands of cases."

"So were there many crimes that you covered up?"

"Hey, there's no need to say things like that. I'm old enough to be your father. And besides, every case has its own context. Are you still eighteen years old and you think the world's black and white?"

"Yes, in your case it has to be black and white. You were the key to justice. When it turns gray, the world turns black for everyone else."

"So what would you have wanted me to do?"

"You could have defended the truth. You could have been an honorable and decent person, or at least you could have resigned and not taken part in these crimes."

"One can admit to oneself that it's wrong. That's the least one can do."

"That's what you can tell God if you're lucky enough to meet Him. But in this world, there's no such thing as taking part in murder and saying your heart's not in it, though it's nice to know you actually have a conscience."

"What's the point of this now? Why have you come here? In just a few days I'll be saying goodbye to the world and everyone in it. What do you want me to do now? Apologize to you?"

"No, I'm not one for apologies. I've come to settle the score, as I told you. I just wanted to check that you didn't have some excuse for what you did."

"The truth is I don't. Call it human weakness, or that sometimes we lose touch with reality."

"And I'm the one who paid the price."

"I'm sorry."

"I reject your apology. This is not a personal debt, it's a public debt. You helped to destroy a whole generation, a whole society. You helped to undermine truth and justice, which you should have upheld."

"I know my apology won't do you any good. But what you're doing won't do you any good either."

"At least I'm balancing the scales."

"If you're planning to do that, then lots of people will have to die."

"Don't worry. With perseverance, hopefully, I'll get there. Do you have anything else to say?"

"Anything to say? You seem to think we're in court here. It's wrong what you're doing."

At this point, Fakhreddin took out a knife and plunged it straight into the man's chest. He twisted the knife a little to let the air get into the heart and accelerate death. The man shuddered and clung onto Fakhreddin's arm. Then his eyes gradually dimmed until he gave up the ghost. Fakhreddin waited a few minutes, and pulled the knife out of his chest. He wiped any traces of his hand off the man's fists and made sure he hadn't left anything on the bed. He picked up his file and the knife, covered the body, and left. He walked down Taha Hussein Street to his taxi, which he had left outside a café on July 26 Street. He got in, headed to the hospital, and arrived before seven o'clock in the evening. He thanked Leila, told her she could go, and took her place looking after his sick aunt.

Dr. Shayma gave Aunt Maria special attention. Her hours on duty gradually changed until she was always there in the afternoon. When Fakhreddin arrived in the afternoon he would ask the nurse how his aunt was, and the nurse would smile and reply that the doctor would come shortly. When Dr. Shayma arrived, she went straight to her office, changed into her work clothes, and went over department matters with the nurse. She would start her round of the patients with Aunt Maria. She'd go into the room, smile at her, and greet Fakhreddin, who would stand up and move aside. She'd consult the charts for the day and the test results, and take the pulse of the patient, who peppered her with questions and remarks that bore no relation to anything in particular. Shayma would smile and make small talk to distract her while she went on with the examination. Shayma would spend longer than usual examining her. The nurse noticed this and smiled to herself. Just before the end of the examination, Shayma suggested Fakhreddin leave the room. A few minutes later Shayma would come out and explain in detail how Aunt Maria's condition was progressing, the new tests she had requested, the changes she was going to make in the dosages of medicine Aunt Maria was taking, and what she aimed to achieve by this. He would ask her how long his aunt would have to stay and she replied with her estimates.

Shayma would talk to him at length and tried to stretch out the conversation as long as possible, encouraging him to ask questions. She gave him her cell phone number and asked him to call her if his aunt's condition deteriorated or if he noticed any shortcomings on the part of the nursing team. But he didn't call her. The nurses did their work well and she dropped in on Aunt Maria every day. Sometimes Shayma would bring up subjects that encroached onto his personal life, but were also relevant to Aunt Maria's health, such as whether there was anyone at home who could look after Aunt Maria after she was discharged, where they lived, what he did for a living, and whether he had the means to hire a nurse. But his answers were always terse. She asked him directly if it was true, as the nurses said, that he had been a lawyer and had studied in France before coming back and working as a taxi driver. He nodded, but nothing more. She understood that he didn't want to talk or be more friendly, so she stopped trying and would just explain Aunt Maria's medical situation, though she didn't stop scheduling her shift for the afternoon, when Farkhreddin would be there.

Tamer came two or three times a week and spent some time with Aunt Maria in the afternoon. Tamer and Fakhreddin spent hours together in the waiting room. Tamer saw his visits as an opportunity to be friendly with his uncle and get to know him better, but Fakhreddin was still reluctant to talk. He sat in silence most of the time watching the patients' relatives. One day, a patient's family would be cheerful: they would take the patient and go home. Another day, the mood would be distraught and many people would be crying, and then the relatives would finish off the paperwork, and pay their bill.

"Hospitals make you think about life differently," Tamer said.

Fakhreddin nodded but didn't say anything. Tamer didn't let his uncle's silence stop him. He spoke to him about his fiancée, and Fakhreddin asked him if he was really engaged, since he hadn't heard about this from Leila. Tamer smiled and said they were as good as engaged. Then he explained his relationship with his girlfriend and the questions they asked about themselves, their anxieties, the future, society, family, the nature of relationships, and the fate of love. Fakhreddin listened to all this and tried to appear really interested in what Tamer was saying, but deep inside he wasn't really listening. His gaze wandered and he thought to himself that nothing had changed.

At night, he'd slip into Aunt Maria's room and sit beside her, listening to her regular breathing. Sometimes she woke up and found him there and smiled at him or nodded, then went back to sleep, while he stayed seated. He went about his other business as necessary, but his heart wasn't in it. He no longer felt anything, neither when he was putting a bullet in someone's head, nor when he was giving his aunt her medicine. He asked himself if this was what it meant to be brutalized. Was it a return to human nature, which was instinctively savage? He looked at his aunt lying sick, between life and death, and wondered how it was that he no longer loved this woman, who came as close as possible to being a mother to him. He worried about her and was upset when her health was in danger, but it wasn't love. Aunt Maria had to survive: that was the natural order of things and he would be uneasy if this order was disturbed. But it wasn't love. Sometimes he grew weary of her negativity and constant complaints, and almost hated her for that. Then he felt he was being intolerably brutal and he tried harder to look after her. He changed the urine bags and carried them to the bathroom during the night, bathed her when she would be only half awake, but he did so without emotion.

Hind brought him plenty of information about the former president of the Bar Association who had plotted his disbarring long ago. He had left that office long ago to become a provincial governor and then a government minister. As a minister, he had been assigned a security detail more elaborate than ministers usually had, because of fears that his victims might seek revenge. Fakhreddin had also gathered lots

255

of information through his conversations with the detectives, the police officers, and their families. He knew where the man lived, who protected him and how, where he spent his winter and summer vacations, where he bought clothes, which school his only daughter went to, and other details that couldn't be concealed in a small community like that of Cairo's powerful people. Fakhreddin had a choice of three locations in which to carry out the operation: his office, his home in Cairo, or the coastal resort of Ain Sukhna, where he spent his days off. Killing him with a sniper rifle would be almost impossible in his place of work because the heavy security was bound to detect him. If he tried to assassinate him at home, his family might be there and they would see the dead body and the blood and so on, and that was something that Fakhreddin preferred to avoid. Fakhreddin chose the road to his beach house in Ain Sukhna as the place to act. He studied the site carefully and found a rocky hideout that overlooked the road, with another site nearby where Hind could watch the road and give him a signal that his vehicle was coming.

He spent four months preparing for the operation. He monitored the target's movements and routines, and his daily and weekly habits. He noticed that his security detail changed their routines so often that it was hard to find a pattern. But after tracking them a long time, he worked out the logic behind the changes in the routine. They followed a three-week schedule of changes, and at the end of this three-week schedule they followed the same schedule in reverse. He tested the accuracy of his theory and every time his predictions turned out to be right. Now that he understood the pattern, it was just a question of time.

He would kill him on the Friday of the third week of the cycle. On that day, the minister would leave home at nine o'clock in the morning and drive to Ain Sukhna without any family. He would leave at nine o'clock on that day, not at 8:15, 7:30 or any other time. The third Friday in the cycle was a nine a.m. day. He and his staff would take Salah Salem Road, then the Suez Road, and not the ring road. That was the route on the third Friday. Fakhreddin was right. Standing at his rocky hideout overlooking the Ain Sukhna road, he felt elated when the hands on his watch marked half past ten and he received a text message on his Swiss phone asking him to drop in on her within five minutes. That was the signal. Exactly five minutes later he saw the front of the minister's motorcade coming along the road. Fakhreddin had a good look at his car in the telescopic sight of his rifle. He took aim and pulled the trigger. The car turned over immediately. Fakhreddin looked again and aimed at the tank and the car blew up. Within seconds, Fakhreddin had abandoned his hideout. He didn't leave a trace, nothing that could point to him or to Hind. No fingerprint, nothing, not even an empty cartridge case.

He felt a deep sense of relief as he drove the Regata back toward home. He had almost settled all his scores. He drove silently, with Hind now sitting in the back. The road was narrow between the rocky hills and the seashore. It twisted sharply from time to time and then straightened out. The rays of the sun reflected off the surface of the deep blue sea, sometimes dazzling him. He turned the sun visor down and tried to concentrate on the road.

"Are we almost done?" asked Hind.

He looked at her quizzically in the mirror.

"Are we done, or are there many more?" she added.

"No, we're almost done. Only two left."

"Be careful. This last operation will cause an uproar."

"Definitely."

"They're going to be putting much more effort into looking for the people behind these operations. If they were on level one before, now they'll be on level ten."

"Definitely."

"Be careful. You're getting too close to the fire, and one mistake would finish you off."

"Definitely. But notice that there's no link between these operations. So far there are only three operations that have attracted attention—Sayyed Aboul-Kheir, the former prosecutor-general, and today's operation. And there's no thread between these people that leads to me. Besides, they're focusing on the Islamist groups. And there's nothing in my record about the Islamist groups. Plus, they think they have eyes on me all the time and I don't think anyone thinks I do anything of importance, other than driving."

"Not necessarily. Someone might have been watching you in Afghanistan or Sudan or in any of the danger zones you were involved in."

"Don't worry. Besides, you've forgotten the most important thing that prevents them suspecting me."

"What's that?"

"That they think they know everything and control everything, which prevents them from examining the foundations of their work and their assumptions. At the end of the day, they don't know anything and don't control anything. Everything happens right in front of their eyes but if they do discover anything it's mostly by chance or because other people make mistakes."

"And you never make mistakes?"

"I'm bound to make some, but there's not long left, and I hope I don't make any big mistake before I'm done."

"Okay, now can you explain to me why you're *really* killing these people?"

"Why are you killing them?"

"I'm having fun and helping you. But you?"

"You could see me as something like a sentence implementation committee."

"And, of course, you were the court too?"

"Hind, there's no need for you to be like that."

"We're killing people! We're a grim reaper committee, not a sentence enforcement committee."

"There's no need to joke. These are people who've been proved to be involved in unforgivable crimes. These are criminals by any known system of law. These are people who have hijacked the legal system, abused it, and deprived people of justice. I'm setting the balance right. I'm carrying out the sentences that should have been imposed on them if there was any justice."

"And when you carry out these sentences of yours, do you feel relieved?"

"Yes."

"Really? Do you feel relieved right now?"

"I feel like I'm doing what I have to do. I'm fulfilling a promise that I made to myself."

"What exactly was that? Like the Count of Monte Cristo? Anwar Wagdi in the film *The Prince of Vengeance*?"

"It's a question of settling scores, adjusting the balance, and that's enough joking."

"That's nonsense. What you're doing is worthless. Who else are you going to kill—General Samir himself? Of course, if he doesn't get to you first. And what use would that be? The same day you kill General Samir someone else will come and take his place that's no different from him. Instead of General Samir, you'll have General Munir. And then, nice Captain Ayman will get older and understand the game and become General Ayman, who's not so nice, and so on. Are you going to kill them all? And the truck driver who cut us off just now and almost killed us? And the driver who was driving on the wrong side of the road with his lights off, isn't he a threat to people's lives as well? Are you going to pursue them all to kill them? And the guy who gave them driving licenses, isn't he responsible? And those are only two parts of the Interior Ministry—the traffic police and State Security. And the rest? What do you think of the Ministry of Health, for example? You've got the food safety inspectorate, aren't they responsible for dozens of people dying? And the people in charge of

259

irrigation and the Nile and the canals and water pollution? So, Fakhreddin, am I the one who's joking or is it you?"

Fakhreddin drove on. They didn't speak again till they reached Cairo. He drove her to her house and then went straight home. The kids would come to do their homework at five o'clock. End-of-year exams were coming soon and Fakhreddin had agreed to spend more time with them. They turned up at exactly five o'clock and Fakhreddin reviewed their Arabic with them till nine o'clock.

Fakhreddin heard from the detectives that State Security was on high alert and vacations had been canceled. In his taxi he heard Captain Ayman's wife telling her mother that her husband came home very late at night most days and sometimes spent the night at the office. She said she was fed up with the situation. Her mother asked if she was sure he was telling the truth, and she said his colleagues' wives were saying the same thing about their husbands and there was an emergency because they were trying to catch the members of the organization that had killed the minister and other public figures that hadn't been announced. Her mother suggested she move in with her until the state of emergency ended, and she mumbled that she would ask Ayman and give her an answer.

The next day a plainclothes policeman passed by and told him to be ready to go out on a raid at ten o'clock that evening. The police had used Fakhreddin's taxi in the past to pick up wanted men when there wasn't a car available. Fakhreddin stopped outside the man's house at the appointed time, and called him. His wife sent him a cup of tea with her young daughter, who asked him to wait for her father to come down. A quarter of an hour later, he came down and told Fakhreddin to go the station on Subki Street. Another young policeman joined them there.

"Where are we going?" Fakhreddin asked.

"Kerdasa."

Fakhreddin's heart sank. He hadn't been there since he'd taken refuge in Hussein's house. He drove slowly. They went to a house in the main street and they asked him to stop. The street was deserted: all the shops had closed and the tourists were gone. Fakhreddin remembered the area well. One of the men got out, came back ten minutes later, and gave Fakhreddin new directions. They went into a narrow lane and stopped outside a small house. The policemen got out. A quarter of an hour later they came back with a woman wearing a niqab and a young girl. Fakhreddin's heart sank even farther. They put the two of them in the taxi and the elder policeman sat next to them while the younger one sat in the passenger seat in front. The woman was trembling and clutching the girl, and every now and then she would convulse and burst into sobs. The girl looked out of the window in silence. The policeman alternated between scolding her and assuring her that they would soon go back home. Fakhreddin drove them to the station fast. He watched them go in, and then called the young policeman over to ask who these people were.

"How would I know?" the man said. "We've been doing this every day for ten days now. I swear I never get a chance to go home."

"What's it all about?"

"It's a big operation and they're rounding people up. They're looking for the members of this new organization. And if someone isn't around, they'll turn up to look for their relatives."

"Okay. Do you want me for anything now?"

"No. Off you go before you get roped into one of the dawn raids. We're working around the clock."

Fakhreddin hadn't reckoned on this. He had made his preparations to strike his blows without them being able to catch him, and hadn't thought they would detain other people. This was their usual method and he knew it, so he should have taken that into account. He was going to harm many

261

innocent people and now he felt partially responsible for their ordeal. They didn't know where the attacks were coming from so they were striking out, in revenge and preemptively, in the places they knew: here, in Upper Egypt, and abroad. He felt uneasy, but decided to press on anyway.

Aunt Maria's health improved and stabilized in the fifth week, and at the start of the sixth week Dr. Shayma told them to get ready to take her home. She explained to Fakhreddin and Leila exactly how to look after her at home. Shayma did some final tests and then allowed Maria to be discharged, as long as she went back for tests once a week. They thanked the doctor and asked her to recommend a doctor close to Bayn al-Sarayat because they were worried that Maria might find it too much to go to the hospital and wait every week. Shayma gave them the name and telephone number of a colleague in Dokki. Fakhreddin completed the paperwork, while Leila gathered Maria's things together and they prepared to leave. Shayma said goodbye to Fakhreddin and left her hand in his a little longer than was necessary. She told him to get in touch with her if he changed his mind and wanted to bring his aunt in for a checkup. Fakhreddin thanked her sincerely and left to bring the taxi up to the main door.

As Fakhreddin drove, Hind started to take pictures of the shore. Then she left him at the Qaitbay Citadel in Alexandria and asked him to come back in two hours. He parked the car and walked toward Manshiya Square. Within minutes he was outside the building where Hisham al-Rasi lived—an officer who had retired in the wake of the war over Kuwait. He climbed the stairs to the third floor and rang the doorbell. The brigadier opened the door, and was surprised, but not that surprised. He left the door open and went back inside. Fakhreddin went in after him and shut the door.

"How are you, my boy?" the brigadier asked.

"You remember me?"

Hisham looked at him and gave half a sigh. "Remember you? Of course I remember you. Sit down. Would you like something to drink?"

"No, thanks."

"What have you been doing? In life, I mean? Are you happy? Have you done what you wanted to do?"

"No, thanks to you."

"Thanks to you too."

"Why, when I'm the person you sentenced to death?"

"Of course I sentenced you to death."

"Then how come you're not to blame?"

"You're just the same. You haven't changed. Well, that's good. At least it wasn't all a waste."

"Tell me how."

"What do you expect when you disobey orders during wartime? I opened several doors for you, but you seemed to want me to sentence you to death. I didn't have any other option. I implored you. I told you it was the hardest thing for me to do, but you were dead set on me sentencing you."

"So I was the one who was dead set on that? It wasn't your decision?"

"As I was saying, not just mine. You were complicit, just as much as I was. What could I do to avoid enforcing the law? Start a revolution in Hafr al-Batin? Have the unit secede and proclaim the Fakhreddin Republic?"

"So you remember my name as well?"

"I remember everything. That was the worst day in my life. That day I told you I agreed with you. Almost all of us agreed that it wasn't our war and that we were acting under duress. But you took the easy way—'I can do what I want and you deal with it. I can defy the world but you have to take responsibility for it.'"

"And you, when you went along with the commanders, although they were wrong, you were taking the hard way?"

"Yes, I took the hard way. Do you think it was easy for me to give my troops an order to execute their comrade? Just for your information, when the missile hit the base at the start of hostilities, I was delighted. It was the first time a commander has ever rejoiced when his unit is hit. I tore up the minutes of the court-martial and acted as if nothing had ever happened. If you go to the military records you won't find any trace of the story or else you'd now be listed as dead, or as wanted for arrest. I told them the records had been destroyed in the bombing. But I couldn't go back to the army. I couldn't go back to being an officer. So here I am. I left the army and came here and I run a tourism company, and I swear I should have called it Fakhreddin Corp."

"Why couldn't you go back to being an officer, for heaven's sake? You were just acting on orders."

"Why are we again discussing something we discussed seventeen years ago?"

"I wanted to give you a chance to defend yourself, just as you did to me at the time."

"I think you issued your verdict before you came!"

"And didn't you make up your mind before the court-martial? You gave me a choice between death in a war that I refused to take part in and death at your hands. At the time it was fate that saved me, not you. You're a murderer, brigadier, however much you may have regretted it later. And it was me who paid for your crime with my life, not you. Now I'm strong enough to stand up to you and the state that's behind you. At last the day has come when I can restore justice."

"What a shame, Fakhreddin. I'd hoped you'd come to terms with it but it's clear you ended up a victim of what happened. I've said what I have to say. Over to you, do what you came to do."

Fakhreddin raised his pistol, which was fitted with a silencer, and aimed it at the head of the retired brigadier.

Hisham looked at him and calmly recited the two Islamic professions of faith. Fakhreddin released the safety catch, put his finger to the trigger, and fired.

Leila was serious when she announced that she planned to set up a center in the neighborhood to help elderly people avoid what had happened to Aunt Maria. One morning, she told Fakhreddin she had discussed the idea with Tamer and Dr. Shayma and had come up with a practical and effective model for her project. Fakhreddin looked at her puzzled and she gave an elaborate explanation.

"What I'm going to do is compile a list of the local people who have diabetes, high blood pressure, or chronic diseases that need monitoring. And next to each name I'll make a note of the diet the doctor says they should follow and the medication they should take, and at regular intervals I'll check they're sticking to the program," she said.

"Wouldn't that require nurses and doctors?"

"I won't be ruling on anything medical. I won't be prescribing any medicine. I'll keep everyone's prescriptions, dietary instructions, and the schedules for tests, and I'll remind everyone of the dates and if anyone needs a push, I'll give them a push."

"And how will you remember all that? Aren't you worried you'll get confused? That's quite a responsibility."

"Tamer will make me an app where I can insert all the details and every day it reminds me what's needed that day. Dr. Shayma likes the idea and says she could drop by once a week to see how it's going and I could send her the cases that don't have a doctor."

"You'll probably all end up in jail."

"There's only one thing missing—buying and preparing the drugs for everyone. And that can be your task, my dear, so that you can come to jail with us too."

"Me?"

"Yes, when you get medicine for Aunt Maria at the beginning of every month, you could get the rest. I've made a deal with the drugstore and they'll give us a ten percent discount. But you'll be in control of the process, the receipts for the drugs and so on, because I'm not so good when it comes to finance."

"No, thanks, I don't have time for this charity work of yours. Have your son Tamer do it."

Leila carried out her plan, she gradually overcame the obstacles that any new idea faces, and things settled down. Leila didn't work so she found the project to be a useful activity on which she could spend her time. She also found helping the old people in the neighborhood to be an expression of loyalty and service to her aunt, as if they were all part of the same thing. These people were no longer able to look after themselves, and needed someone able-bodied and with a quick mind to help them. Tamer liked the project: he designed the app he had promised and he developed and improved it, week by week. Then he launched it and passed it on to his online friends in the hope that others might start similar projects. Shayma started visiting the neighborhood once a week, but Fakhreddin was always away when she came. Although he obviously wasn't enthusiastic about the project, as usual he did his duty—going at the start of every month to his favorite drugstore on Qasr al-Aini Street, where he had managed to negotiate an even bigger discount, and buying drugs for all the participants in Leila's project. He then spent the day putting the pills in little boxes that were color-coded for morning and evening, or for before meals or after.

Hind was right. Fakhreddin didn't find comfort in settling scores with the people who had betrayed him, sold him out, tried to kill him, or killed those he loved. When he killed one of them he felt a certain satisfaction. He felt he had done his duty and had regained his dignity, but the satisfaction didn't last. The same day, he would go for a drive through the streets of Cairo and face new situations that took him back to the way he had been. Then the policemen would call him and take him on a visit to fetch more victims and he shuddered at the thought that the victim might be someone he knew. Then he asked himself what the difference was between the people he knew and the unknown people he drove to their ruin.

He felt he needed a rest and time to think. He called his old friend Bishoy and asked if he could visit. He told one of his police friends with that he was going to Alexandria with a group of tourists for a few days, so that he would tell Captain Ayman if he asked, and then he left. Bishoy met him and put him up in his old room. Fakhreddin went back to the same routine. He kept himself busy with the monastery work as if he were running away from himself. Bishoy watched and finally asked him what was wrong and what was behind the deep anxiety that gnawed away at him all the time. Fakhreddin told him he was like a man who had been dreaming of something all his life and the closer he came to achieving it the less satisfied he felt. He looked at his friend and admitted that he no longer knew what to do with the rest of his life. Bishoy asked him how he couldn't know what to do when he was only a little over forty. He reminded him that the Prophet Mohamed's mission didn't start until after he had turned forty, so really Fakhreddin was just beginning his life, so why did he feel that he was done with it? They talked at length and Fakhreddin opened his heart to his friend without giving away any details of his activities. He asked Bishoy about the path to salvation and peace of mind. Bishoy explained how he had found his own peace serving the Lord through serving humanity, in meditation, in remembering God's smaller and greater blessings, in beauty, and in serenity. Bishoy said a lot, but halfway through his speech he noticed that Fakhreddin's mind had wandered. He smiled and urged him to have some rest, which might help to clear his mind.

Neither rest, meditation, nor staying in the monastery helped Fakhreddin. A week later he thanked Bishoy and went back to Cairo. No, he didn't regret anything he had done. He didn't regret the throats he had slit and the wounds he had inflicted. He had done what he had had to do. But after spending all those years preparing to get even with those who had done him harm and when he was about to settle his last score, he realized that he would then have nothing to do. He had one target left and after that he would leave the scene, but he did not yet know where he would go. Once he'd settled all his scores and restored justice, he would face the same problems as he'd faced when he was in his twenties. Nothing had changed and he didn't think he could change anything. That's what he had come to understand after all these years. Words wouldn't change things, and neither would bullets. The most that words could do was make our lives a little more beautiful and more humane. The most that bullets could do was protect someone weak on one occasion, carry out a sentence against a fugitive from justice, or settle an old score, but nothing more.

Only General Samir was left and he wasn't an easy target. After the general had succeeded in infiltrating and destroying various student groups and giving the security agencies complete control over university life, he had been promoted to other positions and had achieved stunning successes in them all. He became one of the top officials in the field of political security. He had made hundreds of enemies through his tireless work, and so he now surrounded himself with complex security. He was the general who had beaten him up in detention during the university demonstrations, who had recruited his peers and some of his friends, who had later pursued him, and who had himself led the assassination operation in which his cousin Eissa was murdered. It was he who had murdered Yahya Ibrahim and Ali. General Samir was his prime target and principal test of strength.

But he decided to postpone it until the security agencies were no longer on a state of high alert and stopped pursuing the unknown organization. He decided to leave them on high alert until it exhausted them, but as soon as they stood down, he would strike his blow.

He wondered, though, if that really was the reason for delay, or if he postponing it to avoid having to ask himself: what he would do once he had finished with Samir?

Over the following months, Fakhreddin settled into a routine that didn't vary much. He started the day washing and polishing the Regata, as thoroughly as someone polishing the lenses in his glasses, then he drove people around and observed the streets and the people in them. In the rearview mirror of the taxi, he watched faces and lips move, hands pointing or waving, and people coming and going. This lovesick girl looking at her cell phone every two minutes in the hope it would ring; that sullen mother dragging her querulous child along without listening to what he was saying: the thin man, who was close to sixty, holding a newspaper and faithful to his old frayed suit, putting on his glasses firmly and silently calculating how much the fare would be and how much money he would have left in his pocket. That tourist with disheveled hair and clothes, who was amused to see the chaos, pointing out yet another extraordinary sight to his girlfriend, who looked like him. That bearded man who pushed his wife, in her niqab, and a daughter, in her hijab, into the backseat of the taxi, put the bags next to them, and came to sit in front next to him. He stopped on the October flyover at the beginning of Tahrir Square, when the police held up the traffic for some VIP's motorcade to go past. The wait dragged on and the sun beat down on the windows of the stifling Regata, then the traffic started to move but stopped again because of the usual congestion, and the siren of a decrepit ambulance could be heard in the distance. He couldn't make out whether the sound was coming from behind or from in front. He thought for a moment about the injured person in the vehicle that was trapped and what he or she might be thinking about, if they were even thinking.

He drove the Regata around and around and would sometimes stop in the city center to have a rest, buy some sandwiches, and watch a traffic policeman circling around him, telling him it was a no-parking zone and preparing to be paid off to leave him alone. The policeman would snatch the pound Fakhreddin proffered and the expression on his face soon changed from satisfaction to embarrassment to impatience to slip the pound safely into his pocket. Then he'd turn away as though to pretend all this had never happened and to go back to being a traffic policeman. He watched the shop-keepers sitting waiting for good times, busy persecuting their workers, or trying to sell things to customers when they knew that the customers had as little intention of buying as they had the means to do so: the needy waiting for help from the needy.

He drove alongside people in important positions who sat in the backseats of cars pretending to read the newspaper through the constant shaking from the potholes and the stop-start traffic. They looked out of the window and tried not to see the people around them or how they were living. The driver, pretending he could hear and see only the road, wondered whether his boss was happy with his driving and whether it might be a good time to ask for an increase in his meager salary, whether he would manage to get home early, and what he would say to his mother, who wanted to go to the doctor, or to his fiancée, who was fed up with waiting, or to his wife, if he had a wife, who was fed up with him being out all the time.

He sat through heavy traffic and watched brash young men, who accelerated into the ten meters available and then slammed on the brakes, making their tires screech; who tried to squeeze an expensive car between a minibus and a big bus. These young men who looked in the mirror to check that their hair was still properly styled and that the stubble on their chin looked good, and not too untidy, and that the girl at their side was still at their side, or that the one who wasn't at their side had sent a text message, while they changed the music again and again.

Fakhreddin had a cup of tea in the little plant nursery next to the Nile and watched the young couples sitting on the Agouza riverbank and trying to focus on each other's eyes or hands, ignoring the hundreds of cars driving past behind them making enough noise and pollution to wipe out a whole population. The young man asking himself if this was really the girl he should marry or should he wait for the next girl, while she asked herself whether she should take things to the next level with him, or whether he would think ill of her if she did.

He drove the Regata around and at an intersection a man with a smile came up to him trying without success to sell him a few red roses, then offering them to the passengers in the backseat. They told him off, and he went on smiling to the next car, as if nothing had happened. He moved forward a little, the traffic was stopped again, and the traffic policemen shouted at each other about letting the traffic move or not and persuading an impatient driver to wait and not drive out of lane and block all the traffic, as they silently cursed the day that had brought them to this street and this intersection far from their families and from what mattered to them in life. He stopped, children raced to the car windows carrying fresh mint and limes, and the drivers closed their windows or edged forward a few inches to escape being pestered. A passenger scolded the children selling mint, and his son sitting next to him watched the scene and, maybe, thought to himself that his father was a hard-hearted man, but at the same time, the scene left an impression in his memory and he would behave exactly like him when he was a man.

He drove through the streets and watched an old woman looking for an even sidewalk to walk along from the door of her building to a nearby shop, and a disabled man sitting in his wheelchair, waiting for someone to volunteer to help him maneuver through the dangers that he faced. He caught sight of a young man who grabbed at the breasts of a passing girl and laughed, while she had tears in her eyes. He saw an old man driving a broken-down taxi next to him, leaving a trail of exhaust fumes that did many times more damage to the health of passers-by than could be justified by the money the driver earned from his livelihood. He saw a man standing at a bus stop that was hardly recognizable as a bus stop, and wondering whether he should run after the bus that had just gone by and whether he would find space on the bus.

He watched schoolchildren wandering aimlessly in the streets, troops of them coming out of the school gate, fleeing one hell to enter another that awaited them. He took one customer to the train station, and passed through a crowd of soldiers, either coming back or going somewhere unwillingly. He waited behind a car driven by a Christian priest and wondered whether the policeman had turned the stopped the traffic as he arrived by chance or as a form of discrimination. He was stopped by a fat woman after a minibus driver didn't want to stop for her, and she asked him how much he would charge to take her to Giza Square. Then she decided not to get in and pulled back to the side of the street to wait for another minibus. Fakhreddin pretended he hadn't heard the woman passenger in the back ask if he had any foreign clients and he didn't listen to the student with the big hair and iPod headphones in his ears when he asked where he could buy some weed. In his mirror, he watched two young women sitting behind him as one of them complained to the other, in French because she thought he wouldn't understand, about her absent father who wasn't interested in her, and she didn't know who she should talk to about her problem because her mother would get hysterical and lose it if she heard her story and wouldn't be any help. He drove on and thought that if he had a heart in his ribcage it would break. He thanked God that his heart had died long ago.

He suppressed his anger, then saved it up to vent it all on someone he thought deserved it—like a suicidal driver who cut in front of him. There were many drivers who seemed determined to ignore other people and other vehicles on the road. Someone might block the whole road to go to buy cigarettes, or drive the wrong way down a one-way street, refuse to go back, and instead, turn off his engine in an idiotic show of defiance. Or they might stop suddenly, having perhaps been reminded of something by someone in the car with them, causing the cars behind to drive into the back of them. One of them might stop on the bend of the access ramp to a flyover, where you couldn't see him until you crashed into him, or another might lurch out into the middle of the road, endangering anyone coming from behind or giving them a nervous breakdown. A hero such as this would be asking for the anger Fakhreddin had saved up over the day. He recognized him as soon as he appeared, as if there was a mark on his face by which to identify him. He would drive behind him until he reached a quiet road with no one behind him or around him, then he would drive up alongside the other driver and put a bullet in his head that blew his skull apart, finishing off both him and the ancient vehicle he had been driving. Fakhreddin would continue to work for the rest of the day and then go home, always by eight o'clock to be in time to help the children with their homework.

Fakhreddin set a rule for himself—he wouldn't kill more than one person a day, whatever the circumstances. On some days, he would meet his "hero" off the road, since not all heroes are drivers. One day, he woke up in alarm to the sound of a voice shouting in the street. When he was fully alert he realized it was the new imam of the privately financed mosque that had opened at the bottom of the building opposite. The imam wasn't giving the call to prayer or reciting from the Quran. He was praying into the microphone. *God is Great.* Silence. *God is Great.* Silence. *God listens to those who praise Him. God is Great.*

Silence. *God is Great.* Silence. *God is Great.* Silence. *God is Great.* The first prostration was done. There was nothing but his sudden and repeated shouting of *God is Great* every time he bowed or stood up or prostrated himself or sat down. Then silence. Fakhreddin couldn't see the sense in this, so he got up, got dressed, went to the mosque, washed for prayers, and prayed. After prayers he had a private conversation with the imam and suggested he make do with using the loudspeakers for the call to prayer if he wanted, and to recite some verses of the Quran if he thought it necessary. But he said that praying into the microphone made no sense, since the prayer was meant to be silent anyway. The imam agreed with him and commended him for his advice, but the next day, he did exactly the same thing. In the evening, Fakhreddin spoke to him about it again, and the same conversation took place between them day after day without any change. One day at dawn, Fakhreddin got up and went down to the mosque, went in while the imam was prostrated, and put a silenced bullet in the back of his head. He left before anyone noticed anything. On that day, for example, he didn't look for any other "hero" in the streets.

Another time, Leila asked him if he could find work for a local girl who was working in a cell phone shop and who was being harassed by her boss. Fakhreddin went and spoke with the man, who denied the allegations and flew into a rage, summoned the girl, slapped her in the face, and fired her. All that happened within minutes. He went home and asked Leila to tell her friend to go back to work the next day as if nothing had happened. The next day the girl went back to the shop, to which she still had the keys, but the shop owner didn't turn up. He didn't come the next day either, nor for the rest of the month, so the girl decided to open up every day and run the shop until the missing man showed up, but he never came back.

Hind disappeared during this period. Fakhreddin called her and she said she was in Upper Egypt covering the feast of the Virgin Mary in Asyut and she had taken the opportunity to write some other stories about Upper Egypt and Nubia, and then she disappeared again.

Boredom was seeping in further. Everything seemed pointless. Everything he did was just a sedative until he could find something else to do. But what could he do? Nothing meaningful. He wanted to do something meaningful but he didn't know what that was. What could have meaning in such a world? As he drove around the city, he thought a thousand times what the mysterious thing might be that brought meaning and every time he came to the same conclusion: there was nothing. Legal activism didn't lead anywhere. Words didn't lead anywhere. Killing had its limits: it wouldn't teach a father to be kind to his daughter or bring her up well. It wouldn't stop the children who sold mint in the street from falling into the abyss. It wouldn't teach people how to drive properly. It wouldn't establish justice or bring back what was lost. Killing wouldn't do much, and words wouldn't do much either. So was Nasser al-Khudari right: there was no point? This was something he refused to accept. There must be something that was useful and until he found it he would keep driving around in the Regata and administer a little justice his own way.

Fakhreddin rushed up the old staircase. He stood at the door to the apartment. He wiped the dust off the old copper plaque and read the name of the former resident. He took a sharp instrument out of his pocket and applied it to the lock. A minute later he heard the bolt click open. He pushed the door and it opened. A cloud of dust descended on him. No one had been here for years. He went in and quickly closed the door.

He stood still, till his eyes had grown used to the dark. He took a pair of flat slippers out of his little bag and put them on his feet. There was dust on everything. The furniture was covered in white sheets. The little kitchen had a white fridge and an old Frigidaire gas stove. He walked through the bedrooms and the living room. It was a small apartment and it felt like a relic from the past, as if he were walking around in a black and white movie. The noise from Qasr al-Aini Street brought him back to reality. He headed to the study, but he didn't find what he wanted in there. The place had been cleaned carefully before it was closed up. He was surprised that Omar Fares had tidied up his papers so carefully before he suddenly died. There wasn't a single piece of paper in the study. Omar's mother had told him that she hadn't been into the apartment and that she had sent the maid to clean it and pick up his clothes. Someone else must have made sure all the papers were removed from the apartment.

He went into Omar's bedroom and looked in the bedding, under the bed, and in the wardrobe but couldn't find anything. He moved on to the other rooms and found nothing remarkable there. He stood in the middle of the living room and looked around him. Hadn't Omar Fares left any trace of the investigation on which he had spent a whole year? Or had they gotten here first and wiped out all traces of their crime? He looked around at the dining table and the eight chairs, the sideboard, the rocking chair, the bar, the tea table, and the antique piano under its cover. Then he caught sight of a bear's head. On the piano stool, he could see the teddy bear that Shireen had given him the first time they had celebrated his birthday together. He went up to it slowly, examining it carefully. He was sure it was the same one. He pulled off the sheet that covered the stool and picked up the bear. There was no doubt about it. Even its smell hadn't changed, and smells don't lie. What was the bear doing here? Why had Omar Fares taken it and why had he kept it here? Fakhreddin stood gazing at the bear, his mind working fast. Then he reached out and slit open the bear's belly with his penknife. There! Yes! Well done, Omar Fares!

Fakhreddin found an envelope buried carefully inside a plastic bag hidden in the bear's stuffing. He took the envelope out quickly and opened it. His eyes first fell on the copper casing of a bullet. He held it and remembered how hot it had been on the day he picked it up off the ground and felt his heart sink. He looked at the papers and soon realized what they were: Omar Fares's complete report. He skimmed through it and his heart sank further with each page and tears welled up in his eyes. The report took him back to the tiniest details of his past life. He didn't notice the passage of time and he didn't move from where he was until he had finished the whole report. For the first time in many years, tears fell from his eyes as he put the report carefully in his little bag, picked up the bear with its gaping belly, and left Omar Fares's apartment.

"Why are you wasting time?" asked Hind. "Why don't you do something?"

"Do what?"

"Didn't you find Omar Fares's report? So publish it!"

"Publish it how? Print off copies and give them away to people in the street?"

"No, print it as if it's a novel."

"Now that's an idea, and what good would that do?"

"It would get it off your chest."

"No, what I have on my chest is too big, too heavy to be gotten rid of with a novel."

"Okay then, enough procrastination. Let's get back to work and finish the job."

"What do you mean?"

"You know very well what I mean. The one you've left till the end. The main target. The one you've been pursuing and who's been pursuing you. Come on, I'm fed up with the two of you."

"I'm fed up, too."

"So, we're agreed, and this will be our last operation together."

"What? You're going to pull out?"

"If you don't mind. I'll help you with this operation and then that's it."

"It really is the last operation."

"It's a deal, then."

They reached this agreement as he was driving her to Heliopolis. She went home and put on a plain black dress that reached just below the knees, put on large round sunglasses, and gathered her hair in a ponytail. She looked like a businesswoman or a senior official in a bank. She picked up the Egyptian passport she had forged in the name of Ilham Wanis and set off to meet Amm Mohamed, the realtor who had promised to show her some apartments in the neighborhood where General Samir lived.

"I want somewhere good in a large building, on a high floor, and close to the club," she said.

Amm Mohamed showed her several apartments and she chose two in different buildings that overlooked, at different angles, the area around the target's house. She chose the first apartment for herself—on the eighth floor of a twelve-story building. She told Amm Mohamed that a friend of hers who worked with her in the same bank wanted a similar apartment. Her friend would be coming in three days and so she asked Amm Mohamed to hold the other apartment for her. Two days later she signed the contract and got the keys to the first apartment. The owner, based on instructions from the security people, warned her not to go up on the roof. She assured him she had no need to use the roof and she would never allow her young children to go up on any roofs. She paid three months' rent in advance, as the contract required, and gave them a photocopy of her passport. She gave Amm Mohamed one month's rent as the commission upon which they had agreed.

Fakhreddin went to meet Captain Ayman and told him he was going to Hurghada to work as a driver for a tourism company for a few months. Captain Ayman looked at him at length, and for a moment Fakhreddin thought the captain doubted his word. The captain asked him what he would be doing with the taxi while he was away and Fakhreddin said he would leave it in Bayn al-Sarayat. After a pause, Ayman told him to leave the keys with his aunt and tell her that one of the plainclothes policemen might come by every now and then to take the taxi. Fakhreddin nodded without discussing it and the captain gave him leave to go.

The meeting had been uncomfortable and Fakhreddin was worried that Ayman might be suspicious of his story or was testing him. It would have been better to resist leaving the taxi keys, which would have been the natural behavior of anyone who owned a taxi. But what had happened had happened. Even if Ayman was suspicious, Fakhreddin would disappear for a few months and when he reappeared he would have finished his mission, and he could cross that bridge when he came to it.

Four days later, Huda Karim, a blond woman with clear blue eyes who had just arrived from Geneva and who wore a suit that was revealing without being outrageous, signed the lease for the other apartment and was given the keys. Fakhreddin slipped into the apartment closest to the target's house when workmen were coming and going, while Hind moved into the other apartment and used it as a monitoring post. They didn't communicate by telephone, whether cell or landline, nor online, because the area was under surveillance and they might be discovered. Hind would go to Fakhreddin's apartment and write out what she wanted to say. He would then reply or ask questions in writing, and then burn the scraps of paper in a clay pot. She would take away his dirty clothes and the remains of his food and give him supplies for the next day, then move on. When she went to that apartment she would become Ilham Wanis, dressed as Ilham, and then she went back to Huda Karim's house and changed her appearance there, so that none of the doormen or security people would ask her who she was coming to visit. She was at home in both cases and as the weeks passed both women became familiar to everyone in the two buildings. She had told Amm Mohamed that the children were going to stay on in Geneva a while with their father since it turned out to be difficult to find them places in equivalent schools in Cairo during term time.

It was hard spending so much time stuck in the apartment, but Fakhreddin was well trained. He restored contact with his spiritual side during the long weeks of waiting in his hideaway. Hind's daily visits also cheered him up. He started marking the day by the timing of her visits. He also did more yoga and breathing exercises because reconnaissance work requires high levels of self-control. He had to spend many hours watching the target's house from the apartment, sometimes with a telescope and sometimes without. There were many hours when nothing happened: no one moved, no one came or went. At other times it would be chaotic, with fleets of cars arriving and then leaving, without anyone getting out. Sometimes the target would arrive on one of several helicopters that landed, and then the helicopters would fly off with some of his family members. Sometimes helicopters would fly off and come back without any passengers. Some of the activity seemed to be for decoy purposes and some of it made no sense. But much of the time passed with nothing at all happening. Sometimes, after hours of futile waiting, Fakhreddin would go to the bathroom and when he came back something had changed, as if they had been waiting for him to leave his post before they moved. Usually two or three teams of two people each would carry out a surveillance operation of this kind, but he didn't want to take any risks. This was his operation and he would do it alone.

The security measures around the target were complex and well thought-out. But anyone who works in security or in the assassination business is well aware that no plan is a hundred percent foolproof and that however complicated the security measures are, and however strict the procedures, there are bound to be loopholes. If someone is determined, smart, and well trained, they will be able to evade any security measures in the end. That's why security agencies depend more on intelligence information than on direct protection to prevent attacks. That was another source of strength for Fakhreddin: he wasn't working with a group so he couldn't be infiltrated and his intentions could not be known. He was also patient, intelligent, well trained, and definitely determined. He was just the type of person that security agencies fear most.

Hind was taciturn. She did her support work from the other apartment without speaking. After the six weeks of intensive reconnaissance that Hind had done from her building, which overlooked the other side of the house, and her chats with the doormen, the man in charge of parking, the grocer, and everyone else she could talk to, she knew enough about the target's movements for Fakhreddin to carry out the operation. He wanted to choose a time when no one from the general's family would be at home. He didn't want his wife, children, or grandchildren to come and see him lying dead on the ground in a shroud. At that point the target would cease to be a target and go back to being a man who had been killed in front of his family, and Fakhreddin would see himself as a man who had murdered a father, a husband, and a grandfather in front of his relatives. He was willing to postpone implementation in order to avoid such a situation. By the eighth week, Fakhreddin was ready, but he kept waiting. On Tuesdays, the target's wife went out early in the morning, the children went to their various places of work, and the grandchildren were in school. The target had some meetings at home and had a few of his aides with him. When an important visitor arrived, he would come out of the house with him and walk to the end of the garden. This was the moment awaited by our sniper, who was lurking on the eighth floor, not far off. These are the most difficult periods in a sniper's assignment—the long hours of nerve-racking tension. The target might appear at any moment and you don't have much time—a few seconds, or minutes if luck is on your side. Then you have to get your rifle into position without losing sight of the target. You have to be ready to strike at any moment, and to pick up your equipment and move off without ever coming back, without even thinking of looking behind you.

The first Tuesday passed without the target coming to the door. The next Tuesday his wife didn't go out for some reason. The following Tuesday was in the last week of March and by that time Hind was worried she might not be able to prevent the doormen and the people around from growing suspicious. But that day the target came out to say goodbye to some guests and then had a short walk in the garden with one of his aides. The target turned to his aide to listen to something he was whispering and Fakhreddin could make out his facial features clearly. He increased the magnification on his scope. He raised the rifle a little till the crosshairs were on the man's head. General Samir's head was in the center of the crosshairs when Fakhreddin's phone started to vibrate. His hand shook and the target was no longer in his sights. Fakhreddin hesitated: only a few special friends knew the number of that phone. He focused on the target again. He moved the crosshairs left and right across the general's head. He held his breath. General Samir turned to his aide to hear something he was whispering as he looked through the folder he was holding. Fakhreddin could make out his features clearly. There was no way he could be mistaken. The crosshairs were steady on his forehead. The telephone kept vibrating insistently. Fakhreddin tensed. General Samir suddenly looked up and Fakhreddin imagined that their eyes met. That's when he pulled the trigger. He fired one bullet that landed between General Samir's eyes, which were looking toward him, and the general collapsed immediately. The folder fell from his hands and flew through the air.

General Samir fell onto the asphalt path that ran from the front door of the house to the heavily protected metal gate. Fakhreddin heard the sound of his head hitting the asphalt and saw blood streaming from his nose and mouth. He looked through the telescopic sight and on the face of the dead man he saw the smile of someone who at the last moment understood what was happening. Fakhreddin took a deep breath and pulled back from the edge of his lookout, out of sight. He took the small phone, which was still vibrating, out of his pocket and answered it.

7

The Eagle's Desert

"So here I am," Fakhreddin mumbled to himself as he sat on a bare rock and cast glances left and right, without seeing anyone. Here he was, alone as always. Omar was asleep, maybe from exhaustion, maybe so he wouldn't have to see his father. That didn't bother him any longer. He was used to the idea that his son didn't like him, or hated him to be more precise. But he was determined to set him right and win his affection. His attempts had failed so far but he would try a second time, and a third, and a tenth. He would keep trying, here in the desert, and they wouldn't leave till they had come to terms with what had happened or died, one or both of them. He knew he had a limited chance of success, but what else could he do? When he realized that Omar didn't like him, he was shocked and felt the world shaking around him. He hadn't taken this possibility into account. He had never imagined it could happen to him, but it had happened. After Omar's long silence, after he had refused food and drink and had come close to death, after Fakhreddin had carried him in his arms and looked after him for many days and nights, and after Omar had woken up and looked at him and it was clear how much he hated coming back to life and seeing him again, Fakhreddin realized that his son hated him. Maybe Omar thought Fakhreddin didn't deserve to be his father, or to be a father at all, and Fakhreddin thought that his son might be right.

Fakhreddin sat down to relax and think. He went over what had happened in the past few weeks. He had swum against the tide to save his son from the clutches of killers. He had picked him up in his arms and escaped, without thinking of anything but his immediate objective. But Omar had started to wriggle out of his grip. When he broke free, he started to fall and Fakhreddin had to reach down as quickly as possible and catch him. If he had hesitated for a moment, the hungry wolves watching from the ground would have devoured Omar. Then he had carried Omar out of danger and set him on a high rock in the middle of a remote desert. He stopped for the two of them to catch their breath. But Omar continued to wriggle, as if he were determined to let the wolves devour him. Then Fakhreddin realized that his son would rather submit to the wild beasts that sought his blood than be with his father. Omar did not want to stay with him, even if he had nowhere else to go.

He thought about this and about Shireen, who wanted to be with him but couldn't, and who couldn't be anywhere else. He didn't know where to take his son or where to go himself. He knew that Shireen had been a victim of her social class, which had trapped her and crippled her, but Omar was a victim of his own father and no one else. After thinking it over at length, Fakhreddin realized that Omar had been angry with him when he did what he did. He had committed one crime after another to take revenge on his father, and then he had tried to end his own life in a way that would hurt him. When Fakhreddin saved him, he was even angrier, and now he wanted to die right in front of him to punish him further. That's why he was furious when he woke up and found he was still alive, thanks to his father. The son wanted to die at the hands of his father in order to make him suffer, and Fakhreddin wanted to forgive him in order to save him. So there they were: the famous beast of the air and his son the little beast, face-to-face in the desert, watching each other and not knowing where to go next.

Fakhreddin wondered if his son hated him because he had fathered him, because he had neglected him, or because he didn't know him. When he thought about it, he didn't blame Omar. Where had he been all those years? What would it matter to Omar that his father had been a mujahid in Afghanistan, or even Che Guevara? Maybe Che's children hated their father, maybe he hadn't looked after them, hadn't hugged them when they were little or made them happy. Che hadn't held his son's hand and taken him anywhere. He hadn't given him a chance to grow up around him, feel safe, or see him as a role model. What did it matter to the sons that their father was the liberator of Latin America? Maybe they secretly hated him. But Omar made no secret of it: he said it, in every possible way. At least there was that: he was brave enough to tell his father. Fakhreddin wondered hopefully whether it was courage or a desire that his father would win him over, hug him, prove him wrong, and show him that he loved him and had abandoned him only under duress.

But he knew this was only a faint glimmer of hope. He had abandoned Omar deliberately and Omar felt that and wouldn't forgive him. Fakhreddin hadn't been unaware that he had a young son who needed him, but without much thought he had decided to "postpone" him, as if he were something that could be kept for later, until he restored justice. He thought that then he could bring his son back to life and they would live together in the new world of justice. He had abandoned him temporarily, and then forgotten him for years. When he remembered him he found reasons to hope that he was in good hands with Umm Yasser, that they were living as a family and that this was best for him. He didn't think about it often so that he wouldn't see something he didn't want to see: that his son was his responsibility and that he needed him and should be with him. He didn't want anyone to become attached to him and—now he started to understand—he didn't want Omar to grow too close to anyone else. Only now did he start to see what he had failed to see over all the years: that all he really wanted was to be alone—in this desert, in those mountains in Afghanistan, or in that monastery on the coast, without the monks. He wanted to be alone in a sky where he could spread his large wings and fly so high that no one could reach him.

Did he secretly blame his son for Shireen's death? Although it was rather cruel, deep down inside, he admitted there was some truth to this. At the end of the day, hadn't Shireen died so that she could give birth to Omar? Didn't the pregnancy and the delivery kill her? There were times when he thought that Shireen had deliberately gotten pregnant with Omar and that this was her way of being with him, because she knew from the start that she wasn't strong enough to go off with him and defy the world around her. The only way out she could find was to die and leave her son with Fakhreddin. She couldn't go off with Fakhreddin and she couldn't stay in her own world, which was killing her, so she left and stayed with him by giving him Omar. He had said this to himself for years. But if he had really believed it, he would have kept Omar with him. He would have picked him up and taken him away and wouldn't have abandoned him. Yes, he was bound to blame Omar secretly for the death of Shireen.

He sat on the rock and understood the enormity of the crime he had committed. But he couldn't believe he had committed such a crime against his closest relative, after wandering across half the world in search of truth and justice. And here he was, on a rock in the desert, staring his inadequacy in the face and trying to find a way to pull himself together again, recover some of his composure, and remedy the mess for which he was responsible. He no longer blamed anyone but himself—neither Omar, nor Umm Yasser, Hamza, or the group. When he went to rescue Omar, he had blamed Sheikh Hamza. He had told him it was blowing up the consulate that had earned them the enmity and vengeance of the security agencies, but now he realized that this was only half the truth and that the security people wanted to take revenge on him, even if they didn't know who he was. Fakhreddin had to learn that his deeds would not go unavenged by Samir and his aides and that, just as he knew how Samir operated, Samir knew how he and those like him operated. He was the one who had poked the beast in the eye, not Hamza. He forgot that he, himself, also had an eye that was unprotected. He forgot that there was always an eye that was unprotected. He had taken revenge on everyone who had taken part in the plot to kill him in the past until he had reached the mastermind. But the mastermind had beaten him to it and struck back at him before he could fire his last bullet. Samir had killed him with a smile before Fakhreddin killed him, and only now did he understand what the smile meant.

He told himself that he wasn't much better than Hamza, that he was no better than anyone. He had hurt those he loved and abandoned his son. He should have stayed with Omar and been a father to him, but he hadn't. Omar knew his father was the one responsible: when he spoke, that's what he said. He said his father was the reason for everything that had happened and that he didn't like him. Then he shut up. There he was, face-to-face with a simple truth: that he had turned his son, by mistake, inadvertently or through negligence, into a traitor, a conspirator, and a murderer. In his attempt to kill the beast, he had become like him, just as Damian had predicted, and turned his son into a monster like himself. The original monster he had been chasing had died, and there they were—the two surviving monsters sitting face-to-face in this silent desert.

He wouldn't carry Omar against his will. He couldn't and he knew he couldn't. Omar would wriggle free again and again and again, until he perished. If Fakhreddin saved him against his will, Omar would hate him even more and would find a way to kill himself, just to hurt his father. They wouldn't get back to Cairo within a week. The old plan had failed and there couldn't be a new plan without Omar cooperating. They would stay there, perched on this rock, in this desert, circling around each other until they came to terms or died together. There was a well not far off and they had enough provisions to last a forty-day journey. Toward the end of that period they could slaughter one of the two camels since the provisions it was carrying would have run out by then, and they could live off its meat for some days longer. They would stay where they were until Omar decided whether or not he wanted to give Fakhreddin another chance and accept him as his father. And if he didn't want to do that, maybe he would agree to give himself another chance. He might understand that Fakhreddin didn't need him to die in order to recognize the mistake he had made. He did recognize it and accepted responsibility for it and for himself, and wanted forgiveness from Omar. He would stay with his son in the hope that Omar would forgive him, for Omar's sake. Until that happened, they wouldn't move.

Omar sat at the mouth of the cave, wondering how this man had suddenly appeared in his life and what he wanted from him. At first he thought Fakhreddin had come to kill him, to atone for the shame of Omar's actions and so that it wouldn't be said that he was soft or cowardly. So Omar decided to let himself die in order to thwart his father's plan. But his father had saved him from death. Omar was still expecting his father to kill him, even if he hadn't done so yet. He didn't understand what he wanted. Did he really want to take him back to Cairo? If so, why? As a cover to mislead the security agencies? Was he going to set up a new organization and did he want Omar's help? He must be mad to think that Omar could help him after what Sheikh Hamza had told him. Did he, like Sheikh Hamza, want to send him on a suicide mission to "atone for his sins"? Omar smiled, as he remembered Sheikh Hamza's face when Omar told the sheikh that *he* should go and blow himself up to atone for *his* sins. He would say the same to Fakhreddin if he brought up the subject. If that was his objective, then Fakhreddin didn't know how much Omar hated him and the whole group. He was waiting for the moment when he could surprise Fakhreddin by his ability to do him harm. Fakhreddin didn't know yet. He didn't know that Omar was capable of plunging a dagger into his heart and could watch him struggle with death. He told himself that all his father knew about him was what he had heard from Umm Yasser and Sheikh Hamza, but he didn't know what he was capable of. He looked at Fakhreddin from where he was sitting, and smiled to himself. He thought it was the security people who had deceived Fakhreddin and told him about Omar cooperating with them. Fakhreddin didn't know what had happened, not yet. Omar sat and waited. He would tell his father the truth when he decided it was time.

He played in the ground with his dagger and regretted that his conspiracy had failed. If his partner hadn't been so weak, it wouldn't have failed. If that novice hadn't confessed to his father, the plan would have succeeded and the leaders of the group would have been blown to pieces and no one would have known which parts belonged to whom. If that coward hadn't confessed, he would have detonated the bomb during the meeting and wiped them all out in one fell swoop. The boy had wrecked the plan. He had broken down and begged for forgiveness. They had forgiven him and now he would become one of them again and, who knows, maybe he would be a commander in the future. But Omar hadn't sought forgiveness. On the contrary, he had enjoyed telling them how much he hated them. He had thrown it in their faces. He had confirmed the plot and told them he knew the penalty and he wasn't afraid of it. He had stood in front of the whole judicial council and told them, slowly and clearly, that he hated them all and would rather die than ask for a pardon. He remembered Umm Yasser, the poor woman. She didn't understand anything he had done and didn't believe it. She hugged him and cried, as he pushed her away. The last thing he wanted was her tears. All he wanted them to do was leave him alone, but they insisted on "reforming" him and they sent him to the sharia units for him to "repent." He looked at his father and remembered their reaction. They didn't believe the son of the Eagle could do this to them. "You of all people, Omar! What will your father say?" They didn't understand him, they didn't understand a word he said. They thought they were immune from dissent and couldn't believe that one of their own could hate them. Omar smiled to himself, knowing that he was the one who had gone to the intelligence officer and led him on. After that, when they sent him to the sharia units for indoctrination, he had turned the units against them. He had tricked the kids there, recruited some of them, and spent whole weeks wreaking havoc until they woke up to what he was doing. Omar had laughed when they accused him of corrupting the children there. He asked them with a sneer how he could have corrupted them in three weeks if they had been virtuous in the first place. Then he asked them about the people that Sheikh Hamza and the other leaders had corrupted and he enjoyed seeing their faces contorted in discomfort. He loved throwing insults in their faces. If his father was an eagle who killed from above, he was a panther that attacked face-to-face and looked his opponents in the eye as he felled them with his dagger. He was content, because they would always remember the panther that had almost wiped them all out in a single stroke.

But then the Eagle had swooped on him, completely out of the blue, and saved him. He was angry because he hadn't asked him for help and he didn't want to see him. For years he had adapted to his father's absence. From an early age he had realized that Fakhreddin had brought him into the world, abandoned him to these monsters, and flown away. He had accepted that and grown used to it, and now he didn't want anything else. He only wanted to continue the arrangement he was used to. But no, the annoying Eagle had returned as suddenly as he had disappeared and he was depriving him of the only death that would make them remember him. He looked at his father and felt a wave of hatred for him. He wished Sheikh Hamza had killed his father and spared him from him forever.

Two weeks passed, and they didn't go anywhere. Omar was still silent most of the time, but he started saying a word or two a day. Fakhreddin tried to teach him how to ride horses but he didn't show any interest. Fakhreddin acted as if Omar was keen and explained the difference between various kinds of horses and how to deal with each kind, how to break in a horse and train it without being cruel. Omar didn't look at him and didn't seem to be listening, but Fakhreddin assumed his son could hear him, even if he was pretending otherwise, unless he had been struck deaf. Fakhreddin would pause suddenly in the middle of a sentence, feeling that Omar was about to ask him to continue, but he didn't, so Fakhreddin would continue anyway, in the hope that he was at least listening.

Despite Omar's silence, Fakhreddin set rules for their life together—waking up, eating, and going to sleep. Even if Omar resisted his role as a father, he had to understand that there were limits. He didn't force him to do anything, but there are rules for matters of survival and Fakhreddin was responsible for both their lives, at least for now. They had to wake up by seven o'clock at the latest. At first, when Fakhreddin woke him up, Omar pretended he was still asleep, but he couldn't go back to sleep, especially after Fakhreddin lifted the awning that covered the mouth of the cave and the sun poured in. Omar still lazed a while, but then he gave in and got up. A few days later, he started waking up before seven o'clock so that he could get up in his own time. Fakhreddin looked on and told himself this was fine. He asked Omar what he would like for lunch and when Omar didn't respond, he chose on his behalf.

After a few days eating the same food, Omar started giving an answer to this question. So he said at least one word a day and took part in one decision.

Fakhreddin asked him to help with certain chores, like looking for firewood, tying up the animals, taking them for walks, cleaning out the area where the animals slept, or checking that the tents that protected them at night were well secured. Omar ignored him for a whole week, then started to do some small things without talking. Then he chose to gather firewood and look after the animals. He took on these jobs without being asked. When Fakhreddin asked about such things, he made gestures to indicate that he had taken care of it. Every now and then, at least once a day, Omar would do something aggressive. He broke something, threw some water in the sand, or he wouldn't reply when Fakhreddin asked him to take care of something or help him with something. When he acted this way, he looked at Fakhreddin defiantly as if he were inviting him to punish him, as if he were looking for the cruelty he thought was latent in his father. But Fakhreddin took it in his stride and told him this was the wrong way to behave. Then he went and did the job without adding another word.

Fakhreddin spoke to him every day over lunch and in the evening before they went to sleep. Omar didn't respond but Fakhreddin went on talking. He told him about simple things, the foods that he liked and hated, how to prepare food in the desert, about hunting, driving cars, boats and the sea, the stars, the winds, and the sands, about Cairo and Bayn al-Sarayat, about his aunt Maria and her illness and Leila and her medical charity work. He asked Omar about himself and what he liked. Omar didn't answer, of course, but his father spoke at length. Once he talked to Omar about Shireen, and Omar stood up, went off to bed, and didn't come back for the rest of the day. Fakhreddin didn't talk about her again.

Twice Fakhreddin offered to take him hunting gazelles or wild rabbits, assuring him he would like that. Omar looked at

him for some time but didn't answer. Fakhreddin assured him
he could soon learn to ride the horse or he could ride behind
him, and again he didn't reply. When he asked him with a smile
if he was frightened of falling off the horse, Omar just looked
at him contemptuously and didn't reply. That was the first time
Omar had looked at him with an expression other than hatred.

Omar grew tired of this game, tired of this barren desert. He
couldn't see the point of waiting. The provisions would soon
run out. Did Fakhreddin want to waste time and provisions
and then run off with what was left, leaving him alone to die
of hunger and thirst? Was this the form of punishment he had
finally decided to inflict? But nothing in Fakhreddin's behavior
suggested he was planning to punish him, and that was what
worried him. He seemed like a normal father. Every day he
fed the animals, went out hunting, and brought water, while
Omar gathered firewood. Then they did the cooking and so
on. Omar wondered what this meant. Was this the sharia unit
version of Fakhreddin? Would the next step be teaching him
to memorize the Quran and asking him to repent? And if he
didn't repent, would Fakhreddin feel exonerated and carry out
the execution? If that was what he intended, he was wasting
his time, because Omar didn't intend to repent or recant.

But what puzzled Omar most was that his father didn't
ask him what he had done with the group or what had happened. He didn't ask about the intelligence officer and his
relationship with him, about the children he had won over,
the explosives, the betrayal, and all that. Omar wanted him
to ask so that he could tell him and see the impact it had on
him. He wanted to tell him to his face, slowly and clearly,
how his friend Sheikh Hamza was the first to abuse him,
to tell in detail how it happened, gradually, day after day,
to the point that he found Hamza pressed against him, felt
his body heaving on top of him, felt that pain, and couldn't
escape his grip. He wanted to see his father's face when he

heard that, when he heard from his son how his whole body began to shake, and how he cried in silence under the weight of Hamza, the rapist, submitting to him in the knowledge that he was weak and defenseless. He wanted to tell him how he tried to explain this to Umm Yasser, who had married Sheikh Hamza, and how she cut him off, scolded him, and refused to listen to what he was about to say. He wanted to tell him how Sheikh Hamza had repeatedly summoned him on the pretext of "having a talk" and how the sheikh had told everyone he had adopted him. He wanted this heroic Eagle to ask him, so that he could tell him how he started to enjoy these sessions with Sheikh Hamza because they were the only times when someone hugged him, stroked his hair, or asked him what he wanted, at least until he mounted him and hurt him again. He wanted to tell him how he came to like the fact that Sheikh Hamza had adopted him because it made the other boys envious of him. He wanted his father to ask him about the bombing plan so that he could torment his father with the truth and tell him that he didn't do it in revenge for Sheikh Hamza's repeated assaults but because, after a while, Hamza cast him aside and adopted another boy. He wanted him to ask about the intelligence officer so that he could explain why he tricked the poor man, who thought he was a conquering hero and didn't understand that Omar was using him to destroy his enemies. But Fakhreddin didn't ask and didn't bring up the subject in any way whatsoever. All he did was cook, look after the animals, and talk about horses, stars, and relatives Omar knew nothing about. What exactly was his game? What was he trying to achieve?

He didn't understand this man. He knew his father hated him for causing Shireen's death and that he had abandoned him because he had more important things to do, like the other leaders of the group. But he could see that he was different from them. He wasn't as coarse as them and, except at his meeting with Sheikh Hamza, he hadn't seen him being violent or cruel. He hadn't hit him ever. He wasn't even harsh with him when he was stubborn, broke things, spilled water onto the sand, or wasted provisions. Fakhreddin would just tell him that a boy like him shouldn't do such things, and then moved on. That's all he did and that amazed Omar, who was used to corporal punishment. Even when they went out hunting, he was gentle with the rabbits he caught. Omar didn't understand him. Sometimes he saw him talking to himself as if there were a third person present. He didn't understand all the questions he asked him: what he liked, what he ate, and what he didn't eat. The boy didn't understand why his father didn't leave him alone and do what he had come to do, and he didn't understand what he had come to do.

Deep down inside, Omar was hopeful and fearful. He hoped he had his father back, that Fakhreddin would take him back and be a father and protector. But he didn't believe this was possible, and whenever it occurred to him that Fakhreddin might have honest intentions, he quickly dismissed the idea. He simply didn't want to think about this possibility. He wouldn't allow himself to just go along with his father and believe him. No, he would never allow himself to be weak.

He would leave rather than wait to find out what his father intended by his indecision. He would take revenge in the way he had always wanted, but directly on his father. It was clear that Fakhreddin wanted to win his trust. He didn't know exactly why, but that was the purpose of all his attempts to win him over—the stories he told and the time he spent with him. He would humor him in his game and make his father trust him, and then he would inflict his punishment on him. That was the decision he made, so that he wouldn't give in to his father's sweet talk and the hope that tempted him from afar. He would humor his father until his father trusted him completely, and then he would deal the fatal blow.

*

Then Hind turned up.

Fakhreddin was sitting in the cave when he saw her coming through the entrance. He was startled. She smiled and walked toward him, stumbling as she came. She was wearing a dark skirt suit, stockings, and high-heeled shoes, and carrying her usual leather purse. He looked at her in disbelief: how had she gotten here? How did she know where they were in the middle of the Gilf Kebir? Why was she dressed like that and how had she crossed the desert in those clothes? This time, he was frightened. He looked at her and at Omar sitting alone in the other corner of the cave, but Omar showed no sign of being upset. She smiled and said, "Don't worry. He can't see me."

Fakhreddin scowled and asked, "What do you mean, can't see you?"

"Haven't I always told you I'm an ethereal being?"

He called Omar and looked up toward him, but Omar didn't answer. Fakhreddin signaled to him to look at Hind but Omar kept looking at Fakhreddin blankly. Looking at Omar to see if he really hadn't seen Hind, he asked, "How did you get here?"

"I always know how to find you. Look, I'm sorry to report that the boat broke down on me and I couldn't take it back. It was going to sink and I was going to drown. Never mind, I thought, and jumped in and swam ashore. Then I made my way as best I could. If you remember, I'd told you the Heliopolis operation was the last one I'd help you with. I swear I only came to Sudan with you for your son's sake. And how is he your son? He's a hundred times more handsome than you."

"How did you get here?"

"Don't you believe I'm ethereal?"

"What do you mean by 'ethereal,' Hind?"

"Haven't you noticed?"

"Noticed what?"

She smiled tenderly and put her hand on his shoulder.

"Fakhreddin, my dear. Think for a moment. I'm sure you know, deep inside you."

"Know what, you crazy woman?"

"Know that God sent me to you and that no one but you ever has anything to do with me."

"Sorry?"

"Fakhreddin, don't tell me you've never thought about this before."

"Omar! Omar!"

"Let Omar be. Don't make him more confused than he is already. May God help you with him. He's the one who'll show you that God is truth. Are you trying to tell me you've never noticed that no one else ever sees us when we're together? You want me to believe the thought has never crossed your mind?"

"What's wrong with you?"

He looked at her, but couldn't speak. He didn't know how to talk to her. He couldn't even think. His tongue was tied and his brain had stopped working. He froze. In a way, she was right—he seemed to know, and yet he didn't know. Part of him was not completely surprised, but he couldn't believe it. What did all this mean? What did it mean that she was here in the middle of the desert, when no one in the world knew where they were, and wearing these extraordinary clothes? Even if she had discovered their route by some miracle, how would she get here alone without animals to ride or provisions, if she was a normal human being? But how could Hind not be real? What about everything they had been through together—the killings, the conversations, and their adventures in Afghanistan and Peshawar? Who had he been with all this time? He looked at her and wondered how real it all was. Was she an ethereal creature as she claimed? Was it all fantasies and delusions? For all this time?

"Don't be so shocked. You can think of me as part of yourself—the ethereal part," she said with a laugh.

He rubbed his eyes, stood up, sat down again, and saw her sitting and smiling. He went and immersed his face in the basin of water and came back. He found her irritated that he was skeptical, but still smiling. He went toward her and touched her shoulder, and she seemed real enough. She was as he had known her, and she felt just as he remembered her well. She looked at him and shook her head impatiently. He looked at Omar again. Omar really didn't seem to see her. He went to where Omar was sitting and tried to speak to him, looking at Hind to check that she was visible from where Omar was sitting. Hind laughed and made a gesture that meant, "You're crazy." Fakhreddin turned Omar's head to face her and asked him if he could see anything. Omar turned his head back, looked at his father irritably, and didn't respond. He went back to her, but he couldn't stay close to her while Omar might see them. He went outside, lit a fire, and sat down in front of it. She joined him. He went back and forth between the cave and the fire all night, while she sat immobile by the fire. Toward dawn, she yawned and said she was leaving: she would leave him with his son, who needed lots of his time and energy, and she added that taking his son back might be the best thing he had done. He asked her where she would go and she said she would go back the way she had come and pointed to his head. Then she added she would check on him discreetly and would come back if she felt he needed her, though she didn't think that would happen. She leaned over, planted a warm kiss on his lips, picked up her elegant purse, and walked off into the desert in her high-heeled shoes, stumbling and grumbling.

When the fifth week had passed and their supplies were running short, Fakhreddin began to feel uneasy. He reminded himself of the decision he had settled on: that he wouldn't move from this spot until Omar showed a clear desire to go to Cairo. He wouldn't change his position now. Even if the provisions ran out he wouldn't force Omar to leave.

At the beginning of the sixth week, Omar's behavior was noticeably different. He started speaking more. Instead of pointing, he would tell Fakhreddin he had cleaned out the area where the animals were tethered, or he would ask what kind of firewood he should look for or about a kind of food that Fakhreddin had cooked some weeks earlier and that he didn't seem to have noticed at the time. Then he suggested they go out hunting and asked Fakhreddin to teach him how to find prey and catch it. He told his father he was the fastest and most agile man he had ever seen. The praise made Fakhreddin smile. This was the first time Omar had said anything positive, and Fakhreddin started to feel some kind of relationship between them was about to develop. That brought some comfort to his heart.

They went hunting, came back with a gazelle, and did the cooking together. In the evening, they sat together and Omar asked him about his life in Cairo. Fakhreddin told him about his aunt Maria, about Leila and Tamer, and then stopped. For the first time, he realized that he didn't know much about his family or life in Cairo beyond the world of killing. To find something to tell Omar, he had to think hard to remember details that were worth mentioning or that would attract Omar to the life that awaited them when they went to Cairo. He told him about the two kids he helped with their homework every evening and how they had done amazingly well that year. He told him how their success had changed the way they thought about themselves. The year before, they had been introverted, they didn't like school, and they felt victimized. When they were better able to learn at school, they felt more self-confident and were on better terms with their classmates and teachers. They were also more cheerful. Omar asked Fakhreddin if he missed them and he replied with a nod, then smiled and said he was waiting for the start of the new school year so that he could go back to teaching them.

He told him about Tamer and his passion for computers and the Internet and the websites he was setting up for his young friends. Omar asked him for more details and remarked that he and his friends had done similar things, but for the group. Fakhreddin smiled and admitted he was ignorant about such matters. When he thought hard, he remembered that Tamer was helping his young colleagues set up their own websites to write blogs, share information, or sell products, and that Tamer had met his fiancée though this work. He had shown Fakhreddin dozens of websites he had set up for bloggers. He also remembered what Tamer had said about developing a toolbox for young people to set up their own websites and putting it on his own website. He added that Tamer was helping his mother run the center that helped old people in the neighborhood manage their medication and diet through an application he had designed and a website that supported it. Fakhreddin said this was what Tamer had said, although he didn't understand exactly how it worked. Omar asked if the website had "resources" for users, and Fakhreddin looked at him cluelessly.

Omar listened with interest. He asked his father what he was going to do when he went back and if he would continue with what he was doing in Sudan and Afghanistan. Fakhreddin looked down and shook his head. Then he said he was done with that kind of work and was looking for a new path, but didn't know what it was yet. Omar asked him about his life and how he had come to be a jihadi. The trace of a smile showed on his face and he said it was long, boring story and he might tell Omar about it at a later stage. When they reached the middle of the desert they would have plenty of time for that. Omar suggested he write it down and Fakhreddin said he had a complete and well-documented report on his life. Omar was surprised, and asked if he could have it published, maybe as a novel. Fakhreddin shook his head dismissively, unable to believe that his son too had suggested this. Omar asked him about Leila and how old she was, if she was tall or short, thin or fat, what color her eyes and hair were, how she spoke, whether she tended to be funny or serious, what kind of food she cooked, and so on. Once again, Fakhreddin found that he had to think hard to answer. He asked about the medical network she had set up, the patients that it tracked, their social circumstances, what had happened to their families, why Leila had to track their medication and diets, and what Leila gained from it. Fakhreddin told him about these things, and explained how Leila enjoyed helping their elderly neighbors. He told him that the nurses and doctors who had treated Aunt Maria had done so with the kind of selfless devotion that could not be explained by their professional obligations alone, and that there was something humanitarian about helping the sick and the powerless to overcome their ordeals. He described how the patients' families felt when one of them died and the families took away their bodies for burial. It was like a shared disaster that had struck them all. He told Omar that this sense of human weakness and solidarity with other weak people was felt only by those who had spent days at the hospital, following that red line to the ward, and asking themselves every day if they would find their loved ones still alive or, when they left the hospital, if this was the last time they would see them. Omar asked him about the red line and the hospital staff, and Fakhreddin told him what he remembered—the intensive care unit, the nurses, and Dr. Shayma. Yet again, Fakhreddin was surprised how much information one could remember without noticing it at the time. He remembered what the doctor looked like, the color of her eyes, her hairstyle, how tall she was, her posture, her gait, the way she spoke, how she paused absentmindedly in the middle of a conversation, her broad smile, her cheeks when she blushed, and the way she looked down with a restrained smile before turning and walking off. This time Fakhreddin gave Omar a lengthy description without him asking. Then he discovered that his son had fallen asleep while he was talking.

Omar asked his father to teach him to ride horses properly. They went out to have a walk and to play with the horse. Fakhreddin held Omar up and helped him to mount the horse and showed him how to jump down, if necessary. Sometimes he rode with him to show him complicated maneuvers, how to control the horse, and how to persuade it to do things it was afraid to do. At first Omar flinched when his father touched him, but he gradually grew used to it. Toward the end of that week, Omar put out the fire and, before going off to bed, said, "Goodnight, Abu Omar." Fakhreddin smiled. "Goodnight, Omar," he replied tenderly.

In the morning, Omar said that, unless Fakhreddin objected, he wanted to start the journey to Cairo. His father's face lit up and he agreed immediately. They spent the day gathering their things, preparing the two camels, the horse, and the two donkeys and, as far as possible, removing all traces that they had stayed there. It wasn't possible to remove every trace. They left the remains of the fire, the smoke marks on the walls of the cave, traces of the animals and their food, their footprints in the area, and so on. They removed what they could and left the rest for a sandstorm or two to take care of. They put their provisions on the backs of the donkeys, tied the horse to them, and mounted the camels that were kneeling on the ground. Fakhreddin smiled with satisfaction as the camels stood up and started walking. He thought about how far he and Omar had progressed in the time they had been together.

They set off as the sun was setting and traveled all night. Omar rode alongside Fakhreddin and asked him about the route and how to navigate by the stars and the waterholes along the way. He asked about the oases and who lived there and about other aspects of traveling in the desert. From time to time, he asked Fakhreddin about himself, how he had learned all this, and whether he had often traveled alone in the desert. Fakhreddin was delighted to be asked such questions. If Fakhreddin had spoken his mind, he would have told him everything in detail and explained his emotions, thoughts, and anguish over the years. But he restrained himself so as not to frighten the boy and consoled himself by thinking there would be plenty of time to teach Omar everything he knew and have discussions with him as he grew up. At daybreak, they found a hill, set up their tent in its shadow, and rested a while. Then they went out to gather firewood and look for water, meeting up again an hour later. Omar found some firewood, but Fakhreddin didn't find any water. There was a well nearby but it was dry. Never mind, he said, they had enough water to last for some days. They rested for the remainder of the day and resumed their journey at sunset. They rode all night, as on the previous day, and rested the next day at another site where, yet again, the well was dry. Toward sunset, as they were preparing to move on, Omar said he was tired and would like to rest that night. Fakhreddin objected, saying it would be wiser to find a well first. But Omar insisted, saying his back was hurting and they had enough water to last five days. Fakhreddin backed down and they went to sleep early. In the morning, Fakhreddin woke up and couldn't find Omar or the horse. He thought Omar had gone off for a ride or to look for water, but he wasn't back by midmorning. He went and looked at the place where they had left the animals and the provisions. The other animals were there but most of the food and water had disappeared. Omar had fled.

Fakhreddin spent three days and nights looking for Omar, without success. He went off on his camel in the morning and searched in one direction, came back at sunset, and went off on the other camel in another direction until the morning. At sunset, he took the first camel and searched in a third direction. Omar had run off with the only horse, and however fast the camels ran they wouldn't be able to match the speed of a man on a horse. Where in the desert had he gone and why had he done it, after Fakhreddin had thought that they had a chance at reconciliation? He was heartsick as he roamed the emptiness of the desert on a tired camel. Omar wouldn't know the way in this treacherous wasteland. The questions Omar had asked him wouldn't help: only someone who had personal experience of the Gilf Kebir and had learned the tracks again and again would be able to cross it. He looked everywhere that came to mind. He traveled in all directions without finding a trace of Omar. Had he run into trouble while escaping? If that had happened he would have found a trace of him or the horse, but he didn't find anything. The boy seemed to have vanished into thin air. Fakhreddin crisscrossed the area in all directions looking for his son or any sign of him, to no avail. With every hour that passed, his hopes faded and his heart sank. Omar couldn't survive in the desert alone. Neither the horse nor the provisions he was carrying would hold out, and the nearest oasis was days away. The fourth day came, and Fakhreddin was riding under the desert sun, again to no avail. The sun was bright and Fakhreddin's eyes, after days without sleep, were squinting in the glare. He closed them against the glare from the sun and the grains of sand in the wind, and opened them again, but there was still no sign of Omar or his horse. He spent another day searching desperately. He understood what his angry son had done. He had decided to take revenge on him. He had given Fakhreddin hope and then dashed it cruelly. By day, he went back to the places he had searched by night, but he was sinking into despair with every hour. Four days had passed, his supplies were running low, the animals were ailing, and Fakhreddin didn't have enough water or food for them or for himself. He hadn't slept for four days. He slipped in and out of consciousness. At one point he thought he saw dates to eat in front of him, but he didn't know if they were real, memories, or just figments of his imagination. On the fifth day, he realized it was time to stop and decided to go back to the cave where they had sheltered for the past few weeks because there was water nearby for him and the animals. It was a two-day journey and he and the animals, exhausted by hunger and thirst, might not reach it alive. But there was no other hope left. He might find Omar there or he might perish. He had promised himself that he wouldn't go back to Cairo without Omar and he would fulfill his promise. He mounted his camel and headed south toward the cave. He rode without stopping, through a haze of sky, sun, and night, until the world went dark and silent around him.

Dr. Shayma's soft brown face was the first thing he saw when he opened his eyes. He examined her features and the pores of her smooth skin. He caught the trace of a smile on her lips and in the corner of her eyes. He looked at her and she nodded. "Welcome back," she said.

"Where am I?"

"In the hospital. How do you feel?"

"How come I'm in the hospital?"

"Ah, you and your endless questions! Lie down, keep quiet, and behave yourself. Let us look after you."

Fakhreddin scowled. He wasn't used to anyone speaking to him like that. How had he reached the hospital? And where was Omar? He tried to get out of bed but found he was chained to the bed frame. Shayma stood by the bed looking through his medical reports. He pointed to the chains and she nodded to indicate that this was normal. She came toward him and sat on a chair next to his head. He caught a glimpse of her brown knees and her white doctor's coat riding up her legs. He slipped in and out of consciousness as she spoke. She talked about her mother and her family and the restricted life a conservative society imposed on a young woman like her. She spoke about her desire to specialize in preventive medicine and the projects she dreamed of setting up that could improve public health at very little expense. She said that she wasn't happy with her situation but she couldn't break out of it alone, that she realized she was weak and was trying to find a way to improve her life in a way that suited her talents.

Leila came into the room, propping up Aunt Maria, and they sat down in silence. Shayma kept talking. She asked him if Leila had told him that they had agreed to convert Leila's project into an integrated preventive clinic and that she would be the doctor in charge of the clinic. She would devote some of her time to it without giving up her day job. She stood up and examined him again. She unbuttoned his white shirt, massaged his chest, then kissed his chest tenderly, and asked him if he liked her. The question took him by surprise, but when he tried to answer he found his mouth was covered with sticky electrical insulating tape. He looked at Leila and Aunt Maria, but they didn't seem surprised by Shayma's bold question and actions. Shayma touched the sticky tape and smiled, then explained that she had liked him at first sight and was sure he had noticed this, though he had ignored her. She looked at Aunt Maria, who nodded to confirm that women knew such things without words. Shayma added that seeing him every day made her whole body feel warm, including her heart, and that she never heard half of what he was saying because his voice made her flustered. She reached out and touched his face and chest as she spoke. She told him not to worry: she knew all about his past and had no objections to any of it, so they could put all that behind them and start a new life together. Her gaze wandered but her hand was still on his chest. She added that there were many things in life more pleasant than killing people and that her vocation was to treat people's diseases, not to punish them for them. Patting his hand, she looked back into his eyes and told him to rest assured that they could have plenty of children to make up for the people he had killed. She leaned over him and took the sticky tape off his mouth, without him feeling any pain. She planted a long warm kiss on his lips, put the tape back on, and left.

Leila stood up, patted his hand, and congratulated him that he had survived and that Omar had come too. She said that Tamer had taken Omar on a tour of Cairo to show him his new home and was very happy that his cousin had turned up. Reproachfully, she asked why it had taken him so long to bring Omar and whether he thought Umm Yasser could be a better mother than her. He tried to reply but she tapped the tape on his mouth and added that it didn't matter now, because she was happy that Omar was back and that he had married Shayma. He replied that he hadn't married Shayma, at least not yet, and was surprised that this time his voice came out clearly despite the sticky tape. Leila reminded him that he couldn't speak because of the tape over his mouth, and he apologized. She assured him she had no objection to his relationship with Shayma because Shayma suited him better than she did, and better than any other woman he had met. It was a sign that God was pleased with him, she added, that He had given him such an opportunity to start afresh. She said she had been like a sister to him since they were children and they would stay that way. She begged him not to worry and thanked him for everything he had done for her. She looked at Aunt Maria, who nodded to confirm what she had said, and then Aunt Maria asked him about her medicine and whether he was going to help the two kids with their homework, as usual, or if he couldn't because of the sticky tape.

Omar's face was the first thing Fakhreddin saw when he opened his eyes. Omar was wiping his father's face with a wet cloth and dripping water onto his lips. The boy's face looked stern. He did his work mechanically, without even the trace of a smile when he saw that his father had regained consciousness. When Fakhreddin opened his eyes, the ghosts of Aunt Maria, Leila, and Shayma disappeared. He shut his eyes, opened them again, and looked at the cave to figure out where he was. Omar stood up, moved to the end of the cave, and crouched there. Beside him, Fakhreddin found a small bowl with pieces of dry bread and a small glass of water sweetened with honey. He wanted to ask Omar a thousand questions. He wanted to stand up and hold onto him, to make sure he was real and not a dream or another hallucination. But he couldn't move. A week without sleep or food had almost finished him off. He wanted to speak but he could only say disconnected words. He looked at Omar, who was going in and out of the cave, picking things up and putting them down, disappearing and reappearing without a glance in his direction. Then Fakhreddin went back to sleep.

He woke up, ate some bread, and drank some water. Sometimes he found an olive, some honey, or a date before him. He recognized the food. It was the stuff he had bought weeks before and he was surprised that Omar had kept some of it and that they were still alive. The provisions had lasted longer than they should have. He picked up a piece of bread or took a drink of water, stayed awake a while, and then dozed off. With time, he stayed awake longer but he wasn't strong enough to get out of bed. The sunlight came into the cave midmorning. Fakhreddin regained strength and sat facing it. Then the sunlight went and he lay back again. Omar came and went without looking at him. They seemed to have reverted to the way they were at the start of the journey, but Omar seemed older. He had organized everything around them properly. He had looked after the animals, fed them, and watered them, and was using the provisions frugally. He had fetched enough water and filled the saddlebags as a precaution. The place was clean and tidy, the firewood stacked in bundles at the back of the cave, and there were the remains of a grill. Omar had gone hunting by himself. He put more water in front of his father. "Thanks," Fakhreddin said with a smile.

Omar looked at him warily and said, "You're welcome."

"What are we going to do now?"

"I don't know."

"What made you come back here?"

"I didn't know the way to the oases. I was worried I'd get lost."

"Really? After you asked me about every detail?"

"I decided to wait till you'd given up looking for me."

"I wouldn't have given up till I died."

"I would have waited till you died," Omar said right out and looked his father in the eye.

"And when I died, what would you have done?" he asked.

"When you died, you'd be dead and you wouldn't be asking me these questions."

"You have much in common with me, you know."

"How did that come about? I've barely ever met you."

"It's in the genes."

"That's what you think. No one's ever said I'm like you. If there are things we have in common through our genes, I'll give them up. There's nothing I can't do."

"Didn't I tell you?"

"Listen. I'm fed up with all this talk and playing around and beating around the bush. What do you want? What do you want from me? Why did you come back? Did anyone ask you to come? Did anyone tell you I wanted to see you?"

"I came back because you're my son and I'm your father."

"Since when, for God's sake? You're not my father and I'm not your son and you're well aware of it. How many times have you seen me? How many times have you spoken to me? What do you know about me? Where were you when I was living through one painful disaster after another, when I was being abused and humiliated and trampled underfoot because I was an orphan and didn't have a father? I wish I really had been an orphan, but my father was alive and had abandoned me. Where were you when they had me completely under their control?"

"I was . . ."

"I know. You were waging jihad like the rest of them. You and the other adventurers who abandoned their children and went to Afghanistan—Abu Musaab and Abu Mushal and Abu Qatada and Abu Ubeida and Abu Whoever Else. May the Lord take revenge on you and on them. Isn't it rather strange that you all named yourselves after the children you'd abandoned?"

"I'm sorry. I'm really sorry."

"I want to know one thing—what did you do? What did you achieve? You sacrificed me, but what did you gain?"

Fakhreddin was speechless. Omar paused for a few moments. The sound of his breathing grew louder. Staring into space, he continued: "I want to tell you something so that we can keep it short. First, don't speak to me as if you're my father. You're nothing to me. You're just someone who made my mother pregnant. I don't have any obligations toward you. The second thing you have to understand is that I hate you and if I let go of myself, I'd kill you."

"So why didn't you leave me to die?"

"I planned to, and I was watching you as you came and went, turning in circles. All I had to do was not do anything and let you fall. But I didn't want to be like you."

"You've grown up quickly, Omar, very quickly, and you've grown very cruel."

"You're the reason. You have to understand that you're the reason for everything bad that's happened to me."

"I know, and I admit I'm responsible. I know I've been remiss and neglected you. It wasn't deliberate or because I didn't love you, but there were other things I pursued. I know I was wrong. We all make mistakes. We forget things and get things wrong. One mistake you make can follow you for the rest of your life. I admit my error and I came to set it right."

"I don't need you. That's it. But I want to know why. Why did you abandon me?"

"I didn't abandon you. Not at all. I thought it was for the best, for you to live with a family and with other boys and girls. I should have thought about it more. I should have taken more interest. I should have realized that having you with me was more important. I won't look for a justification, but the truth is I grew up without a mother or father and I didn't have an example to follow. I didn't think."

"You should have thought, and your excuse is no excuse. On the contrary, the fact that you grew up an orphan should have made you more sensitive."

They discussed it for many hours without reaching any definitive conclusion. They said what they wanted to say to each other, and that was that. In the end, Fakhreddin asked Omar to forgive him and give him another chance. The boy said he couldn't trust him, since he had let him down once and there was no guarantee he wouldn't do so again. At that point, there was a long silence, and neither of them added a word. Omar got up and went to bed. Fakhreddin lay on his makeshift bed, covered himself up, and closed his eyes.

In the morning, Omar gathered up their things, prepared the animals, and told his father they were going. Fakhreddin asked him where and the boy replied firmly that they would go to Cairo. Fakhreddin said he wasn't strong enough to travel and the boy ordered him to pull himself together. He said they had no choice and if they didn't leave now they would perish in the desert. Fakhreddin asked him if he would like to go back to Sudan, so that he could recuperate and take revenge on Sheikh Hamza on Omar's behalf. The boy replied that he didn't want to take revenge on anyone, that he was stronger than Hamza, and that he preferred to let Hamza stew in his own juices, rather than become a killer like him. The boy urged his father to make haste, saying it was a long journey, and they had little food left. He told him that all he had to do was stay alive on top of his camel and show him the way so that he didn't get lost. They would economize on food and water and take a chance and hope that God would provide them with a well or something to hunt. The boy looked at his sick father and said it would be an adventure and they couldn't be sure they would reach their destination alive, but he was prepared to try.

Fakhreddin wanted to object but his son pressed him to hurry. He helped him out of the cave, wrapped in a thick blanket to protect him from the wind, the sand, and the temperature fluctuations at night. He made Fakhreddin's camel kneel and helped him sit straight on it. The other animals were loaded with the few provisions that remained. The water bags were full. Omar mounted one camel, pulled the other camel behind him, and signaled to his father to move off. He asked him to hold on tight as well as he could because they had a long journey ahead of them.

Omar glanced from time to time at his father, who was huddled on the back of his camel. He was now convinced that his father had a kind heart, much kinder than he had thought, but he was definitely naive and slightly stupid. He couldn't believe how quickly the man had trusted him. It hadn't taken more than a week, some smiles, some running and horse-riding, and some conversation in the evenings. Although Omar didn't like anyone to touch him, he had allowed his father to pat him on his shoulder and to think this meant they were now really father and son. Fakhreddin had trusted him, just like that. If Fakhreddin had been evil, as he had thought, he wouldn't have trusted him so quickly. In fact he wouldn't have trusted him at all.

But why hadn't he left his father to die? Omar asked himself the question, but avoided answering it. Did he feel sorry for Fakhreddin? When he decided to go along with his father, had he tricked him or had he deceived himself? Didn't he really long to share affection with his father, if only temporarily, even if he had begun by pretending? Could he have forgiven him just because he had seen how good it felt to have his father there? And if he didn't want his father to stay with him, why hadn't he left him to die in his wanderings in the desert? He had watched him day after day crisscrossing the desert like a blind man stung by a scorpion, trying to escape it but not knowing where he was or where he was going. It wasn't the Fakhreddin he had heard about, Fakhreddin the eagle that felled his prey with a single bullet, between sips of tea. Fakhreddin had been lost and had allowed himself and his camel to stumble toward death. The eagle he had heard about wouldn't have allowed himself to grow so weak. He would have gone on his way, because whatever benefit he would gain from Omar coming back with him would not have made his death worthwhile. The only explanation Omar could find was that Fakhreddin really wanted him. A conscience had stirred or, who knows, maybe an emotion. Maybe he had remembered him when he found out that the group was going to kill him.

He sat on his horse and remembered how Fakhreddin hadn't argued with him the previous day. He hadn't looked for an excuse or tried to defend himself. He hadn't expected that. He had expected his father to get angry, to get up and smash things, to hit him, to draw a gun on him or fire it at him, or to strike him down with one of his famous punches. But he'd lain calmly in his makeshift bed, apologizing again and again, admitting his mistake and almost crying. He hadn't expected that at all. He'd tried to provoke his anger, as much as he could. He had been crueler to him than he felt at the time, but his father hadn't been angry or flown into a rage. He'd just kept apologizing and asking for another chance.

Another chance? If only he knew how much Omar longed for another chance, for a real father, protection, a house, a school, a street with neighbors who didn't kill anyone, and friends, a mother or someone like a mother. Sitting on his camel, he sometimes dreamed that his father had married Leila or Shayma, or both of them, and that they were living together as a family. Then he thought about what he would do in Cairo. Would his father go back to fighting? He didn't know what would be worse—if this was all a cover for another organization, or if the Eagle was really this kind and had really taken him back. Could he let himself hope for a father again? Should he allow himself to hope and believe, or was his father suffering from a temporary bout of insanity? If so, and if he then recovered from it, would Omar find himself on the streets, without a father?

Omar led the little caravan and looked at his ailing father. He was worried his father's condition might be worsening and, at the same time, he was worried he would recover. He wouldn't know what to do with him in either case. If Fakhreddin was really as kind and loving as he seemed to be, why hadn't he come ages ago? Fakhreddin had laughed heartily when they had races. His father wasn't good at racing but he was stronger. Omar was sure he would beat him after a few months' training. He would start with running, and Fakhreddin had also promised to teach him to swim in a sports club near their house. He told him how kind Tamer was and assured him he would be happy to have Omar take part in the computer projects he was working on. He also told him there was another boy and another girl that he helped with their homework every day, and Omar asked him at once why he hadn't helped him, when he hadn't understood anything at ordinary school, or in the Quran school, and when his teachers beat him all the time. Fakhreddin replied that he could help the three of them. He said he hadn't gone to school when he was Omar's age, but he had lessons at home and sat the exams. He said Omar could do that, and then go to university. Omar wondered what he would study at university. He wouldn't study law like his father, or explosives either. He wouldn't go to the military academy. Maybe medicine: he could be a good surgeon. That's what one of the doctors in the group had told him when he helped him with some operations at the farm. He thought that he could consult Dr. Shayma if she turned out to be nice, as Fakhreddin said she was. He also thought he could help Leila in the strange clinic she had set up. He could take on the tasks that Fakhreddin

316

had been doing—buying the medicines and distributing them. That way he would get to know the local people and maybe meet some girls. He had never gotten to know any girls. On the farm, they kept the girls with their mothers, away from the boys. He was bound to meet lots of them in the neighborhood and, who knows, maybe he would meet a girl like him, orphaned or abandoned by her father and looking for someone to talk to and share things with. What else would he do? He could take Aunt Maria for the daily walk that the doctor recommended. She might tell him his father's story from the start, and the stories of his grandfather and grandmother. His heart skipped a beat when he wondered whether Aunt Maria had known his mother. He didn't want Fakhreddin to talk about her. Maybe Leila would tell him things about her or about people who had known her. They must have a picture of her. He wanted to know what she looked like. After that he could look for his sister Maryam and meet her: she was bound to have pictures and stories about their mother.

"When we go to Cairo, I want to see Maryam," he said.

"Which Maryam?"

"My sister. Isn't she called Maryam?"

"Yes, but I don't know if she's in Cairo or in Paris with her father."

"Look for her. I want to see her. I want her to come and live with me for a while and for me to go and live with her for a while. I want to see my sister. Is that strange?"

"No, it's not strange at all. Okay, when we get to Cairo."

Omar realized he was no longer weak or frightened of Fakhreddin. In fact, he felt he was the stronger one. He was the one protecting his father now. He was the one in charge. Fakhreddin was just a compass and it was Omar who was leading the caravan. He was going to watch his father and, if he abandoned him again, he would show no mercy. Omar sat upright on the camel and told himself he would watch carefully to see how things went between him and Fakhreddin in

317

the future. But for the moment, he had to concentrate on the route so that they didn't both die in the desert.

Fakhreddin grew tired. All he wanted to do was lie down on the ground and sleep for a long time, as long as possible. The idea stuck in his mind as he slipped in and out of sleep on the back of the old camel, which pitched up and down in the sea of sand around him. The light filtered into his eyes, along with images that could have been real or just delusions. Omar had strapped him on well so he wouldn't fall off, and every now and then he asked him a question about the route, to make sure he was still alive and awake. Fakhreddin would answer him and then doze off again. The upheavals of recent weeks had worn him down and his hallucination about Hind had undermined his confidence in his own sanity. Omar and his duplicity had then broken what remained of his resolve.

He only wanted to rest. He longed to spend the daytime hours lying on level ground but Omar had decided to keep moving by day. They would stop for just one hour to let the animals rest. Omar said there was no other choice if they wanted to get there alive. Fakhreddin didn't argue. He no longer had the strength to argue. Omar seemed to be leading the caravan well and, if not well, at least he was leading it, whereas Fakhreddin could no longer do that. All he wanted to do was lie on the ground and sleep. He wanted to spread out on the sand and drift across the soft warm surface like a tent in the wind. He didn't care if his body was dried out by the sun, washed away by rain, or blasted by sandstorms till it was rough and strong and pliant like a living palm frond. He no longer wanted anything. His days were done and all he wanted now was to lie down and waste away slowly. He imagined his soul taking flight in the form of little butterflies that fluttered in the air forever.

His strength gave out. He had voyaged across mountains and valleys, along streets, down rivers, across seas and deserts, and all he could do now was admit that he had reached his limit. He couldn't go further than this. His plans had collapsed. He had lost control and things had started happening to him, instead of him making them happen. He urged Omar to leave with the food and water that was left and abandon him because there was no way he could endure the long journey back. But Omar insisted on sticking with him, saying he wouldn't allow him to abdicate his responsibility toward Aunt Maria, Leila, and Tamer and make the same mistake with them as he had made with him.

Omar asked him why he had led his life as if he were responsible for the whole world, and Fakhreddin said nothing. He had been trying to promote justice and resist injustice. Was that arrogance or was he just naive? Should he have abandoned the world to its corrupt ways and looked after his aunt, his son, educating those two children, and helping some old sick people? If he had done that, who would have taken a stand against injustice? But now he wondered whether he had failed on both counts and spent his life as a phantom chasing phantoms. He had traveled far and wide in search of a goal that had eluded him, and hadn't seen any of the things that were worth seeing along the way. He woke, looked into the distance, and could see nothing but sandy hills. He wished he had seen the things that were close as well as he had seen those in the distance. Maybe if he had seen Shireen properly and really known her, he could have saved her or, if he had understood, he would have left her in the world where she belonged. And where was Aunt Maria? Why had he abandoned her? He asked himself if he had really known Nasser and Ali, if he had known any of the people he had loved. Or had he just preached sermons, while he sought out a dragon to slay it?

Omar said that all he asked of his father was to stay alive. Fakhreddin wanted to try. He loved this boy. The more Omar spoke, the more Fakhreddin knew that this wounded angel was his son and a part of him. But he wasn't sure he could stay alive as he had promised. He didn't have anything to go back to. Life had lost its savor long ago, and then he had lost the goal that kept him going. He had slain the dragon, only to discover that he had no life beyond what he now saw to be phantoms. Omar checked on him every hour. He gave him food and water and encouraged him. Every morning, he made him promise to hold out for another day. Fakhreddin watched him and saw how he was growing closer to him day by day. Fakhreddin gave his promise, but he didn't know if he could hold out, or whether he would submit to his overwhelming desire to perish in the sands of this desert, which he knew so well and which knew him too.

SELECTED HOOPOE TITLES

Embrace on Brookylyn Bridge
by Ezzedine C. Fishere, translated by John Peate

In the Spider's Room
by Muhammad Abdelnabi, translated by Jonathan Wright

Guard of the Dead
by George Yarak, translated by Raphael Cohen

*

hoopoe is an imprint for engaged, open-minded readers hungry for outstanding fiction that challenges headlines, re-imagines histories, and celebrates original storytelling. Through elegant paperback and digital editions, **hoopoe** champions bold, contemporary writers from across the Middle East alongside some of the finest, groundbreaking authors of earlier generations.

At hoopoefiction.com, curious and adventurous readers from around the world will find new writing, interviews, and criticism from our authors, translators, and editors.